A Party To Die For

A Cape Cod Cozy Mystery

A Party To Die For

Margaret Stockley

Alva Glen Press

Copyright 2024 by Margaret Stockley

Alva Glen Press

All rights reserved.

This book contains material protected under International and Federal Copyright Laws and Treaties. Any unauthorized reprint or use of this material is prohibited. No part of this book may be reproduced or transmitted in any form or by any mean, electronic or mechanical, including photocopying, recording, or by any information storage and retrieval system without express written permission from the author/publisher.

This is a work of fiction.

ISBN: 978-0-9969825-5-9

eISBN: 978-0-9969825-6-6

This book is for those who savor the feeling of being transported to a quaint town, where secrets lurk behind every charming facade. So sit back, relax, and let yourself be swept away by the pages of this cozy mystery.

Chapter One

The ear-splitting scream emanating from my cell phone was so loud that I thought my neighbors would come running. Even Duke, my German Shepherd, raised his head with a start, instantly alert from a deep sleep and concerned that something important was happening that required his immediate intervention. I gave his quirky ears a reassuring rub, the right one erect, the left one droopy, and offered him a broad smile. Moments ago, I had phoned my friend Gabby and told her that not only had I been invited to the prestigious Suzie Wilde event, but I was calling to invite her to be my plus one.

I continued to hold my phone away from my ear until I was sure that she had calmed down. "Seriously?" she asked, having taken a deep breath. "For real?"

"Yes, for real Gabby." Unlike me, she was prone to showing her emotions openly. However this was no ordinary invitation. Even I had let out a breathy 'oh, my, gosh' when I saw the thick white envelope poking out of my mail, wedged between the weekly supermarket flyers. I checked the envelope twice in case it had been addressed to someone else, (recognizing the famous name on the return address and admiring how the initials S and W were embossed on the back flap, then opened it carefully so as not to damage the contents.

After easing out the sturdy white and gold card that looked like a wedding invitation and reading the formal script that was indeed addressed to me, Marnie Frazer, I plonked myself down on one of my hard metallic kitchen counter stools and wondered if life in Legacy Cove could get any better.

Receiving an invitation to the party was not unlike winning a Willie Wonka Golden Ticket and I was one of the lucky few people in town to receive an invite.

From the thumps coming from the phone I could imagine Gabby jumping up and down like an over-excited toddler. "What does it say?" she asked breathlessly.

"The invitation is for me and a guest and given that you're one of the few people that I know outside of my work, well, I thought it only fair to see if you were free." We both laughed. Neither fire nor flood would prevent either of us from going to the event.

"Read every word," she continued.

I held the card carefully at the edges so as not to smudge the invitation or crease it in some way and cleared my throat in dramatic emphasis. "Here goes, 'Dear Marnie Frazer, you and a guest are formally invited to attend the annual Suzie Wilde Event, to be held on July 31st at 6 PM at the Suzie Wilde Estate, Ocean's View Island, Legacy Cove, Massachusetts. Please be at Harbor Bay by 5:25 PM with this invitation where a Wilde Estate tender will transport you to the island. Black Tie Reception.' That's it. Plus, there's an RSVP email, Team@WildeEvent.com."

"Oh, it all sounds fabulous," Gabby gushed. "I've heard that her private island is simply spectacular." There was a pause, and I thought I picked up a hesitancy in her voice.

"Do you still want to go with me?"

"What? Of course. Who wouldn't want to go. It's just that I was wondering how you managed to get an invitation?"

I had been wondering the same thing too and my stomach did a flip that somehow it was all a mistake. Or a bad joke. Even after two decades, I occasionally had to suppress the jarring jolt of not feeling good enough, despite being a leader in my field of archaeology and the youngest professor at Legacy College. I just couldn't seem to shed the emotion of feeling like a fraud and not being good enough.

"I mean, you've not been here that long," she continued.

"I know. I thought maybe there was a typo, and it was for another Marnie Frazer, or somehow, I got a sympathy vote."

"No way it's a mistake. You're the only Marnie Frazer that I know. There has to be something that you've done that you've forgotten about. Suzie Wilde is not only one of the best country music stars on the planet, but she also only invites a few people each year to her extravaganza and they've all done something remarkable."

"I can't think of anything. I've not started a charity, or made a huge donation, or invented some life-enhancing product. Plus, as you said, I'm relatively new to the community. It's been a little over two years since I came here. And I don't think that being a researcher and overseeing archaeological digs for Legacy College counts as a good deed to the community. Even though what I uncover about the past can often help us understand today's society."

"Well, your students, volunteers, and all those international historians might think otherwise. You're quite the famous researcher you know, and you make ancient history sound fascinating when you're sharing your latest escapades with me over one of my weekly sundowners. Either way, this is the best news I've had all day, actually all week. No, it's the best news all month. Oh, it's only six weeks away and it's already the middle of June. We'll need something to wear, we need to go shopping."

I groaned. I didn't shop for fun. My taller than average height usually made shopping challenging and I'd learned as a young teenager to buy multiples of items that fitted my lanky frame so that I wouldn't have to keep searching boutiques or department stores only to have zero positive results. This meant that as I grew older, and thankfully stopped growing at five foot eight inches tall, I only shopped when absolutely necessary, such as for a friend's wedding or when a favorite pair of jeans had worn out and were so thin that I was afraid my knickers would shine through. "The event will be here before we know it," I said. "Any idea what we should wear? It all seems so formal if the beautiful invitation is anything to go by."

"Haven't you seen photos from previous Suzie Wilde events?"

The truth was, I hadn't. I'd only heard about Suzie and the event from colleagues and from my friends. I wasn't one to scroll through social media, and I explained as much to Gabby.

"I mean, I love her music. Apart from owning a few of her albums, I know little of what she does when she's not making music. I mean, I've heard that she's someone who donates a lot of money to charities and has even set up a few of her own, such as the ones that help children and animals.

"Well," she said, "you should start checking out everything related to past parties. You'll see what I mean. What we wear needs to be something elegant, yet fun, not whimsical, but definitely sexy and flattering. Something that goes well with sipping glasses of chilled champagne and nibbling scrumptious dainty canapes with delectable delights such as smoked salmon and caviar." She giggled. "And I know the perfect little boutique where we can go in the village. Although I hope that all the best outfits haven't already been snapped up," she added.

"Great," I said with real enthusiasm. Gabby would be a good help when it came to choosing the right outfit, so long as I could get one to fit. Trousers were always an issue as they never were quite long enough. Fortunately, finding a dress that didn't look like I'd squeezed into a short frock from the junior's department was usually less of an issue. "Only, my budget isn't the same as yours," I reminded her. She owned a software development company and while not showy with her wealth, she had shared with me that her company was about to become a publicly traded company, making her an overnight multi-millionaire. "A professor's salary has to go a long way to reach your status Gabriella Martinez," I teased, calling her by her full name.

"My company isn't trading yet, and you know what's said about not counting your chickens, or eggs, or whatever it is."

"It's chickens. Don't count your chickens."

"Well anyway, I don't want to jinx it. All the same, we need something spectacular to wear. Think of the clothes as an investment. Once word gets out about you going to the Suzie Wilde event, you're going to be asked to even more soirées and clients will be lining up to attend one of your classes or volunteer at a dig."

"Apart from sipping sundowners on your porch, the most I've been out since I got to Legacy Cove is to the dig at Heritage Hole with my students and volunteers, or taking Duke to the dog park or Wolf Swamp. And German Shepherds aren't exactly good conversationalists."

"And wait until I tell Adam. He'll be so jealous."

"You've been dating him for how long now?"

"Three months next weekend."

"How's it going?"

"Okay. I'm just really busy at work though, to think about deepening a relationship."

"I'm sure he can find something else to do when we're at the Suzie Wilde event."

"Hmm. I wonder who else is going to be there?" she mused. "I know! You should ask Troy," she stated.

"Well, he is the best realtor on all of Cape Cod and the Islands. He should know a thing or two about what's going on. I'll call him later this evening," I said, saying bye to Gabby after agreeing to see her for our regular sundowners on her porch at six o'clock on Friday evening and setting a firm time to go shopping together in a week's time on the following Saturday morning. Troy Norton, who started out as my realtor and quickly became a friend along with his long-time partner Patrick Hamlin, seemed to know everyone in the town as well as what was happening and when. If anyone knew who else was going to the event, and why, it would be Troy.

I looked again at the invitation in my hand. Its weight was substantial, indicating quality, and not from some made-in-bulk box off the shelf. The wording and embossed lettering, no doubt chosen with care, also indicated that this was a social gathering that meant something of importance to the sender.

I was still flabbergasted as to why I was invited. The last time I was surprised without warning was thirty-two months ago and that event left me stunned, seething, and freaking mad for many months.

I smarted as the unwelcome memory popped up in my mind. Looking back, moving here to the ocean where I once lived as a child, and away from my familiar adult surroundings of institutions of higher learning, seemed a logical next step to me although to many of my colleagues it was an emotional and irrational response. In fact, quite a few of them told me so, telling me I was throwing away my hard-earned career and that I'd never be taken seriously again.

But I'd learned from harsh experience that my happiness was not predetermined by events that directly impacted my life. Nor by what people said to me, whether to advise me or to bully me. Life, I'd come to see, was just one big ocean, sometimes with ripples and at other times with huge waves that threatened to wash me ashore flat on my face in the sand. And each of us bobbing around had a choice, to either give back as good as we got, or put a stop to the flow of violence once and for all.

For me, the ripple effect of the past would only affect my present if I let it, and I sure as heck wasn't going to give it an inch of room. Nope, no way, not even a teeny sliver of hope. Sure, leaving the excitement of Boston seemed a reckless thing to have done, but I calmly and logically felt that I was doing the right thing in returning to Legacy Cove and I had no fear of standing out.

After all, we are all connected to each other, whether we realize it or not.

But now, my predictable, safe, Legacy Cove life had now been thrown a curve ball and it was an unsettling mystery as to why I was invited to one of the most important social events of the year.

Chapter Two

Walking Duke always cleared my head, and he was due for his early evening walk. His ears pricked up when he heard me put on my navy-blue Converse shoes and he clambered to his four paws, his thick tail swishing back and forth as he stretched languidly then ambled to my side, his soft fur brushing against my bare legs. No need to ask him if he was ready. Slipping his harness over his hairy shoulders I attached his leash and opened the door.

The view to my left as I stepped outside onto the front porch of my house (while avoiding looking at the ever-growing weeds in my hydrangea and azalea beds) never ceased to disappoint, no matter the weather. My little Cape Cod cottage was situated at the end of a dead-end road that overlooked a salt pond. Ducks and blue herons would often be seen picking at pond grasses or feasting on small fishes trapped by low tide. About two hundred feet long and seventy-five feet wide, the pond was encircled by reeds that grew thick and tall and beyond the pond was the bay and the strip of water that opened directly into the ocean one mile away to the south, providing boat access to Martha's Vineyard. Black cormorants, their wings spread to dry their feathery armpits, sat listlessly on the cabins of fishing boats and the masts of yachts that were gently rocked by the waves lapping against their moorings. Right now, the water glinted dark blue and sparkled like it was carrying a flotilla of diamonds out to sea.

I could have afforded a larger, grander house, but what I needed was comfortable surroundings and a feeling of belonging within a neighborhood.

My favorite part of living here was the narrow strip of sandy beach about twelve feet wide that ran the full length of the water's edge all the way to the ocean. It was rarely busy except on the Fourth of July weekend when families and groups of visitors appeared in their droves. Otherwise, on a hot summer's day there wasn't anything better than to bring my beach towel and sit there, reviewing my notes from the current dig, or read up in journals about other dig sites around the world. Then, a quick dip in the water when it got too warm.

A Cape Cod cottage with a water view and what I considered my own little beach hideaway. I sighed. A perfect life.

Turning right at the end of my street I headed to the dog park. This evening, the cooling easterly wind helped ease the warmth of the day providing a little respite for neighbors' homes, that unlike mine, had no air-conditioning, as evidenced by windows that were open from one end of the various cottages to the other allowing a through-flow of air.

I'd only gone about two hundred yards when I heard a car slow down and cruise beside me. Two toots of the horn made me stop and turn. I recognized the car that had come to a standstill at the curb, and I beamed as the passenger window of the gleaming white Mercedes rolled down and the driver leaned over. Duke tugged on his leash, and I had to keep a strong grip on it in case Duke decided to put his paws on the vehicle in order to investigate who was inside.

"Well, hello Troy, fancy meeting you here."

"I was just heading home from the office Marnie. Lovely to see you and your furry friend."

Troy could have been heading home, he did live nearby with his partner Patrick, but he would have been driving in the other direction if he'd come directly from his office. This was Troy at his best, I chuckled to myself.

"I hear congrats are in order." He raised an eyebrow in eager anticipation of hearing more.

So, I was right. Digging for gossip was the reason he 'just so happened' to be cruising through my neighborhood. Suppressing a smile, I pressed him on how he found out. "Let me guess," I beamed. "Gabby told you."

"Well, who else could it be?" He flashed a broad smile showing his perfect teeth. "Although, I want to hear everything about it from you."

I gave a little shrug, conscious of the fact that this was what was going to consume my interactions with most people in my life over the next few weeks. The only individual who was completely indifferent was Duke who was now uninterested in the arrival of Troy and was pulling in the direction of the park. "I was going to call you next. To be honest, I'm still processing what happened."

Troy's reaction was elated to say the least. "I'm so happy for you, Marnie," he said cheerfully. "I can't think of anyone who deserves this more than you."

"Thank you Troy. By the way, could you do me a huge favor that day?"

"Let me guess, you need someone to watch our favorite furry friend."

I rubbed Duke's ears. "Just pop round, and make sure he's okay. Even though he loves spending time with you and Patrick. I'll have walked and fed him, but it's not the first time he's stepped on his water bowl and tipped it over."

"Consider it done."

"You're such a good guy, you know that?" He had been a solid friend to me since I arrived on the Cape. "I'll be in touch nearer the day to finalize a drop-off and pick-up time."

"When I heard the news about your invitation, I had to come over and see you straight away. Listen, are you free a week on Saturday in the afternoon?"

"I should be. Providing Gabby and I have found outfits to wear for the Suzie Wilde event. We're going shopping on that Saturday morning, you see. Why?"

"Hold your horses, I'll get to that. But first I want to let you know that I'm hearing good things about your research in the dig down by Heritage Hole."

"You bet. We've had a lot of excitement recently too. We had an injection of funding for the dig through a donor to the college, which in my experience rarely happens. So, I'm really thrilled at the moment."

"Fabulous. Fabulous. Anyway, I digress. What I wanted to say was there's a yacht race in Vineyard Sound sailing out of the Harbor Yacht Club next Saturday afternoon. A scholarship fundraiser. The race starts at 3 o'clock so get there earlier if you can."

I really wasn't keen on going and sharing small-talk with a group of strangers. Socializing was never one of my strengths, and small-talk even less. "I'm not sure, Troy."

"Nonsense. It'll do you good to meet people outside of the college. Plus, I have it on good authority that there will be people there who are also going to the Suzie Wilde event."

"You have it on good authority?" Now it was my turn to raise an eyebrow.

"Okay, okay," he said, raising his arms and feigning being caught out. "I began inviting them when I heard that the first of the invitations had been sent out."

I sighed and shook my head, smiling at him. "Okay. I'll bring Gabby."

"Well, that's just super. And of course, with Gabbs' new wealthy status just around the corner she'll be very welcome at a fundraiser. Plus, no occasion's complete without her. She's always fun to have around."

"And I'm not?"

"On the contrary. You know what they say about quiet types," he said with a wink.

"Whatever could you mean," I said laughing.

"It's going to be a good networking event and there's about, oh, seven or eight so far who I know of who're going to the Suzie Wilde event." He paused. "In fact, come to think of it, there may be a couple of people that you know from way back."

I frowned slightly and shrugged. "Like whom?"

"Amber Clarke?"

I shook my head. "Nope. Not someone I remember."

"Rupert Boyden, then."

I felt a sudden tightness in my chest when I heard the name, and stuffed down the stomach flip that sprang up without warning. I knew when I moved back here that there was a chance that I'd stumble across some of the people I knew as a child, however I hadn't been too concerned. We were all adults now. I was stronger today than I was back then. I'd survived and heck, I was thriving. But still, I hadn't expected to have such a gut-wrenching reaction to that name. I took a deep calming breath. "The name sounds familiar," I managed to reply calmly after a few moments.

"Super. Dr Rupert, as some of us call him, he's a great guy. Although his ex-wife probably thinks otherwise." He laughed at his joke. "And I'm not letting you back out of this."

"With you there it'll be fun Troy. Plus, it'll be quite a change from the classroom or digging around in a field searching for ancient artifacts." Even if Rupert Boyden was there. I'd surely be able to melt into the midst of the attendees and stay clear of him.

"You clean up pretty good Marnie."

"Oh thanks, Prince Charming. I don't know how Patrick puts up with you, because you sure know how not to sweep someone off their feet. More like knock them over."

"I'll pretend I heard nothing. I'll even buy a round of drinks for all my guests. A nice incentive for some of your fellow schemers to turn up, don't you think?"

"Schemers? What do you mean?"

"Well, how else do you think they get an invite? They smooch and press the flesh to influence the right people all year in the hope that they get their coveted invitation."

"And yet, here I am, getting an invite and I've no idea why."

"You must have done something, Marnie. You just have to think harder, that's all." He paused and lowered his sunglasses so that I could see his dark brown eyes. "Although I do know," he said slowly "one or two of the guests' secrets."

"Secrets? You make it sound very mysterious Troy." I tried to read his eyes to see what he meant by secrets, but I couldn't tell if he was being funny or serious.

"Well, someone's spirited temper and another's venomous tongue have incited quite a few arguments creating no end of enemies, and then there's the ubiquitous dancing twosome between three people if you follow me."

I thought I did but let it pass. I'd noodle on it later.

He nudged his sunglasses back up to where they belonged. "Life just keeps getting better and better." He laughed. "Oh, don't mind me and my gossip. They're a great bunch of people. Really." He paused briefly for a breath, pursing his lips. "Most of the time."

Duke nudged me with his wet nose on my leg as if to say, 'wrap it up.' Taking the hint, I made my excuses to leave and blew Troy a parting kiss.

"Ciao, Marnie. See you at Gabbs on Friday evening for sundowners," he called, driving off as his tinted window rolled up.

As I picked up my stride with Duke to get to the park, I thought about what Troy had shared about the other guests, and about what he believed some of their secrets were. Rupert Boyden in particular. What would it be like to see him in person? Would he even remember who I was? The me I used to be? Marnie Hitson? Echoes of name-calling and cruel bullying arose as I walked, increasing my pace and stomping out every dark memory. 'Shitty Hitty.' That's what he called me, getting the other kids to join in. And then there was Melissa Cooke. She was a nasty kid who seemed to thrive on putting other kids down. Probably a nasty adult by now if she lived that long.

Although I did remember one kid, who was also being bullied by Rupert. I think he was called JJ, although I doubted that was his given name. He had a much older brother who put a stop to JJ being bullied, and gave me a break too by taking me under his watchful eye until he left school the following semester. I couldn't quite recall the older brother's name: Trey, or Trig, or Tick. Something like that. Those months definitely gave me hope that life wouldn't always be bad. I learned the hard way though that it's what people do that gives them away, not just what they say. My then social-worker, who later became my aunt because she was my adopted mother's sister, once said that an action always betrays a person's thoughts, whether benevolent or vengeful. I never forgot that.

I sighed heavily, realizing how much of an impact the mention of Rupert Boyden and the memory of the other awful kids was having on me. I hadn't thought of any of them for years and now the thought of seeing any of them was making me feel angry at how I had been treated by them, and how most of the adults at the time ignored what was happening. Now Rupert was apparently a doctor of some sort, so perhaps he had changed.

Or perhaps not.

Enough I decided! The past was the past. I wasn't going to let anything, or anyone, extinguish my earlier excitement. I had a great career that I loved, I was successful in my field of work, and I had just been invited to the most prestigious event in the whole of Cape Cod. No one could take that from me.

What Troy referred to as secrets sounded more to me like gossip, otherwise not a lot of people would know about them, now would they? If there was one thing that I'd learned over the years it was to never listen to gossip. Although, I mused, that wasn't to say that there weren't actual secrets to be uncovered. All the same, I wondered what I'd learn about my fellow Suzie Wilde guests at the yacht club. Rupert Boyden included.

And what they would discover about me.

Chapter Three

The following Saturday, after what turned out to be an unsuccessful morning shopping, Gabby and I clambered out of a Legacy Cove taxi at a quarter to three on Saturday afternoon, and crunched our way on the crushed shell path that wound its way from the car park overlooking the harbor to the yacht club. Loud laughter, raucous enough to fill a football stadium, made us glance at each other with eyes wide. Gabby nudged me and laughed, "They've started before us."

When we reached the corner of the building we could see Troy up on the wooden balcony on the first level, holding court with his partner Patrick and seven other people, four women and three men. One of the men had dark cropped hair and was almost a head taller than everyone in the group and he was the one who was apparently responsible for most of the racket, judging by the way everyone around him was laughing. The men sported beige or Nantucket red shorts and an array of pastel polo shirts while the women wore comfortable clothes that ranged from long floaty floral dresses to white jeans and a top.

"Ready?" I asked.

Gabby nodded and adjusted her navy bag hanging over her left shoulder and we climbed the stairs to join Troy. The ocean breeze was warm and gentle, only enough to ruffle a hemline rather than cause an upset with our hair. There appeared to be about eight other loud groups mingling on the balcony, all dressed in similar Cape Cod attire. Taller than Gabby by five inches, I easily spotted Troy as we reached the top of the stairs and waved to him.

"Follow me," I said and led the way through the various groups toward the rear of the balcony where Troy was holding court.

"Marnie. Gabby," he said as he greeted both of us warmly with pecks on our cheeks. "So good you could both make it. I've been so busy I've not had a chance to pop round and see either of you. Anyway, let me get you both a glass of something. What would you like?"

"Sauvignon Blanc please," I said. "And me too," said Gabby.

"Good, good. Let me first introduce you to some wonderful people who will also be going to the Suzie Wilde event." Drawing us forward to the group, he waved a hand to intrude the conversation. "Ladies and gentlemen, I'd like you to meet my good friends Marnie Frazer and Gabriella Martinez who are also fortunate to be joining you at the

Suzie Wilde event. Take a moment to get to know each other; share why you're so special that you got the illustrious ticket too. You all know the routine." He slipped away to get the drinks while the round of introductions began.

First up was the tall man with the dark hair and booming voice that I had heard before I'd seen him. His hair was obviously dyed as it had an almost blue tinge to it and he must have been in his fifties or even older based on the age spots on his hand holding his glass of red wine. His powder-blue polo shirt hung loose over his Nantucket shorts, in an attempt to minimize his abdomen that, while not straining beneath the shirt, was definitely ample. "Bernard Lazenby, of Lazenby Commercial Real Estate, and this is my lovely wife, Celia." he said, raising his glass as a means of acknowledging everyone. Celia squeezed her husband on the arm playfully, her rings flashing in the sunlight.

He was even louder now that we were standing a few feet from him. And his wife was significantly younger than him with cropped spiky hair, closer to my age I thought, although their May-December relationship really wasn't any of my business.

"Ah," said Gabby. "I read about your company. You raised a phenomenal amount of money for a local family charity during their fundraising drive last December."

He grinned and laughed, or rather bellowed. "That's us. Always willing to help out our community. In fact, my company contributed an additional two million dollars for the Surfside Family organization during a fundraising drive last November and December. Tell me about yourself."

"I'm the CEO of APP-APP," enthused Gabby. "We make it easy for software development companies to significantly reduce their development costs and use their apps on multiple platforms. That in turn makes it easy for users to implement the apps." She paused and looked at the group. "I guess I'm going on too much about technical things." She gave a light laugh. "I love what I do though.

"I'd say we all appreciate your enthusiasm. It's no wonder that you're the lucky gal who got the invitation," he thundered.

Gabby leaned back slightly. "Actually, no. It's my good friend Marnie."

His eyebrows lifted above his sunglasses as he gave me the once-over. I couldn't believe that relics like Brash Bernard existed. Plus, I was uncomfortably aware of other attendees glancing briefly over at our little group, alerted no doubt by Bernard's pomposity.

Standing next to Bernard was a man with sandy-colored hair, not as tall but possessing a wider chest and shoulders, giving him the appearance of an athlete. I guessed he and I were around the same age. "Hi there," he smiled with perfect teeth. "Dr Rupert Boyden. I'm in charge of a pediatric oncology practice covering the Cape and Islands."

My body suddenly tensed, but I forced myself to keep breathing normally. He seemed older than when I remembered him, exuding self-assurance. Even so, I wasn't planning on revealing that I knew him from before—unless he brought it up first. Half listening to Rupert explaining how their clinic was making progress with treating young patients, I prepared for whatever might come next, though I had no idea what it could be.

"…as well as advising the Artemis Group in their charity work providing support for family members of those unfortunate to be addicted to opioids," Rupert finished with a self-satisfied grin.

"That's very important work," Bernard remarked.

In spite of my reservations about being around a bully from my childhood, it was hard to find fault with what he was doing professionally. "Hopefully one day your services won't be required. I've unfortunately seen the effects of drugs on some students."

"You're a teacher?"

"A professor actually. At Legacy College. Archaeology."

"Oh, a professor." He leaned ever so slightly forward, studying me carefully, chuckled, and shook his head. But even with sunglasses on to mask much of his expression, I got the sense that he wasn't particularly impressed by what I did. Thankfully, it didn't appear as though he remembered me from our teenage days. After all, I had changed my last name. "And you were invited to the Suzie Wilde event?"

"Yes." I smiled broadly, my self-confidence returning, and left it at that, conscious of this group of new people looking at me, wondering why I had been invited. I still wasn't convinced that my invitation was correct. What was more likely was that another Marnie Frazer or some other woman whose last name was Frazer was sitting at home alone, wringing her hands, and wondering why her good deeds had gone unnoticed by the Suzie Wilde organization.

"I'm Kaylee Bardot," smiled a young woman next to him, "and this is my friend Sabrina." Both women looked to be in their late-twenties and standing side-by-side they were like yin and yang with Kaylee having dark hair and Sabrina, with no last name, white hair. Although both hair colors would likely be changed in a few months if my students at the college were a good guide as to everchanging trending tints. Sporting tattoos on their inner arms, piercings on their eyebrows and ears, it was Kaylee who was the chatty one of the pair, and as she spoke, I was in awe of what she'd been able to achieve. "Six years ago," she explained, "when I became clean and sober, I created a drug rehab center and now we have additional funding from sponsors to provide assistance for people who want help but can't afford a private center. We've launched a mobile unit too and I have plans to expand the program throughout New England next year, and into neighboring states the following year."

Here was yet another brilliant idea that directly assisted the public. "It's incredible what you've achieved," I said, "and in such a relatively short period of time too. In fact, every person I've met so far has created a much-needed organization that directly benefits our community."

There were nods all around and agreement with the sentiment.

"Hi, I'm Liz Tanner," the petite brunette said. Her dark locks were pulled back to minimize the bedraggling effect of the ocean breeze if it chose to spring up, as it frequently did in this part of the Cape, in the late afternoons. I had learned during my first week living here that it was best to keep beach hair on the beach. She took a sip from her glass of white wine as thin ankles daintily poked out from beneath her cropped trousers and struggled to support her slender frame. On top of all this was her voluptuous chest which was trying desperately to escape its floral blouse.

"Hi," Gabby and I said.

"Are you part of the dig at Heritage Hole?" she asked me.

"Yes. I'm the lead researcher."

"It sounds super interesting. Have you found any treasure?" Liz's eyes widened as she leaned closer to me, as did the others in the group at the mention of treasure.

I smiled inwardly. It was a common question, asked by children and adults alike. "Sorry, no. Not this time." Her face fell slightly, as did both Bernard's and Rupert's. "My students and I are primarily historical archeologists, and we're fortunate to be assisted at the moment by local volunteers who are also members of the Legacy Cove Archaeological Society."

"So, what do you look for then, if not buried treasure?" asked Bernard.

"Oh, we find all manner of fascinating artifacts, like bits of pottery, the remains of wooden boats, glass, seeds, tools, even human remains sometimes."

Bernard screwed his face up. "I'll pass on the dead bodies."

"Me too," said Liz, "but I'd love to see the glass. I'm always looking for unique natural items for the products that I make."

"Unfortunately, what we find on a dig is protected and not for sale."

"Well, that's a pity. I'll just have to continue scouring the shoreline for sea-glass then."

"I love doing that," said Celia. Her voice was shrill yet raspy at the same time.

"I've never tried it," confessed Gabby.

"I've got an idea," I said to Liz. "While the archaeological items we've found aren't for sale, they are on display at the Heritage Hole museum. You might find they offer you some ideas for your own original pieces. Plus, there may be similar items from other digs that you could use for research or inspiration. Do you sell your jewelry locally?"

"Yes, and I've actually taken it further and created an online franchise called Earth and Moon Aromatherapy. I love to source ingredients that are indigenous to New England and use them in my products."

I sighed wistfully. "Well, I'm always impressed by people who are artistic. I'm too focused on specifics to let my mind wander into the unknown imaginative world of an artistic personality."

Liz inclined her head slightly, giving the impression she understood what it was like to focus on only details and facts, but I wasn't so sure. Most artists that I knew were wildly erratic. They may get lost in the flow when composing music or painting for example, and the building could fall down around them and they wouldn't notice, but despite living in a state of organized chaos I couldn't deny that they produced wonderful works of art.

"You know," I continued, "I marvel at creatives like you who use their imagination, rather than relying solely on facts and data like many of the people I work with. Sure, some of us also cook while others excel at playing an instrument, but those of us who do that are the outliers."

"It comes naturally to me. I see something and everything sort of flows from there."

"I'm such a nerdy person, always so focused on the minutiae. It can sometimes take me a while to see the wider picture. But I was wondering, where do you source your ingredients?"

"Oh, here and there. I do a fair bit of hiking in the woods. I like the feeling of being surrounded by tall trees. I find it much cooler than hiking in open fields. Then, there's the ocean." She swept her arms expansively in the direction of Vineyard Sound. "I love SCUBA diving too and being at one with all aspects of nature. There's no end to the inspiration I get when I simply embrace life and let ideas for new products flow to me."

"I like walking too with my dog, although I'm a bit wary of walking him in the woods because of ticks. Plus, he's likely to go off chasing rabbits."

Liz laughed. "That's a drawback, for sure. Although I think the benefits outweigh the negative."

"That's true."

"It's helped me so much especially since I sold my first business manufacturing organic bee products to a large conglomerate."

"I may need to come to you for some advice," laughed Gabby. "I'm about to do something very similar with my company."

"I'd be happy to," smiled Liz. "Having the additional funds has enabled me to use my products as a luxury treat in my charity," she continued.

"Oh? What does your charity do?"

"We help mothers with premature babies that are hospitalized by providing products such as tiny clothing, donated breast milk that gets sterilized and treated so that it's suitable for these special children, and sling pouches that the mother can wear and keep the baby nestled inside so that the baby can be kept close directly against the mother's skin to help the baby thrive. We even provide funding for lodging and travel for the mother so that she can be with her baby as much as possible," she explained. She took a sip of her wine and shrugged casually. "It's no biggie. I usually provide an item of jewelry for the family as a memento of their time spent using our organization."

"That's so impressive," I said. "Have you helped many women and babies?"

"Over one hundred and fifty so far, since I started four years ago."

"You're supporting families during what is a particularly stressful time," said Celia. who had been listening carefully with Gabby.

Liz chewed her bottom lip, her brow furrowing before choosing to answer. "Yes, I found out from personal experience how painful it is to lose a baby. That's why I do what I do."

Celia touched Liz on her nearest forearm. "I've been through it too, Liz. But you can always try again. Perhaps it will work out for you?"

Liz shook her head quickly, drawing her arm away. "It's too late for me. There was an accident, you see." She shook her head. "It was a long time ago. No point in dwelling on the past now, is there." She smiled broadly. "Not when there are people who need my help."

I understood now why she was so keen to help others out. And I wondered again why I was invited to the Wilde Event, as I hadn't done anything worthwhile like the people I'd met so far.

"Well," continued Celia, "you're an absolute treasure. Isn't she everyone?"

We all agreed whole-heartedly.

Rupert cleared his throat and spoke directly to Liz. "I remember the accident. It's a wonder no-one was killed. I'm glad that life has turned out well for you. You deserve it."

She gave a small smile and a nod of her head in thanks, then focused on what was happening out on the water.

"Talking of bodies at your dig sites," Rupert asked me, "didn't someone get injured or die at Heritage Hole a while back?"

Chapter Four

"Ah, you heard about that." The group were now very interested in hearing more about someone else's mishaps.

"Around here, it would be hard not to," he quipped.

Before I could answer, a clipped female voice butted in. "Well, well. Isn't this nice."

We turned as one to look at the speaker who had squeezed her way into our group and was addressing us all. Her snippy attitude snapped everyone out of their interest in what had happened at the latest dig site.

The new woman came almost to the height of my shoulders but what was most striking was her dark hair. The effect was almost magnetic, and I did my best not to stare, but I just could not take my eyes off the sleekness and precision of the most perfect bob, cut sharply to meet the woman's jaw. My right hand went unconsciously to my own hair with its straggly blonde layers, and I tucked a stray lock behind my ear to tame it.

My adopted mother's Scottish accent, as clear as if she was standing beside me whispering 'don't gawk!' broke through my thoughts and the conversations swirling around the yacht club balcony. Images of myself watching my mother wrapping her fingers absent mindedly through her unruly tangle of Kathrine Hepburn-style hair flashed up as clear as day. Forgive me mum, I thought, (being British she preferred mum to mom,) but even you would stare at this woman's hair.

"Melissa. Fancy meeting you here of all places," said Liz.

"Well, I did receive an invitation, you know. I'm not the hired help," she sniffed. "Hi everyone, I'm Melissa Maxwell," she announced. "General Manager of the Saltside Hotel Group. You're probably familiar with our flagship hotel located in the north part of Legacy Cove."

Rupert appeared by her side and gave her a quick peck on a cheek. "It's thanks to Melissa that one of the hotel chains that she manages now provides long-stay accommodations for free for some of the families that I treat, as well as those of children receiving care at New England Children's Hospital."

She smiled coyly at him.

Saltside was the private luxury group hotel on the Cape. And according to Troy, it was reportedly booked out two years in advance for weddings and at least three times more expensive than other local hotels, although on a par with the big names in Boston.

"Hey Liz, hi guys," chimed a happy voice as another woman joined us on Liz's left, linking an arm through one of Rupert's and kissing him on both cheeks before introducing herself to the whole group. "Lashawna White, of Washashore Animal Rescue."

Rupert pecked Lashawna back. "Lashawna is amazing. Her no kill shelter saves hundreds of animals each year."

"You're such a smooth talker you," she said, giving his arm a playful squeeze. "I will say though that this is our fifth and best year so far," she enthused, "with over four hundred animals saved and either fostered or adopted." Lashawna had a warm round face, and white hair that flowed in wiry curls past her shoulders. Her hair was tied back lightly by a long and colorful abstract scarf that added a splash of color against her full length loose-fitting red and powder-blue flowery linen dress. She looked a similar age to Bernard.

I smiled warmly at Lashawna. "Who doesn't love dogs? And cats too, I guess." We all laughed. "Actually, it's great to meet you in person. I rescued my dog Duke from Washashore three months after coming to Legacy Cove, when he was only a year old," I explained, just as Troy sidled up between Gabby and I with two glasses of chilled white wine for us and a broad grin on his face.

"Introductions over? I'm sure you'll all find today very beneficial in some way for you. Now, while we're waiting on a few more people to arrive it's time to start the bidding on a few items, the highlight being an all-expenses paid trip to

Boston to stay at the Ritz for a weekend in August, attend the premiere of the latest production of the *Les Miserables* musical on the Saturday evening, all with a limo driver to take you and a companion there and back. You probably all know '*Les Mis*' is sold out, so the highest bidder is going to be really lucky to attend it."

"This sounds wonderful," said Celia, nudging her husband Bernard. "Go make a bid for it darling. You know how much I love musicals."

"In a moment dear."

Liz beamed at Troy. "I'm a fan of musicals too. Where do I make the bid?"

Troy pointed over the heads of the assembled guests to the left of the bar. "There's a table set up with display stands showing all the donated items to bid on."

"I'm going now," she said. "Anyone else want to come?"

"Count me in," said Melissa.

"Me too," said Lashawna.

The three of them left and squeezed their way through the crowd.

"Why don't we move our group over to the railing to watch the start of the race until the last of my guests arrive," said Troy. He waved an arm in the direction of the long side of the balcony overlooking the carpark and the ocean beyond it. "And don't worry, I've arranged for a server to be right over to take any more drink orders. It's so busy at the bar, a person could collapse from thirst first."

We moved to the side of the balcony overlooking Vineyard Sound, the body of ocean between the Cape and Martha's Vineyard. Twenty small sailboats, each with a different colored sail bobbed on the waves about three hundred yards offshore and maneuvered around each other like horses before a race. Just over six miles away, the hazy shoreline of Martha's Vineyard was in view from East to West, while to my right was Heritage Hole where several of my colleagues in other departments worked on marine biology research ships and oceanic related projects. The sun caught the water and I marveled at the way it shimmered and sparkled. I never tire of seeing the ocean.

I felt a presence on my right shoulder accompanied by a strong whiff of a florally perfume and looked at the owner. It was Celia. She leaned in close and glanced over at Rupert. "He's quite the catch now that he's divorced, you know." Her voice sounded even more raspy as she tried to speak so that she couldn't be overheard, yet there was so much noise from the other attendees that I think she could have stood on a table to address me and very few people would have heard her.

"Oh really?" I did remember Troy mentioning something similar the day that I received the Wilde invitation, although I wasn't about to let on that I was aware of his marital status in case people thought I was keeping tabs on him. Plus, the last person I would ever want to date would be him. His poor wife had probably had enough of his meanness, and I wasn't about to share my dislike of the man with Celia as she was obviously smitten with him.

"Even though," she continued, "he comes with one piece of baggage. If you know what I mean." She raised an eyebrow.

I shook my head. "I'm sorry, I'm not following you."

"He has a son. Stevie. He's twelve or thirteen now, I think."

"Are you trying to set me up Celia?"

She smiled coyly. "Just saying, you know. Doesn't do any harm to share."

"He's not my type," I said curtly. The startled look on her face made me realize I'd either responded too strongly, or she'd misinterpreted what I meant. "What I mean is, I prefer a different type of guy."

"Oh well, you can't blame me for simply letting you know the facts," she said laughing.

We were now in a small group chatting about the events in town, from the latest controversy of the location of a large housing development to the latest sighting of a great white shark. The race had just started when Troy bounded back with another man who was about my height and inserted him into our ever-growing group. Bernard Lazenby's body stiffened. "I didn't realize you would be here Stadler," he said touchily. "Not your type of thing, is it?"

"Gather round, gather round everyone," said Troy merrily, choosing to ignore Bernard's dig at the man called Stadler. "This chap here," he said turning to the man on his other side "is none other than Simon Stadler who owns Stadler Construction and Landscaping."

The name meant nothing to me, but clearly meant a lot to Bernard as he visibly bristled at the man in front of us. "Still designing your cheap homes, Stadler?" he quipped.

Simon straightened visibly and adjusted his Maui Jim's, giving a glimpse of narrow eyes behind the tinted lenses as they bore into Bernard Lazenby. "My design team is innovative, and our work is impeccable and you know it," he hissed between clenched teeth. "You only wish you could come up with the creative ideas that we do." He took a sip of what appeared to be a cloudy lager or an IPA from the tall glass he was holding.

"Creative shortcuts, you mean."

Simon Stadler shifted his stance to ignore Bernard, who had resumed talking, louder if that was possible, with Rupert Boyden, and turned instead to address Gabby, essentially ignoring me and by default the other women too, even though we were a small informal group. From where I stood, I could eavesdrop on his conversation in case Gabby needed someone to bail her out.

"I'm so pleased to finally get a chance to meet you Gabriella," he said. "I recognized you from the last Chamber meeting," referring presumably to the Legacy Cove Chamber of Commerce. "You're the talk of the Chamber, if not the town," he said smoothly.

"The talk of the Chamber?" repeated Gabby. She stared at me with a poker face. I knew that look. It said I've got this.

"Why, yes. You must be one of the most successful Legacy Cove companies that we've had in years, including mine I may add. You're probably up there with my own company of course. We've all heard about the major investors who are backing your organization and we hope that you'll continue the expansion here in town."

"Ah, I see. The rumor mill is quite a unique entity isn't it," she said as she cleared her throat. "Unfortunately, I'm not at liberty to share any information at this stage." Then without missing a beat she turned to me. "Simon, have you met my friend Dr. Marnie Frazer?"

Simon smiled an acknowledgement.

Liz and Lashawna joined us from placing their bids. Gabby and I would need to do likewise when she finished talking with Simon. I scanned the crowd and spotted Melissa sidling up to Rupert. They were well suited.

"And these wonderful women here," Gabby continued, "are Liz, Lashawna, Kaylee and Sabrina, and Celia."

Simon raised his beer glass. "Ladies." He then turned back to Gabby.

"Excuse me," said Liz rummaging in her handbag and pulling out a white paper tissue and wiping the corners of her eyes before stuffing the tissue back in the depths of her bag. "Allergies. They're awful when I'm surrounded by lots of perfume. I can't even go into the beauty section at Nordstrom's without sneezing or my eyes watering."

She gave a little shrug as though putting up with the clouds of perfume and other fragrances from lotions that drifted languidly in the balcony space was an everyday occurrence. "I'm used to it though, so it's not really a big deal."

Liz then leaned closer to us so that Simon couldn't overhear her. "He's such a crook," she said as quietly as she could manage given the increasing volume of the guests, nodding her head slightly in Simon's direction. "The way he always makes a killing snatching up the best land zoned for development. And of course, that's all before he does perk tests and the like and then sells it off for a huge profit. But I've heard that he has big debts to pay off."

"Apparently he's under investigation," added Lashawna. "Money problems."

Celia cleared her throat. "I don't know about him being investigated but from what I hear he doesn't have any problems with money." She raised an eyebrow and pursed her lips. "In fact, he's splashing it around buying all sorts of expensive items."

"Like what?" asked Kaylee, leaning in with Sabrina.

"Well, apparently, he's just bought a boat that has not two, not three, but four outboard engines. It retails at over 400K."

"Wow!" we all said.

"I know. No-one knows where he got the money to throw around like that."

"You could buy a small cottage or an apartment for that amount of money," stated Sabrina.

"Could it be from the land deals that Liz mentioned?" Kaylee asked.

Celia shook her head. "Unlikely," she said. "In his type of business, he has to reinvest the money otherwise he's liable for a huge tax bill at the end of the year. By reinvesting he avoids paying up, but it does mean that while he's wealthy on paper, in reality he doesn't have any spare cash floating around."

I was going to ask Liz and Lashawna what the big debts and money problems were that they were referring to when I felt Gabby and Simon beside me.

"Gabriela tells me that you're a professor at Legacy College Marnie," Simon stated.

"Yes. I'm head of the archaeology department."

"Well, I'm glad my company has never unearthed any artifacts on our sites. We couldn't afford the stoppage on a job for old bones and bits of pottery and other crap that's going to get stuck in a glass case and never see the light of day again." He laughed and raised his beer glass. "Anyhoo, the Wilde event is proving to be quite an unusual affair this year. Apparently, she's invited a special guest."

I was uncomfortably aware that I'd been given the quick once over as his gaze flicked up and down me. I was beginning to see why Bernard in particular had bristled when he saw that Simon Stadler was present.

Simon looked at me expectantly. Was he wondering if I was the extra person? More likely, I thought, there was an extra person because it was a mistake and Suzie Wilde was in the awkward position where the invitation had gone out and it was absolutely unheard of to say, 'oops, sorry,' and take the invitation away. Nevertheless, I simply smiled and shrugged. "You're more in touch with this than I am. Thanks for the inside scoop."

He cleared his throat. "Nice to meet you all. I see some other people I need to catch up with. I look forward to catching up at the big event," he said as he drained his glass and slipped off into the crowd, presumably heading to the bar.

Not if I can help it, I thought, just as an ever-smiling Troy joined us, with a harried yet helpful server carrying a bar stool. I caught a glimpse of a dark-haired woman, who stood at least two inches taller than Troy, and three inches taller than me, walking behind him. Troy appeared to be in his element mixing and mingling within the ever-expanding group and had done a good job at bringing in people to the fund-raiser. One thing that I'd grown to appreciate through my teens and adult life was the generosity of human beings, as I had also found out with the many volunteers on dig sites around the world. Many people on the Cape were generous in helping others not only with their time, but with their wallets and creative talents as well.

With several 'do you mind' and 'excuse me' and even a couple of 'oops' our small group shuffled and bumped elbows and maneuvered enough space to make room for the addition of a barstool and two more people. "Troy, thanks again for the invite, and sorry we're late," the woman said slightly out of breath. Her voice had a warm, smooth tone. "Hey everyone," she said, smiling at the small group. "Sorry I'm late. Let me get a seat. After a stiff G and T, I'll feel better."

"Everyone," announced Troy, "this is Amoy Johnson. Her partner Mark Kleinman will be here soon."

"I'm right behind you," added a dark-haired man who had successfully squeezed his way through the crowd to our group.

Shorter than Amoy by at least six inches he was the afore-mentioned Mark, carrying a dark beer in a frosted glass and a tall glass rattling with ice floating in what was presumably a gin and tonic for Amoy. They clinked glasses and smiled at each other as they said 'cheers'.

"Now don't forget to bid on the donated items," said Troy. "Remember it's all for a good cause." He paused briefly before adding, "especially the item for the Les Miserables musical."

We all introduced ourselves yet again, each of us sharing a little bit of information about our businesses or, in my case, my occupation. I liked Amoy's openness and friendly demeanor, as she touched briefly on her life growing up in Miami before her parents moved to Massachusetts when she was in fifth-grade. We all laughed out loud when she told us about seeing snow for the first time. Now she worked as a Massachusetts lawyer specializing in family law, while her husband Mark owned a law firm working primarily in conveyancing in commercial real estate. "Life is good," she laughed. "If you don't include a vandalized car."

"That's awful, Amoy," said Troy. "What happened?"

"Someone keyed my car, that's what. And I'm still fuming."

"Have you reported it?" asked Celia.

"Absolutely I reported it. That's why Mark and I were late getting here. I was hoping when we went to the police station that they'd tell me that this was one of many vehicles damaged, and that they had an idea of who was behind the spate of vandalism, but sadly no. We're no further forward in finding out who's behind it."

"We have to put a stop to this," insisted Celia. "People work hard to earn nice property."

Amoy took a gulp of her drink. "It's probably kids, or someone drunk or high that did it and we'll never find out who."

"At least you have insurance," added Bernard.

"Absolutely. It's not the fact that my Range Rover is a bloody expensive car, it's the principle, don't you think. Otherwise, there'd be no repercussions. Plus, there's the inconvenience of not having a vehicle when it's in the shop being repaired."

Mark raised an eyebrow in Bernard's direction. "I wouldn't try to tangle with Amoy. She's one of the best family lawyers in the state, and once she's decided on something, there's no stopping her. Isn't that right dear," he said, winking at his wife.

She winked back. "Well thanks for the high praise honey, and yes, I'm determined to find out who did this and when I do, I'll make sure he or she has to do community service cleaning and polishing cars until they get the message that other people's property isn't to be messed with." She took a deep breath and shook her head slowly. "I can dream, I suppose," she laughed. "Talking of dreams, I'm looking forward to going to the Wilde event and seeing what all the fuss is about."

We all laughed then Troy, ever the social mixer, took Mark, Bernard, and Rupert to meet some other guests.

"It's just us now ladies," I said. Another round of drinks ordered, we settled in with our little group watching the yachts racing in the bay and getting to know each other. I enjoyed chatting with everyone, and Gabby and Lashawna were adept at keeping us all laughing with their stories. My sauvignon blanc seemed to be growing warmer with each sip and I considered switching to an iced soda water while I scanned the guests in the other groups who were all growing louder.

The group on my left were four men, with Simon Stadler in the mix, fresh from the bar, silent and brooding as he gripped another glass of beer.

Bernard was in the next group over on the right with Rupert, Mark, Troy and two other men and unlike Simon Stadler, he was loud and now appeared slightly drunk as he flung his arms up to emphasize the story he was sharing. His wine glass was empty on the high-top table they were standing beside.

"The men always seem to do this don't they," remarked Amoy, nodding to where Troy and Mark and the other men were now huddled in groups ignoring the yacht race.

"Definitely," I agreed, looking at the all-male groups. "No matter whether it's a house party or a formal event they always seem to be able to separate themselves into a huddle…" I saw Bernard staring towards the entrance with the ocean behind it. Rupert turned, apparently mid-sentence, to see what Bernard was looking at. He was about to break away from the group but stopped and turned to look in the direction of my group instead. Liz was listening intently to Gabby, wiping her eyes with a tissue and giving a little sniffle as she did so. Allergies, I overheard her say.

As though there was a communal thought, all the attendees turned as one mass, straining to peer over the heads of the other guests to see what everyone was looking at. Amoy and I had a clear view, given our height. "It's a late arrival," I informed the group.

It appeared that everyone on the balcony had now turned to stare at the newcomer, or rather the latecomer. The crowd parted to reveal a woman wearing a yellow sundress that clung to her body as she walked. It appeared to reflect onto her hair and catch the late afternoon sunshine creating the illusion that she too was golden and not made of flesh and blood. She was unflustered and didn't seem to be bothered by the fact that everyone was looking at her. I got the impression she was used to such a reaction; that everyone was waiting just for her.

A petite Gucci canvas bag was slung casually over her left shoulder, its signature horse-bit and red and green colors on show, and even from where I stood, I could see the woman's moist lips shimmer with red gloss.

"Who is she?" I mouthed to Gabby.

"Don't know," she mouthed back.

We watched Troy greet the woman as men and women moved aside to allow them to pass through while giving themselves a chance to gaze a little longer at her.

Celia leaned in close to me. "Oh, oh. This will be interesting. She's one of Rupert's past girlfriends."

I looked sideways at her.

Celia raised an eyebrow while nodding conspiratorially at me. "Plus, her organization has had a very successful year," she stated, emphasizing the word very. "Apparently, it's solely her vision that has increased the company's profits."

"That's impressive."

"That's not all. There's what she has done for the community," continued Celia. "Bernard and I heard that she won yet another municipal contract to provide low-cost lottery housing. It's heavily subsidized for the home-owners and good for the company's bottom line, you see. And that's not all." She tilted her head quickly in Melissa's direction. "They don't get on. That's what happens when you both date the same guy."

I sipped my wine. I couldn't think of a response to that piece of information. But the afternoon was surely going to get even more livelier if the two women interacted with each other.

After a stop at the bar, Troy guided the vision, who was still being tracked openly by the other guests, to where my little group was stationed. "Ladies, let me introduce you to Amber Clarke. Amber works at the Artemis Group where she's a specialist in medical research, and she's also going to the Suzie Wilde event."

Amber slid effortlessly into our group between Gabby and Liz and myself. She smiled broadly at each of us. "Hi everyone. Lovely to meet you all."

A quick round of introductions was fired off with Amber giving the highlights of her organization and its success with helping sick children and their families. I marveled at Amber. Even her name evoked feelings of being rare and special.

Liz turned to Amber, smiling broadly at her. "Remember me? Nice to see you again, JC, I mean Amber. It's been too long," she said as Troy departed to mingle yet again.

Honestly, I thought. The man could teach classes at the college on how to socialize and network effectively.

"Liz? Oh my gosh. Liz Tanner. How long has it been?" Amber beamed a perfect white smile as a waitress arrived with a glass of white wine for her.

"Too long. After spending the last fifteen years on the Outer Cape building up my company, I returned to Legacy Cove ten months ago to expand into the Upper Cape. I'm friends with Troy…"

"Aren't we all though," she laughed.

"Yes, of course, it's Troy we're talking about, so anyway, when he invited me here he mentioned some people who would also be here, and you were one of them."

"Oh? I didn't know that many people knew about me and my work." She smiled coyly.

"Seems like you're very well known, and appreciated I might add."

"Who did you talk to?"

"Rupert. I bumped into him by chance a couple of months ago at the supermarket near the harbor. I thought you had moved from the area as I couldn't find you listed anywhere. He told me all about you; that you'd changed your first name, what you've been doing, even who you've been dating since."

"Dating? Ha! That's a joke." Amber looked at each of us and laughed. "I just simply don't have the time." She shrugged. "Not that it matters anyway."

I smiled at her. "I feel the same way."

"Me too," chimed Gabby.

"Not me," said Celia.

"Nor me," added Lashawna.

Amber beamed at Liz. "Liz and I knew each other when we were teens," she explained. "This was back when we were in school and had nicknames. Mine was JC, but of course we're all grown up now, and I go by my middle name, rather than my first name of Janie. Anyway I think Amber is more professional sounding."

I always liked the name Janie. It was very popular in my Scottish mother's family, with an aunt and a cousin both with the same first name.

"I'm intrigued," said Celia, turning to face Liz. "What was your nickname?"

"Just Liz," she said with a straight face, then a broad smile lit up her face.

We all burst out laughing.

"Well, 'Just Liz'," continued Celia, "I think it's really wonderful that you still have old friends here and that you'll now be able to stay in touch. Staying connected with anyone, for that matter, is a hard thing to do."

We all voiced our agreement to that. I knew for myself how hard it was to forge long-term friends, due to the nature of my work pulling me away for long stretches at a time. I traveled less once I was appointed as an assistant professor and subsequently got married, but by then I was focused on my work and our friends were really Craig's friends. It wasn't until I came to Legacy Cove that I found myself with friends who were mine, not the friends of someone else.

Amber flashed a warm smile. "You've never changed Liz. Always the joker amongst us. We could never tell if you were being funny or serious until your face crinkled up and you'd erupt in a fit of laughter at catching us out."

"What? You don't think I've changed?" grinned Liz feigning mock horror, her hands fanned out on both cheeks.

Amber nudged her gently with an elbow.

I envied their friendship, and that they could pick it up so easily like it had been only yesterday they'd seen each other.

Then Amber turned to me, her head cocked slightly to one side suddenly interested in me. "Hey, I heard that you don't know why you were invited to Suzie's event. Is that really true?"

I took a breath in and realized I was holding it. I didn't like where this was going, not one little bit. I felt the others staring at me, waiting on my answer. Why indeed had I had received an invitation? "Actually it's not for me to question why any of us, me included, warranted an invitation. I'm just happy that I received one."

Having put on my best professorial tone, I hoped that I sounded competent in my response and that I was successful in diverting the potential flow of curiosity away from me. Amber's interest was a natural one, and even I wanted to know the answer as to why I had been invited to the event.

Amber's expression was dead-pan. "Well said. I reckon we're all glad we got an invitation." With a public humiliation averted we resumed chatting about our work, each one of us passionate about our fields of work.

My reverie was short-lived and I groaned inwardly as Rupert rejoined us, sidling up to Amber, Melissa by his side.

Melissa leaned in to Amber and said something to her that I couldn't catch due to the elevated voices around us.

"Ha, ha" laughed Amber loudly and sarcastically to whatever it was that Melissa had said to her. "What have you done for someone else that brought you to the well-meaning attention of Suzie Wilde and her organization, I wonder."

Now each of us turned our attention to the bickering women. It was hard to ignore the spitefulness between both of them.

"Actually," remarked Rupert, draping an arm around Melissa and attempting to intercede between her and Amber, "Melissa is doing a fine job."

Gabby caught my eye and moved to come over to stand beside me, visibly relieved at being able to distance herself from the bickering duo.

Rupert continued his defense of Melissa. "If it wasn't for Melissa's initiative, a lot more families would be significantly impacted financially, as well as emotionally, as they struggle with all that's involved in dealing with a sick child."

"Thank you, Dr Rupert," cooed Melissa, snuggling up to him.

Amber visibly bristled. "She's not personally involved in that though, is she?" Looking at Amber's reaction to Rupert sticking up for Melissa, it was highly possible that she had had a past relationship with Rupert.

"Of course, I am," huffed Melissa. "I oversee it as the General Manager."

"I'm lucky," added Rupert, addressing our group, "to personally know both Melissa *and* Amber, both of whom are two very successful women."

"Thank you, Rupert," said Melissa. Her perfect haircut swung as she leaned into him. "You know I don't like to talk about myself."

I almost choked as I took a sip of wine, as did Amoy and Celia.

"In fact," continued Rupert, patting her gently on her upper back, "it's rumored that Melissa is going to be this year's 'Person of The Year' at the Legacy Cove Chamber of Commerce."

I glanced at Gabby quickly, then back to Rupert. As far as I knew, it was Gabby who was tipped to be this year's recipient, and from what I'd seen this afternoon, I don't think that Melissa was the type to let that award slip through her tiny grasping fingers.

Melisa wasn't finished though and straightened up, smiling coyly at Rupert. "You of all people should know that I don't like to count my chickens before they're hatched."

I paused mid-sip. That was the same phrase that Gabby had used a few weeks ago when I assured her that she was likely to do exceptionally well with the public launch of her company. I hoped that Melissa didn't know that Gabby was also a contender for the 'Person of The Year'.

Amber shook her head slowly, her golden blond hair shimmering in the warmth of the late afternoon sunlight. "I hardly think you'd have anything to do with the well-being of children," she said softly so that likely only Melissa, Rupert, and Gabby and I could hear as we were standing closest to her. She took a tiny step forward towards Melissa. "Isn't that why your husband left you? For another woman who was pregnant with his child because you refused to have any?"

Melissa ignored the jibe and lowered her voice. "I'm sure your little projects are very nice, dear. But Suzie's party is for the elite, not for struggling wannabees."

Amber clenched her fist that wasn't holding her wineglass, her eyes flashing with fury. "At least I wasn't a plastic surgeon's wife who had him rebuild my entire face!"

Meow! I thought. I decided to squash this little spat before it grew into something worse and addressed our group. "It was good of Troy to invite us all today so that we can get to know each other before the big event. How do each of you know Troy?"

Amber remained noticeably quiet as the conversation shifted to laughing and reminiscing about how each person knew Troy and for how long. Gabby had known him the longest; ten years, while the others all thought they'd known him for at least five years or so. Gabby had met Troy when she graduated from Harvard with two masters, one in computer science and one in business studies. Troy had helped her find office space for her start-up and also her cottage, as the Cape also had great tax incentives for women-owned businesses. She was a 'washashore', having grown up with her family in San Antonio Texas before being accepted to study at Harvard.

I had known him for a little over two years and while I listened to the other women chat, I cast a side-ways glance at Melissa Maxwell who I was now coming to think of as BobCat. It wasn't so much the bob-cut hairstyle, but the slinky way she stole up to the group and the way her green eyes moved from person to person, watching. There was something else about her that bothered me though. It went deeper than superficial feline qualities. Something lurked deep down, hidden. The woman's face seemed familiar, yet there was more to it than a vague shadow of a past connection. The facial expressions were perfectly poised just like the hair, her body language open and non-threatening.

Despite this, I felt that there was something decidedly off about Melissa.

I felt her shaded gaze bore into me.

Searching.

"Marnie, Marnie, Marnie," she repeated. I locked eyes with her and stood straighter. "I knew a Marnie once," she continued slowly. "I wonder if you are the same one?"

"Oh, but Marnie's not really from around here," Gabby piped in. "She's from Boston. Her parents are professors. Like Marnie."

"Hmm. Pity, it would have been lovely to get reacquainted."

I'll bet it would, I thought. I wasn't about to share with Melissa that in junior high school my name was Marnie Hitson and that when I left, I took my adoptive parents' surname. The past was the past and that was where it belonged. Although, shedding the past was proving to be harder than I realized and now, after twenty-five years, it was still a work in progress.

I felt Rupert's gaze on me. Did I remind him of someone he knew when we were children?

Glancing quickly around I saw the opportune moment to escape from any further probing and prying. Amber was chatting with Amoy, Lashawna, Liz, and Celia. I gripped Gabby by the elbow, smiled quickly at Melissa and Rupert, and with a quick 'lovely to meet you all, see you later,' I moved Gabby and myself over to join the other women.

"Of course, it was a wonderful surprise for my company to be nominated this year," said Amber as we joined her and the others. "We're primarily involved in the research of clinical depression, and in particular the correlation between biological and environmental factors. That said, we help women who are in need because we want to, not for any personal gain. However, the rewards just seem to continue coming our way."

Unfortunately, Melissa and Rupert fell in behind us. Melissa sniffed like she didn't believe a word and took a small sip of her red wine, failing to hide her distaste of Amber's virtuous comment. "It's not only women who need help," she chimed in as she stared steadily at Amber. "There are single men too, raising a child or children if the mother has died," she shrugged, "or they just upped and left. Drugs or something." She sniffed and drew herself up while pursing her lips. "What about them? Hmm?"

I sensed another squabble starting and interceded again. "Everyone who has been invited has done something of merit. And of course, we can all continue to do something each year to help one another."

"And what would you know about it?" Melissa spat back. "You didn't earn an invitation. You're only going because you're friends with Gabriella Martinez and she's been successful with her company."

I felt like I'd been slapped in public. I took a deep calming breath but Gabby stepped in to set the record straight. "Just to clarify Melissa, it is in fact I who is the plus one."

Before I could add anything else, a ruckus erupted in Troy's group where Bernard Lazenby, his hair and bushy brow aglow with perspiration, was poking a finger repeatedly into Simon Stadler's chest with Stadler swiping Lazenby's hand away like it was a flying pest. Those nearest to the incident backed away slightly while turning to watch the commotion as Troy, ever the diplomat, pushed his way in-between them and said something that was apparently funny causing both men to laugh and push each other away. To look at them now they seemed to be saying we're only having a bit of 'boys being boys' type of fun.

Simon Stadler's slouched back was to me as he pushed his way through to the bar, with Bernard Lazenby's glare following him, reflecting a look of sheer loathing. I recalled that Bernard Lazenby, with his thunderous temperament, was involved in commercial real estate and his company had raised a ton of money for a local family charity with their fundraising drive since last December.

Simon Stadler, on the other hand, with his own construction company, was in my opinion equally matched against Lazenby with his hands-on approach to helping to ease homelessness for families by providing labor, lumber, and other resources to build the homes. How much more they could achieve by working together instead of fighting.

And why were they in a direct dispute with each other? Troy would likely know the answer. I made a mental note to ask him later.

The uproar over, people resumed their conversations, chatting and drinking and laughing. Friends and family of the crews out in the bay were the ones actually watching the race and cheering for people by name (although the teams were so far offshore that those sailing wouldn't hear the cheering) and the conversation in our group moved onto the race and did anyone know who was winning.

I chose to ignore Melissa's previous dig at me, but I could still feel her icy stare boring into me as I gazed over at the race with the small yachts with their colorful little sails turning around floating markers and passing each other with barely an inch to spare from my distant vantage point.

Smashing glass and icy cold liquid on my legs jolted me from my reverie and it took me a second to realize that Amber's wine glass now lay shattered on the deck and her chilled wine was spreading amongst my sandals and bare toes.

We all jumped back to get away from the glass and spilled liquid while at the same time Amber was bent over, wheezing and gasping for breath. Her little Gucci bag swayed in her hands as she fumbled with it, trying to open the clasp and failing with each attempt. She was becoming bluer in the face with each passing second.

Chapter Five

I sprang into action, wrapping my arms around Amber and lowering her to the wooden deck while opening her bag and reaching inside.

"What are you doing," demanded Melissa. "Someone stop her. Call for help!"

Amber slumped against me. "Pen," she choked, her lips cyanotic. Her eyes closed and I feared that she had passed out, or worse, that she'd stopped breathing entirely.

I rummaged frantically inside her bag and pulled out what looked like a blue pen and removed the cap, revealing a small orange tip. "Ready?"

Amber barely responded as I pushed up part of her dress to expose her right upper thigh and swiftly plunged the orange tip into her bare leg. I pushed the top of the device down feeling it click, confirming that the epinephrine inside had been administered. After the count of three I removed the pen and waited for a positive response from her.

An interminable age passed, but was in fact only a few seconds. Had I reached her in time?

The crowd jostled for a better position. "I'm a doctor," I heard a man say. "Let me through." I looked up as Rupert pushed his way through the last of the crowd. He crouched down beside me, and lifted one of Amber's hands and checked the pulse in her wrist. "What happened?" he asked me. He appeared calm, which contrasted to how I was feeling with my racing pulse and shaking hands. I was experiencing an extreme rush of adrenaline. I explained as much as I knew, and as succinctly as I could muster, showing him the EpiPen that I had retrieved from Amber's bag.

"And you gave her one shot?" he asked.

"Yes." I averted my eyes from his and forced myself to concentrate on Amber. She moaned and her eyes fluttered open. Rupert smiled as she regained focus, and she gave a hint of a smile back. Remarkably, her breathing steadied itself, although, despite her bronzer make-up, her lips remained blue-tinged.

"Thanks," she muttered faintly, a light spritz of perspiration erupting on her forehead and neck.

"No problem," I said, trying to reassure her. She turned her head slowly to me. A flicker of a smile turned up the corners of her mouth, and she leaned into me. I ignored the crowd of onlookers pressing forward, many watching slightly aghast at what had just transpired. Reluctantly I addressed Rupert. "Has an ambulance been called?"

He nodded. "Did it myself. Although I gather several other guests also did the same."

Satisfied that Amber would soon get professional help, I was curious as to what had happened to her and wanted to ensure that whatever had harmed her was not still in the vicinity. "Do you know what you came in contact with that triggered the allergic reaction?"

She shook her head feebly. "I'm allergic to peanuts. I didn't eat any." She stopped for breath and licked her lips that were now visibly dry. "Unless someone nearby was eating them… and breathed on me?"

I looked up at the crowd that had gathered around us. "Did anyone see anyone with peanuts?" I called out. "Anything like that?"

They all shook their heads, murmurs of negativity filtering through to us. But then again, most of us had been distracted by the dispute between Bernard and Simon. Sirens grew closer and there was the audible rumble of tires on the gravel beneath the balcony.

"The ambulance is here," someone in the crowd called out. Moments later the people parted as the ambulance crew climbed the stairs to check on Amber. "I'm fine," she insisted. "Really."

"You should go with them," I said firmly.

"Definitely," agreed Rupert. "In case there's a delayed secondary response. In fact, I'll follow the ambulance in your car. Drive you back."

She sighed, but without much energy, and then proceeded to rummage in her bag, slowly handing Rupert the keys. "It's the blue Range Rover. The fob will show you the right one."

Rupert and I stood up, and the assembled guests parted ways to allow Amber to be escorted out by the paramedics and into the waiting ambulance. I walked over to Gabby and smiled wearily. I was relieved that Amber was going to be okay.

Melissa lifted her chin and sniffed. "Hmm," she muttered as she made to leave the event. She looked back over her shoulder to face me. "She likely did it on purpose for attention."

I bit my tongue so that I didn't respond to the idiotic comment. What was wrong with the woman? Couldn't she see that Amber would likely have died of anaphylactic shock without help?

I froze.

A memory arose from over two decades ago of a girl I knew called Melissa. Could it be the same one? The one who was a bully and enjoyed making anyone that she deemed beneath her miserable?

Back then in junior high, the girl was called Melissa Cooke.

Some things never change though.

I looked at her directly. The eyes and tone of voice gave her away.

Melissa Maxwell was Melissa Cooke.

That explained why she was so condescending and snarky to everyone. Did she know who I was?

Probably. If not now, then soon. Very few people beyond Gabby, Troy, and my department colleagues knew I was adopted and that I had spent my early childhood here in Legacy Cove. But I'm not the same person that I was as a child. And I'm not going to let anyone drag me down. The bullying by Melissa and her crew ended when I left Legacy Cove with my new Scottish-American parents for a life in Boston, with summers spent helping at digs in countries that many of my teenage peers had only ever seen on a map.

If she wanted to pick up where she left off all those years ago, well, she had better think again. She didn't know what I was capable of.

I scanned the group of men and women who had now resumed chatting in their groups. What happened to Amber didn't concern them.

"C'mon Gabby," I said. "Time to leave. It's been way too much for one afternoon."

We waited in the parking lot for a local taxi to pick us up. The guests' cars varied in size and price. A few Audis and BMWs along with several pick-up trucks, a Tesla, a couple of Toyotas, and at least three Jeep Wranglers completed the stable of cars as designated drivers drifted downstairs with their passengers and poured them into the vehicles. I mused on the fact that there were actually two blue Range Rovers owned by invitees to the Suzie Wilde event; one was Amber's, and one was Amoy's with the keyed scratch running from the driver's front wing to the rear panel.

And the other pressing question was where did the source of the peanuts come from?

And was it an accident?

Chapter Six

"You were amazing acting so quickly like that," said Gabby on the taxi ride home. "I still can't get over it. You literally saved her life!"

"It's nothing really. Like I said, it's what I'm trained to do. Having a first-aid qualification is required in my profession. After all, when you're in the middle of nowhere, dealing with sharp tools and sometimes having to crawl into generally unsafe places, all in close proximity with other people, it's easy to see that accidents can happen. Plus, there's also the natural injuries that can occur when someone collapses due to sun stroke, dehydration, or even serious heart issues like the event that happened suddenly four months ago with one of our volunteers."

"Wow, I never considered the variety of things that you have to do in your profession. I thought it was just research and analysis. You're quite the "Jill of all trades".

"I'm still a little shook up, to tell the truth. I kind of did it on auto-pilot. If she wasn't carrying the EpiPen she could have died before the ambulance crew arrived."

"You don't think that she was harmed deliberately, do you?"

I'd actually thought that there was every likelihood that someone had done this on purpose, given that I hadn't seen Amber, or anyone in the group, consume any nuts. But if it was deliberate, how did it happen? I didn't want to share my morbid thoughts though as I had no proof. All I had was merely a hunch as I didn't believe in coincidences. I gave a shrug in reply.

"I have people," continued Gabby, "from my HR department who are in charge of first-aid and the regular fire drills, but I think the last, and come to think of it the only time we've had to have an ambulance is when one of the programmers went into early labor when her waters broke, six weeks before her due date. That was quite the event."

I agreed. "So was this. I'd much rather stick to what I love to do and leave the heroics to the professionals."

"Hopefully your quick thinking and training won't be needed anytime soon."

The taxi dropped Gabby off first, and I put the events of the yacht club fundraiser firmly out of my mind as the taxi pulled up outside my driveway.

The next morning, I climbed out of bed having had a restless night, dreaming of the yacht club and being unable to save Amber.

I threw on white shorts, socks, a navy t-shirt, brushed my hair, and went into the kitchen. Duke was sitting half on and half off his memory foam bed, his thick tail thumping rhythmically on the wooden floor, waiting impatiently on me for his morning walk.

"I know Duke. I'm sorry I'm late this morning."

I opened a cupboard and took out my water bottle and filled it from the fridge filter.

"It looks like it's another hot one today. We'll stick to the shade and grassy areas to protect your paws."

He woofed, clearly understanding what I was telling him

I sat down on the bench in the hall and slid on my navy Converse shoes. Slipping his harness over his hairy shoulders, I checked it was secure then attached his leash with the little bone shaped container that held his poop bags swinging from the handle.

All that I needed now was my cell phone, a tissue, and my sunglasses. I put on my sunglasses and stuffed the phone and tissue in my shorts pockets, then grabbed my water bottle and opened the door. Duke slid past me first and I had to pull him back in order to close the door and hit the door code to lock it.

Walking Duke in the morning was always a good way for me to start my day, especially after the disturbed night that I had had.

A sharp tug of the leash snapped me out of the torturous mental trail I was wandering down as Duke stopped abruptly to sniff at a hydrangea bush, thick with blue flower heads that were the size of my two hands clasped together.

I took a few deep breaths and looked around me. Familiar silvery-sided cottages with white seashell paths sat gracefully along each side of the road to the dog park. Some of the residents sat in the shade beneath small pergolas sipping coffee and eating their breakfast, while others pottered around in the shady areas of their gardens, inspecting their rose bushes. The heady scent of cascading pink roses drifted heavily around me.

Several cars drove by and a Jeep Wrangler, its four doors and roof removed, cruised past me, reggae music wafting from the vehicle. Two laughing couples were squished inside between bags overflowing with towels and beach paraphernalia, a Yeti cooler with four colorful Tommy Bahama deck chairs nestled on top lay in the rear compartment. They were clearly going to be one of the first people on one of the beaches today, most of them likely being full by ten o'clock. I was surrounded by harmony and happiness and the potential of a new day.

Then I heard a scream and realized almost at the same time that it came from me. Tires screeched as a vehicle came skidding and swerving and slamming, with an almighty bang, to an immediate stop into the base of an oak tree fifty yards ahead of me. "Oh no," I gasped and ran as fast as I could to see what could be done to help the driver, with Duke pulling me frantically to the car that now had steam and smoke pouring from underneath it.

I reached the car, a white Lexus, and tugged on the passenger door as it was nearest me.

Nothing happened. The door was locked or stuck.

I dashed around the rear of the vehicle with Duke in tow to the driver side, dropped his leash and stood on it in one single move and tried the driver's door.

It gave way slightly. Buoyed up by this glimmer of hope I grasped it with both my hands overlapping each other and tugged at the door again with strength that I didn't know that I possessed.

Almost. But not quite. It was getting harder to see the vehicle despite standing right next to it because of the smoke billowing from underneath the vehicle.

Large hairy hands came into view and hovered in front of the handle grip. "I'll do it," said a gruff voice, just as I made one more determined tug and was able to free the door.

Still grasping the handle with both hands, I swung the door wide. Inside was a blonde-haired woman, her head tilted backwards onto the headrest, the airbags deployed. Her nose looked broken and blood ran down her lips and jaw onto her pale blue cotton sundress. Blood trickled down through her matted hair from a deep gash at the front of her skull onto her forehead and down her face, the rest of her blonde hair piled on top of her head and held in place with a diamante-trimmed blue ribbon. The contrast between the woman's busted-up face and body and her sparkly hair decoration made me pause as the realization of the fragility of our lives struck me. Her lips moved and I leaned in closer to hear her.

"Help is coming," I said to her as distant sirens drew closer. "Don't try to move."

Duke, meanwhile, nudged past me with his wet nose to sniff the woman's hand. She seemed to sense he was there, and reached out her fingers to gently graze his soft fur. As her hand traveled down to stroke his floppy left ear, Duke's tail wagged happily, offering comfort and support as only dogs can. He nuzzled against her hand, his presence a steady source of strength and reassurance in this moment of uncertainty.

Duke had always been amazing, but in moments like these, it was clear just how much he truly understood and cared for those around him.

Some men who'd ran out from their homes and gardens were now crouched down, attempting to peer beneath the Lexus, but the smoke was making it difficult to see if there was a serious issue. I gently drew Duke away from the woman and kept him on a short leash beside me. "Is it safe?" I asked the man who'd offered to tug open the door.

He shrugged. "Too difficult to tell."

The woman groaned as tried to move. "My car," she said weakly. She inhaled no more than a sip of air. "Not working."

"I know. You've been in an accident."

"Brakes. Not working."

"Don't try to talk. The first responders will be here soon."

She sunk back into her seat; her eyes closed. Her legs were trapped where the parts of the interior had become wedged into the footwell.

She muttered incomprehensively and I leaned in close to try to understand what she was saying, but I couldn't make it out. I spotted her handbag on the dashboard where the shock of the smash must have thrown it, and reached inside for it while trying my best not to lean on the injured woman.

I called out to a silver-haired female bystander standing a few feet away from me and waved her over to me, quickly explaining that I was going to open the injured woman's bag. "I'm Marnie," I said quickly.

"Jean," she replied.

We had no time for other formalities. A quick rummage in a narrow front compartment of the handbag revealed the driver's license. Julia Musto. I didn't know her, neither did Jean.

Julia blearily opened one eye but there was barely any reaction as she stared off to the side. I doubted if she was actually focusing on anything.

People of all ages and abilities were now surrounding the vehicle and I was relieved when sirens indicated the arrival of a police car, closely followed by both a Legacy Cove fire truck and fire department ambulance. Right now, I felt all my senses heightened just like I'd chugged down a double shot of espresso. I leaned in close so she could hear me above the din from sirens and people's alarmed voices. "Help's here now Julia. Is there anyone I can call for you? Let them know what's happened?"

There was no response as she drifted off into unconsciousness.

I opened her handbag again to return the driver's license that I was clutching and that's when I saw it. A thick white envelope addressed to Ms. Julia Musto; return address, The Wilde Estate. I tucked the driver's license firmly into the front compartment of the bag and sighed. Poor Julia. She wasn't going to be going anywhere soon, other than the hospital. I stepped away to let the emergency workers take over. I thought about the woman and how her life had taken a dramatic turn in a matter of seconds. Once again I was struck by the stark contrast of the sparkling diamante ribbon against the blood pooling around her face. Was this pretty ribbon something that she wore regularly, or had she taken time today to select it and tie it carefully in her hair in front of the mirror because of the invitation to the Wilde event? Was she driving to show the invitation in person to someone? Perhaps the person she was going to invite to go with her?

An hour later, after sharing with the police what I had seen and heard, I was finally at the dog park, walking around the perimeter trying and failing to clear my head from what I'd witnessed. Life was so fragile. I kept thinking about Julia and how she must have felt wrapping the sparkly blue ribbon in her hair and how excited she must have felt when she discovered that she had an invitation. Try as I might, I couldn't shake the image of the blood-soaked hair and the shimmering blue ribbon.

I sat down on a wooden bench in the dog park. Duke stopped sniffing the grass and came up to me. He put his head on my lap and looked up at me with his big brown eyes full of concern. I stroked his head gently, grateful for his silent comfort.

"Good boy today, Duke. Now off you go and play. You deserve it." He looked up at me as if to say, 'are you sure?' then stood up and loped off in search of other things to smell.

I called Gabby to tell her what had happened.

"I heard what happened," she said.

"So quickly? How?" I had no sooner asked the question when the answer popped into my mind.

"Troy."

I might have known. "So, what did he tell you?" I was curious to know what he knew, and very curious about how he found out. The man was a veritable fountain of information that all sorts of news and gossip flowed into, rather than from.

Gabby shared what Troy had told her and sure enough, it was like he had actually been there with me. Then the narrative changed, and as she spoke, the trees, bushes, and fences around me melted away, and I listened intently to every word.

"He only told me what he knew as fact," she continued, "but according to the police, there had been a threatening note left on her windshield that they found inside her bag. She was on her way to the police station to report the threat when the accident happened. Although, between you and me, it wasn't an accident."

"I'd agree with that," I said slowly. I realized that in the commotion of the moment, and the fact that I'd been further distracted by seeing the Suzie Wilde invitation, I'd overlooked the note. Not that I could have done anything with it of course. That was definitely for the police or the detectives or whoever followed up with this type of menacing crime.

However, Gabby wasn't done yet. "And do you know what else Troy found out?"

"No. Tell me."

"This is the really disturbing part of the whole incident."

"Get to the point Gabriella."

"The person who wrote the note said that Julia would never live long enough to go to the Suzie Wilde event." She paused. "The police think that guests are being deliberately targeted."

Chapter Seven

My objective to focus on my work was well intentioned but short-lived. The Monday after the yacht club fundraiser word leaked out at the college that I was going to the Suzie Wilde event. It shouldn't have been a surprise, but it actually was. Even though I was working in one of the world's biggest sieves, namely a place of education. Nowadays, very little surprises me although I remain an eternal optimist that humanity is continuing to evolve in a positive manner, and not descending into an abyss where kindness is frowned upon and friendship is based solely upon your political affiliation, or the size of your bank balance, or your family name.

Anyway, the texts just kept on coming and fell into three unequal camps. The smallest was from colleagues who had heard the news and wanted to say congratulations, hope you have fun, and the largest was from my students who were amazed that their professor was going to a country music star's event. My students' emails and texts, while often brief, included smiley face emojis and jumping for joy memes. Receiving this kind of communication brightened my day.

The middle group was people who began with congratulations, and quickly followed it up by asking for photographs of Suzie, or details of the food served, or the music that was played, or… The list was never-ending, and I found it to be a dismal reflection of today's society as I read their superficial list of requests, which were quite frankly exhausting. I promptly deleted these types of communications making a mental note in future to be even more selective with the people that I associated with. Colleagues I couldn't ignore, but I could ensure that I was even more professional with them and not invite them to be any closer than was necessary. My students, on the other hand, were one of the reasons I loved my job and to be able to create a positive and safe learning experience that was better than my own when I was in elementary and junior high school was a powerful driving force, albeit that most of students were young adults, except of course for the majority of the PhD students who were closer to my age.

The remaining weeks leading up to the Wide event blew by like a gentle ocean breeze.

In-between classes at the college and supervising graduate students and local archaeology enthusiasts at the dig at Heritage Hole, there was still more clothes shopping to do. The event was black tie and early evening in the summer, so I was looking for a formal dress that wasn't too 'weddingy' in its style. Shopping with Gabby eventually went better than I expected, as she mulled over a selection of accessories and outfits of varying colors and textures before she splurged on a strappy peach sequined dress that flowed as she moved and was a bright contrast to her brunette hair.

Much to my surprise, I found a fabulous silvery shimmery long dress and a pair of white flat sandals, with silvery buckles and pearl details, that would make it easier to walk on grass. I always opted for practicality over prettiness anyway, but I had to admit that the dress was really lovely.

For accessories, I didn't have to look far. I chose my favorite silver Celtic pendant, handed down to me from my Scottish mother, and a black vintage Chanel handbag with a black and silver chain strap, also my mother's.

Once home, I tried on the ensemble in front of the full-length mirror in my bedroom just to double-check that the outfit was as lovely as I remembered. As I turned from side to side, inspecting the way the dress swayed and ensuring that it revealed just enough skin to not be sexy or prudish, I thought, not for the first time, of how my life could have turned out so differently.

The day of the Wilde event finally arrived and I could barely sleep the night before from excitement and anticipation of what it was going to be like. With my hair freshly highlighted plus a blow out, mani-pedi done, Duke walked, fed, and suitably tired, Gabby came over to my house and we got ready together. And after asking Gabby's opinion on my outfit for the tenth time and having her check that I hadn't got any labels sticking out or a hem tucked in my knickers, I was finally satisfied that I was ready.

Our Legacy Cove taxi pulled up outside my house promptly at 5PM for the fifteen-minute ride to Harbor Bay where we would then be taken in one of several tenders for the short trip to the Wilde Estate island. There was no suggestion of even being the remotest bit fashionably late. No way.

We exchanged little conversation in the vehicle, Gabby doing this fidgety thing with her thumbs rolling over and over each other while she gazed out the window. I, on the other hand, remained relatively still by staring at the invitation yet again as I tried not to fidget with it in case I crushed an edge or transferred a trace of make-up onto the crisp white embossed card with my name on it. I was finally, after four weeks of wondering if it was indeed all an awful mistake, either going to be turned away as a gate-crasher or was about to finally meet the famous Suzie Wilde and discover why me, Marnie Fraser, had been invited to the event.

Pushing my nervousness aside, I checked my watch. Ten more minutes until we reached the harbor. I watched the now familiar streets and shops of Main Street pass by with people strolling casually along the sidewalks, stopping to look at menus in restaurants or entering and leaving shops with bags stuffed with the one-of-a-kind items that gave Legacy Cove its reputation as a pearl in an oyster. This gave way to streets that overlooked the calm dark-blue ocean on one side flanked by broad swathes of silvery sand. Cozy vintage two-storied silver-gray cedar shingled cottages lined up in disorderly fashion opposite, some with modern large picture windows to maximize the view over to Martha's Vineyard, others with modest windows and gardens overflowing with hydrangeas heavy with blue blooms the size of my head and quintessential pink roses cascading over white picket fences. Small family-run hotels, several well over one hundred years old, were dotted along this stretch of beachfront and the mix of cottages and hotels were randomly interspersed by newer construction elevated by ten feet to avoid storm surges, where an old cottage once stood.

The taxi turned a wide sweeping bend as it passed the last of the cottages on the street and gave way to Beach Drive, where three-season beach cottages stood on stilts directly on the sandy shore, and the ocean lapped or crashed against the stairs leading up to the living space depending on the time of year. These rickety looking shacks with their modest interior and one small bedroom were pricey and cost as much as a three-bedroom cottage further inland, away from shore and any water views. Location, location, location, as Troy had reminded me when I bought my own cottage, with its magnificent water view over the bay and a salt pond that attracted herons, ospreys, and other sea birds in summer and swans and ducks in the winter.

Then the paved road ended, and the taxi trundled over a well-worn gravel path where two shallow troughs were formed by repeated vehicles going to and from a parking area that already held about ten vehicles. We came to a stop, I paid the driver, then Gabby and I stepped out of the taxi into the sunshine. A dozen or so people were milling around, some leaning against the harbor wall looking out across to the Vineyard, while others took selfies and group photographs. Seagulls made their presence known by either swooping overhead or cawing loudly from the harbor wall, their screeching seemingly laughing at the ineffective shooing by visitors.

About one hundred yards from the shore, small center-console boats and motor cruisers, each one varying from around thirty to thirty-eight feet in length, bobbed in the water tied up next to buoys. A warm breeze ruffled our dresses softly, and I marveled yet again at the beautiful way that sunlight caught on the tips of the small waves making them sparkle like jewels, before they lapped against the side wall that separated the ocean from the road and disappeared, only to be replaced seconds later with more glittering gems. The sound of the small waves was rhythmic and gentle, and the smell of seaweed hung in the air. Even the seagulls flew languidly in the air above us before settling on the railings of nearby boats.

From where we stood looking over to the west, a string of small islands that were little more than dark blips against the blue sky, and appearing no bigger than the steamship ferry but were probably several acres in size, dotted the horizon. One of those islands was where Suzie Wilde lived, and we would be taken soon. I glanced at the other people who were ambling around the harbor wall and wondered if any of them were going to the same place that we were, or if they were all visitors on vacation.

I peered over the edge of the harbor wall to the floating dock where the yacht club had rows of small dinghies tied up to use in their sailing club for children and teenagers. Tucked to one side I spied a small tent, the kind often seen at county fairs with four poles and a roof for protection from the elements, but no sides. Sandbags held the poles in place but there was hardly a breath of wind so the tent was in no danger of flying off. A small sign no bigger than twelve inches hung on the front of the tent with the words 'Wilde Estate' inscribed in blue writing. A red rope, like the one you see outside valet parking at hotels and restaurants, created a level of security around the tent and there was an entranceway staged between a pair of hibiscus plants sitting in raised planters. It was all very elegant.

"That's where we should be heading," I said to Gabby. "It's a security checkpoint to make sure no-one tries to sneak aboard one of the tenders."

We made our way down the flight of concrete steps to the wooden boards of the floating doc. Sure enough, a man stood up from a folding chair as we approached the cordoned off area, adjusting his sunglasses. In the shade of the tent I saw a woman seated at a table, a clipboard in front of her. They were both dressed in navy shorts and matching white polo shirts embroidered with intertwined SW letters and tan boat shoes. They each wore name tags. The man's showed he was Charles, the woman Linda.

"Good afternoon," he said politely. "Can I help you?"

"Yes. I have an invitation to the Suzie Wilde event and the instructions said to arrive here at the harbor at this time."

His manner was professional yet relaxed as he held out a hand. "May I see the invitation to verify the details, and proof of your identity please?"

Anticipating this request, I was already carefully lifting my invitation from my bag, not wanting to let the precious envelope and its contents slip from my fingers or be blown away into the ocean by a rogue gust of wind that happened to materialize on this tranquil afternoon.

"And you too Ma'am," he said to Gabby, who was already reaching into her small bag for her driver's license.

There was a moment of held breaths as he handed over my invitation, and both of our drivers licenses to his colleague Linda for inspection. The seconds ticked by as she examined the invitation and licenses and checked my name against the typed list securely attached to her clipboard.

Satisfied, she smiled and returned all the materials to Charles who then handed me back my invitation, and our licenses back to each of us. "Please come through." He unhooked the heavy rope and indicated that we should enter to wait in the shade of the tent. "The tenders are just approaching now."

I saw two Boston Whalers about sixty yards away, weaving between the anchored boats and pointed them out to Gabby. "There's our ride," I beamed excitedly. I sighed long and slow as I gazed at the ocean and the bay of the harbor that we were in. It was a tranquil start to the evening. All is well, I thought, so long as the seagulls stay away. "Beautiful, isn't it," I said to Gabby.

"Mmm."

"Are we late?" I asked Charles as I didn't see anyone else waiting to ride with us.

"No Ma'am. The timing for the guests arrival is staggered, so as not to overwhelm the boats or have guests waiting in lines."

"That's very considerate."

"Miss Wilde is like that. Always thinking of others."

The two Boston Whalers approached the harbor wall where we were standing, one in front of the other, the name Wilde Estate printed in silver lettering on both top sides of the sturdy boats. These were the tenders that would take us to the Wilde Estate Island. I thought that each boat looked big enough to hold about six people comfortably, plus the driver of the boat, without anyone being squished in.

"Ahoy," called out the female captain of the Boston Whaler as she drew up alongside us, giving us a friendly wave.

We all watched as the first Boston Whaler slid expertly around the deep harbor and pull in alongside the tent, Charles expertly catching the rope that was thrown to him from the first boat. He tied it off securely on one of the metal cleats that was on the floor of the walkway nearest to the ocean. Then he repeated the action with the second boat, securing it to a cleat about five yards from the first boat.

With our names and the invitation verified we climbed aboard our little boat that would ferry us to the island. "I'm glad the weather's calm," whispered Gabby to me. "I don't do well on water."

"Now you tell me, I whispered back.

Our captain introduced herself as Irene. "I'm your water captain and I've been sailing and boating for over thirty years. First we'll cover a few safety checks." Once she had delivered the instructions to sit and not stand while the boat was in motion and invited us to wear a life vest, Irene asked Charles to throw her the ropes which she then expertly caught, then coiled on the deck near her center console. Then, she eased the boat out from the side of the sailing school dock and expertly turned the Boston Whaler around to face forward in the direction of the islands.

I looked back to wave goodbye to Charles and Linda but I saw that another couple had arrived, Charles greeting them as he had us earlier. They would no doubt get the second boat to ferry them to the island. I wondered how many more people were due to arrive or if we were one of the later ones. I didn't recognize the couple on the dock as they hadn't been to the Yacht Club fundraiser a few weeks ago. The woman had dark red hair and looked older than the man, although he was much taller than her.

The trip to the island took around seven minutes and we pulled into a slip where we disembarked from the tender and admired what little we could see of the sprawling estate ahead of us. Magnificent rhododendrons, at least twelve feet tall with traces of pink still visible in their papery foliage lined an informal path that led to the house, its gray shingled roof just visible between a mass of pines and oaks.

I glanced at my watch. 5:40. "Not too early, and not late either!"

Irene told us she was going to set off to pick up the last of the guests before she would moor the tender at a quay for the evening.

We were greeted by two beefy security guards also wearing navy shorts and matching white polo shirts embroidered with intertwined SW letters just as Charles and Linda had, right down to the tan boat shoes. Their name tags indicated that one man was Hank, and the other Jerry. There was a moment of held breaths while my invitation and our ID's were inspected yet again.

"Feel free to explore the property Ms. Frazer," said Hank with a smile, as I once again returned my precious invitation and ID to my bag, and Gabby did likewise with her license. He was the taller and according to his name tag, the more senior of the two men. "There is a marquee where food and beverages are being served, and if you wish to freshen up there are bathrooms in the pool house."

A server stood beside them in the shade of a row of leafy maples next to a table draped in white linen with a variety of glasses neatly lined up and assorted drinks chilling on ice. "Champagne please," we both said in response to being offered a beverage.

My excitement mounted as we strolled along the winding white gravel path, not wanting to appear too much in a hurry. "We made it," I said with a smile to Gabby.

She beamed back the biggest grin. "This is going to be awesome."

"I'm glad we opted for flat sandals," I said as we were inadvertently kicking up dust from small white crunchy stones underfoot, while trying not to hurry, because if we did we were in danger of spilling tour chilled glasses of bubbly.

No chance of arriving unannounced though, what with the racket we were making. I estimated that the path from the ocean to the house was a little over one hundred yards long as it curved gently to eventually lie perpendicular to the ocean.

And then, there it was.

The sprawling two story silvery cedar-shingled house was west-facing with a wall of sliders that opened out onto the expansive lawn and overlooked the ocean, making it perfectly positioned to catch the sun-sets over the horizon. To the right-hand side of the main house stood a cute little single-story cottage with loungers and tables and sun umbrellas placed around a sparkling blue swimming pool. That was presumably the pool house, accessed from both the house and a wide shaded path from the lawn.

I could see other guests making their way towards a cream-colored marquee, its sides rolled up to provide an unobscured panorama of the magnificent ocean view, while the marquee itself provided welcome shade. Tiki lights were strategically placed around the lawn, still to be lit, while small white lights twinkled around the branches of trees and were strung between strategically placed posts.

The scene was elegant, with servers smartly dressed in tan Bermuda shorts and white polo shirts walking amidst the guests offering silver platters with small hors d'oeuvres while a ten-piece jazz band was playing traditional jazz tunes under the shade of a small marquee. Off to the far sides, I spotted a couple of other security personnel positioned discreetly in the background, passively monitoring the guests. I wasn't sure what I expected. Certainly not this. It wasn't the house I thought that a country music singer would live in either, or even the town they would live in for that matter. But perhaps Ms. Wilde needed peace and quiet too, after traveling for months on end and performing most of those evenings away from her home and any family she might have, even though from what little I knew about Ms. Wilde she only gave a few summer concerts each year now.

I nudged Gabby gently on her left elbow. "Look at that. I think we're going to be treated to a private concert." To the far left of the lawn, with the ocean and a million-dollar view as the backdrop, a stage about four feet high and thirty feet by thirty feet was set up with a single wooden stool situated front and center, and four microphones and equipment placed to the rear of the stage, presumably for other musicians.

"Oh, this just keeps getting better and better," she enthused.

A raucous male voice bellowed out over the verdant manicured lawn before we even saw who was dominating the airspace. "Bernard Lazenby," we both said together with a smile. A quick glance showed Bernard, dressed in a dark suit and bowtie, unmissable because of his shocking mop of jet-black hair and boisterous manner. His wife Celia, wearing a tight ankle-length navy silk dress, was laughing along with Bernard.

"I'm surprised people don't need to wear earplugs when they're up close to Bernard," Gabby said. "He's loud enough outside, I wouldn't like to be in an enclosed room with him."

"I agree, I don't know how Celia can bear it. But he does seem like a happy person, doesn't he?"

"Except when he's near Simon Stadler," she said with a knowing look.

"True. So, apart from Bernard and Celia, do you know who the two men are?"

"No idea. But I wonder if Amoy and Lashawna are here with their partners. I propose we go look for them."

"Oh, Bernard's spotted us." Bernard waved a hand at us to join him. "C'mon Gabby. We'd better join him and Celia for a few minutes then go look for the others." Not one to be left behind, she strode along beside me, and we joined Bernard and Celia, sporting friendly smiles.

"…And my company raised a ton of money for the local family charity with our fundraising drive last winter," we heard Bernard say. It was the same elevator pitch that he used with us and probably always used when introducing himself to new people. Short and succinct, I supposed. "Ah, here's a couple of interesting people I'd like you all to meet," he said warmly as we joined his group. "This is Professor Marnie Frazer and with her is one of Legacy Cove's most successful entrepreneurs, Gabriella Martinez. Why don't you share a bit about yourself Henry?"

Henry was the politician look-alike. "Henry Grant, Laurent Academy. My school is number one in the state." He smiled, but not with his eyes, I noted. The other man was his partner, Benjamin Pearce, a lawyer. Ray-Bans atop his cropped brown hair, he had a cheeky smile and a twinkle in his eyes to match and I wondered what on earth he saw in Henry. Opposites attract, I supposed. Like Celia and Bernard.

"I'm so glad to see you again," Celia said to us warmly, her raspy voice seeming higher than I remembered. Her hair was elegantly side-swept into a low bun, and a pair of Gucci sunglasses and a small Gucci bag completed her ensemble. She smoothed down the front of her navy silk dress to stop it from clinging too much.

"Us too," said Gabby.

"So," I asked, "when do you think we'll get to meet the famous Suzie Wilde?"

"I've heard," said Celia, "that she just turns up and sings, does a little meet and greet, then hands out an award and leaves."

"I think I'd do the same, even if the people invited here were chosen by me."

"But why?" she asked. "Probably more than half of the people here are huge fans of hers."

I laughed. "That's why I'm not a famous singing star. Can't abide the publicity and intrusion of privacy."

"Personally, I'd love it," said Celia, with a faraway look on her face.

"Me too," agreed Gabby. "Publicity has been good for my business, having me as a figurehead for my company." She steered the conversation to a topic she enjoyed, other than coding and computers. "Wherever did you get such a chic dress," she asked Celia. "It's simply stunning."

Gabby and Celia discussed boutiques, as I half-listened to Henry chatting with Bernard. The other half of me looked around us at the variety of high-top and low tables and chairs set up in the marquee, with pink carnations and white daisies arranged in simple round glass vases on plain white tablecloths, set against a backdrop of lush green grass and blue sky.

Simple elegance.

I sighed and fought to squash a small voice that I thought I had buried a long time ago, one that now rose in my head and whispered, 'You're not good enough'.

I excused myself and took a tiny step back from the group and allowed my gaze to casually drift over the other guests to where I spied Melissa Maxwell, wearing a black and white striped dress that skimmed her ankles. She was standing next to a taller svelte woman who wore a long iridescent green dress and sported fiery red wavy hair. I recognized her as the woman from the harbor who was waiting to climb aboard the next tender a few minutes behind me and Gabby with a younger dark-haired male. The red-haired woman's wrists jangled with silvery bangles that shimmered in the sunlight as she waved her hands animatedly in front of Melissa's ample breasts. Melissa reached to swipe a hand away, but the taller woman was feisty and smacked her hand away first and continued her with her spirited reprimand.

Well, well, I thought. Someone is standing up to Melissa. Maybe the bully has lost her touch after all.

Offering a large friendly smile, I reinserted myself beside Gabby and Celia, trying to quash my insecurities from spoiling what was promising to be a fabulous evening. After a few minutes, I looked at Gabby with a 'time to mingle?' expression and we said our goodbyes, promising to catch up later in the evening and headed in the direction of the marquee. "Geez, Gabby," I said. "We've only just got here and someone's having an argument already." I inclined my head slightly to indicate Melissa and the other women fifty yards away.

Gabby casually allowed her gaze to wander in that direction while sipping from her glass to take in her surroundings as the other woman strode off, leaving Melissa staring at the woman's back, before turning back to me. "Wow, she really had it in for Melissa. And here of all places."

I stifled a comment and released the image of Melissa glowering after the other woman, choosing instead to focus on the blue sky, the sparkling ocean in the distance and the mellow jazz music playing in the background. We sauntered over to where a waitress was working her way between two other small groups. Gabby clinked her empty glass with mine. "More bubbles?"

"Absolutely!"

Two minutes later, each of us with glasses refreshed and two dainty smoked salmon choux puffs and two Italian-style fresh fig, honey, and goat cheese crostini ingested, we were not the only guests eager to mingle. I felt Gabby's elbow nudge me on the arm holding her champagne glass, causing some to spill over the rim onto my newly manicured fingers. The wetness bothered me. I'd made a huge effort and if I wasn't careful the drips from my fingers were going to land on my new dress and spoil it. I wanted to make a good impression when we finally met our host.

I quickly scanned the other guests. A defensive skill I had honed as a child, always having to check that my surroundings were safe. People were milling around, chatting briefly then moving along to the next group. Laughter gushed as the champagne and other beverages flowed. "Let's introduce ourselves to the woman with the energetic hands." Anyone who can put Melissa Maxwell in her place can't be all bad, I thought.

A few seconds later we were shaking hands with none other than Madame Helene Gauthier, the owner of the renowned Gauthier French bakery and restaurant (according to Troy from our previous discussions of the best items on the menus in various restaurants around the Village).

Madame Gauthier's personality was allegedly temperamental, apparently exaggerated by the confidence that she exuded through her flamboyant style, her red hair seeming to shout danger. Despite her hair's subtle warning to back off, she radiated a musical air as she laughed in tune with the tinkling of her wrists as they jingled from the layers of silvery bangles, a sound she seemed to barely notice as she passionately waved her hands while she spoke.

"I'm so excited to be here, aren't you *mademoiselles*?"

"Absolutely," agreed Gabby and I together. "And," I continued, "I have to say Madame Gauthier, that I'm such a fan of not only your restaurant, but your raisin roulade, and your croissants of course. And the bread with the olives…"

"…And the mini chocolate gateau," added Gabby, licking her lips.

"Ah, *oui*," said Madame Gauthier, nodding and smiling. "So many of my products are special, and each one is made with such a passion that you will not find anywhere else." She paused briefly in the way someone did when mentally savoring one of her creations. "And please do call me Helene."

Her smile was warm and inviting, just like one of her croissants.

We gushed over the wonderful breads and pastries that she and her staff, led as it turned out by her son Max, created six days a week in the Fall and Spring and seven days weekly from the Fourth of July to Labor Day. "*Naturellement*, we return each winter to spend time with family *en France*."

"Beautiful at any time of year, Helene," I remarked. "When I was a teenager, I visited several archaeological sites in Burgundy and Brittany a number of times with my parents. They are also archaeologists and specialize in Roman sites both in Europe and the UK."

"Ah, *oui*, there are many such places throughout France."

"I love France too," said Gabby with a sigh. "But I've only been to Paris once. Are you here at this event by yourself?"

"Oh, no," she smiled broadly. "My son Max is here with me. He saw some people that he knows and stopped by to say hello." She waved a jingling arm to where Simon Stadler and a short auburn-haired woman were talking with a tall dark-haired man who resembled Helen Gauthier. He was really handsome. "That's him with Simon and his girlfriend Stella. I had other people to see, in the meantime."

Yes, I thought to myself. Melissa Maxwell. I wondered what the disagreement had been all about.

"But I digress," continued Helene, "I'd love to introduce you both to my son, Max, at some time this evening. And perhaps I can reconnect with both of you at some point in the future. Perhaps have a coffee and pastry?"

We both agreed that we would love that, and we exchanged numbers with Helene. I wanted to whisper to Gabby that I saw him first, but I wasn't really interested in a relationship, although the Frenchman might make me amend my decision to not date anyone ever again, after my debacle of a marriage to cheating Craig.

"Ladies," bellowed Bernard, making me jump slightly as he strode up behind us with a small entourage in tow. "Do you mind if we join you?"

We all turned as one, taking in Bernard and his wife Celia who were closely followed by Henry and Benjamin and a stout, busty woman sporting cropped silver hair brought up the rear with a balding man who had a bit of a paunch and appeared to be in his late forties or early fifties. They were all making their way towards us from the marquee with small white plates topped with more of the tasty hors d'oeuvres.

About twenty yards away I could make out Liz Tanner, wearing a long flowing beige dress, a thin cream shawl, flat sandals and carrying a mid-sized shoulder bag with a gold chain, hand-in-hand with a broad-shouldered man, his hair tied back in a short ponytail, wearing chino pants, a pale blue polo shirt and tan Sperry boat shoes. I hadn't known that Liz was going to be here. She was definitely modest as she hadn't mentioned anything about attending this event when we had all met at the yacht club a few weeks previously.

They were laughing with Rupert Boyden who didn't appear to have a companion. Rupert's firm shoulders were emphasized by a crisp navy blazer, white shirt with a blue floral trim on the collar and where the button holes were, and cream chinos. All in all, I thought he looked smart. Handsome even. But I wondered what people would think of him if they ever found out about his past behavior as a young teenager.

"Helene," Bernard said, reaching for a surprised Helene and giving her an air kiss on each cheek. "Many of you either know Madame Helene Gauthier of Gauthier Bakery and Restaurant fame, or have been to one or both of her fine establishments." He patted his ample abdomen. "In my opinion," he stated, "it's one of the finest restaurants, and bakeries too might I add, in Legacy Cove, if not the entire Cape."

"We do too," agreed Gabby. "My friend Marnie and I had a lovely meal there with some of our friends only last week."

Helene smiled warmly at everyone, clearly not expecting any other response. "Thank you, Bernard. Everyone."

"Have you met this lovely lady by my side?" he asked, smiling at the silver-haired woman. "Georgina Maloney, but better known to us all as Ginger," said Bernard.

Approximately the same height as Gabby and wearing a long pale green satin dress and sturdy one-inch heeled tan sandals, Ginger sniffed and pursed her lips and eased herself in-between Helene Gauthier and Gabby. From the side, I noted that beneath the woman's wide sunglasses, she also had narrow, wily eyes that quickly scanned the group. I got the impression that not much escaped Ginger Maloney.

"She has a pharmaceutical research lab," continued Bernard, "and, well, I'll let Ginger share the exciting news with you. Come on dear," he said to his wife Celia, offering her his arm. "Let's go and say a quick hello to Amoy and Mark. They've just arrived." Celia clung to Bernard's arm as she tottered beside him, keeping her free arm down by her side to prevent her dress from riding up as they walked to join Amoy and her husband.

"So," remarked Gabby to Ginger, "Bernard mentioned that you had exciting news to share."

We all leaned in to hear what she was going to tell us.

She tilted her small chin up, barely looking at anyone, focusing instead on the ocean beyond with its gentle waves. "Yes, my pharmaceutical research company, Ginglab, has discovered a compound that has the potential to treat early-onset aging."

"Early-onset aging?" asked Gabby.

"Yes," prickled Ginger visibly. "Aging affects us all. The impact can be psychological as well as physical. Plus, it's a big area in the beauty industry. We've successfully completed all the research, had the molecules patented, and we've had them approved by the Food and Drug Administration. All that remains is for a final round of funding, a small amount I may add, for marketing etc."

Wrinkles, I thought. We all smiled broadly as we agreed that it was indeed an important medical breakthrough. "That's super exciting, I'm very happy for you."

"Thank you. Our team has worked for many years on the development of what will become an important product for millions of people."

That was when I saw that Helene Gauthier was not paying attention. From where I was standing, Helene was staring, no, scowling was more accurate, her brows furrowed and her lips pressed tightly together. Her intense interest appeared to be directed at a group of six people, one of whom was Rupert Boyden who I'd been doing my best to avoid and another man who looked similar to him and was likely his brother or a relative. Amber and another woman who had her back to me, along with Liz Tanner and her partner concluded the group. Simon Stadler and his girlfriend Sandy were beyond them, still chatting amiably with Laurent.

I couldn't tell which of them was taking up all of Helene's attention.

And making her so angry.

Chapter Eight

I turned my gaze away slowly while taking a sip of champagne. "I think I recognize Amoy and Lashawna," I said. I did and I groaned inwardly. "They're chatting with Melissa Maxwell. But I also see Amber and some of the people I met at the yacht club fundraiser from a few weeks ago. Gabby, I'd like to go and check on Amber and see how she's doing since her allergic reaction." I had no desire whatsoever to be near Melissa Maxwell. Chatting with Amoy and Lashawna would have to wait a little longer.

This appeared to refocus Helene. "Yes, I heard about the nut episode. Most unfortunate."

"I'll come with you," said Gabby.

Ginger didn't appear interested in what had happened to Amber as she began to explain to Helene how she discovered her company's molecular breakthrough. Helene was still distracted and was barely paying attention to Ginger.

But Ginger reminded me of some of my colleagues who were equally passionate about their work and didn't realize that not everyone felt the same way about their chosen field of work. And from experience I could tell that she was all set to provide a lengthy explanation on her work.

As for me, asking after Amber was an excuse as I had texted with her a few times since the yacht club event and she appeared to be doing okay, being doubly careful over potential allergens she might be exposed to.

As we sauntered over to where Amber and her friend were chatting with Rupert and the others, I looked back and caught Helene staring at the little group again before quickly turning back to resume chatting with Ginger.

Odd, I thought. Must be some past history there. But who was Helene scowling at? And in which group?

Parts of other conversations drifted to us from the assembled small groups.

"... Well, you can guess who got that contract, and how he got it."

"... I wonder who she'll bring? I heard that she's having an affair, or her husband is."

"... I heard that she faked the allergic reaction."

With that last remark I swung round in the direction of the voice but couldn't tell who had said it, except that it was a woman who had spoken.

"What is it," asked Gabby.

"Oh nothing." Each person who had received an invitation had either a brilliant mind or were generous in the manner in which their unique ideas or efforts now served the community. This didn't make them saints. Not by any shape of the imagination.

But then, I wasn't aware that any of the assembled guests had done anything terrible other than gossip or be overly confident in their abilities. I'd honed my 'jerk-sense' in the way that Spiderman had a 'spidey-sense' and over the years I now kept my friends close and ultimately small in number as a means of preserving my privacy and having people around me that I could trust. Although I hadn't exactly fared well with my misplaced faith in my ex-husband Craig Thomas's ability to stay true to his marriage vows.

Tinkling laughter reached us as we joined Amber, Rupert Boyden, Liz Tanner, and two men and a blonde woman that I didn't recognize. "Hi there, good to see you two again," said Amber raising her champagne flute as we walked up. She was wearing a cream-colored flowy cotton dress that skimmed her sandals. Its scooped neckline showed enough of a decolletage to be tasteful. "Quite the event, don't you think?" she said as she popped a dainty cucumber sandwich square into her mouth. Her pale manicured nails complimented her peach-colored pedicure and she looked so well put together that I glanced down at my own dress to ensure I looked okay and hadn't dribbled anything on myself. Thankfully, I was good.

I stood near Amber to create distance between myself and Rupert Boyden.

"Hi," said the tall blonde woman next to Amber. Her smile was similar to Amber's and revealed perfectly white teeth. "I'm Fee Gibson. A colleague of Amber's," she giggled as she introduced herself. I couldn't tell initially whether it was the alcohol, or Fee's manner to overcome nerves, or just a habit to find everything slightly funny. The perfect white teeth were the only similarity. Fee couldn't be more opposite to her cool colleague. Fee had her hair piled up in a straggly ponytail, a diamond stud in her right nostril, and was wearing a mid-length pink dress. "We've known each other since high school."

The contrast served as a means of highlighting Amber's professional demeanor, thereby showing Amber in a very positive light.

Amber straightened her spine a little, but laughed. "Unlike Fiona, I grew up. That's what happened. We can't all continue to use nick-names like 'Fee' from school."

"And I'm Jim Thacker," said the man in a smart dark suit and colorful bowtie, "but everyone calls me JT." He raised an eyebrow to the fact that he was an adult who also used a nickname. "I'm with Liz." Liz lowered her eyes as she took a sip from her champagne flute. Her flowy pale blue cotton dress skimmed her slim ankles and had a high neckline that masked her voluptuous breasts. JT seemed relaxed and comfortable in the group. "So how do you all know each other?" he asked.

Amber gave another laugh. "Many of us only met a few weeks ago at an event at the Harbor Yacht Club."

"A bit like Liz and me. We've only known each other a few months," he said.

"Hi," said the man with Rupert Boyden. "I'm Anthony. Rupert's younger brother. The smarter one," he added with a grin.

Rupert gave him a brotherly punch in the back. "Watch it, you." He then glanced at me and there was a small parting of his lips.

I hoped he wasn't going to speak to me. I hurriedly looked away.

Rupert's phone rang and I was literally saved by the bell as he glanced at the screen before excusing himself to take the call.

Liz leaned into our little group conspiratorially, addressing me. "We never quite got to the bottom of the mystery at your dig site, when several of us met at the fundraiser last month." She looked at each of us, nodding slowly.

Now everyone was intrigued and looked at me, waiting.

"Mystery? What do you mean?" I was a little worried as I wasn't sure what she was talking about.

She lowered her voice a shade for effect, which was challenging given the background music and the many conversations from the assembled guests and their partners. However we all heard what Liz said next, loud and clear.

"The dead body."

"What dead body?" I was confused. "We uncover many artifacts at my dig sites and if there was a body I would have known about it."

Liz shook her head. "It's common knowledge that one of your students collapsed and died at the Legacy Cove dig."

Fee's eyes widened. "Is it cursed?"

My brain was now firing on all cylinders when suddenly everything clicked into place!

"Well, I have to tell you all," I too leaned into the group, mirroring Liz's actions for double the effect, "someone did collapse." Fee's eyes widened and I struggled to keep a straight face. "Happily no-one died."

Their faces fell.

What was the attraction of other people's misfortunes I wondered. "A volunteer had a heart attack and collapsed into a trench," I explained. "Fortunately, I was first on the scene. Several of us, myself included, are certified in first-aid and CPR. We're trained to handle this exact type of situation, especially as we're not often close to a town and you never know when we might be required to administer life-saving care."

"You're quite the heroine," remarked Bernard.

I shrugged. "All in a day's work."

"Tragedy seems to follow you, though, doesn't it," said Rupert, slipping his phone into a pocket in his suit jacket.

I looked at him, unclear what he was referring to, and all too conscious of the others in the group studying me. "I'm not sure what you're talking about?"

"The incident with Julia Musto. You were first on the scene there too, weren't you?"

I had to think who that was, then I remembered. "Ah, the car crash a few weeks ago. It was the day after the yacht club fundraiser. Yes, I was. I only did what most people would have done. Plus, there were plenty of people who heard the crash and came over to help too."

"You're too modest."

"Who is Julia Musto?" demanded Bernard, turning to Rupert.

"She was a lovely young woman who incidentally was also invited to the Wilde event," said Rupert.

"Never heard of her. What happened to her?"

"She sustained a severe head injury in a car accident. Marnie was there and saw it happen."

"That's bad news. I take it Julia is a friend of yours?"

Rupert looked out across Vineyard Sound briefly before turning back to us, his unwavering gaze fixed on my face. "Yes. Julia was a close friend of mine. The call I took just now was a family member. After being in a coma since the accident, Julia died an hour ago."

"She what?" I gasped and placed a hand over my mouth as tears welled up in my eyes. I didn't know Julia personally but I had been thinking about her daily and wondering how she was doing.

Celia, who'd been quiet most of the time since we arrived, finally spoke up. "Well, that's tragic. Such an awful waste of a person who was doing so much for the community."

"Did you know the woman?" her husband asked her.

"No dear, but everyone who was sent an invite has done something worthwhile with their life. They're not wasters, as you well know."

"Hmph," grumped Bernard, before turning to Rupert again. "A car accident you say?"

Rupert nodded. "Although apparently the police believe that her car was tampered with."

Recovering from the shock of the news, Rupert's remark triggered a memory of something that Julia was able to say to me before she fell unconscious. "Julia was awake briefly before the ambulance crew arrived. She said that her car wasn't working, or responding. Something like that. I told the police what she told me."

"That fits in with what the police are suspecting," said Rupert. "Brake fluid would have been gushing out each time she hit the brakes."

"So, now you're saying it was a deliberate attempt to harm her?"

"That's exactly what it was. A calculated, premeditated effort to hurt her. Basically, lack of brake fluid transformed her vehicle into a missile, with her strapped to the inside of it."

"This is so messed up. Who on earth would want to harm her?"

He paused and looked across the ocean where an osprey was circling high in the sky, hunting for a fish, before turning to face us again. "That's what I'd like to know. Now it's a murder investigation."

Chapter Nine

We were all silent and I shivered involuntarily. The image of Julia and her sparkling ribbon rose vividly to mind. As did the conversation that I'd had with Gabby when she said that according to Troy, someone was actively targeting guests of this year's Suzie Wilde Event. I'd forgotten all about that dire prediction.

"I'm sorry for your loss, Rupert," I said. My interaction with Julia had been brief, nevertheless, I was genuinely sorry.

He nodded and cleared his throat. "Thank you. I appreciate it."

Everyone else added their condolences.

Laughter from other groups drifted towards us. Rupert pulled out his phone again. "Excuse me a moment, won't you all." He stepped away and made another phone call.

Liz raised her glass of champagne, "I love Moët, the real kind. Not the fake sparkling wine kind I had when I was twenty-one. It is wonderful to be able to sip real champagne any time you feel like it," she said as she took a healthy gulp, squinting in one eye as the bubbles from her too-quick guzzle danced up her nose.

"My ex-husband was cheap like that too," I said.

"Amber always says life's too short to drink cheap wine, or cheap champagne too for that matter," quipped Fee. "Don't you."

Amber only raised her glass in a mock toast.

Liz gave a shy laugh. "I remember a time when you drank shots behind the bleachers Amber, and never looked at the label to see what you were drinking."

Fee laughed. "Really? That's right. You were at the same school as us although different years."

"We were one year apart, me being the younger one, but hey, look where we've all ended up."

"I have a question," I said, addressing the group. "Has anyone here met Suzie Wilde before?"

"Not me," laughed Fee.

"Nor me," said Amber. "Her music is great though. Kind of like Pat Benatar meets Dolly Parton."

"And she does look amazing," remarked Anthony. "She must be in her fifties or sixties now."

"Mid-fifties, I think," said Amber. "She's still good-looking for a woman her age."

"I'm looking forward to meeting her," added Liz.

Gabby began chatting with Amber, while I started to engage with Liz and Fee. Anthony and JT slipped easily into a discussion of tomorrow's Red Sox game when Rupert returned and joined them. I was acutely aware of Rupert's presence and the fact that he was not so subtly watching me.

"All of the guests here are quite the mixed bunch, aren't we all?" I said.

"Speak for yourself," said a snipped voice behind me.

We all turned in the direction of the speaker.

"Good to see you again Melissa," smiled Anthony broadly at the new arrival, but then I noticed that he took a small step closer to Amber.

"Well, hello everybody. Good to see some friendly faces." Melissa smiled, her lips colored with a vibrant ruby-red matt lipstick, a stark contrast to her long black and white stripy dress, beamingly white teeth, and jet-black hair. Her bob cut was shiny and immaculately groomed, and once again I felt a strong urge to tuck an unruly strand of my own hair behind an ear in an attempt to tame it. "This is my friend Carrie Abrams."

Introductions were made, both Anthony and Rupert giving Melissa a hug.

"Melissa," said Amber. "Turning up, just like a bad penny."

Melissa glowered at Amber but didn't ignore the snide comment. "Wormed your way in, did you?"

"I don't know what you're talking about. You're clearly confused."

"Well, I am a little confused. I was talking with Bernard earlier today and quite frankly we can't fathom as to why you of all people were invited here."

Was it my imagination or did Amber stiffen and clench her jaw at the mention of Bernard? Time to bale away from this mini dispute that was threatening to put a serious dampener on the whole event. I waved to Gabby and gave a little flick of my head for her to follow me.

We had barely gone twenty steps when a hand lightly touched the small of my back.

"I knew it was you," a low voice whispered at my shoulder.

Chapter Ten

I stopped on the spot. I knew who was there before I turned around, but I swore a long time ago that I wasn't going to be intimidated ever again so I moved slowly, deliberately, and with as much self-poise as I could muster. Rupert Boyden.

"I must say though, you've changed quite a bit," he said.

I didn't say anything at first. I just stared back at him. He wore a grin like it was tattooed permanently on his face.

I sensed Gabby standing quietly by my side.

"Oh?" was all I could say.

He looked down at his feet before raising his eyes to meet mine. "Marnie Hitson. That was your name before, wasn't it?"

I bristled slightly at the mention of my original name, but didn't reply. I merely nodded.

He looked around but no-one, apart from Gabby and I, was able to hear him. He leaned in a little closer. I waited for him to speak. Say the taunting words. 'Shitty Hitty'.

Gabby turned to me, no doubt wondering what was going on. I placed my right hand on her left arm to reassure her. This was my fight and I'd tackle it. I was determined to not only win it, but finish the festering war once and for all.

Rupert straightened up and cleared his throat. "I want to say I'm sorry for what I said as a kid. Being a kid isn't an excuse. I knew better and yet I still said those things."

I was stunned and at a loss for words. I was all prepared for a continuation of his verbal abuse and I searched his face for a tell-tale smirk that would indicate that his apology wasn't genuine, that he was only mocking me.

His lips were pressed together, and despite my intense scrutiny he didn't blurt out any name-calling.

Now I felt his and Gabby's stares burrowing into me, clearly waiting for a reaction from me.

What did he expect me to do? Should I slap him, shout at him, kick him in the pants?

In the periphery I was aware of the marquee and the ocean, Melissa bickering with Amber, the jazz music wafting around us, and the other guests still having a really good time.

My eyes never left his face as I extended my right hand towards him. His warm fingers enveloped mine firmly. I didn't flinch. "Thank you Rupert. I'd actually forgotten all about what happened at that school," I lied. What I'd actually done was push the memory of being bullied into a corner of my mind where it lay until I heard Troy mention Rupert's name, the evening that I received my invitation.

We shook hands briefly and he inched closer to me. "I'm glad. I was worried that you might loathe me."

"Not at all."

"If you like, could I call you someday, perhaps meet for a coffee?"

Huh! I wasn't exactly jumping for joy at the chance to catch up on the 'good' old days with him, couldn't he see that? I glanced at Gabby and she had her eyebrows raised, darting her eyes from me to Rupert, egging me to reply to him. So what I actually said was, "Sure. That would be lovely."

Why I said that I'll never know, but I certainly had no intention of meeting up with the man and certainly not sitting chatting over a cup of coffee.

"Great. I only have your office number. It was listed on the college website. Here, let me give you my card. It's got my cell phone, email etc. on it too." He handed me a pristine business card and waited expectantly, but I hesitated to share my cell phone number with him.

"I didn't bring cards," I said.

"No problem," he said, pulling out his phone. "Send me a text and that way I'll have your private number and be able to reach you faster."

There was no way of getting out of this without being rude. I sighed inwardly. Get it over and done then, I told myself. You can always ignore his calls or be too busy to talk if he does in fact call to set a day and time to meet for coffee.

So I sent one word in a text to him. '*Hi.*'

His phone pinged and he grinned at me. "Fabulous. Can't wait to catch up."

Across the lawn, and over the heads of Helene Gauthier and Ginger, I spotted the welcome sight of Amoy Johnson and her husband Mark Kleinman.

"Excuse us," I said, clutching Gabby by the elbow. "I see some people I need to talk with," and promptly steered a bewildered Gabby hurriedly away, leaving him watching us.

"What was that all about? Where are we going?" she hissed.

"Amoy and Mark," I hissed back. "We'll be able to have a normal conversation with them, and not be stuck having to listen to some awful bitching party between old enemies or deal with the likes of Rupert Boyden."

Gabby was undeterred. "I didn't know that you knew Dr Rupert. Or that you have a past together." She looked behind her to where I was certain that Rupert was still watching me. "He's so well-liked around here." Her voice trailed off, but not for long. "I think he's interested in you."

I stopped abruptly. "You're joking right?"

"No, I'm not joking."

"That man…" I caught myself, breathing heavily. "That man doesn't interest me in the slightest."

Gabby merely raised an eyebrow, but said nothing else and resumed walking.

I had shared a few things about my personal life with Gabby and Troy; enough, I hoped, to stop anyone from digging deeper. They knew that I was adopted and had spent my early childhood here in Legacy Cove before my new parents whisked me away for a life in Boston. I had a script of sorts that I shared with anyone new that I met, explaining how happy my adopted life was, omitting to mention the past other than that my birth mother was an addict who had died when I was thirteen.

As far as I was concerned, adversity either breaks you or makes you stronger.

We took a direct path over the thick lawn that bounced softly beneath our sandals, due to the tightly packed blades of grass, and were greeted by warm smiles from both Amoy and Mark.

"Good to see you both," I said, as I fixed a broad smile on my face.

"Isn't this great," beamed Amoy, as she walked towards us in a long pale blue linen dress trimmed with pearls and a small white bag. "We're so happy to be here. What a place. What a view," she said while gazing to where the edge of the property met the dark blue ocean, the water interspersed with gently rolling oyster-colored waves.

"Yes, it is great," I enthused. "Most people are enjoying themselves."

"Oh, what would it be like to live here, in this beautiful estate," she sighed.

"We're not moving," insisted Mark.

"A bit out of our price range too, honey. We'll have to work a few more years before a smaller version would even be affordable."

"And then the upkeep would be too much. And all that lawyering work we'd have to do to pay for it, we wouldn't be home to enjoy it."

"You're always the practical one," she said, giving her husband a friendly squeeze around his middle. "What would I do without you?"

"You'd think of something."

We all laughed. "It's nice to dream though," sighed Amoy. "Isn't it?" Her gaze lingered over the view where distant yachts sailed slowly across the ocean.

Despite my best attempt at being aloof, at that moment I couldn't help searching for Rupert Boyden again and I found him quickly. Too quickly? Well, Amber is hard to miss, I told myself, as she was now leaning in towards him.

Nevertheless, I thought, it also didn't take her long to get rid of Melissa, wherever she'd slunk off to. Perhaps the BobCat was losing her spiteful touch after all.

And I got the impression that Rupert and Amber were more than just friends. Troy did mention a dancing twosome, or was it threesome? Was it Amber, the Golden Girl he was talking about who had two men vying for her affection? If so, who else was she seeing?

Or was it Rupert who was seeing someone else? Or both? Oh Troy, you really have a way of messing with my head with all your talk of who is seeing who.

Voices around us got louder as the champagne and other beverages continued to flow. Was it my imagination, or had the music increased in volume too? The atmosphere was wonderful, a warm breeze and blue sky with light cumulonimbus clouds, the happy little clouds that I'd learned about from my mother one summer when we were in her native Scotland on an archaeology dig outside of Aberdeen. Most summers that I can remember were spent in one field or another, and on one occasion spent near a very windy beach on the Isle of Skye on the rugged west coast of Scotland, with views not dissimilar to the one here where I was standing, yet all the way across the ocean.

A group of couples about thirty yards away were laughing and heading to the marquee and as they moved, I got a glimpse of another person hidden behind them and heading straight towards me.

"Hey Gabby, I think there's someone else that I know who's also been invited." I waved and called out as they got closer. "Hi."

"What are you doing?" hissed Gabby, tugging at my arm and deliberately trying to pull me back. "It'll be so embarrassing. That's Suzie Wilde!"

Chapter Eleven

"It's not Suzie I'm talking about," I said, watching the woman that was apparently our host, pausing to chat with Henry Grant and his partner Benjamin. "It's the man beside her."

"No, no" she hissed again.

"C'mon. Follow me and I'll introduce us."

I ignored her. We weren't going to meet our host Suzie Wilde. We were going to meet one of my special friends.

"Hey Harry," I said, almost running to give him a hug as we met up. "I didn't know you'd be here!" To be honest, I was completely thrown to see him.

I glanced over my left shoulder at Gabby and I honestly thought she would have looked more relieved about who I was in such a hurry to meet than she currently did, as she fidgeted with her handbag in an attempt to appear nonchalant.

Harry gave me a hug back. He winked at me. "I'm only here because of you, you know," he said as he gave me a hug back.

For a man in his sixties, Harry looked thinner, but fitter and dare I say younger, than he did four months ago when he collapsed at the most recent Legacy College dig in late February from a heart attack. His previously rotund abdomen was definitely more svelte beneath his crisp white and blue striped shirt and he had a spring in his step that I'd never noticed before.

"Harry, I want to introduce you to my friend Gabby Martinez. Gabby is the founder of the software company APP-APP."

Gabby smiled warmly as she shook Harry's extended hand.

"Harry is more than a volunteer at the dig site," I explained, fending off Harry's protestations at my support of him. "He sends out daily updates to staff and students, everything from the weather so we know what we need to do to protect ourselves from the elements, what's been found at a dig, and any professional successes that we can celebrate. He's the gel that unites us and makes us such a productive team."

"Oh, stop it," he said with a grin. "It's you who's our leader and rockstar of the team, not me."

"Well, my teaching life is so much easier with you around. Don't underestimate how valuable you are."

I had only met his wife Dottie in person in the ER room when Harry was being triaged, as I had accompanied him there in the ambulance. She asked me to stay with her for support at the hospital until she learned from the doctors exactly what had happened to Harry and what was going to happen in the coming hours and days. During the four hours that we waited there, we had chatted about Harry mostly, and about his passion for historical facts and archeology. Thankfully Harry didn't require cardiac surgery.

Since his medical emergency, I had made a point of checking in with Dottie and Harry every two weeks via video call initially and most recently by email to see how he was doing, and I had been truly delighted with his progress and looking forward to his return to the dig site

Dottie and Harry had been effusive in their gratitude, sending flowers to me at my office at the college with a handwritten card expressing how thankful they were for my quick thinking in saving Harry's life. The card also contained a gift card to my favorite restaurant (I must have mentioned yet another wonderful meal I'd had during a conversation with Harry on a previous dig).

There was also the gift of a year's supply of the fresh dog food I fed to Duke. And yes, Harry and Dottie knew the exact type of food I was giving Duke since the day my lovable hound had come into my life, and that not only did he love to eat it, but it was keeping him healthy. Now, thanks to good nutrition and daily exercise, he was one of the hairiest and fittest German Shepherds I'd ever known.

Although I'd only met Dottie in person once, I felt I knew her through our conversations when she or I checked in with each other about how he was doing.

"I can't believe you're here," I said to Harry. "Is Dottie here too?"

"Careful now," said the glamorous woman coming up beside him. "Tongues will be wagging if we're not careful." She opened her arms and gave me a welcoming hug. "Marnie, so glad you could make it to our party. Harry and I are so happy to have you here after all you did for him. We can't thank you enough."

If I was thrown earlier at seeing Harry here, I was now completely flummoxed as I gazed at the glamorous woman with an arm linked through one of Harry's. She was tanned, had shoulder-length soft blonde curls, and wore fitted blue jeans teamed with a black sequined top and sequined white jacket. White cowboy boots completed what was apparently the trademark stage ensemble of non-other than Suzie Wilde.

That's when I noticed the security person standing next to Suzie. It was Hank from the check-in point when we arrived on Wilde island.

Suzie Wilde slid her Chanel sunglasses up to the top of her head, and I clasped both my hands over my mouth as I peered directly through her dark false eyelashes into a beautiful pair of very familiar smiling brown eyes.

I felt my knees wobble.

"Oh, my, gosh!" I gasped with my mouth agape. The woman that was our host and everyone knew as Suzie Wilde was none other than Dottie Knight who I knew as Harry's wife. Off to the side, I was vaguely aware of other guests taking pictures of Suzie and our intimate group.

"Dottie," I muttered, confused by what I was seeing and aligning the vision before me with the person I'd come to know during video and phone calls over the past four months. "What a fantastic surprise. What I mean is …" I was rambling and I knew it. "I had no idea," I blurted out, hurling a wide-eyed glance at Harry who I saw could barely contain his excitement at the big reveal. "You never said anything." I avoided calling him a rotter for hiding this pertinent fact from me, but I was sure that both he and Dottie had a good reason for it.

He shrugged. "What was the point. You and Dottie get on really well."

That was true. We do get along well.

Suzie smiled lovingly at her husband. "I hope you can forgive us our subterfuge, Marnie. I wanted to tell you about my career when we knew that Harry was really on the mend, but once we'd set our minds on inviting you to today's event, he said he'd like it to be a surprise."

"Oh, yes," I said. "It is a *real* surprise. You both got me good with this." I looked at Dottie. "So, what do I call you then?"

"Call me Suzie. Everyone does, apart from Harry, that is. You see, when I'm with Harry I get to be me," she explained. "That's why when I arrived at the ER I introduced myself as Dottie Knight. It's my real name, and I use it when during legal situations or when I don't want any fuss. Although sometimes it can get a bit confusing, for example when I forget which name a hotel booking's been made under." Both Dottie and Harry laughed and winked at each other. "But," she continued, "Suzie's kind of my alter ego, honey. I like who she is too. Otherwise, it would be too complicated to try to keep track of who I am."

"Oh Dottie, I mean Suzie, that's too funny. I'm glad I don't have to remember who I am." At least, I thought, I know who I am as an adult.

"It'll be easier than you think honey." She slipped her sunglasses back on and turned towards Gabby.

Quickly, I introduced Gabby who, from the looks of her, was struggling to keep her mouth from dangling open. "Suzie and Harry, this is my good friend Gabriella Martinez, better known as Gabby. She's also my neighbor and has done a great job of helping me fit into town these past two years." It felt odd calling Dottie Suzie, but I had to admit the woman before me looked every bit a glamorous music star and was the polar opposite to the worried woman I'd first encountered at the hospital emergency department.

Gabby was remarkably composed. "It's lovely to meet you both. I didn't know until just now that you are both friends with Marnie."

"Marnie's been a godsend," explained Suzie. "Checking in on Harry, and me for that matter too."

Harry squeezed his wife's hand. "We've been together since we were teenagers, and I couldn't imagine what Dottie must have been feeling when she learned that I'd collapsed and had to be given CPR. She's a worrier."

"No wonder I worry," teased Dottie. "I nearly lost you. If it wasn't for Marnie's quick thinking and knowing what to do, my life would be very different from what it is today."

I was a little embarrassed by how much they were emphasizing what I had done. "The doctors and nurses took over. They did the rest."

"I know, but if it hadn't been for your quick thinking, my Harry wouldn't be here." She laughed heartily. Beneath her sparkly clothes, make-up, and confident stage persona I could see that she was still the woman-next-door I knew as Dottie. Both she and Harry leaned in conspiratorially. "That's why Harry and I made the next decision together and …"

Gabby and I waited, eyes widening.

"… and I'm going to dedicate my next single to you Marnie, and I'll be performing an acoustic version of it exclusively this evening."

"What!" This was amazing. Could this evening get any better? "But, but …" I clasped a hand over my mouth. I couldn't speak coherently. Tears stung my eyes. Shoot, it was going to be an evening I'd never forget.

"Now, go off and enjoy yourselves. You are, aren't you?"

"Oh yes," Gabby and I exclaimed together. I had to resist jumping up and down. I was so excited, and so happy that my dear friends Dottie, aka Suzie Wilde, and Harry were here.

"Good. I have a bit of mingling to do. Oh, and before I forget, there's a photographer and social media person here that my publicist arranged. They'll showcase the event and write good things about what the various companies here have done to help people in the community. When you're as well-known as I am, it's helpful to control the narrative. So, if you see anyone lurking in the bushes with a telescopic lens …" She shook her head and laughed loudly. Her laughter was infectious, and we all chuckled at the lengths some paparazzi would go to snap a photograph of a celebrity. "Simply ignore that they're there and they'll blend into the background."

"I'll try. I don't know how you deal with all the intrusion."

"Oh, it's not always intrusion, honey. Sometimes it is. But I've learned to be picky about where I go, who I'm seen with, that sort of thing. And of course," she added with a flourish of her hands, "I'm always on my very best behavior when out in public."

All four of us laughed out loud. This was the Dottie humor that I had come to know. Gosh, was there no end to the surprises this woman delivered?

"I promise, you'll hardly know the media are there," she continued. "Oh, and Harry's going to stay out of the way in our home. It's round the other side of the pool house and the cabanas." She pointed over her left shoulder to two rows of hydrangea bushes that lined a shell path. The sprawling property was laid out with various areas designated for a specific purpose. It was all beautifully designed and well-managed.

"Plus," she continued, "we've got Dolly and Blake waiting at home for him to wrangle. They're our two feisty Westies," she explained to Gabby, seeing the puzzled look on her face. "Harry will need to keep an eye on them. They already know something's happening here today. Plus, Harry doesn't do the whole fan and publicity thing." She squeezed Harry's arm playfully. They were always touching each other lightly either for reassurance or simply to let the other person know they were there.

"I'll bet you'll have a great time," said Harry to me.

"I will," I said. "And you know," I said, putting on a pouty face and pretending I was upset with him. "You never gave anything away, you rotter," I said.

"See! Isn't this what I told you?" exclaimed Harry, laughing.

I looked at him and rolled my eyes. "I've done it again, haven't I?"

He nodded, a smile broadening over his face. "You're American, yet every now and then you come up with these doozies, where you sound 'Bloody British,' and those of us around you have to pause and think what the heck you just said."

"Ah, yes. Mea culpa. British parents will do that to you every time. As a child I soaked up the culture through books, mysteries mostly, and the vagaries of both American and British English. They're similar, yet as you all probably know, really dissimilar at times."

"Well," continued Harry, "like you Marnie, I'm more focused on archaeology and digging for artifacts. When it comes to what is happening with the music industry, I leave all that to my darling here." With a peck on her cheek and a brief wave to us, Harry headed off in the direction of their house.

Suzie reached out to me and touched me lightly on the shoulder. "That's my cue too honey. Now you and Gabby here, go off and have a great time with all the folks here. If there's anything you need, don't hesitate to ask any of the staff who're mingling amongst us with food and beverages."

Suzie gave me a peck on the cheek and then, with Hank in tow, was off happily mingling with her other guests.

"Scallops?" Gabby and I swung around in unison in the direction of the male voice. A smiling young server held a platter with an assortment of bite-sized puff pastry hors d'oeuvres that were indeed filled with small bay scallops, while deftly holding small white napkins in his other hand. I noted a small card on the platter that said that the food was locally sourced.

"Yes please," I said, carefully taking a warm cloud of pastry and a napkin and juggling them with my now empty champagne glass all while keeping my shoulder bag in place on my shoulder. "Mmm. That was delicious."

Gabby took a pastry and was able to delicately place it into her mouth without even spilling a flake. "Yes, it was," she mumbled. "C'mon. Let's mingle. And by the way," she said, shaking her head at me. "I can't believe you didn't know that Dottie was Suzie, or the other way around." She took two steps ahead then turned back to look at me with a broad grin. "You know something Marnie Frazer? You're a worse nerd than I am!"

Almost one hour later we'd freshened up in the bathroom near to the pool house with its adjoining cabanas, mingled with each of the guests and their partners that we met at the yacht club event.

The music stopped and a man's deep voice made an announcement. "Ladies and gentlemen. Please gather around the stage for an intimate musical performance by your host, Ms Suzie Wilde. Suzie will give a special performance at 7 PM and you won't want to miss a thing." I glanced down at my watch; fifteen minutes until Suzie came on stage. "She will of course sing several of her famous hits. This will be followed by live music from a local band, The Clammers."

"Oh, I can't wait for the show to start," said Gabby as we drifted along with the other attendees to gather at the stage. Amoy and Mark joined us, along with Henry Grant and his partner Benjamin, Rupert's brother Anthony, Lashawna and her husband Richard, Amber's friend Fee who was chatting with Melissa's friend Carrie, and Helene Gauthier. I was surrounded by laughter, and I could feel the electricity around us as we all waited with heighten anticipation for Suzie to come on stage and start her performance. Then I noticed that the professional photographer and reporter were off to the right of the stage. That was the first time I'd seen them this whole evening. They sure knew how to blend in.

Four band members walked on stage and began testing and tuning their instruments and confirming sound checks with a hidden crew who, going by the trail of wires, were located somewhere behind some magnificent old rhododendrons that were as big as cherry trees. I spotted Jerry, the security guard who was one of the security personnel who greeted Gabby and myself when we arrived at the island on the tender, lingering, or was he lurking, to the left side of the stage where it was in shadow. He wasn't obvious, but I'd learned as a child to be alert to potential hazards, be they of the material kind or the human kind. I didn't think for a moment that Suzie, who I was now comfortably thinking of by that name instead of Dottie, was in any danger from any of the guests, or band members, or servers. But I guess he was paid to be observant, so I shrugged him off and went back to focusing on enjoying myself.

I looked around for the others. In the back of the marquee, I saw Bernard and Celia who were now in a small group with Liz and JT facing the ocean. Rupert and Melissa stood chatting at a high-top table with Helene's good-looking son Max. I didn't know whether it was too much champagne or the exuberance I was now feeling about being here, but something was giving me the confidence to want to approach the tall, tanned Frenchman. Although I didn't know if I was going to have competition, based on the sultry way that Melissa was acting.

Simon Stadler and his girlfriend Stella were in a cozy huddle in the opposite corner nearest to the entrance to the marquee. Ginger Maloney was with a man walking to the stage from the direction of the marquee. Striding to the stage from the opposite direction was Madame Gauthier.

Gabby leaned into me, "We've got about fifteen minutes, and I need to go to the loo. I'll be back in time for the start of the show."

"We only went about half an hour ago."

"Well, I need to go again," she called back as she strode off in the direction of the pool house bathroom.

"I'll keep us a place in the front row."

Servers walked among the guests, both in the marquee and those of us milling around the front of the stage, plying us with yet more food and beverages. A welcome light cooling breeze was wafting across the tiny island, ruffling the hems of dresses and hairstyles alike. Beyond the edge of the lawn, ospreys swooped and called in their high-pitched song as they hovered above us before plunging into the ocean, claws spread to catch the fish they needed for themselves and their hungry young chicks in their nests.

The excitement was mounting as the four musicians on stage took their place behind their microphones and struck a chord in unison, causing those who knew the intro to the song to erupt with loud cheers and applause. The musicians played what seemed like an intro or a first verse, while some of the guests sang the lyrics. Others, like me, danced on the grass in front of the stage, enjoying the thrill of being here on this exclusive island as a special guest. Then, when I thought the crowd couldn't get any louder, Suzie strode out from where she had been waiting behind the large rhododendron and began belting out the lyrics to the song as she climbed the five stairs at the right-hand side of the stage to eventually move to the front of the stage and sing. Suzie was great, and I loved everything about her performance. Why hadn't I listened to of her music?

As one song transitioned to another, I craned my neck searching the crowd for Gabby. Despite the relatively small audience by concert standards, by any standards, my friend was nowhere to be seen. I wasn't worried though. Gabby was a great mingler. She was probably talking with someone. Yet, I knew how much she was looking forward to Suzie's concert. Being this close to Suzie was a rare event. Why was she missing it?

Two songs into Suzie's show, I checked my watch, more than ten minutes had gone by since the concert had started. Plus, Gabby had left for the restroom fifteen minutes prior and there was no sign of her. Why hadn't she come to let me know she was talking with someone else? I'm not her keeper for goodness sake, but this was bordering on being rude!

Suzie stopped singing after the third song. "Thanks for coming, everyone. Are you having a good time?"

"Yeees!" came the resounding reply.

"I have a big announcement to make."

This caused another roar and cheers from the crowd.

"You are all winners," continued Suzie. "Each and every one of you. Your contribution to the community is remarkable and as such it is always my pleasure to host tonight's Give Back Event, which is now in its 15th year."

There was another round of cheers, this time accompanied by applause.

"I'm not done yet," she laughed. "One of you will have the special honor of receiving the Suzie Wilde Trophy, which is given for outstanding work."

There was more applause and loud whispers and nudging as I watched the attendees speculate as to who was going to be this year's recipient.

I scanned the guests in case Gabby was talking to someone else, knowing what a chatterbox she could be, but I still couldn't see her.

"I'll make the announcement after the next five songs. And later I'll sing the acoustic version of my new single that will be released tomorrow, and dedicate it to a special guest." The crowd went wild in response to the mention of the new music, wondering who the special guest was to receive the honor of a dedication. Suzie caught my eye and I beamed warmly.

That settled it.

Suzie began singing again and I squeezed my way through the crowd. From the looks of it, everyone appeared to be watching the show, with the exception of the missing Gabby, and I headed swiftly in the direction of the pool house bathroom to check on her, as she definitely wasn't with the guests watching the show. She was not only going to miss the entire show, but she was going to miss Suzie's new single.

I marched directly over the lawn, its tightly packed grass spongy beneath my sandals. After ten steps I altered my fast pace and slowed it down a bit and that's when I noticed the little bounce beneath each footstep. It was like walking on a quality carpet, I thought. Except this one has to be cut and trimmed regularly. I hoped that Suzie didn't mind me sneaking off like this and hurried as quickly as I could without breaking into a run and creating a fuss. Gabby was going to be fine. There were security guards all over the place, for goodness sake. She would have texted me or called if there was a problem. No, I assured myself, she was probably talking with someone, even though I didn't think anyone else was missing from watching the show, and she either forgot the time or it was difficult to get away.

And I sure as heck was more than a little annoyed with how she was behaving.

The music drifted behind me as I reached the end of the lawn and stepped onto a sun-bleached seashell path that wound its way to the swimming pool and pool house. The contrast of the shells was instantly apparent, and the sensation was hard and crunchy underfoot. The openness of the party area gave way to spotty filtered shade with muted sounds of the band and Suzie's singing. A hedge of hip-height evergreen bushes marked the pathway, and I hummed a little of the catchy chorus and followed the straight route to the pool area. The path opened up and gave way to a clearing where the pool house was now visible, flanked by low hedges of blue hydrangeas with blooms the size of a human head. There was one large rhododendron bush with heavy faded blooms that drooped over the path, shedding dry crispy petals onto the black mulch below their branches.

I saw a sandal sticking out from the corner of the bush on the path. That's a nice sandal, I thought. They're like the ones that… I stopped mid-thought and walked cautiously past the bush and bent down to look at the sandal. A woman was lying on her right side, asleep. "Are you okay?" I asked softly while bending down to check for a pulse in the woman's neck. My fingers felt no arterial pulsation and I abruptly drew back my hand in horror. That was when I noticed the small white froth that bubbled over the woman's blue lips and now lay in an amalgamated pool in her golden hair.

Chapter Twelve

Over the course of my career I've seen many human remains; except they were typically hundreds of years old and frequently reduced to dry bones. What I had now uncovered was very different, and oh so shockingly real.

I went to straighten up and almost fell on my butt as I struggled to make sense of what I had found.

A woman was dead. And not just any woman.

It was Amber.

I forced myself to look at her. Her lips were cyanotic and covered in a grayish froth that appeared to be a mix of spittle and something else. Her purse was open and her epipen lay beside her untouched. Her blue eyes were open and stared sightlessly at the gnarly base of the bush, her pupils dilated. I hoped that her death had been swift and that she hadn't suffered any more than she must have by trying to breathe and cling onto life. Her once tanned and glowing skin had already taken on a grayish hue.

It appeared that she had been exposed to an allergen and couldn't reach her life-saving EpiPen in time. And yet, there was something about the way she was lying on her side, one hand beside her bag, the other placed on her chest. Her long cream dress was stained and partially ruched around her mid-thighs. The way she was lying had a familiarity about it, but I pushed the thought away. Focus, I told myself.

I needed to remain objective, and not allow my heightened emotions to cloud what I was doing.

My archaeology training and site experience took over and I regarded the scene around me just as I would if I was beginning the initial exploration of an archaeological dig. At this early stage I wasn't sure what was relevant information or if anything that I identified would help drive forward any subsequent investigation into her death. And having participated in digs across the world since my teens and led my own dig teams from my mid-twenties onwards, I was confident that I knew enough to make a positive difference.

I pulled my phone out from my bag and opened up the camera. It didn't take me long to get into what I called my work-zone mode. Treating it like an exploration site, I was careful where I stood, and I noticed that there were several sets of small footprints intercrossing in the soil where the black mulch had been scraped away. A woman perhaps? Or a man with small feet? Either way, I could tell that the person was wearing shoes or flat sandals.

Working quickly but shakily I set about the various tasks that would help me to adequately describe what I was witnessing and in turn help the police and their experts analyze my findings in order to subsequently interpret and classify the evidence.

I snapped images of where I'd been walking when I saw her sandal and foot peeking out on the path. I forced myself to hone in on the froth around her lips, and her hands and fingernails without staring at those areas directly. I wasn't looking for anything specific, merely trying to capture the fresh scene in case it got contaminated or the curious froth evaporated while making sure that I hadn't inadvertently caused damage to the area where Amber was lying in.

That said, I took nothing at face value. The filtered early evening sunlight cast alternating long fingers of light and dark everywhere I looked, intermingled with splodges of light.

I'd have to tell Suzie and Harry. My arms hung heavily by my side, and I pressed my lips together feeling even more sadder, and angry too, as the seconds drifted by. I didn't relish breaking the news as the evening of celebration would now come screeching to a terrible stop. Everyone would be devastated. And what about Amber's friend Fee? Someone would have to break the awful news to her. And her family too. I definitely didn't want to be the one to do that.

And the police would need to be called. I would need to do that first before I told Suzie.

Silently, I continued to scroll speedily through the sequence of events that would subsequently unfold. It would also mean an investigation and questioning of everyone here.

Gabby!

I'd forgotten that I'd gone in search of her when I stumbled across Amber's body. She'd probably made her way back to the stage and was looking for me. Unless…

I shivered and felt the small hairs on the back of my neck stand up as though all the warmth and color of the day had been sucked out of the air around me and I was suddenly plunged into a frozen land devoid of all that was good.

"Hey you! What are you doing?"

I spun around only to find myself face to face with none other than Melissa Maxwell. Crap, this day was going downhill fast.

Chapter Thirteen

"Back away Melissa." I couldn't think of what else to say as I took one step closer to her to shoo her away and prevent her from seeing Amber.

"I asked you what you are doing. And I demand an answer."

"I don't need to say anything to you. Right now, though, it's in your own best interest to move away from here."

Melissa didn't leave. If anything, she spread her feet apart, standing her ground and readying for an argument. "I don't trust you, Marnie Frazer. I've been asking around about you. You're trouble, you know that? You shouldn't even have been invited to this event. You're nobody." She almost spat out the word nobody.

I didn't have time for this. I had to get back to the main event and break the news to Suzie, but I couldn't leave Melissa here to sniff around and risk her contaminating the scene where Amber now lay a few feet away, partially hidden by the bush. "Let's go back to the party. We're missing the concert." I pushed past her and started to walk back to the lawn in the hope that she would follow.

I should have known better.

"What have you done," Melissa gasped.

I swung around and saw her bent over with one hand raised softly to her mouth. She backed away from where Amber's body lay and stared at me, her dark eyes wide, before she turned and fled towards the pool house. Once there, she would reach the lawn which stood between the swimming pool and the main house, and circle around to the stage where she would no doubt be able to alert Suzie and the security personnel.

I had to get to Suzie before Melissa did. There was no telling what damage she would do, what scathing assumptions she would make if she shared what she mistook as evidence. And I could guess who she would be pointing her manicured finger at.

I was breathing heavily as I ran on the seashell path to the lawn, my heart pounding from fear of what I'd stumbled across and what Melissa might do and say. I'd only been so traumatized once before in my life. That was the day I'd found my birth mother unconscious, prior to her eventually dying three days later, and the subsequent fear of what was going to happen to me and whether I would be put in a state-run children's home or put into foster care. Neither option gave me the warm and fuzzies.

I reached the lawn and quickened my pace as I pulled out my phone and called the emergency services. Cell coverage wasn't good. Only two bars. But it was enough as the call was answered after the third ring. I explained as succinctly as I could to the dispatcher why I needed the police and a medical crew and any other first responders she thought we would need, given the circumstances.

My heart pounding, I was halfway to the stage as the call ended. I quickly scanned the crowd for any sign of Melissa. Had she somehow managed to reach here before I did? Suzie was slowing her singing, indicating she was about to end the song soon, watching me. I wasn't sure if she had caught sight of me emerging from the pool house path. I spotted Hank, and headed straight to where he was standing off to the left side of the stage near one of the tall stage speakers. Jerry was nowhere to be seen. The photographer and reporter had moved to the right hand side of the stage and were taking random images of the attendees. They didn't appear to notice me hurrying. To them I was probably just someone keen to listen to Suzie singing.

I beckoned to Hank, my face alone probably letting him know that something was wrong. The music was loud so close to the stage though, plus I had to stand on my tip-toes to try to tell him what I had discovered, trying to make him hear above the music without forewarning the groups of people nearest us. I failed in my attempt to alert him to what had happened, but I couldn't give up trying. Goodness only knows what trouble Melissa was stirring up while I attempted to make Hank understand the severity of the situation.

He glanced around us and with a flick of his head, indicated that I should follow him to the area behind the stage. I followed right behind him into an area strewn with cables and heavy-duty boxes with shiny silvery hinges. This was where the backing band had left their equipment cases for their musical instruments and other items they needed to perform. Two men sat at a sound desk, ignoring us, as they fiddled with information on their computers, speaking occasionally to either each other or a band member via their headphones.

Hank cocked his head towards me, his brow furrowed, reading my body language and trying to gauge whether I posed a threat. I could feel his warm breath on my neck as he drew slightly closer. "Tell me again what appears to be upsetting you so much."

I repeated what I'd said to him moments earlier, speaking slower but still as loud. "I've found one of the guests and they appear to be dead."

He jerked back as if I'd slapped him, causing the sound engineer nearest us to glance briefly in our direction before returning to stare at his computer. I doubt he heard anything; only that he saw Hank's reaction to what I'd said to him.

Hank pulled off his sunglasses and squinted at me. "Did I hear you correctly, ma'am?"

I nodded stiffly. Resisting the urge to point, I said, "Do you want to follow me? I'll show you where she is."

"A woman? Sure she's not had too much of the bubbly stuff?"

I lifted my chin and glared at him. Hard. "I know a dead body when I see one. It's not my first time you know." This came out all wrong. I was trying to be professional, not snarky, and to hurry this guy along. Thinking quickly, I said, "Come on, we need to hurry in case another guest finds her and tramples over the scene."

After a moment's hesitation we set off, me striding forth as fast I could without running and causing people to look at me and deciding to follow Hank behind me. "You've done this before?" he huffed. "Seen dead bodies?"

Sort of, I thought. "I'm a professor at the college," I said hurriedly. That's when I saw Melissa talking animatedly to Jerry, one of the other security professionals and pointing back in the direction of the pool house. I quickened my pace, no longer caring if people saw me hurrying with Hank in tow. "And I've got plenty of experience in preserving data where objects, human or otherwise, have been buried." I left it at that and did my best to run on the seashells as we entered the pool house path.

Hank kept close behind me, his footsteps landing heavily on the crushed shell path.

With a mix of relief at getting here before Melissa, or anyone else for that matter, I stopped before the large rhododendron and looked at where its lower branches skimmed the mulch and earth. Amber's body was still there behind the bush, her peach nail-polished toes a stark reminder of the fragility of human life.

But even so, I was scared I'd imagined what had happened to her or that someone had been watching and subsequently hidden her. Weird I know, but so many awful thoughts were flowing through me right now it was hard to think straight.

Hank drew up beside me, our bodies close. We looked on silently. Flies were now settling on Amber's face, and I forced back the urge to swipe them away from her. Small brown sugar ants were already snaking a line to her pale dress.

Now that I'd had time to process what I'd seen when I'd first found Amber, my subconscious kicked in. I knew what I was seeing. Her body was staged.

Chapter Fourteen

I heard him exhale. He shook his head in denial at what he was seeing. I wanted to touch his arm in reassurance but hesitated in reaching out to him. It's not easy seeing a dead body and I didn't know if this was the first one he had seen. I don't know if it gets easier. This was only my second body and they were over two decades apart. That's not counting the numerous bones and skeletons I'd come across over my decades of research, but even the bones, regardless of age, were also treated with respect. They were once a living, human being. But that didn't invoke the same guttural reaction as seeing a flesh and blood person that I'd known, now dead.

"I've already called the emergency services. We need paramedics and things like that."

He looked back at me. "Police too?"

"Yes. Them too. Shouldn't you call your colleagues and let them know what's happened? They'll need to keep the guests back until help gets here."

Hank unclipped his cell phone and made a call. "Jerry, it's me. Get over to the pool house as quickly as you can. There's been an incident." He listened to Jerry while looking at me, and I guessed that Melissa was now spinning a tale. It was going to come down to her word against mine, I thought, as my stomach began to flutter and do flips. "The police are on their way," he added as he concluded the call.

Mindful of Melissa's scheming, I knew that I needed to be proactive here, and fast. "We need to tell Suzie as soon as possible," I told Hank, all too conscious that I was breathing heavily. "I'll go and break the news if you keep an eye on things here, stop anyone from trampling over the surrounding area."

He moved his jaw around as he mulled over what I'd said. "Gee, I'm not sure about that. I'll call one of the other security guys to tell her. After all, this needn't stop the party. Unless…"

Unless he suspected foul play? "It's better if I break it to Suzie. I know her and her husband personally. Plus, your colleagues will be needed to watch the guests and keep them calm until the police get here and take over."

He chewed his bottom lip, trying to decide, then nodded and I turned on my flat heels and headed swiftly back to the lawn before Hank could change his mind, feeling his eyes boring into my back as he watched me leave. Back in the evening sunlight, I saw that Suzie had in fact finished her concert and had left the stage.

She headed straight towards me; arms open wide ready to give me a huge hug.

I'd missed the dedication and hearing her new single. I squashed that thought. How could I be thinking of that when a young woman was dead. This particular Suzie Wilde event was going to be remembered for all the wrong reasons.

"Hey Marnie," she said as she squeezed me tight before holding me at arm's length to look me squarely in the eyes. "What's up? I saw you going back and forth while I was singing. Do you have an upset tummy? Are there issues with the pool house plumbing?"

"No Suzie. Listen, I've got bad news about one of your guests. You need to prepare yourself for a shock."

Suzie took me by the elbow and guided me over to the shade of a giant red oak. She looked me straight in the eyes. "Break it to me honey."

"It's Amber Clarke. One of your guests."

"Amber. Which one is she now?"

"Tall, blonde, works at the Artemis Group."

"Ah, yes. Artemis. They've done a great job this year …" Her voice trailed off. "How bad is it?"

"Let's make our way to the pool house. I'll tell you as much as I know on the way there. But we need to hurry."

Keeping the details succinct, I effectively gave Suzie the Cliff Notes version of what I had stumbled upon.

We met up with Hank. Jerry was with him and, surprisingly, no sign of Melissa. There was no telling where she was now and what mischief she was causing, or about to cause. "Brace yourself Suzie," I told her.

"Ms Wilde," said Hank, raising an arm to prevent her going any further. "We're not sure what happened to the guest. The police and emergency services have been notified though."

"Thank you Hank. Marnie filled me in on what she found. Surely you don't think that it's a suspicious death?"

We shrugged as one. "Unlikely," said Hank, "but we need to be sure."

"She did have a serious allergic response at an earlier event," I said, "but I don't see how she could have ended up behind a bush."

Suzie sighed heavily. "Let me see the poor woman."

Hank stepped aside.

I stayed close to Suzie. "Try not to touch anything," I gently advised her as she visibly steadied herself and leaned gingerly towards Amber.

Suzie drew her shoulders back and her lips parted and moved just as they would if saying a prayer. Hank, Jerry, and I watched her gaze down at Amber's body. After a few breaths, Suzie stepped back and joined us. "What a sad day. I wasn't able to talk with the woman prior to the concert. She was on the roster to chat with afterwards. And now, well …" She looked at Hank. "Who did she come here with?"

"I'll check that," he said.

"No need," I told them. "She came with her friend, Fee Gibson. I spoke with them earlier this evening. Ideally though, we should wait for the police. Have them officially confirm the death and notify Amber's family. However, that also means that we run the risk of another guest telling her."

"Another guest?"

"Yes. Melissa Maxwell also knows that Amber is dead. She arrived just after I found Amber's body, then she ran off towards the lawn."

"That could be a problem, Ms. Wilde," said Hank. "I can have one of my security team find her and isolate her, prevent her from talking to too many people before we know for sure what has happened."

"Thanks Hank," said Suzie, "but I think the damage is done. I know how fast both good and bad news travels. It only takes minutes before a tragedy or a celebration is all over social media. Oh, this is awful. It's my event and I can't help feeling responsible for what's happened."

"How will the police and the medic crew get here?" I asked. "Boat? Helicopter?"

"Boat and road, honey. It shouldn't take them long."

"Road?" I was puzzled. We had arrived here via a Boston Whaler. I wasn't aware of any roads leading to and from the island.

Suzie raised her eyebrows at me. "There's also a causeway to get on and off my island," she explained.

"I should have realized that that would be the case." I groaned internally. I had been too caught up in the thrill of being invited to the event that I hadn't dug more into the Suzie Wilde persona and her background as well as what was known about the island. "That's much more practical," I continued, "although I'm also relieved that there's more than one way off the island."

"It's a little longer, but necessary during bad weather and for practical reasons such as large deliveries."

"We have to let the guests know that there's been an incident," said Hank. "Explain that the pool house bathrooms are out of use. We can't have anyone coming here and trampling over the area."

Suzie sighed heavily and pursed her lips thoughtfully. "You're right. No need to cause any further alarm. I'll call Harry. Let him know what's happened and what to expect. I'll redirect the guests to my house. They can use the powder room there." She turned to Hank. "Hank, I want you to notify Cindy. She's somewhere around, keeping an eye on things. Send her to my house so that she can ensure that no-one gets lost in the house," she gave air-quotes as she emphasized the word lost. "And make sure she stays there until I know what's happening once the emergency services get here." She looked at me, seeing me puzzling over who Cindy was. "Cindy's one of my security team," she explained. "Ready to come with me to break the news to the guests that we're going to have a few more unexpected visitors?"

"Definitely. But we'd better hurry. The police were notified about ten minutes ago. My guess is they'll be here really soon."

"I hope we don't meet anyone," said Suzie. "It's going to be really awkward otherwise."

We reached the lawn and headed straight for the stage where the local band, The Clammers, were now playing lively music and several groups were dancing, oblivious to the tragic events of the past few minutes.

I gave a quick glance over to the ocean beyond us and I saw a boat speeding towards the island, a blue light flashing from the center console. It was maybe five minutes away. Sirens were audible from the causeway which I now knew was behind Suzie's house and I reckoned we had a minute or two before the police vehicles and their occupants arrived.

I suddenly remembered that Gabby was missing. There was still no sign of her and a squirrely feeling rose in my stomach.

Was there a connection between Amber's death and Gabby being missing?

We reached the stage and Suzie exhaled slowly to calm herself as she prepared herself to climb the steps to the stage. With her flamboyant clothes, hair and make-up she evoked the aura of a country music star, albeit a subdued one.

That momentary pause was the gap that Melissa needed. She clambered onto the stage before Suzie or any of us could realize what was happening and grabbed the nearest microphone from a stand, surprising each of the band members who all stopped mid-chord. "Listen to me, everyone," she announced clearly and confidently. Everyone hushed and watched her on the stage. She tucked both sides of her perfect bob haircut behind her ears to show she meant business. It was a bit like watching a politician walking around with her sleeves rolled up. "There's been a murder."

Chapter Fifteen

The band stepped away from her, likely thinking she was either deranged or drunk. Either way, I didn't actually disagree with their surmise. A man and a woman, both broad-shouldered and each wearing security personnel outfits climbed onto the stage. Melissa ignored them and continued addressing all the invited guests who were now present in front of her. "There's a dead body over by the pool house," she continued, "and they don't want you to know about it. Any one of us could be next."

Now she had everyone's attention. Mutterings of disbelief came first, followed by shaking of heads, then I saw Bernard, Celia, Kayla and Sabrina rush off in the direction of the pool house, no doubt to verify what they'd just heard.

Suzie's photographer stood stock still by the stage, mouth agape, before starting to take photos of Melissa.

Suzie charged forward and made a wave with her left hand and the drummer of the band leaned over and flipped a switch, effectively cutting off the sound to Melissa's microphone. Switching on her small lavalier lapel microphone, Suzie climbed the stage swiftly and faced the concerned faces gazing up at her. "Hey guys. Listen to me." Her husky Suzie Wilde voice came over the microphone loud and clear as Melissa was escorted off the stage by the two security personnel and was now arguing with both of them. "Ladies and gentlemen, your attention please." She was now transformed into Suzie Wilde, commanding the crowd with a well-worn ease that belied the fact that about seventy-five yards away, a woman was dead, most likely murdered. "One of our guests has sadly died, perhaps from natural causes. The emergency personnel have arrived and they're going to take care of everything. Please remain calm and assist the first responders and the police with any questions they may have. And, because of the ongoing situation there, please feel free to use the powder room in my house, instead of the pool house bathroom."

Instantly, huddles formed and discussions ensued from the assembled guests, each small group keeping their comments to a chosen few, along with pointing back and forth from the stage to Suzie's house. Some faces were smiling. Others were casting glances towards the direction of the pool house. There was a discernible shift as sandals and boat shoes huddled closer to give the wearer a better position to talk with their partner. All were moving as one into their pockets and handbags retrieving their phones.

"Might be best if y'all head on over to the marquee where the excellent servers will provide you with more food and beverages," urged Suzie. "We'll let you know what's happening as soon as possible."

Her words fell on mostly deaf ears as her guests turned their united backs on her. Suzie hurried down off the stage and rushed to meet me. "They're all going to go see what happened for themselves, aren't they?"

"We'll get there before them." I hoped I sounded more certain than I felt. I reckoned we had only minutes before the guests decided to swarm en masse in the direction of the pool house.

She pointed towards her house. "The emergency services people have arrived. I saw them from the stage. I'll send Jerry to meet them."

"Good idea. Let's head on over to meet up with Hank at the pool house."

We reached Hank and Jerry, and found Bernard and his wife Celia, along with Kaylee and Sabrina already there with their cell phones out, snapping pictures of, well, anything really. The trees, pool house, Hank and Jerry, each other. Taking selfies to show that they were at the scene of the crime, so to speak. I hadn't had a chance to chat with Kaylee this evening. The last time we had spoken was at the yacht club fundraiser a few weeks ago.

"Hey, Hank, Jerry," Suzie called out, panting slightly. "The emergency services have arrived," she announced. "Jerry, I want you to go over and meet them. Fill them in on what's happened and bring them here as fast as you can."

Jerry sped off just as raised voices and the sound of feet crunching over the white seashell path reached us. Guests appeared about fifty yards away, some squeezing their way to the front of what looked like a fat conga line.

Hank stepped forward. "Move back everyone. Don't come any closer."

It appeared that the guests, wait staff, and security had now descended on the area surrounding the pool house path hoping to see something. People were standing between the hedge and the lawn, phones out, flashes and clicking and nudging all to get to the front of the crowd. I stood tall, my spine as straight as I could muster given the shocking events that were unfolding.

"Stay back everyone," Hank repeated.

As one, there was a surge as the crowd edged closer, ignoring Hank. There was a shout out from the back of the crowd demanding answers. Was it Bernard Lazenby? He was certainly the loudest of the attendees. Who it was didn't matter now as the initial call triggered a heavy chorus demanding answers.

The swarm, as I was now thinking of them, rather than guests, began to murmur as one. The same male voice, hidden of course by the swarm, called out, "How could this happen?"

"Are we safe?" shouted a female voice.

"How do we leave this place?" cried out another man, or was it the same one. The swarm was abuzz with questions all demanding immediate answers.

I'd mistakenly assumed at the moment when they saw Suzie that everyone would be respectful. How wrong I was.

Ignoring the thrust of the questions with their barbed insinuations that somehow, she was to blame for what had occurred, Suzie marched forward to stand beside Hank while avoiding looking in the direction of where the body lay under the bush. She thrust her hands on her hips. "Everyone," she called out firmly in her deep raspy voice, "listen carefully. My security people are escorting the paramedics and police officers across the property. In the meantime, we need to move back to the lawn and give them space to work. Please follow their instructions when they arrive."

Mumbling and grumbling erupted from the guests milling around in front of us. On the perimeter, I spotted Suzie's official photographer taking photographs and the media person looking around her and making copious notes. What a scoop they were having.

"You can't do this," called out a man from the mid-section of the crowd.

Suzie turned to Hank. "Hank, keep moving everyone back."

Most people moved back a few steps, trying to be cooperative for the benefit of their host while also trying to see more from a slightly new position in the crowd while deciding if, and when they should head back to the lawn. They spilled out between the lawn and the evergreen hedge, trampling the freshly laid mulch and kicking up large chunks of it onto the seashell path. Several seemed oblivious to the snags from the hedge on their skin and clothes.

Phones continue to click away, most held up recording the unfolding scene. How many photos could these people take, I wondered. Apart from some shuffling feet, the guests were taking little notice to stay back, talking on their phones and texting. Loud voices of dissention and agreement all muddled in as one.

Suddenly there was a wave that flooded through the crowd. They swayed as one organism, emitting gasps and loud mutterings.

Then a woman screamed, pointing behind me.

I swung around to see what she was looking at. I grabbed hold of Suzie as Gabby staggered from behind the pool house, her dress disheveled, blood running through her fingers into her bedraggled hair.

Chapter Sixteen

I rushed swiftly to Gabby's aid; my previous emotions kicked to one side as she slumped against me. I was glad when Hank dashed over and helped me lower her slowly to a semi-prone position against the front facing wall of the pool house, facing the pool and away from prying eyes and snooping phones. A magnificent red oak was next to the pool house. One of several shade trees on the property, it seemed to stand guard over her.

Hank then stood up, legs spread, arms crossed, daring anyone to get any closer. I quickly checked Gabby for the source of her injuries. As gently as I could manage, I pared back her hair that three hours ago was freshly washed and styled into soft curls and was now an amalgam of matted hair and mulch tangled together. She flinched when I touched the back of her head. This was where the blood was oozing from. A quick examination of the scalp showed an extra-large egg-sized contusion at the back of her head. The bleeding from the head-wound appeared to have stopped, but there were regular reports in the news about people who suffered catastrophic head injuries.

Trying not to alarm my friend, I knew that she needed to get checked out in case there was any hidden damage. Maybe a cracked skull. Or worse; a brain bleed. I was only trained in basic first aid, but I was scared for Gabby, given the size of the swelling and the bleeding from her head. All that plus the fact she appeared groggy after being knocked unconscious.

"Do you remember what happened?"

"Not much. Only that I was heading back from the loo," the corners of her mouth lifted into a little smile, "thankfully not on my way to it."

"True. You'd already had several glasses of champagne."

"I was a little wobbly on the seashell path. I remember hearing someone panting and groaning when I left the pool house."

"Did you see who it was?"

"No. It was like the sound you hear at the gym."

"Was it a woman or a man?"

"A man. No. It was a woman." She paused thinking again. "Oh, my head hurts where they whacked me with something, hard, on the back of my head." She probed the back of her head and brought her hand close to her face, surprised at her blood-stained fingers. She closed her eyes and spoke softly. "To be honest Marnie, I either can't remember, or can't tell the difference." She flopped against me, and I struggled to sit her back up. Thankfully Hank, who was diligently standing guard, saw what was happening and helped me ease my friend into a more comfortable position.

I leaned in close to Gabby. "Quickly," I asked her, "did you happen to notice anyone else in the area either going to or coming from the pool house?"

"No, sorry." She wiped her now moist eyes with the backs of both hands. "All I heard was Suzie singing in the distance, and when I came out of the loo to someone grunting."

"Hmm. Do you remember where you were when you were struck? You said you had left the pool house and were on the path, but just now you came from around the rear of the pool house."

She closed her eyes. "Give me a moment. My head is swimming."

I waited.

"There was a foot." Her eyes sprung open. "I remember!" she squeezed her eyes shut then slowly opened them. "Or at least I think I do. I left the bathroom and I saw a sandal sticking out under the bush." She strained to turn her head in the direction where Amber's body lay. "I crouched down to have a closer look and that's all I remember. Then I woke up at the back of the pool house with this horrible headache." She stared at her own sandals. "Look at that. My new sandals are ruined." The previously white strappy sandals were scraped and torn, and scraps of black mulch were stuck between her manicured toes. "How did I manage to do that?"

Oh Gabby, I thought. Your head injury could be much worse than I originally believed. "Someone dragged you out of the way," I said gently.

She began to tremble. "They could have killed me."

I shook my head, trying to reassure her. "Thankfully they only wanted to hide you, rather than seriously harm you." I hope I sounded more confident than I actually felt.

"You're right. I didn't think of that." She closed her eyes as though sleepy.

Both our phones pinged. A quick glance showed it was Troy. He'd likely heard through the Liberty Cove grapevine some of what had happened. Well, as much as I liked Troy, he'd have to get in line for a response.

"I'll be right back with help for you Gabby."

Heavy footsteps crunched behind me. Thinking it might be Suzie, I stood up too quickly and lost my balance, my right heel stepping on a hard shoe, while bumping the owner of the shoes in the stomach with my elbow and grabbing wildly for something to hold onto, which was a firm arm, to stop myself from falling. "Oops, watch out," I called out as I struggled to stay upright, dreading being face-to-face with one of the other guests who might start to demand information or take my photograph yet again. Instead of an imbibed guest I came face to face with a stranger. Or rather, I was face to shoulder with him. I looked up and found myself staring, yes staring, and slightly open-mouthed, into the bluest eyes I had ever seen in a man. His dark cropped hair only enhanced his cheekbones and light brown skin. And, oh my gosh, I thought, that's what a chiseled jaw looks like.

"I'm fine," he said in a firm deep voice, jolting me from the spaced-out moment I was having.

Muttering an incoherent apology, I backed away from the man, noticing his dark chinos and white polo shirt, teamed with a black belt containing an official-looking badge and a gun. He was with another man dressed similarly, but he was shorter by about six inches. This man also wore his hair cropped, but his had silvery flecks that acted like highlights against his heavily tanned skin. Trailing about fifteen yards behind them strode a woman with blonde hair pulled back in a tidy ponytail that reached her shoulders, wearing jeans and a white shirt and carrying a heavy black leather bag that looked similar to a briefcase.

Two female paramedics were right behind her, escorted by Jerry.

Suzie raced over to me and the man I'd bumped into, taking note of Gabby's condition. "Trip, thank goodness you're here," she said, hugging him briefly.

"Are you hurt?" he asked, studying her, then looking around.

She shook her head, her curls shaking.

"It's not me, Trip, nor Harry." She took a deep steadying breath. "One of my guests is dead and another is badly hurt."

His face gave little away. "I got the call about there being a homicide here. There was no name as to who had been found dead, other than it was a woman."

"And you were worried it might be me?"

"Well, I'll admit it was the first thing that crossed my mind. So, I was mighty relieved when I saw you." He turned and looked over his shoulder and raised an arm. "Over here," he called out to the paramedics.

Jerry led them to where we were standing and then joined Hank in a huddled discussion. Suzie hurried over to both men. "Hank, I need you to assist Sergeant Brodie's team with anything they need. Help get them acquainted with the property etcetera.

"Sure thing Miss Wilde," he replied with a nod. "And what about you?"

She looked around her and raised her arms in a wide gesture. "With all these police officers here, I'm good. I feel really comfortable, actually better, knowing that you're helping them do their job better and faster."

"Okay, Miss Wilde."

"I'll call you if I need you, Hank. But stay in touch, and let me know when you're done helping out." She hurried over to rejoin me.

I approached the two paramedics. "It's my friend Gabby," I blurted out. "She's been attacked and needs help."

"Tell us what happened," said the taller of the two women. The other woman was heavier set and more muscular than her companion, and placed her medical bag on the mulch beside Gabby. She opened her bag and pulled out items to help her monitor Gabby's pulse and blood pressure. She then set about shining a pen light in Gabby's eyes, checking for the reaction of her pupils to the intense light.

I filled both women in with what little I knew.

"Thanks. Now, please step back and allow us to see what we can do to help Gabby.

I did as they asked to give them space to check out the extent of Gabby's injuries and walked over to rejoin Suzie, who was bringing the man she called Trip and a woman who carried what appeared to be a medical bag, up to speed with the events that had happened.

Three uniformed officers arrived from the direction of Suzie's house. The colleague who was with the man that Suzie called Trip approached them and appeared to give them instructions. Sure enough, the uniformed officers took over crowd control.

"This is a crime scene folks," called out one of the officers. "We need you to step back." The other two officers were doing a fine job ushering the guests back to the lawn, ensuring that no-one snuck past them to snoop around.

I noticed two additional officers had arrived and were moving swiftly, unfurling yellow and black police caution tape to cordon off a wide perimeter that appeared to encompass not only the bush where Amber lay, but the area behind us where the path led to the pool house restrooms, but the pool too where the cabanas and lounge chairs were neatly arranged around the pool.

It was all very imposing and official.

Turning to me, Suzie introduced me to the couple she was talking with, starting with the woman.

"This is Dr Diane Cowen. She's the medical examiner." Realization dawned on me as I suddenly understood that the doctor was here to examine Amber's body, not attend to the living.

"And this is Detective Sergeant Trip Brodie. Trip's a longtime friend of Harry and myself. He's also a really good detective."

"Diane and Trip, this is Marnie Frazer. Marnie was the one who found Amber and alerted my security team."

"Hi," I said. I decided not to make any reference to how I'd inadvertently collided into him.

Trip thought differently. "We bumped into each other earlier. Nice to see you again Marnie. And I heard what you did for Harry when he had his incident at the dig site."

"You did?" I frowned at Suzie, and she shook her head.

"Don't look at me. All I told Trip was that Harry's professor had saved his life." She nudged him as she continued talking. "I told you he is good at his job. But that aside, I feel better now that he's here."

I gave him a little smile but he didn't smile back, so I backed off a little, uncertain about how everything was going to pan out. I felt nervous around him, yet I had nothing to be guilty about.

Trip pursed his lips. "This is going to be a high priority, Suzie. What's happened here is all over social media. It's only going to be a matter of time before the reporters turn up and hound you for answers."

"I realize that Trip," she said with a heavy sigh.

"Well now," Dr Cowen announced. "Be that as it may, I'm ready to make an assessment of the deceased." The doctor lowered her bag and opened it, and pulled out a white coverall suit from inside the briefcase.

We stepped back onto the seashell path to allow the doctor space to pull on her protective coveralls, in order to examine the body and confirm what we all knew.

Not wanting to just wait around, I pulled out my phone and unlocked it. "Sergeant Brodie, about what Suzie mentioned earlier–that I was the one who found Amber."

"Yes?"

"I took photographs of what might be important."

He raised a skeptical eyebrow at me.

"You know, for footprints and such."

"You took photos?"

Did the man have to be so cynical? "Yes."

I felt his steady gaze burrow into mine.

"And while there didn't appear to be an obvious injury on the body," I continued, "there was something odd."

"Like what?"

"Well, I didn't detect an odor on her, apart from her perfume, that is. But she had some kind of white froth on her lips."

"Show me what you took." He went to take my phone, but I drew it away from him.

My hands trembling as I scrolled through the numerous photos that I had taken, I readied the photos for him to view and held up my phone. "Let me show you."

"I'll need those."

"What email shall I send them to? You can count the number of images on my phone here to be sure I didn't hold any back."

He paused before replying. "Brodie J at Legacy Cove PD dot com."

I highlighted the images and sent off sixteen pictures.

His phone pinged. "Got them," he said, looking at me oddly. "Have you done this before?"

"What, take photographs?"

"Not funny. I'm talking about being at a crime scene."

"No. Just watched a lot of CSI type programs."

His lips curled ever so slightly at my cynical comment. Well, it did make sense, at least to me it did. That, plus my profession gave me some leeway in gathering evidence without knowingly contaminating a location.

"I'd have thought it was the fact that you are a professor of archaeology and skilled at preserving sites."

"You got me."

"And it's Trip. I mean you can call me Trip." He ran a hand through his hair. "Seeing as how we're both friends with Suzie and Harry."

"Trip." It felt a tad strange to be calling him by his first name rather than his professional title. After all, he was here in a professional capacity. "All right Trip." I smiled at him, and he smiled back.

"Well, Professor Frazer, I've got more questions for you, given as how you're the one who found Miss Clarke."

Miss Clarke, I thought with a jolt. Then I realized he was talking about Amber. Miss Clarke seemed old fashioned, like a spinsterly aunt from a hundred years ago. Not the vibrant woman that had been walking amongst us a few hours ago.

He stepped aside as the other detective who'd gone off to utilize the uniformed officers rejoined us, his gaze scrutinizing all of us. "Hey Trip. The medics are making their way over here."

Trip made the introductions. "This is Detective Nate Whitney. Nate, this is Suzie Wilde the homeowner, and Professor Marnie Frazer."

Nate gave a brief grunt by way of an acknowledgment. "What a day, eh?" he remarked. I could see that Detective Nate Whitney had the look of a man who didn't see much in the way of exercise. If you didn't count raising your arm with a pint glass of beer in your hand exercise. His belly was beginning to drop over his belt and his jaw was rounded, unlike Trip's. Detective Whitney sensed that I was watching him and turned slightly and glanced over in my direction, before turning back to Trip.

Dr Cowen rejoined us, unzipping her white coverall suit and unceremoniously stepping out of it, then tugging off her nitrile gloves. Her face bore a tight expression as she turned to Trip.

"I can confirm Amber Clarke is dead," Dr Cowen announced gravely as she reappeared from where Amber lay. "And in my opinion it wasn't an accident."

My heart sank at the confirmation. My deduction that Amber's body had been staged had been correct. I'd share my findings with Trip in a moment.

"Do you have any idea what could have caused her death?" Trip asked Dr Cowen.

The doctor shook her head. "It's difficult to tell without a proper autopsy. What I will say is there are no obvious signs of trauma. I've notified the medical examiner, but given the time, when the crime scene officers are through it will be later this evening before the body can be removed from here. So, in all likelihood there won't be an autopsy until tomorrow morning." She began putting her stethoscope and a thermometer away in her medical bag, then raised an eyebrow. "I gather you have someone who can identify the deceased?"

"Yes we do," said Suzie.

Trip looked at her.

"We haven't had time to fill you in on everyone. Amber came here with a friend. Plus, Marnie knows Amber."

"Well then," continued the doctor. "Time enough for you to notify the family, Trip."

"Isn't there anything else you can tell us?" Trip asked, his eyes glancing over to where Amber's body lay.

Dr Cowen hesitated, as if unsure whether she should say more. "Well, there is one thing..."

"What is it?" he asked.

"Well, I found a small trace of saliva that had foamed around her mouth. It's very possible that she was poisoned." She held up her free hand that wasn't holding her medical mag. "But you need to wait for lab work to confirm anything once the Scenes of Crime folks have been and took note of every detail. And we all know that Annie Osborne and her illustrious team of crime scene officers will take as long as is necessary to sift through everything that she deems of importance when gathering what could potentially be evidence."

"Yeah, we know," said Detective Whitney.

"I'll be off then," said Dr Cowen. "Unless there's anything else anyone needs from me?"

"Nope. Thanks for helping out at short notice," said Sergeant Brodie.

"Perfect, if you'll excuse me, I need to make additional notes into my voice recorder app." She paused and turned to Suzie. "Sorry we had to meet under these sad circumstances."

I watched her head back in the direction of the house where she would have parked her vehicle in the causeway.

Poisoned.

The word echoed in my head like a siren, and suddenly, everything started to make sense. I knew what had bothered me when I saw Amber's body lying on the path. It looked staged, in the way that bodies in some cultures were laid to rest with their feet facing the east, or were buried with items of personal importance. Amber's body was staged to make it appear that she had suffered an allergic response and was unable to reach her life-saving pen.

But now we knew. The frothy saliva, the lack of visible injuries, the failure to reach her EpiPen all pointed to one thing. Murder.

Chapter Seventeen

The detectives stood grim-faced and gathered closer to discuss their next steps. I too was also going through various scenarios. Who could have done this? And why? I didn't know Amber well, but from what I'd seen, she seemed like a nice enough person, although she and Melissa were clearly not fans of each other. And yet, someone had taken her life and left her body to be found by a stranger at one of the most prestigious events in town. It was a chilling thought.

Trip pressed his lips together, steeling himself for the next task. "Wait here, both of you," he ordered Suzie and me. He made no other comment as he and Nate stepped over to see Amber's body.

Trip and Nate crouched down beside Amber's body. I moved to one side so that I could watch them. Her pretty dress was spread on the ground, still tangled around her upper thighs. The men then stood up for a moment in silence with their hands clasped behind their backs, murmuring to each other. Nate kept his eyes on the ground, but Trip turned and stared intently at me. I got the weirdest feeling he was trying to read my mind. I surmised that they were looking for clues and whatever else detectives did in these circumstances.

After the earlier frenzy, there was an air of relative tranquility as though we'd all been holding our breath and had exhaled as one entity, but I suspected that what we were now collectively experiencing was only the calm before the storm.

I looked around at the pool and along the seashell path. Gabby was still being attended to by two female paramedics. Reality hit me hard, and I forced myself to stay focused and professional and not become a hindrance to what was unfolding.

Sergeant Brodie and Detective Whitney stepped away from Amber's body and rejoined us.

"Suzie," Sergeant Brodie began, "sorry about your event. I know how big a deal it is to you and the community. That said, I can't let your guests leave, not yet anyway. We'll need to talk to everyone who is here, and also contact the family. Nate's going off to coordinate the process. You mentioned the deceased came with a friend?"

We heard heavy footfalls on the crushed shell path and turned around to find Liz hurrying towards us, tears streaming down her face. Fee was right behind her clutching her small handbag so hard her knuckles were turning white.

"Amber came here with her friend, Fee Gibson," I said quickly to Sergeant Brodie, keeping my voice low so that only he could hear what I was saying. "That's her on the right. Liz Tanner has known Amber since they were in high school together. Only one other guest knows what's happened, and it looks like she's gone and told whoever will listen."

"Officers," said Liz, her voice trembling. "We need your help. Our friend Amber is missing, and we think she may have had an accident or something."

Sergeant Brodie looked at them, his piercing blue eyes scanning their faces. He took note of their names and after a moment of silence, he spoke to them in an even, gentle tone. "Let's move over to the pool area where it's more private." He looked at Suzie. "Would you walk with us Suzie?"

"Of course Trip." She turned to me. "And Marnie too."

I felt a wave of unease wash over me as I followed Sergeant Brodie and Suzie towards the pool area. The sun was beginning to set, casting an eerie glow over the sparkling water of the pool and the neatly manicured lawns, adding an extra layer of suspense to the unfolding events. The atmosphere had shifted from one of excitement and anticipation to one of fear and apprehension.

The weight of the situation settled heavily on me, and I wondered what secrets and dangers lay hidden within the seemingly glamorous world of Suzie Wilde.

As we reached the pool, I noticed a stillness in the air. Liz and Fee huddled together, their faces etched with worry and fear. My heart went out to them, knowing that they were desperate for answers about Amber. So far they were unaware that Amber was dead.

Sergeant Brodie took charge of the situation, his voice steady yet filled with compassion. "Please, sit everyone."

Liz and Fee sat side-by-side on a lounger, Suzie and myself sitting on chairs on either side of a white plastic circular patio table.

"Tell me everything you know," he urged, his gaze fixed on Liz. "When was the last time you saw Amber?"

Liz and Fee looked at each other through tear-streamed eyes. With trembling lips, Liz began to recount the events leading up to Amber's disappearance. "It was before the concert started," she said, wiping her eyes with the back of her hand. "I went for a refill of champagne. Amber went to the loo. She doesn't drink much." She gave a small laugh. "I mean, not like she used to, when we were younger." She turned to Fee. "Isn't that right?"

Fee took a deep breath and tried to steady her voice. "She used to be quite the party girl when we were younger."

Sergeant Brodie nodded, jotting down notes in his small notebook. "Did any of you notice anything strange or out of the ordinary leading up to Amber's disappearance?"

Fee's eyes were wide with fear as she clutched her handbag tighter. "No. Nothing. We were all together during the cocktail hour, but then she vanished. We've looked everywhere for her, but there's no sign of her."

"We tried calling her phone multiple times," added Liz. "But it just went straight to voicemail every time." She glanced at Fee. "We heard about a body being found and we're worried that it could be Amber."

"Did she mention anything about anyone bothering her or following her?"

Both women shook their heads. "No, nothing like that," said Fee, her voice shaking.

"Can you tell me who else was with you during the cocktail hour?"

Liz pursed her lips. "There were a lot of people, we mingled quite a bit, didn't we?" She looked at Fee.

Fee shook her head. "I don't remember. It's all a blur."

"Apart from you both, I'd like to know who Amber was last with. Can you remember who that was?"

They both looked at each other before Liz spoke up. "I think it was Rupert. He's one of our friends. He went with her to the bar."

I froze at the mention of Rupert's name, barely able to breathe. Could it be that simple? After all, a leopard can't change its spots.

"And how did they seem?"

"Oh, friendly," said Fee. "Very friendly," she added.

That's when I remembered something from earlier. I couldn't interrupt, so it would have to wait a little longer.

Sergeant Brodie made another note in his notebook before looking up at the two friends. "Okay. Can you tell me if Amber was acting strange or out of character before she disappeared?"

Fee shook her head. "No, she seemed fine. Maybe a little quiet, but otherwise normal."

Liz nodded in agreement.

His brows furrowed as he listened intently to their account, his eyes scanning the area around us, searching for any clues or evidence that might help to solve the case. "Thank you both for sharing this information with me. It's crucial that we piece together every detail." He exchanged a meaningful glance with Suzie, and then turned his attention back to Liz and Fee. "I'm afraid I have some bad news," he began gently. "Amber's body was found earlier this evening, not too far from here."

Liz gasped, both of her hands flying up to cover her mouth in horror. Fee slumped forward on the lounger, tears streaming down her face. The weight of the truth settled heavily on them as they grappled with the shocking revelation.

I, too, felt weighed down. I was reliving the shock of finding Amber's lifeless body. Suzie, composed and graceful, walked over to Liz and Fee, placing a comforting hand on each of them. "I am so sorry for your loss," she said softly, her voice filled with genuine sympathy.

Fee wept, her body trembling with grief. Liz sat beside her, clutching her tightly as they both sought solace in each other's presence. The pool area became enveloped in a heavy silence, broken only by the sound of their quiet sobs.

"Was it an allergic reaction?" asked Liz, her voice thick with emotion. "She was always so careful to avoid peanuts."

Sergeant Brodie remained stoic, his expression unwavering. "Actually, we believe that there may have been foul play. But we won't know until tests have been conducted."

Fee wiped away her tears, a glimmer of determination in her eyes. "But, how can that be?"

"That's what we're going to determine," said Trip.

"You have to find out who did this."

"That's exactly what we intend to do," he said firmly. Just as he finished speaking, there was the sound of approaching sirens.

"She was so kind," added Liz. "Always putting others before herself." She stood and helped Fee up. "Are those more police cars?" she asked, her voice trembling.

"Yes. As I said, we're going to do everything we can to find out who is responsible. Please accept my condolences."

"Thank you. We're going to try to find someplace quiet to sit, until we've processed what's just happened." We watched in silence as Liz tearfully hugged Fee tightly and guided her back to the seashell path to the lawn area and the other guests.

Trip," I said. "I was with Amber and a few other people earlier this evening and there was a moment when things got a little tense."

Chapter Eighteen

"Tense how? Was she angry? Upset?"

I thought back to it. "My friend Gabby and I were chatting with Amber, along with Anthony, Rupert, and Liz and her friend JT. Then Melissa Maxwell arrived and while she appeared to get on well with Anthony and Rupert especially," I chose to leave out Melissa's spitefulness towards me, "Melissa and Amber had a clear dislike of each other. Amber accused her of turning up like a bad penny, while Melissa retorted by implying that Amber somehow wormed her way into the event, that she wasn't really worthy of being there."

"I'll bet that went down well."

I nodded. "Spot on. But it's what happened next that has me puzzled."

"Go on."

"Melissa then mentioned that she'd been talking about Amber to Bernard, he's here with his wife Celia. Anyway Melissa seemed to be gloating a little when she said that she was talking with Bernard earlier today and both he and Melissa couldn't understand why Amber had been invited."

"I take it she wasn't too pleased to hear that."

"Exactly. But there was something else. A strange look passed over her face at the mention of Bernard's name. I got the impression she was upset that Bernard had said something derogatory about her. And as for Melissa, she seems to delight in making trouble wherever she goes."

"Well, thanks for the insight. We'll be sure to follow up on it." He stood and extended an arm. "Let's head back. I need you both to rejoin the other guests while my colleagues and I get to work on uncovering what happened."

This did seem the optimal time for Suzie and myself to leave Trip to continue with the investigation, but I felt a sense of unease as we walked in silence to the lawn, both of us lost in our own thoughts. I felt a weight settle in the pit of my stomach, in spite of the warm glow of the evening sunshine on the marquee and the stage. In fact, it almost made everything feel like a different world and seemed to mock the tragedy that had occurred. Everything outside of our bubble was wonderful and we were the ones trapped in a nightmare.

Looking behind me, I saw Trip talking on his cell phone. He stared at me before turning away so that I couldn't hear what he was saying or catch glimpses of his mouth and attempt to lip-read. The remaining guests were now either huddled in small intimate groups in the marquee or walking on the lawn overlooking the ocean. It seemed like everyone was now speaking in hushed tones with furtive glances over to where the police officers were cordoning off another area. Crime scene officers were working inside the perimeter, setting up tall portable spotlights that shone like bright daylight, no doubt getting ready to catalog everything that they were trained to deem relevant, including taking samples from Amber for toxicology screenings.

I put a hand on Suzie's arm, breaking her out of her thoughts. "Are you okay?"

She shook her head. "I'm still trying to process the events of the last few hours. I can't stop thinking about Amber and what happened to her."

I gave her a sympathetic look, trying to push aside the heaviness in my chest. "I know. I feel the same."

The distant sound of waves crashing against the private beach and dock filled the air, a stark contrast to the somber mood of the evening. And yet I had a sense of unease, like something else was off. Looking around, I noticed a few people whispering to each other, casting furtive glances our way.

"Do you think they'll find out who did this?" Suzie asked, her voice trembling.

I shrugged, feeling a sense of frustration wash over me. "I don't know. They're doing their best, but it's not always easy to catch whoever did something like this."

We chose to sit on the edge of the stage, and I decided to take matters into my own hands. I knew that I had to find out more about Amber, her life, her relationships, anything that could give me a clue as to who would want her dead.

I pulled out my cell phone and started digging. I searched for Amber's social media profiles, her employment history, anything that could give me a lead. As I scrolled through page after page of search results, I finally stumbled upon something that caught my eye.

Amber had been working on a project with Rupert Boyden. According to the blurb she'd posted, Rupert wasn't only a pediatrician, he was one of the most respected and well-known figures in his field. I had heard he was popular, but I had no idea he was so highly regarded by his peers. He was apparently advising Amber on what was required to help the patients and their families.

Heavy panting broke me from my concentration, and I swung around just as Harry appeared beside us, out of breath and red in the face. "Suzie are you okay?"

"Okay? I was coping fine until you appeared. What are you doing running like that? You'll have another heart attack!"

"Cindy told me what happened. I came straight here. I was worried there might be a mass murderer on the loose."

"Oh, come here you daft so and so." Suzie wrapped her arms around Harry and planted a subtle kiss on the side of his neck as she hugged him. "Better?"

"You bet," he said, glancing around. "Who's here? Police, medical people?"

"All of them, and I'm sure there'll be more on their way as we speak. C'mon, let's sit down on our bench overlooking the bay."

The bench was beneath the shade of a solid old oak tree. The tree stood about thirty-five feet tall, one of the ubiquitous trees throughout Legacy Cove, and all three of us fitted snugly on the bench. Harry and Suzie sat side-by-side and chatted quietly and as we settled in for a long evening of questioning and waiting, I couldn't help my thoughts as they drifted back to Rupert Boyden. I'd read once that crimes were often committed against another person by someone they knew. If Amber had been collaborating with Rupert on a project as had been implied, could he have had something to do with her death? Sure, it was a long shot, but this was no longer just a party gone wrong–this was murder.

The evening breeze that indicated a turn in the direction of the wind had arrived and it had become noticeably cooler, yet still pleasantly warm, the wind having driven out the humidity. There was no music playing, yet it wasn't quiet. A murmurous drone arose from the guests now that they'd moved away from the area where Amber was found and were milling about the lawn, perhaps hoping for more refreshments. Personally, I'd lost my appetite and my thirst for anything other than iced water.

I noted that while each person was an individual, they wore the same blank expression, giving off the impression that they communicated unconsciously as a group. Did they? Right now, I was struggling to hide my feelings and my emotions were right there for the world to see. This always meant that when I tried to hide what I was really thinking, my facial expressions gave me away. However, that did have its upside. I usually had a clear conscience, although sometimes I did wonder that if I had a sort of on-off switch that could enable me to hide what I was thinking, I might have more friends. However, on second thoughts I was quite happy with the few that I had. Plus, I trusted them.

My phone pinged again.

Troy: *Heard the awful news*

Me: *Will call when I can. Kinda busy here*

Troy: *Patrick and I are here for you if you need help*

Me: *Actually yes. Could you take Duke to your house? I don't know how long we'll be kept here?*

Troy: *Love to. I have ur house code. We're staying up all night until we know you and Gabbs are home safe*

A shadow drifted over my phone screen, and I was surprised to see that Sergeant Brodie had appeared beside us, grim-faced, with a subtle nod exchanged between him and Harry.

I hurriedly ended the text to Troy.

Me: *Thanks TTYL x*

The three of us stood up as it seemed that the detective's arrival required that type of movement, while I hurriedly tucked my phone away in my bag.

"Harry," said the detective. "Let's take a walk over here. I need to ask you a few questions." He pointed to the stage area.

"Of course," Harry replied, his voice now calm and measured. "Anything to help out an old friend."

As they moved away to speak in private, Suzie turned to me, her eyes wide with worry. "What are we going to do, Marnie? This is a disaster. How could something like this happen?"

"I don't know, Suzie," I said. "But we have to help in any way we can. We can't just sit here and do nothing."

Suzie nodded, determination in her eyes. "You're right. We need to do something. But what?"

I explained to her what I'd found about Amber and Rupert, and their latest project. But before we could figure out our next move, Sergeant Brodie returned with Harry and addressed Suzie.

"I'm afraid I'm going to have to ask everyone to stay here until further notice," he said. "And we'll be needing statements from everyone."

Suzie and I exchanged a glance, knowing that this wasn't going to be a quick and easy process. But we also knew that we all had to do our part to help bring Amber's murderer to justice.

"I was afraid you were going to say that, Trip."

His jaw clenched, but that was the only reaction I could read from his face. He would make a solid poker player, that's for sure. He then turned and walked away to rejoin his colleagues over by the cabanas, where interviews of everyone in attendance at the event tonight were about to begin.

I quickly scanned the other guests, one or more of them must know something that would give us a clue as to what happened and who did this terrible act, even if we didn't find out immediately the reason why.

That was when I saw the female paramedics pushing Gabby semi-prone in a wheelchair towards an ambulance parked at the front of the house.

"Suzie, I need to go and check on Gabby. Find out what's happening."

"Good idea. We'll stay here in case we're needed by Trip."

I hurried over to check on Gabby, scanning the assembled guests as I walked over the lawn. Most of the guests were sitting in the shade in the marquee. All looked subdued: Ginger Maloney, the busty ginger-haired woman with the laboratory, was seated next to Madame Helene Gaultier and her son Max. Liz Tanner was now with her friend JT standing next to Simon Stadler and his girlfriend Sandy at a hi-top table.

Rupert Boyden was seated next to his brother Anthony. Sandwiched between them in a tight huddle were none other than Melissa and Amber's friend Fee.

Bernard Lazenby's group was larger and included his wife Celia, Lashawna White of the Washashore Animal Rescue Society and her partner Richard, and Amoy Johnson and her husband Mark Kleinman, and Principal Henry Grant and his friend Ben Pearce. Bernard, normally the type of person you hear before you see, was noticeably quiet.

Every one of them must have been told by Liz and Fee by now that Amber was the person who was dead.

Melissa pecked Rupert on his left cheek and then got up and padded stealthily over to Detective Nate Whitney who appeared to be directing officers to bring people one at a time to Trip beside a cabana with sheer drapes tied back on four sides. It appeared that Trip was starting with the musicians. Melissa's sleek hair swished from side to side like a bobcat's tail. She spoke animatedly, pointing in the direction where she'd found me with Amber's body, her little chin thrust forward determinedly. She stood erect in front of the detective, her left hand resting by her hip on the top of her white Tory Burch shoulder bag like a gunslinger ready for action, the other hand clutching a cell phone at her navel. I couldn't be sure, but I imagined that she was spinning quite the tale about me.

Right now though, I had other things to worry about.

"Hold on. Wait!" I called out as I approached Gabby.

The two paramedics attending her swung around to see who was calling out to them.

"I'm Gabby's friend. How is she?"

"Gabby's stable at the moment, but there is definitely evidence of a severe concussion," the senior of the two explained. "We're leaving for the hospital with her now."

Gabby was sitting slumped in the wheelchair, an IV tube in the back of her left hand with a bag of normal saline hooked to a stand attached to the chair, dripping fluid slowly through the tubing. A thick padded bandage was wrapped around her head like a turban. "It looks like you're growing a second head," I teased.

"I believe you," she said meekly.

"How are you feeling?"

"More comfortable," she said slowly. "I'm just so tired."

I looked to the paramedics for guidance.

"We need to go to the hospital now. We're satisfied Gabby is stable enough to be transported. We've called ahead and they're expecting us."

"That's the one," proclaimed a shrill voice.

I swung around in the direction it came from and saw a wide-eyed Melissa pointing at me, her red shiny nails stabbing the air as if her venomous words weren't spiked enough. "She did it."

Gabby and I looked at each other, shocked by the accusation. Melissa was marching swiftly towards us trying to keep up with Detective Whitney and a uniformed female officer striding ahead of her.

Chapter Nineteen

"I saw her," Melissa spat. "She was bending over the body with her hands around Amber's neck."

I heard a woman utter a small scream. Melissa stood poised and assured in her condemnation of me. Now uttered, her words were taking on a life of their own, fueled by further speculation.

A steady trickle of people seeped from the marquee and other shady spots where they'd been waiting until they would be told they could leave. Now they had something else to draw their attention to.

"She's trying to cover up what she did," Melissa stated with conviction.

I wasn't going to stand for this. "Is there no end to the stories you'll make up?" I turned quickly to the detective.

"She's lying. She doesn't like me. She's making it up." I realized how I was sounding. The Shakespeare quote, 'The lady doth protest too much,' sprung to mind and I stopped and took a deep breath.

Beady lights from phones shone in my direction and I felt all eyes boring into me.

Melissa squeezed her way forward and gave a haughty sniff, as though she smelled something grossly unpleasant. "You think you can deceive everyone, pretending that you're an innocent bystander, but I know what you're really like. I saw you tampering with evidence." She was finding her stride now, pointing out to the rapt audience that it was obvious that I was guilty.

Before I could respond, more calmly this time, she shook her head, her shiny black hair swishing from side to side. "And it's not only you." She paused and leaned ever so slightly towards me. "It's your accomplice too."

The spectators watched avidly as Melissa swung around and pointed at Gabby, then looked over at Detective Whitney. "Well, aren't you going to arrest her?" she demanded. "I don't think it's a coincidence that I saw this one arguing with Amber, and then minutes later I find her friend Marnie Frazer kneeling over poor Amber's broken body.

Detective Whitney cleared his throat. "We just need to ask Ms. Frazer and Ms. Martinez some questions," he said to the paramedics.

I couldn't take any more of this nonsense and was about to challenge her when Suzie marched over, with Harry trailing closely behind. She faced both detectives, subtly ignoring Melissa. "What's going on here?" she asked firmly.

"We're following up on every lead Ms. Wilde," Detective Whitney said.

Suzie gave me a reassuring pat on the arm. "Don't worry, everything will be fine."

But her words did little to calm my nerves. Gabby and I were in deep trouble. I felt a cold sweat break out on my forehead. What evidence might they find that could implicate me or Gabby in Amber's murder? Had I missed something when I stumbled upon her body? Or worse, had I left incriminating evidence behind?

"We can't wait here," stated the senior medic. "The patient needs to get to the hospital." She checked the flow rate of the saline dripping into the intravenous tube in Gabby's left hand.

Detective Whitney turned slightly to address the other guests. "Step back please. There's nothing to see here. We'll get around to taking statements from you all too. So, please move back." I saw Melissa smile smugly at the comment about statements and then slink off to be beside her buddies Rupert and Anthony Boyden. I could only imagine what she was going to say in her statement.

Detective Whitney now stared firmly at Gabby. "Be advised," he continued, "that Officer West will accompany you to Legacy Cove hospital in the ambulance." I noted the surname West on the female uniformed officer's name tag. "And once cleared by the medical personnel there may be further questions." He towered over Gabby as he addressed her. "It will be in your best interests to cooperate fully with us."

"I'm going with Gabby," I insisted.

One of the medics attending to Gabby shook her head. "Not possible. It's one patient per ambulance."

"I'm not a patient. And neither is Officer West." I was pushing my luck and I knew it, but if there was one thing I disliked it was a bully, and Detective Whitney struck me as someone who was extending the powers of his role to the fullest.

Detective Whitney held up the palm of a hand, commanding me to cease speaking. "Miss Martinez is simply helping us with our enquiries."

I pressed my lips together hard in case I said something I would either regret or cause problems for my friend. I reached for Gabby's free hand and held it. "Don't try to say anything else Gabby. You need to go to the hospital and get thoroughly checked out."

Her head sagged and she smiled meekly.

I leaned in closer. "I'll see you as soon as we're done here and we're all free to leave."

"Listen, Officer West," Detective Whitney barked, snapping me out of my frantic thoughts. "I need you to keep an eye on Gabby during the ambulance ride and at the hospital. We can't risk her manipulating any more truths."

I scanned the pool area for Trip, hoping he could help put an end to this madness, but he was nowhere in sight. Surely if anyone could put an end to the misery that Melissa was exerting by manipulating the truth it would be him. Plus, his colleague was treating Gabby like she was a criminal who'd done something wrong. She was incapable of harming anyone. Couldn't Detective Whitney see that?

I was so angry. It was Gabby's word against Melissa's however the fact that no-one saw her, apart from allegedly Melissa, could either work in her favor or be forever damning against her.

I was about to insist again that I accompany Gabby when a raised voice broke through my thoughts, as those of us on the lawn, the police and first responders included, swung round to look at who was causing the commotion. I turned as Melissa stormed into the marquee; her face flushed with anger. I could see her eyes scanning the tent, looking for someone, or perhaps trying to avoid someone. Madame Gauthier was standing to the left of the tent with her son Max, looking out over the ocean. Melissa stormed over to her, gesticulating wildly, her face red with anger, while Madame Gauthier remained stoic.

I turned back to Gabby; her bandaged head lolling forward against her chest and touched her right hand gently. "I'll come see you as soon as we're allowed to leave here," I said firmly.

"Find out who did it," Gabby called out as the wheelchair was bumped rather unceremoniously over the lawn to the gravel driveway to a waiting ambulance. Officer West positioned herself opposite where Gabby was situated, and I held my breath as Gabby's right wrist was then handcuffed to a bar at the side of the gurney that she was lying on. One first responder climbed into the driver's seat while the other climbed into the back of the ambulance and closed the doors firmly. The harsh interior light lit up the three people inside and I saw Gabby's wan face just visible over the rear window as the ambulance drove away.

Chapter Twenty

Over at the marquee, Melissa waved her arms theatrically in Helene's direction. Max intervened on his mother's behalf, causing Melissa to take a step backwards, almost bumping into an empty high-top table.

"C'mon Suzie. We should go over and see what this is all about."

"What on earth is happening to people! Have they no respect for what has happened this evening?"

"I don't know about respect Suzie, but someone on your island, likely one of your guests, has committed murder."

She paused mid-stride and grabbed my elbow, her eyes filled with worry. "Oh, I really hope not Marnie. I'm desperately hoping it's been some rogue intruder. I don't want to believe that I've unknowingly played a role in a murder by inviting the killer."

I forced a reassuring smile, even though my stomach was churning with dread. "You couldn't have known, Suzie. And we can't blame ourselves for someone else's actions. But all of us here have a responsibility to help the police find the killer and bring them to justice." I glanced over at the marquee. "And *our* first task is to find out what the heck is going on between Melissa Maxwell and Helene Gauthier."

We set off with a purpose and arrived just as Trip entered the marquee, talking to someone on his phone. "Aw, I'm glad your presentation went well. I knew you could do it," he told the person on the other end of the call. I wasn't listening, not really, but he was within earshot. "Love you." He hung up.

Suzie wasted no time in going up to him. "Trip Brodie, where the heck have you been. Your colleague," she glowered at Detective Whitney who was talking with two uniformed officers on the driveway beside a cruiser, "is out of control. Do you know what he has done? What he's accusing my friend Marnie of? Hmm? Do you?"

I felt his stern gaze boring into me. The man was unreadable, and I couldn't tell if his unyielding manner was his every-day state of being or if it was reserved for the job.

"You must have heard what Marnie and her friend have just been accused of. We all have," she continued, opening her arms wide to encompass the people surrounding us, "and I can put an end to this right here and now."

Despite the shock of Melissa's awful accusation, or actually because of it, I was keen to hear what Suzie had to share. It was hard to tell what Trip was thinking. I felt that he stared at me a second longer than necessary and I immediately experienced a feeling of guilt, simply because I was under the scrutiny of a detective.

"Well, what do you say? Are you going to listen to me, or do I have to get my media people to tell the world what I know?"

He stared at her for several seconds before giving the briefest of nods. "Let me find out what's going on over here, then we'll talk."

He approached Melissa and Helene who stepped apart as he neared them.

"Good evening Sergeant," said Helene with a smile.

"Good evening Helene, Max." He turned to Melissa. "Miss Maxwell, am I right?"

"Yes." She stuck her chin out again, raising her head in a vain attempt to make her appear taller.

"Is everything all right here?"

"Perfectly Sergeant," Helene remarked. Max nodded and stuffed his hands in the pockets of his dark trousers.

"Good. Let's keep the noise down a bit then." He turned and rejoined Suzie and myself. "Let's step over to one side so we can talk. In fact, the cabanas beside the pool house will give us the privacy that we need."

The path to the pool house was blocked off with yellow and black police caution tape while crime scene personnel worked under the harsh glare of portable floodlights, so we had to walk to the pool house from the side of the main house.

The pool was like something from a resort, complete with a diving board, a pool bar, and a row of four cabanas on one length of the pool, sun loungers on the opposite side, little teak café tables with matching teak chairs, and comfy looking double loungers covered in a navy-blue fabric. It looked different from when we'd sat here earlier with Liz and Fee, as small round lights, strung gaily from four posts cast a warm and inviting ambiance to the area.

We entered the nearest cabana and Suzie and I seated ourselves on the edge of one of the double loungers. Trip lifted one of the café tables and a chair and put them inside the cabana. Once ensconced in semi-privacy out of hearing distance from the guests, he brought out his small notebook and placed it on the table, folded his bare forearms, and directed his attention to Suzie.

"All right then Suzie, let's start at the beginning. What do you know about what happened to Ms Clarke?"

Suzie frowned. "Amber, you mean."

He nodded. "Yes. Amber Clarke."

"I realize," she began, "that my music's not everyone's taste. Even if they are my invited guests."

"So? Go on."

"So, when I was on stage during my performance, I had a good view of the lawn and the marquee." She looked at him to make sure he was following her. "And I could see which groups were where and who was coming and going."

"Ah. So, you saw Amber leave and who followed her?"

"Not exactly."

"What did you see?"

"Well, for starters, I saw Marnie near the front of the stage practically the whole time." She gave me an encouraging smile.

I let out a breath I didn't know I was holding, and my shoulders dropped in relief that someone saw me. And that someone was a person whose integrity and innocence in this evening's events were not in doubt. After all, being on stage the whole time was quite the alibi.

Suzie leaned towards Trip. "Amber's cream dress was rather unique, especially the way it caught the sunlight. Combined with her blonde hair, she made quite the entrance, and exit, I must say."

"When did Amber leave?"

She shook her head slowly, her eyes gazing off over the swimming pool with its inviting water, watching a little motorized object zig-zagging along the sides to keep the pool clean and free from bugs and leaves that may land in the water. "The thing is Trip; I didn't see her at all during the show.

"Could you have missed seeing her?"

"No," she insisted. "As I've explained, the woman was stunning to look at. I would have noticed her leaving."

His jaw tightened and he glanced out of the cabana before turning back to face Suzie. "Did you see anyone else who could have followed her?" I noticed that he asked the same question, just in a different style to prompt a different response.

It appeared to work. "Well, just as I don't remember seeing Amber, there were a couple of other people who I didn't see at the start. Let me think who they were." She paused again, looking through the sides of the cabana and staring out across the lawn in the direction of the stage. "Oh, my gosh. How could I have forgotten." She placed her hands on both sides of her face, in mock horror. "It was the middle of the second song, 'Rockin' All Over' and I distinctly saw Rupert Boyden and his brother Anthony head over to the marquee. It's the height of rudeness to walk away during a song, especially at an intimate event like this."

"So, they went to the marquee. Did they stay there?"

"Give me a sec, honey." Suzie paused, gazing off into the distance. "You know, come to think of it, while they were rude to leave, I saw a figure in the pool house path near the lawn and..."

"And?"

She shook her head. "Sorry Trip. I wasn't really following that person. I was more focused on my audience."

"Male? Female?"

"I'm not sure. I think they had dark hair."

He nodded slowly.

"That's all I can remember at the moment. People were mingling. They weren't all standing around in one place. Groups would mix and then some people would pare off to join another group. Some were dancing and singing along. It was a small, but engaged audience. The ones on the periphery were hard to make eye contact with though."

"I see. What about Gabby Martinez?"

I couldn't remain quiet on this, but at the same time I had to ensure that I didn't come across as being too defensive. He might think I had something to hide. I fought to breathe normally and stop myself from raising my voice in frustration at the line of questioning. "Gabby never squabbled with anyone. I was with her the entire evening." I faltered, realizing that that was not entirely accurate. Gabby had left fifteen minutes prior to the concert starting.

He stared at me thoughtfully, pondering something. Had I finally made him reconsider that Melissa might in fact be wasting his time? That she had an ulterior motive? I couldn't tell for sure as he resumed his questioning of Suzie.

"Suzie, can you confirm that? You saw who was there."

"Oh Trip, you know how much I want to help you, but I can't possibly see everything. I move around the stage so much that sometimes I only see segments of the audience during a song. Even an audience as intimate as this." She smiled and tilted her head at him. "People like it when I sing directly to them." She raised an eyebrow. "You know how that makes people feel."

"Trip," I began, "you don't honestly believe a word that Melissa says, do you?"

"Now why would she say what she did? Hmm?"

I hesitated. Melissa was petty and I was not going to sink to her level. Although I had to say something. Before I could gather my thoughts, he pressed further.

"You heard Suzie," he continued steadily, bringing his focus to me. "She saw you most of the time but not Amber, and now we've got an eye-witness who saw Gabby fighting with Amber earlier."

"A supposed witness," I stressed, trying to keep my voice steady. "You can't trust Melissa. You only have her word that she saw anything."

He held my gaze for what felt like an interminably long moment, and I resisted the urge to squirm where I was sitting. He seemed to ignore what I said as he resumed talking with Suzie. "What else did you see?"

"Bernard Lazenby. He left with someone that I didn't recognize and headed to the marquee. Probably off to have their glasses refilled, I think. Then there was Helene Gauthier."

"I know Helene," he added. "And her son Max."

I noticed that he didn't elaborate how he knew them.

"Yes, I gathered that when I saw you with them in the marquee," Suzie added. "Well, Helene followed Bernard into the marquee."

"Anyone else?" he prompted, making notes in his little notebook.

My stomach lurched. The timeline might be right if it was Melissa that left during the second song, and she did happen to see Gabby and Amber arguing with each other. But what about later when she saw me finding Amber's body? The way that Melissa spoke, Gabby had every reason to kill Amber. Or worse, we had done it together.

The sound of sirens drifted towards us as a fleet of vehicles arrived from the causeway.

Suzie placed a hand on his hand nearest her. "As I said. There's no way that Marnie could have harmed Amber," she insisted. "She was in front of the stage the entire time."

He remained stoically silent for what seemed like an interminably long time, but was probably only a few seconds. "Thanks for your time, Suzie. That's been helpful, especially for you Marnie," he added. "But I may have more questions for both of you later."

Suzie smiled understandingly, seemingly oblivious to the proverbial quicksand that I had previously found myself in, only to be thrown a life-line by Suzie. "I'd expect nothing less from you. You've got a tough job, Trip Brodie."

He stood up and left us alone.

I felt like I was in a nightmare. While on the one hand I felt some relief that what Suzie saw helped to clear me of being actively involved in any wrong-doing, it didn't prove that I wasn't involved somehow. I knew that additional police officers were coming to investigate Amber's murder, and I felt that somehow either Gabby or myself would be blamed, in spite of what Suzie had just told Trip. I squinted against a ray of early evening setting sunlight that broke between the leafy branches of the nearest pine tree, and pointed to where the noise was coming from. "Now that more officers are arriving, I wouldn't be surprised if several of your guests call for a friend or relative to come and pick them up."

Suzie sighed. "More vultures coming to get a look at the scene of the crime."

The first team of police officers had cordoned off about a fifty-yard area around the pool house and lawn where Amber's body had been found. I could see a few guests trying to peer beyond the yellow tape, but two police officers were stopping them from getting too close.

The officers all seemed to be busy with their tasks. I felt a knot form in my stomach and knew that I had to stay calm, but it was becoming increasingly difficult. I didn't trust Melissa and I feared that she had already planted doubts in the minds of the detectives.

The guests milled around, anxiously watching the developments. Some of them appeared to be equally surprised by the arrival of another fleet of vehicles, several of them giving the emergency professionals a wide berth and staying within the shade of the marquee.

Trip approached the new officers. Beyond him were two more ambulances, one vehicle with crime scene investigator livery, and at least three additional police cruisers. A second team of police officers who arrived, were fanning out across the lawn at the side of the house.

We turned and trudged back to the marquee where Melissa had resumed holding court and was arguing again with Madame Helene Gauthier. Max was in the midst of it and DS Whitney had now appeared.

"What do you think this is all about?" asked Suzie.

"I've no idea, but I'm kind of relieved as it takes some of the attention away from me."

Melissa looked furious; her face flushed with frustration. I was curious about what they were arguing about as Suzie approached them.

"I can't believe you would even suggest something so ridiculous," Melissa was saying, while Max kept trying to interject between her and his mother and settle the dispute.

Helene Gauthier's response was firm. "I am simply stating what I have observed."

But Melissa was not to be deterred. "No, I want answers now. Don't try to hide the truth from me."

Helene looked around, noticing the attention that Melissa was drawing. "Not here, Melissa. We can talk in private."

The tension was palpable and I wondered what was really going on between them. I made a mental note to keep an eye on them both.

"Leave this to me," stated Suzie firmly.

She strode determinedly over to Helene and Melissa and after talking for a brief moment, Melissa huffed but begrudgingly apologized to Helene, then stormed off, her hair swishing defiantly as she breezed past everyone and headed down towards the jetty where we had all arrived a few hours previously.

My phone pinged again. I checked thinking it was Troy and if so I was going to get more than a little annoyed. But it was my mother. She'd no doubt heard what had happened, probably from Troy. I texted her back.

Me: *Hi Mum. We're fine*

Mum: *Dad and I are worried*

Me: *All ok. Police here. Suzie W is awesome*

Mum: *Call if you need anything*

Me: *Will do ttyl xxx*

I walked over to meet up again with Suzie.

She straightened up and gave a not-so-subtle sweeping glance at her guests. "Kinda shows humanity at its worst, doesn't it?" She sighed and looked at me directly. "And also shows the best of us." She patted my forearms as she said this.

I blushed. "How are you doing? Really?"

"Me? Oh, I'm fine honey. I've been through tough times before. Although probably not as bad as this." She shook her head slowly and leaned closer to me. "It's Harry I'm worried about. He's not like me. He's not used to publicity, good or bad. He deliberately hides from the public eye. He lets me handle everything where publicity is concerned. Providing he's well away from any cameras, of course."

Suzie gave a subtle scan of the people around us then leaned closer, lowering her voice. "I have an important favor to ask of you," she said.

Chapter Twenty-One

"A favor?" I was curious, that's for sure. "Whatever you need Suzie."

"Let's move away from prying ears." She guided me over to the large oak tree with the little bench beneath it. If I hadn't been standing next to the old tree Suzie's request would have knocked me over. "You want me to do what?" I gasped incredulously.

"Investigate what happened today."

"But the police are here. They're the professionals."

"My Harry says you're the best at what you do, you know, digging up clues to find the truth about what happened. And I need someone to not only be my eyes and ears but be someone who can unearth what's happened here today."

"We know what happened today. Amber was killed. Although I will add that in situations like this, people often have something to say."

"You know what I mean. I want you to find out who did it. From what I've seen over the course of my life, people always have an opinion on something and are only too happy to share it. And they're often guarded when it comes to chatting with the police."

"Talking is one thing, but what if we're talking with the 'you know who?'" I leaned in close. "The murderer," I whispered.

"You'll know who they are," she said confidently.

"I'm not sure Suzie. Each person we talk to is likely wondering, like us, who did it. Let's face it, they may even be considering that you or I are suspects. And anyway, what are we looking for? I'm not sure where to even begin."

"Well, for starters, you're not easily swayed by emotion and from what Harry's told me about how you dealt with your cheating ex-husband, you've got street smarts and you're not easily deterred. You're like Dolly, one of my little Westies. You're feisty, determined, and you'll stop at nothing to ferret out what you're seeking."

Sure, a memory of Craig Thomas, my ex-husband and what he'd done popped up every now and again, but the satisfaction of how I'd been able to get rid of him and end up with a great job in a community that I loved was what snapped me out of any self-doubt. I had trusted my so-called gut instinct to find out what was really going on with cheating Craig. This was also the same instinct that had saved me as a child and if anything, had been further honed over the years.

"You're the expert Marnie. Plus," she continued, "you've got a strong head on your shoulders for digging around and finding evidence that leads to answers."

I thought about that. "My skills are specialized though. We need to have local insights, people who know what's going on, on the ground so to speak."

"Exactly. But have you considered that your skills are transferable?" she asked. "Your ability to research and analyze can be used in multiple situations. Plus, the guests are all local to some extent. Some grew up here while others relocated here from another place."

"Wash-a-shores," I said, referring to the people who had moved to Legacy Cove. "I work on facts Suzie, not hearsay."

"Exactly. Either way, the guests have all been here long enough to know what's going on."

When I thought about it, I realized that what Suzie had said was correct. Each person here knew something, and it was a matter of observing and asking the right questions in order to piece it all together and unmask the murderer. "Talking to them might also highlight if the murder was spontaneous or if it was planned. I mean, who else had a grudge with Amber to such an extent that they would deliberately want to kill her?"

"We owe it to Amber and her loved ones. I don't want to sound mean or anything, but, her murder will taint my children's charity. It's imperative we find out who the killer is. My charity donates tens of millions of dollars each year to children's hospitals across the country, not only here in the northeast. So many families depend on what we can provide for them during one of the most challenging times of their lives. They shouldn't need to worry about finding affordable accommodation while their child is undergoing intrusive and painful procedures. I'm worried that the murder will discourage other people from making future donations or volunteering."

"I hope it doesn't come to that." But, I knew Suzie had a good point, and so finding the murderer as soon as possible was becoming even more urgent. I thought of Gabby and what she had been through so far, wondering how the evening would progress if the police really believed that she had anything remotely to do with Amber's sad demise. The image of Amber's lifeless body was vividly ingrained in my mind. Not only that, but the mystery surrounding her death was niggling at me too. I routinely sought answers from the past and the fact that Amber's death was only a few hours old should make no difference. Except for one glaring fact, my friend's innocence was on the line and possibly mine too.

"Well?" asked Suzie.

"I don't have much choice, do I? Your charity is important as well as clearing Gabby's name. So I either sit back and let circumstances unfold, and we've already seen how that has gone, or I start peeling back the layers of what happened tonight and figure out why." I sighed heavily and looked at the guests milling around on the lawn.

"There's a murderer among us," said Suzie in a hushed voice. "And I'm responsible. I never thought I'd ever say that, and certainly not about someone in my own house. It's my refuge, my place of safety from the craziness of the world and now I feel violated." She shook her head, causing her curls to quiver. "I don't know that I'll ever be able to invite strangers into my house ever again."

"The majority of the guests are likely having similar feelings."

"But I'm responsible for inviting everyone here, including the murderer."

"You can't blame yourself. What happened to Amber was no accident. She was killed deliberately and the murderer would have got to her somewhere, sometime."

"I can't fathom it out, Marnie. I look around at these people and I no longer see individuals who are making a positive difference in the community. All I see are a group of strangers brought together by me. I keep trying not to look at them because it's like looking at a creepy version of 'Where's Waldo' and I'm trying to spot a murderer instead of a skinny guy in a red and white striped shirt, bobble hat, and glasses."

"Looking at them is exactly what needs to be done," I said. "And it needs to be done fast in case the murderer strikes again."

Suzie looked at me, her eyes wide with fear. "Do you really think there will be another murder?"

I nodded. "This murderer was brazen enough to commit murder in the middle of a crowded party, staging it to make it appear that Amber had succumbed to an allergic reaction. If they were willing to kill once, they may be willing to do it again. Especially as their carefully crafted plan has failed."

"Okay," Suzie said, taking a deep breath. "What's our next move?"

I was full of admiration for Suzie. Despite the chaos and horror of the situation, she refused to let it defeat her. She was a fighter, someone who would do whatever it took to get to the bottom of this, and I knew that I had to match her resolve. "We need to look at every guest as a potential suspect, each with their own motives and secrets to hide. We need to find out who stood to gain from Amber's death and who had the means and opportunity to carry it out. This means we need to be one step ahead of the murderer and catch them before they can strike again. Especially if they think they may be caught."

"We?" asked Suzie?

"Yes we." A spark took flame in my thoughts. "The guests are stuck here and I have an idea of how we can start to dig a little deeper and faster than the police can."

She raised an eyebrow at me.

"Well, from what I know of human nature, people are open to you, they want to be seen to be friends with you, to have selfies with you. Your guests are more than a little enamored, should I say, by your celebrity status." I paused as I saw how my comment might come across. "Oh, Dottie, I mean Suzie, I mean, I thought you were one person, then it turns out you're someone else. I see you as a person, not a celebrity."

"Well honey, folks around here know me, or at least they know of me." She patted my hand and then squeezed it.

Hard!

"They can think of me what they want," she continued. "I just try to make the best music that I can and give back to the community."

"Well, here's my idea. Why don't you play the role of the gracious host and I'll follow along with you. Together we can chat with each of the guests, steer them over to a quiet corner where they might be more inclined to spill the beans on another guest, see what we can uncover."

"Oh, I don't know about that. Harry says you're good at uncovering facts. I'm only good at entertaining."

"Nonsense. You're more than a great performer. Plus you know what makes each of the guests special enough to warrant an invitation to your annual event. From what I saw a few weeks ago, and then again tonight, some of them are hiding things that they don't want to see the light of day."

"Enough to make them want to kill Amber?"

"Possibly," I suggested, scanning the guests. "C'mon. Let's see what we can dig up."

Chapter Twenty-Two

"Suzie, Marnie!" We turned around swiftly to see who was calling me. Amoy and Mark were hurrying over in our direction.

"Hey Amoy, Mark. What's wrong? What happened?" she asked. A deep frown spreading across her forehead.

Mark swatted a mosquito in front of his face. "We're concerned about being outdoors much longer."

"Whyever should this be a problem?"

"We're both sailors, we have a 38-foot Hanse and we track the weather daily." He shrugged his shoulders. "It's a habit we got into. All sailors, all good sailors," he clarified, "check the weather daily."

Suzie and I looked up at the sky. There were a few clouds gathering but that could be explained by the sun setting. I was curious what the urgency of the weather forecast was. "And you're telling us this because …?"

"Because a nasty squall is coming. Possibly evolving into a storm. It'll arrive in just over two hours at ten o'clock this evening," said Amoy. She opened up a weather app on her phone. A swathe of dark cloud filled the screen as it swirled from left to right, indicating the speed and direction it was going to travel and the speed it was going to strike us.

"A squall?" I looked out at the horizon again. Everything looked relatively calm.

"The weather's going to change, and it'll change fast. You know the old Samuel Clemens saying about New England."

Suzie and I looked at each other. "If you don't like the weather in New England now, just wait a few minutes," we chanted together.

A strong gust blew from nowhere, whooshing my long dress upwards so fast and revealing my practical white knickers! I grabbed my dress and firmly tugged it back down, glancing around to see who else caught sight of what had happened but no-one, apart from Suzie, Amoy, and Mark saw more than I ever wanted the general public to see.

"Wow! That was a big one," exclaimed Suzie. I hoped that she meant the gust of wind and not the size of my underwear.

Amoy cleared her throat which was as good as clearing the embarrassing air between us. "Everything looks good at the moment, and it will stay humid and buggy. But before long there will be a drastic change bringing torrential rain and strong winds for about an hour and a half."

"That's not good," agreed Suzie slowly.

"Indeed. The police need to let us go now, or we must find better shelter than the marquee. And by better, we mean safer," said Amoy. "Trees could come down with the force of the wind."

Her words hung in the air, and off in the distance we could see long dark clouds tinged with silvery-white rolling over the horizon.

"All right then," agreed Suzie. "I'll check with the police, see what they're thinking. Does that sound okay?"

"It is, if they let us go," Amoy added. "We can't stay outside all night you know."

"Don't worry. I'll make alternative arrangements soon if the police don't let everyone leave. Oh, and thanks for letting us know."

Amoy and Mark thanked Suzie and moved away to the bar; their faces serious as they contemplated what was about to strike us next.

"Well," huffed Suzie. "You can't make this up. A storm!" She looked around at the lawn and the festive appearance. "I see that one of the members of my event committee is working to the schedule though." The lovely twinkle lights that shone upon our arrival a few hours ago were now enhanced by the added glow of flickering tiki lights that had now been lit. It was a surreal image.

"According to Amoy and Mark, we've got just over two hours before the storm comes. Plenty of time for us to find out what we can from the guests and also chat to your friend the sergeant."

We linked arms and headed straight towards the marquee, searching for Fee or Rupert when I had an idea. "Suzie, before we talk directly to the guests, we might also want to see what background info we can acquire, subtly." I nodded to where I'd spotted Helene Gauthier who was deep in conversation with Ginger Maloney. They looked like they were becoming firm friends.

"By background information you mean gossip?"

"Gossip!" I said aghast, feigning shock at such a thought. I smiled coyly at Suzie and gave a wink.

"Helene, Ginger," said Suzie warmly. To say they were surprised to see us, or rather Suzie, approach them was an understatement. Helene, who earlier had plenty to say to Melissa was now apparently at a loss for words, and Ginger couldn't stop staring at Suzie. Their self-assured personas slid away as softly as waves on a sandy shore, and they stood wide-eyed and open-mouthed before us. The expression 'gob-smacked' sprung to mind. "I was hoping to get a chance to check in on you and see how you were doing after what happened today," Suzie continued, "and I thought that now would be a good time."

"Thanks," Helene replied, shaking her head in disbelief. "It's been awful. One minute the woman is walking around, the next she's dead."

"It's been such a shock," agreed Ginger. "We're stunned that this could have happened, and here of all places."

"I know. We're all devastated," said Suzie sympathetically.

I spied four chairs away from prying ears at the left side of the marquee overlooking the ocean. "Suzie," I said, "it's been a difficult evening for everyone. Shall we all sit down over there?"

Taking my lead on what I had suggested moments earlier, Suzie beamed broadly as though the suggestion of going somewhere to sit (and also not be overheard) was a complete and welcome surprise. "Why Marnie, putting my feet up while chatting with these two lovely ladies is just what I need. Let's all go over there where we'll catch some of the ocean breeze. It usually flows through at this time of evening making it one of my favorite times of the day." She chattered away putting Helene and Ginger at ease. "And I don't know about you ladies, but after a day like today I need to sit down." She waved over to a server, who looked relieved to have something to do, to follow us to the table.

The four of us strolled over to where the four chairs were placed at a round table and sat down. "Can I get you ladies anything?" asked Suzie as the female server arrived.

"A red wine for me," said Helene.

"Same," said Ginger.

Susie paused for a brief moment. "I'll have a sparkling iced water."

"Me too," I said.

The server left with the order.

Helene and Ginger sat down facing the interior of the marquee although neither of the two women looked at ease. Was it because they were sitting only a few feet away from a famous music star or because of something else?

"It's not quite the day we thought it was going to be," Suzie said. "How are you both doing? I saw your son Max chatting with some of the guests earlier Helene, and I wasn't sure who came with you Ginger?"

Ginger fidgeted in her seat. "I brought my husband Ian. He's also a scientist at my company Ginglabs."

"Is that who's talking with Bernard Lazenby? They seem to be getting on well together."

"Yes, indeed," said Ginger.

"And Max is very popular," added Suzie.

"*Mais oui*. He's going to have his own TV cooking show, so of course people want to know more about his new project."

"How wonderful," we all agreed.

Helene gave a little cough before she spoke. "Do you know how long it's going to take before the police let us go? They can't keep us here forever."

Suzie leaned in closer to Helene, her face wearing a worried expression just as a motherly aunt like her alternate persona Dottie would wear. Except Suzie was a rock star. And now I was weirdly beginning to think of Suzie as both.

A unique entity who wore dark red lipstick with tremendous staying-power. "I'll talk to them again," she said reassuringly. "I can't promise anything, but at least I'll be able to see what their plans are once they've spoken with everyone. Then I can share with you what's happening next. Will that help?"

Helene and Ginger nodded as one.

Suzie leaned back slightly and smiled sympathetically. She appeared genuinely caring and concerned for their well-being given the outcome of this evening's events, and I knew she was as worried about what had happened and what was occurring as any of the people here. She gazed at me briefly, including me in the general 'will that help?' conversation.

"Suzie's been so supportive," I said. "I mean, she helped me after I found Amber and also in talking with the police."

"You're the one who found Amber!" said Ginger. "What happened to her?"

The server appeared with the drinks, and I welcomed the pause in conversation to decide how much I needed to share.

I took a sip of the ice-cold water. "We don't know. I was heading to the bathroom when I saw her." I omitted to mention that I was actually looking for Gabby.

"And I hope the police find the person who harmed her," Suzie added.

I rested my glass thoughtfully on the table before looking at Helene and Ginger. "Did either of you see anything odd during Suzie's concert? See anyone leave, that sort of thing?"

They gave the briefest of glances in each other's direction. It was fleeting but it was there. Had they seen something, or did they know something? I pressed on a little deeper. "Perhaps there was an argument or someone that was confrontational. Even the smallest piece of information can help."

"Tell them," urged Helene.

Suzie leaned in. "What is it? Did you see or hear anything?"

Ginger pursed her lips in deep thought before finally exhaling. "Bernard Lazenby. He's such a know-it-all at times. And as for Simon Stadler. Honestly, I don't know why he is even here." She looked to Helene. "You know them better than me of course."

Helene huffed, and pursed her red lips. Something was bothering her. But what.

Suzie shifted uncomfortably in her chair and looked off into the distance over the ocean. Was it my imagination or were the waves now flowing faster and choppier than when we'd arrived.

"Simon's a crook," said Helene, "the way he always makes a killing snatching up the best land zoned for development before he sells it off for a huge profit."

This sounded familiar. I remembered someone at the yacht club fundraiser accusing Simon of similar behavior. Could this be connected to something that Amber uncovered in her role in the Artemis Group I wondered? Although I thought that her organization focused more on groups related to opioid drug awareness and in helping those who became addicted.

She leaned closer to us, conspiratorially. "Of course, Amber, poor soul, she didn't have good taste in men."

"What do you mean?"

"I have it on good authority, well, actually from Amber herself, that she was in the midst of a land deal with them."

"They were all in it together?"

This revelation broke through Suzie's reverie. "What?"

Helene nodded. "No. She was playing one off against the other apparently."

"Was it common knowledge?" I asked.

Helene shrugged. "I don't believe so. I think she thought she could play them at their own game and squeeze more money out of them. But both men are too sharp and savvy to fall for that. They must have guessed that she was playing them both one against the other, knowing how competitive they are. Especially against each other. Neither man would want to lose to the other."

"Goodness," said Suzie. "For a minute I thought you were about to say that she was having an affair with one of them." She laughed at her confusion.

"Well, you're not far wrong. She is, I mean was, having an affair, or a relationship actually, with Rupert." She nodded slowly at us for effect. "He's divorced, and all that, so I suppose he's free to be in another relationship, but he can't just be bringing women home anytime he feels like it. Think of his child."

With Rupert, Bernard, and Simon all being involved in some way, it felt like we were getting closer to uncovering some truths. Was one of them her killer?

Just as I was about to speak there was a loud commotion at the entrance of the marquee. I jumped up and swung around to see what was happening. Suzie turned too while Helene and Ginger were facing the fracas and watched from their chairs. Anthony Boyden was embroiled in a heated argument with Simon Stadler, while the other guests stood off to one side observing the fracas. Anthony, Rupert's brother, was inches away from Simon's face and was gripping Simon so tightly at the neck by twisting the man's polo shirt that Simon's feet barely touched the ground.

Suzie and I immediately hurried over to put an end to the disturbance before anyone else was killed; Hank thankfully reached the two men before us.

Rupert then appeared on the scene in an attempt to break up the fight. Usually so cocky and sure of himself, Simon Stadler was red in the face and blustering when Hank forcibly separated him from Anthony. "He should be arrested," Simon croaked, pointing a shaky finger at Anthony as the two men backed away from each other.

Anthony laughed and strutted over to join his brother.

"What's this all about?" demanded Suzie. "Hank, what's happening?"

Hank straightened his broad shoulders. "Sorry Ms. Wilde. I didn't see how it started. When I heard them fighting I rushed over at once and broke them up."

It was probably turning out to be a tougher job for Hank and the other security personnel this evening than they had thought when they signed on for the job. He moved to the bar area of the marquee where he could keep a subtle eye on everyone, including monitoring Suzie to ensure she was safe and not hassled.

Suzie shook her head at Anthony and Simon. Then she looked slowly and steadily at everyone present. "We're all under a lot of pressure because of the tragedy that happened this evening," she said evenly, "but I would like to remind each one of you that you are my guests, and this is my home. I expect everyone to behave and to cooperate with the detectives and the investigation." She was breathing hard, yet her gaze never faltered once as she addressed the crowd, some of whom looked away while others lowered their eyes, almost in shame.

I scanned the faces of each of the assembled guests. Melissa the BobCat was nowhere to be seen, and that was either a good thing as it meant I didn't need to look at her any more than necessary, or she was up to something. She was apparently clinging to a long-held grudge, one that I had zero recollection of. Plus she was also proving to be a vicious liar who was only happy when she was causing misery to those around her. I wondered what despicable mischief she was up to and what else she was going to do as the evening gave way to the darkness of night.

First things first though. Keep the blasted BobCat from doing any more damage. The less she knew about what Suzie and I were doing, or were finding out, the better. Plus, for all I knew, she could be the murderer and was doing her damnedest to throw as much muck in other directions in the hope that some of it sticks, thereby letting her get away, literally, with murder.

Right now though I had a job to do, and as much as I wanted to find out where she was and what Simon Stadler had done to upset Anthony so badly, unfortunately, those things were going to have to wait.

Chapter Twenty-Three

The fracas between Anthony and Simon Stadler drew not only my attention, but the attention of the police too as Sergeant Brodie arrived wanting to know what was going on. "I've had to interrupt the investigation because you're fighting among yourselves like schoolboys." He towered over Anthony and Simon. "I'll get to both of you soon. You can be sure of that."

Rupert came forward and spoke to Trip, with Suzie and I right behind him. "I'm sorry this happened. Simon has been goading Anthony, and this is how my brother apparently solves issues."

"Thanks for letting me know, but like I said, I'll be talking with everyone, including your brother and Simon, to ensure I get a complete picture of what's been going on here today."

Rupert gave a half-smile and drifted off to meet up with his brother, grabbing him firmly by the elbow and taking him off to one side where they couldn't be overheard.

"Trip, I need to have a word with you," insisted Suzie. "How much longer are you going to keep people here?"

He shrugged. "Can't say Suzie. A few more hours at least."

"A few more hours! It will be dark then. The mosquitoes will be munching everyone, and there's a murderer lurking out there, either amongst my guests or in the bushes. Plus there's a god-damned squall or storm or something like it that's going to arrive in a couple of hours. We need to let the guests be allowed to go home."

He shook his head slowly. "Don't you think I know that? Why don't you take everyone inside the house? Find a room for them to stay in while we sort everything out here."

"A room?"

"No need to repeat everything. And it would be helpful if you found a room for Nate and me too. That way we can get statements from people, speed up the process."

"And then can they all go home?"

"Well, most of them," he countered.

"Hmm. And I suppose you'll want something to eat too, Trip?"

"Well, now that you mention it," he said with a charming grin.

Suzie's eyes crinkled and then she smiled and gave him a hug. "Honestly Trip. Okay, I'll head back inside. Check in on how my Harry's doing. And Cindy's there too. She's one of my security team, and she's there to make sure guests don't get 'lost' looking for the restroom, as the pool house is out of use now."

Trip shuffled his feet slightly and hooked his thumbs in the loops of his belt. "Suzie, you should be aware that since the crime scene personnel have arrived, we've obtained a search warrant for the area and we're about to start the process of collecting additional evidence and then interviewing each of your guests as one or more of them could well be potential witnesses, even if they don't know it yet."

"A search warrant, for here?"

"It's a necessary part of the process. It will allow us to establish a chain of custody over any evidence we find in connection to the murder," he added. "And I'll need a complete list of all guests, staff, event personnel etc."

"I understand," she said.

Trip took in a quick sweep around the perimeter of the house and the garden area. "I take it you've got security cameras, either physical cameras or ones that you can track on your phone?"

"Definitely. I have to, given my line of work," she replied.

"Then I'd like you to arrange for me to see all the footage that you have. It might help us to ascertain timelines of who went where, and when."

"And the murderer too?" she asked.

"Unlikely. But you never know. We live in hope."

Suzie reached out and grabbed my arm.

"Are you okay?" I asked.

She looked at me, her blue eyes wide and moist. "I think all that's happened has just hit me."

I was concerned for her and how she was holding up. "Do you want me to walk with you to the house?"

She shook her head, her tousled blonde curls bouncing softly against her forehead. "You stay here, Marnie." She then straightened her spine, drawing her shoulders back slightly. "I've got a lot to organize if I'm going to end up with a houseful of guests. This is beginning to feel more like Hotel California," she said as she turned around, gently singing "You can check out any time you like, but you can never leave…"

I stood squarely in front of Trip. He had a job to do and despite what trouble Melissa had caused for Gabby, I couldn't blame him and I sure as heck couldn't simply sit back and feel sorry for myself. I'd been in tougher situations than this, but I also had a job to do too. There were other guests to talk to, to learn what they knew, discover what they'd heard. I had to see if I could figure out who really did kill Amber and hurt my friend too. "I'll let you get on with your job," I said and turned swiftly on my heels to find someone else to chat with and try to unearth what happened to Amber.

Trip calmly turned away and went off again in the direction of the pool house.

On second thoughts, I turned back to face the Trip and catch up with him. As I did so, two figures caught my attention. DS Whitney was in a close huddle with non-other than Melissa Maxwell. My stomach flipped and I wondered what made-up lies she was sharing with him. Whatever it was, I'd bet it wasn't good news for me or Gabby. Stuffing my thoughts deep inside, I caught up with the elusive sergeant.

"Trip," I called out to him. "Sorry, I know you're busy, but everyone is restless and as you saw some people are getting angry. Could you say a few words to the guests?"

He stopped and swung around to face me, or rather lower his gaze at me, despite my above average height. "I can understand your concerns, Marnie. We'll get around to talking to the guests shortly."

"It would be really helpful," I persisted, "if you, or your colleague, could let them know what you're planning on doing. When they can expect to go home. That sort of thing?"

"Yeah, I'll get Nate to do that."

"I remember you mentioning to Suzie that you had to create a timeline of events, but not everyone knows why they haven't been interviewed yet or probably more important, when they will be told that they can go home."

"You listen well," he noted.

"As do you. It's a good skill to have in my profession."

He nodded. "Likewise. Pity more people don't have it though."

I gave a little smile. "Agreed."

He put his hands on his hips and looked around. "Listen, we've pretty much got every available officer and detective here to help us with the investigation as it unfolds. There will be several of my team taking statements, but I'll also need time to review the statements and discuss with my colleagues what information we've obtained."

"Sounds like a long process. Any idea when we can be released?"

"Oh, I'd say a few hours at least. But don't quote me on that."

I sighed. "I thought as much. But it's best if people find out sooner as many of them are extremely restless and there's no telling what they'll do if they don't have an idea of what's going on or when they'll be allowed to leave. Speculation is killing them."

"Indeed. Hopefully no-one else will die because of it."

I realized what I'd said, and cringed. "Thanks, I'll let you get on with your job."

I left him in a hurry and decided to keep my distance from Melissa; I didn't want to do or say anything that could jeopardize the investigation. Instead, I turned my attention to the other guests, trying to gauge their reactions and gather any information that might be relevant to the case.

Not looking where I was going, I almost fell into the arms of Rupert Boyden on the lawn. Pushing myself off him I straightened up trying to regain some semblance of composure. Standing this close to the man, he had aged twenty years in a matter of hours and his brother Anthony didn't look any better either.

"Rupert!" I flushed crimson as I straightened up. "I hope I didn't stand on you?"

He backed away from me. "I'm fine."

He didn't look fine and that's when I remembered that according to Helene he was apparently dating Amber. I wondered how much he would share about their relationship. Keeping the conversation neutral I started up a conversation. "What happened to Amber is such a tragedy. I gather the two of you were close."

He flinched at the mention of her name. "Yes. It's awful what happened. And here of all places."

"I know. I mean, who would do such a thing?"

Anthony shifted uncomfortably from one large foot to the other, his bulky hands stuffed in his cream linen trousers. "Why are you still here? Shouldn't you be talking to the police or something?"

"I've already spoken to the police," I said, trying not to sound too defensive. "They're talking to everyone."

"They've not got to us yet." He looked down at his feet and shuffled.

I wondered why he was behaving like a sulky teenager.

"Did you know Amber well," I asked him, waiting to see how he would react. He may give more away by his body language, rather than what he said.

Anthony lifted his head. "She was more Rupert's friend than mine." His gaze switched towards his brother where it lingered.

Rupert appeared to take the hint and confirmed what Helene had said. "We'd been seeing each other for a few months," he said with a lingering sigh. "Three actually. But I'd known Amber for years. She was like a bright ray of sunshine whenever she walked in a room." He turned to face the ocean, watching the sun lowering in the sky. Swathes of dark clouds gathered at the horizon. The storm was indeed forming. His breath caught and I heard the tenderness in his voice as he spoke. "Now we'll never see her again."

I waited for him to say more, but he seemed lost in his thoughts.

"I'm so sorry for your loss Rupert," I said gently. His expression crumpled, and he lifted his chin slightly, pain evident on his face. Perhaps things had been serious between Amber and himself, and it wasn't some casual 'friends with benefits' type of thing.

Anthony, on the other hand, now had plenty to say. Pulling his hands out of his pockets, he waved his arms theatrically in the direction of the pool house. "We heard that your friend Gabby is involved in what happened to Amber."

Rupert turned slowly to face both of us, but said nothing. I was excruciatingly aware of him staring at me, even though his brother was addressing me.

"That's nonsense, Anthony," I stated firmly. "The police believe that she is a victim of the same person that harmed Amber." They hadn't confirmed that, but they would if I had anything to do with it.

He raised his eyebrows, clearly unconvinced that Gabby was a victim. Skepticism was written all over his face.

"Hasn't enough damage been done?" said Rupert slowly, his voice bordering on weariness.

"Not according to Melissa," Anthony countered, his broad hands now planted firmly on his hips.

"Well, I say drop it. Don't you get it. Enough is enough."

Anthony acquiesced to his brother, rather reluctantly I thought, as he petulantly stuffed his hands back in his pockets.

I thought about what had just transpired between the two men and Anthony's lack of sensitivity around the fact that his brother was grieving. What was really going on between them? Was Anthony glad that Amber had died?

"Sorry to interrupt," boomed an inappropriately loud male voice that could only belong to Bernard Lazenby. He was hard to ignore with his blue-tinged black hair and a voice like a fog-horn. He carried a large glass of red wine and raised it to all of us before taking a sip that bordered on being a gulp. I noticed that his cheeks were more than a little flushed. His wife Celia was beside him, her face a little rosy and a half-empty glass of white wine in one hand. Lashawna White and her partner Richard were with them, each of them carrying half-full glasses of red wine.

"Hi everyone," we all said to each other, almost in unison.

"What an evening this has turned out to be," Bernard said.

I noticed that Celia clutched her wine glass as though holding on to something solid in an attempt to ground herself. "We really shouldn't be surprised though," she added.

"What do you mean?" I asked.

"Violence is everywhere. Don't you see?" She gave a quick, almost furtive look around us.

I looked around and didn't notice anything immediately threatening. First responders were waiting by their vehicles, two police officers were at the entrance to the driveway, presumably to check vehicles entering or leaving. Two other officers were down at the dock to keep an eye on it and prevent anyone using it as a means of coming onto the island, or off it for that matter. Muffled male voices were audible from the direction of the pool house where Amber's body still lay until it could be taken away to be examined by the coroner. This was likely from the detectives and crime scene officers who were nowhere to be seen but were probably working on analyzing the site and whatever clues they could uncover. I wondered how much progress they were making. The remaining guests were gathered in a huddle by the marquee.

"We're safe here," I insisted. "And with all these law enforcement personnel here, no-one would dream of harming anyone else."

"No place is exempt," added Lashawna.

Celia tapped her wine glass to Lashawna's as an indication of agreement. "None of us are safe, not here, not anywhere." She tightened her grip on her wine glass and I was worried the glass might crack under the pressure.

Amoy and Mark joined us. I was relieved and hoped they would bring a level of optimism and reassurance to the group, given their roles as lawyers who, based on the few I'd known over the years, I always associated as being level-headed and not prone to exaggeration. "How's everyone doing," Amoy asked. Her tone was calm and assertive given the circumstances that had flung each of us together.

The general consensus was 'okay.' The continuous subdued sound of professional voices drifted from the direction of the pool house, carried on the breeze that was billowing off the ocean, reminding each of us that despite our own discomfort at being asked to stay on the island, there was an awful reason why this had to be so. I glanced briefly at each of the people in my little group. There was a growing sense of something: camaraderie, comfort, safety?

Me on the other hand, I was wary. Was one of them the murderer?

Amoy was quite matter of fact with regards to the events that were still unfolding. "Have you seen the latest on social media? The news about what happened here is everywhere. The media's having a field day with this one."

Everyone, me included, pulled out their phones and began to scroll through the various social sites that each of us used.

Just then, a low flying helicopter with the logo of a local news channel emblazoned on the doors flew overhead. They were the first ones on the scene. In the distance, over the mainland, I saw three other helicopters flying towards us. This was going to be a zoo, and we were the mammals on display.

"Oh crap," said Bernard. "This is not good. Not good at all."

Celia chugged down the last of her wine and hugged herself. "This won't be good for business if we're spotted, will it?"

"Not initially, no."

"Why is that?" I asked.

He looked at me aghast, like I was from another planet. "It's quite simple Marnie. Until the professionals find out who did this, my business will suffer. There will always be finger pointing and suggestions, rumors, that sort of thing. Insinuations that I'm somehow responsible for what happened to that unfortunate girl."

"He's right you know," agreed Mark. Amoy stood silently beside him.

"Who's right?" Liz Tanner joined us, with her friend JT beside her. "What're we missing?"

Bernard pointed to the sky. "I'd say we all just found a bucket load of more trouble." He cleared his throat and stood a little straighter. "You were right my dear," he said, addressing his wife. "We can't escape this situation."

"Bernie," said his wife, slipping an arm though one of his. "Let's get under cover. I don't want to be filmed and put on display on the national nightly news."

We all agreed that being under the cover of the marquee was a better idea than simply standing around, offering ourselves up as tabloid fodder. Rupert and Anthony headed swiftly to the marquee, and I made my way over with Celia and the others hoping to glean some more information from them.

"I'm not keen on being too close to that Kaylee Bardot woman, though," said Celia as we all scurried over to the relative safety of the marquee.

"Why not?" I asked.

"Well, she and Amber weren't exactly friends, isn't that right Bernie?"

He nodded. "Not sure why though," he said.

"Well, I did hear that it might have something to do with Kaylee's child."

I was a little taken aback by that. "I didn't know Kaylee had a child. She's never mentioned that she had one. Boy or girl, do you know?"

"A boy I believe, but Amber's friend Fee might know more."

If it was true that Kaylee had a son, what had it to do with Amber? I'd have to tread lightly with Kaylee. I didn't want her to think I was prying but if there was a reason why Kaylee wanted to keep quiet about her son and Amber found out about it, well, it might be the reason why Amber was killed.

As we settled into the marquee, the noise from the helicopters above grew louder. We sat in a huddle as the wind whipped through the open sides of the tent, sending paper napkins and glasses flying. I felt the tension in the marquee continue to grow. The arrival of the media had everyone on edge, and it seemed like every move we made was being watched and recorded.

I was relieved when Suzie rejoined us after alerting her staff about what Sergeant Brodie had requested. "I expected this lot to arrive sooner or later," she said, pointing above us to the circling helicopter, and flopping down into a chair beside me. Earlier, she had been doing her best to keep everyone calm, but it was clear that this was all taking a toll on her.

Movement behind her caught my attention and I tapped Suzie lightly on the shoulder, and inclined my head for her to look outside the marquee. The crime scene spotlights from the pool area were shining brightly, creating an ethereal arc in the sky above the trees. In front of the hedge lining the path to the pool house were two medical personnel wheeling away on a stretcher, what I presumed to be Amber's body, inside a black 'body bag' like the ones used in Hollywood. It was a sobering sight, and it reminded me that we were dealing with a real tragedy. It wasn't just a drama or a mystery to be solved; it was a loss of a human life.

I stood up, giving a light nudge to Celia, who did the same to Bernard and as we turned to watch, all the other guests in the marquee became silent and stood and watched Amber's body being taken away. Liz clutched Fee and wrapped her shawl tightly around herself as they leaned into each other in mutual support. JT stood silently beside Liz.

I noted that as the stretcher trundled along, it left two deep grooves in the grass. Death was leaving us a reminder that it had been here. But as the stretcher disappeared from view, I was instantly brought back to the here and now. The media circus was still in full swing with helicopters hovering overhead. It was starting to feel claustrophobic.

I scanned the faces of the assembled guests.

Everyone was subdued after what felt like a feeding frenzy of piranhas eating raw flesh, between the pressure above from the media helicopters, the incessant typing on phones, glowers from people to those who's phones were pinging, or the hissing of 'can't you put that damn thing on silent?' All that, while waiting to be interviewed by the police.

Suzie stood up. "Time for me to let everyone know what Trip wants to happen next. You know, have the guests settle themselves in my house when it gets dark so he can complete the interviews."

I settled myself on a chair at one of the square tables with the drapey white tablecloths, happy to stretch my legs out beneath the table and remove my sandals. They were new flats with cushioned insoles and started out super comfy, but now they were pinching over the toes and at the heel strap, perhaps because of all the standing I'd been doing since I'd arrived at the event.

"Hi everyone," announced Suzie. "Thanks for your attention. The lead detective has told me that things appear to be moving forward and I wanted to let you know that as it's starting to get dark, and we can't stay out here all night, you're welcome to come into my house and wait in some of the rooms on the ground floor. Much more comfortable, don't you think?"

A few people clapped and gave a tired little cheer that also sounded more than a little tipsy.

"You should plan to head to my house no later than 8:45. I'll arrange for food and refreshments to be served there until the police say that everyone can leave."

Now it appeared that everyone was onboard with the plan to move to the house. To actually be inside Suzie's Wilde's house was an experience many of them may have thought they would never have.

"In the meantime, I'm going to come around and chat with each of you. Let you know how grateful I am for your service to the community." She smiled broadly at everyone and made her way back to me.

I wiggled my feet back into my sandals then checked my watch and groaned.

"What's up, honey?" asked Suzie.

"It's only been about forty-five minutes since I found Amber and called the police. It seems so much longer."

I had so many questions, theories, and possibilities running through my mind. All I knew for sure was that we needed to find the murderer before they struck again. "I can't just sit here Suzie. C'mon. Let's mingle. I think we should talk with Kaylee next."

She leaned in, conspiratorially. "Why, what have you heard?"

I filled her in on what Celia had told me about Kaylee Bardot and her son earlier. The fact that Kaylee had a child and had been keeping it from her friends made me wonder what else she was hiding.

I thought about who could have killed Amber and why. It was by some kind of poison, that much we knew. But what was it and how did she ingest it?

I started to realize that there could have been any number of reasons why someone would want to harm Amber, whether it was due to jealousy, revenge, or something else entirely. But the more I thought about it, the more I started to believe that the murderer was someone who had a personal connection to Amber. It wasn't just a random attack.

I spotted Kaylee and her friend Sabrina tucked in the far-left corner away from everyone where, incidentally I noticed, they had a grand view of the entire marquee. Talk about the best seat in the house!

I'd learned over the years that warmth went a long way in helping people to unburden themselves of whatever they were holding onto, helping them to release what they were keeping to themselves for fear of what other people may think. I knew only too well what that particular fear felt like, and in my case, it was one of never quite feeling good enough. Although being invited to Suzie's event was definitely making me reconsider if I'd been too hard on myself for too long.

I nudged Suzie gently and indicated with the slightest tilt of my head that we should head in that specific direction. I discovered right there and then that Suzie is an excellent follower of nuanced looks and eyebrow twitching and whatever else I was doing to indicate without speaking where we needed to go. Clearly a skill she had honed on stage over several decades. Her face remained placid until we approached the two young women, and then Suzie the rockstar burst onto the scene and she gushed forward to greet Kaylee and Sabrina.

Chapter Twenty-Four

Kaylee and Sabrina greeted us warmly, offering us seats next to them. I thanked them and sat down, glancing around to see if anyone was watching us too closely. It was important to keep a low profile while we gathered information.

"I can't believe what's happened," said Kaylee. "I just can't wrap my head around it."

"I know," said Suzie. "It's hard to believe something like this could happen."

Sabrina nodded in agreement. "Yeah, Amber was always willing to help out our organization and she was really talented. She had a good eye for details."

Sabrina was studying us intently. It was almost as if she was sizing us up, trying to figure us out.

"Do you know of anyone who might have had a problem with Amber?" I asked.

Kaylee and Sabrina both shook their heads.

"Did you know Amber well?" asked Suzie casually.

Kaylee and Sabrina exchanged a look before Kaylee spoke up.

"She was always there for her friends and like we said, she was also incredibly talented."

"And driven," added Sabrina. "Yeah, she was really passionate about her work and always pushing herself to be better."

I made a mental note to look into Amber's work at her firm. It could potentially give us some leads on who she may have crossed paths with and who might want to do her harm. And then, there was the rumor that Kaylee had a son and somehow Amber was embroiled in the mystery surrounding him and his whereabouts.

"Yes," remarked Suzie. "We'd heard that Amber's work was important to her. Especially her volunteer work. I heard that she was particularly interested in helping women and children. What can you share about that?"

Sabrina shifted in her seat while Kaylee sat poker-faced. "We did hear something," said Sabrina slowly. "Didn't we Kaylee?"

Kaylee glowered at her friend, and I thought it was a good thing that looks could not kill. "Yeah. She was quite the little Mother Theresa when it came to wanting to help people out. That's all I'm sayin'. That's all I know."

"And what about her personal life?" I asked, trying to keep my tone neutral.

Kaylee hesitated before answering. "I don't really know much about it. She was very private."

Sabrina spoke up. "But she did mention once that she was having some trouble with a guy she was seeing. Don't you remember Kaylee?"

Kaylee shrugged.

"I don't know the details," continued Sabrina leaning towards us conspiratorially, "but it seemed like he was being more than a bit possessive."

"That's interesting," I said. "Do you know who this guy is?"

Sabrina shook her head. "No, she didn't mention his name."

I thought back to the earlier fight between Anthony and Simon. Could one of them have killed Amber. Certainly, Simon was here with Stella, and they seemed like a genuine couple, however Anthony had shown us all that he had a temper. If the rumors were true that Amber had more than one lover, it might not have taken much to push Anthony over the edge and kill her in a jealous rage. Could he be the possessive guy they were talking about?

"Did either of you meet with Amber often?"

"Not really," said Kaylee. "We weren't really friends. We were more or less what you'd call business acquaintances." She sat back at that and folded her arms.

"I see," I said. "Do you think her work had anything to do with what happened to her?"

Kaylee and Sabrina both looked at each other before shrugging in unison. "I wouldn't know," said Kaylee. "Amber was always really careful. She had a plan and she worked towards it."

"You could say she was focused and always got what she wanted." Sabrina nodded in agreement.

"What kind of work did you and she do?" I pressed, trying to steer the conversation towards something more specific.

Before Kaylee could answer, there was a commotion behind me. I turned around and saw that DS Nate Whitney was there, raising his arms, hands spread. Two uniformed officers, one male and one female stood quietly beside him, the woman holding a clipboard. "Ladies and gentlemen, your attention please. We're now at a point in the investigation where we will ask those of you that we've not spoken with yet for your help."

"Are we under arrest?" asked Helene Gauthier.

"Do we need a lawyer?" called out another woman's voice.

"No. Nothing like that. You are all potential witnesses and as such we want to determine who was where during the evening and if anyone was missing during the time when we believe the murder took place."

Mutterings and grumblings filled the tent.

Detective Whitney turned to the female officer and held out his hand. She handed him the clipboard and he cleared his throat. "Helene Gauthier. Please step forward."

All eyes turned towards Helene, who in turn hesitated, reluctant to approach the detective, but the other guests had parted, creating a broad swath and exposing her for everyone to see. She turned back to look at her handsome son Max and gave him a hint of a smile. Helene had wonderful deportment and held her chin ever so slightly elevated and walked forward the ten or so steps in the marquee until she was in front of Detective Whitney.

I couldn't hear what was said but they left the tent with the female officer walking beside Helene, Detective Whitney leading the way in the direction of the cabanas, where it was not only more private, but the area was also still brightly illuminated by the powerful portable spotlights that the crime scene officers were using.

Suzie stood up and we said our goodbyes to Kaylee and Sabrina. Suzie was the perfect host and knew what to say to make them feel especially welcome. "Thank you Kaylee. You too Sabrina. It's been lovely chatting with you. Such a pity it's now under such sad circumstances."

As we walked away I remembered that Kaylee hadn't had a chance to tell us what kind of work she did with Amber. I would have to ask her later.

Suzie nudged my elbow, and we made our way to where Amoy and her husband Mark were seated. "Mind if we join you, darlin'?" Suzie asked with a smile.

"Oh, please sit, sit," said Amoy indicating the two spare chairs at their table. Mark pulled a chair out for Suzie, and we sat down. The server was working her way around the tables, and Suzie and I both ordered a glass of sparkling water when she reached us. We'd no sooner ordered when Lashawna and her partner Richard made their way to where we were sitting. "Hey guys, what an evening," they said, raising their glasses of red wine they were carrying. "Room for two more?"

We smiled and made them welcome, eager to find out how their evening had been progressing too. They pulled up two spare chairs from the empty table next to us and sat down.

"I'm eager to learn more about what you've been doing with your charity work," said Suzie. "I hear you've created a wonderful organization protecting animals."

"That's good of you to say so," said Lashawna, and she proceeded to share how she had first started her animal shelter and what it took to run it with volunteers and donations of everything from not only money and training animals, but food, to bedding, and equipment such as leashes and food bowls.

"Oh, oh, watch out everyone," said Amoy.

"Why," asked Suzie. "What's going on now?"

Amoy gave a brief sideways flick of her eyes in the direction of Simon Stadler who had just stormed into the marquee, his girlfriend Stella tottering several steps behind him, trying not to get the heels of her stilettos stuck in the grass.

"I wonder what's got him all riled up," I asked.

"Doesn't take much, from what I heard."

She lowered her voice. "I can't fathom why Stella sticks by him. I heard he's now in even bigger trouble financially." She gave a little nod and sat back and settled in, waiting.

I thought about what she'd said about Simon. I'd heard someone recently mentioning pretty much the same thing. Then I remembered. It was at the yacht club fundraiser. That's where I'd first heard talk about Simon and his suspect business practices.

Simon settled Stella at an empty small table and then went straight to the bar and ordered drinks.

So he could be a gentleman after all, I mused. I watched him walk back to where Stella was seated and rub her shoulders before sitting in the chair beside her. Something wasn't adding up and I couldn't figure out what it was.

Everyone at our table was now talking about animals or pets that they either have or had once. Mostly, the voices in the marquee, our table included, were hushed but surprisingly, it wasn't quiet. Waves could be heard breaking on the rocks near the boat ramp, crickets and cicadas were noisily calling out from the long beach grasses, and predominantly male voices drifted on the wind from the vicinity of the pool house. Some guests were scrolling through their phones, no doubt checking for, or adding to, updates on what was happening here on Suzie's island.

On the opposite side of the marquee, Bernard only had eyes for Simon and scowled at him over the top of his wine glass. Simon and Stella's drinks were served, and they toasted each other before Simon stared hard at Bernard, clearly daring the other man to come over and start a fight, much in the same way that he had fought earlier with Anthony.

Talking of whom, I looked around for him, but Anthony was nowhere to be seen. Neither, for that matter, was Liz or JT. I envied their alone time together. They made quite a couple. I wouldn't call them cute, but there was a bond, a connection between them that, looking back on my own love life, had been sorely lacking. I'd thought that intellect and good conversation could make up for what was missing on the touchy feely front. Oh, how wrong I was. And all it took was perky bum Ashley to drive that point home, or rather drive Craig from home and straight into her bed.

I took a drink of the sparkling water in an attempt to clear my head and wash away those memories that I thought I was well and truly done with. Amoy made a 'hmph' sound before turning back to us.

"The way he came into the tent I thought for sure he was going to pick up where he left off with Anthony." She looked around searching. "Either him or Bernard," she added, sounding more than a little disappointed.

"I only see Bernard talking with Ginger Maloney, but I got the impression Bernard was not exactly Simon's biggest fan." Ginger and Bernard's body language was interesting though. They were speaking in hushed tones, but they seemed to be arguing about something. He was drawing away from her while she was definitely impeding his personal body space. All of a sudden she got up, straightened down her dress, and stormed out of the marquee. "What's the story behind Bernard and Simon anyway," I asked, already dismissing the scene between Bernard and Ginger.

Lashawna perked up. She seemed to know a lot about everyone. I even wondered briefly what she knew about me. "Well, Bernard and Simon go back a long way. But apparently it's the age-old threesome dilemma."

Suzie's eyebrows furrowed. "Whatever do you mean, darlin'?"

"Apparently Simon used to go out with Celia, but she chose Bernard instead. So naturally, Simon's been harboring a grudge ever since."

"Oh? I didn't know that," said Suzie. "You know, the world would be a sad place if every jilted person was filled with resentment over a lost lover. But it does give me another idea for a song," she said with what I could swear was accompanied with a wink and a smile.

I looked at each man in turn. I was going to have to check out that little tidbit of information and I knew exactly who to talk to. "But Bernard and Celia have been married a long time, haven't they?"

Lashawna shrugged. "I believe that Simon losing Celia to Bernard was what started it. That's all I know."

That was much the same as what Melissa, aka BobCat, was doing with me. The woman was unable, or incapable, of letting the past go. She was either upset with me for some reason that I had either forgotten about or knew nothing about, or it was just her nature to be mean.

Talk of the devil.

BobCat sashayed into the marquee and made her way over to Rupert and Anthony who were chatting with her companion Carrie Abrams. She was back from wherever she'd been prowling and from the smirk on her face and the way she slunk into the marquee, she was like the cat who's got the cream.

Where had she been and what had she been doing? Her sandals and the hem of her dress were smudged with white powdery dust, and she brushed them lightly with her hands as she sat down next to Rupert. Sensing me staring at her, Melissa frowned in my direction. I held her gaze. I was not going to be intimidated by her. Never again. Whatever had transpired between us was long gone; at least as far as I was concerned. On the other hand, I don't think she saw it that way. No, whatever it was, it was a seemingly unmovable obstacle between her past and her life now. I had no idea how to move it out of the way as right now I had no clue what it was. But one thing was clear, it had to be gotten rid of once and for all otherwise she was going to forever be a thorn in my side.

She whispered something to Rupert and the two of them got up and left the marquee, disappearing into the gloom and heading goodness knows where.

Lashawna snuggled up to her husband Richard. She looked sideways at him and he responded by gently rubbing her on the back of her neck like a mini-massage. Oh, how I could do with a massage right now. In fact I was going to make an appointment as soon as this was all behind us.

I spent the next ten-minutes chatting with Amoy. She was still no further forward in discovering who had scratched her Range Rover, but she wasn't going to rest until she found the culprit. Good luck with that, I thought. The sun had almost set, and the last remaining vestiges of light were almost gone. Large fans, about two feet in diameter, were discretely positioned on the perimeter of the marquee between the myriad of twinkle lights and tiki lights, pointing towards the ocean. The fans were switched on and their persistent hum was welcome as they whooshed mosquitoes and other bugs on their merry way so they would not be a pest to us humans. Not this evening anyway.

An ear-splitting scream interrupted us, and I bounded to my feet, all thoughts of a future massage gone.

Celia came running into the marquee towards Bernard screaming and stamping her feet, shaking her hands in the air.

"Stay back everyone," I called out as I dashed over to Celia. She was shrieking at what I surmised was the top of her lungs and pointing out of the marquee in a disoriented manner.

Chapter Twenty-Five

I reached Celia with Suzie right behind me just as Bernard caught his wife, enveloping his wife in his broad arms. "What's happened, Celia. Are you hurt?" he asked urgently.

She was gasping for air and pointing behind her towards the path to the jetty.

"Celia," I asked. "What's happened? Are you okay?"

"There's a woman. She's on the path–to the jetty." She clung onto Bernard. "I think she's dead."

I looked around us and saw Hank approaching from the rear of the marquee. "Hank," I called out, "alert the detectives or a police officer. Tell them what's happened."

"Right. I'm on it."

Meanwhile, mutterings were floating all around us. I grabbed hold of Suzie. "C'mon. We'd better go check," I said urgently.

We left Celia with her husband, the other guests watching. We quickly made our way to the gravel path that led to the jetty, Suzie leading the way. It had only been a few hours since I'd arrived on the Wilde Estate, never imagining how the evening was going to end up. We slowed our pace as we approached the entrance to the path. Our footsteps sounded suddenly harsh after the softness of the grass. I searched in the twilight beyond where the glow from the tiki lights and white twinkle lights ended. There was definitely a dark shape on the ground. We stopped and peered into the gloom.

"Can you make out what that is? asked Suzie in a hushed voice.

"No," I whispered. Somehow, the scene before us didn't warrant loud voices. "There's only one thing to do."

"I was afraid you'd say that."

"I can go alone," I responded.

"No. I'll go with you. Fingers crossed it's only an animal. Not a you-know-what."

I pulled out my phone and switched on the flashlight to see better. We made our way forward again slowly, step by step. The shape in front of us never moved. We'd only gone five steps when it became clear what we were looking at. The shape appeared to morph into a human form, chunky bare feet protruding from one end, a shock of cropped silvery hair topping the other.

"It's Ginger Maloney," I gasped.

"Ginger? Is she dead?"

"I can't tell. Wait a mo while I check." I leaned closer, mindful that if Ginger had been killed we were effectively tampering or contaminating a crime scene, or both. I crouched down and peered closely at the body, using two fingers of my right hand to check for a pulse in her wrist. I couldn't detect one. Her body was warm though, but devoid of any detectable heartbeat.

"Well?"

"No pulse Suzie. I'm sorry."

"Please tell me it's a natural death, not something sinister."

I peered closely at the body, then at the surrounding path but the sun was almost gone, and it was becoming harder to see anything clearly without adequate lighting.

"Quick!" hissed Suzie. "People are coming."

My phone cast long shadows around the path and seemed to extend the length of the body into the evening beyond, but the light caught on a familiar sight, and I let the light linger on a frothy substance around her mouth. I quickly snapped several pictures on my phone then I inched forward for a better look then sighed, mindful of the dusty sharp white stones that lined the path. I felt my shoulders sag. I stood up and turned away from Ginger's body, flicking away any stone dust that may have touched the hem of my dress, just as Trip appeared beside Suzie.

"You again," he said flatly.

I wasn't sure how to respond but Suzie put him at ease. "Yes, Trip. And me too. So don't act so surprised. As you no doubt already knew that we'd be here from what Celia told everyone. We had to know if we needed to get help for the woman who may have been injured." She shook her head. "Sadly it was too late."

He huffed a little, but turned to the entourage that had followed him here. "Everyone, get back to the marquee. Officers will ensure that you all stay there until we can take you to Ms. Wilde's house where you will be interviewed."

Two uniformed officers hurriedly appeared as he finished speaking and helped guide the crowd back to the marquee, though not without much grumbling and dissent from many of the guests.

"Okay, what can either of you tell me," he asked. Which I thought was generous of him as I half expected him to send us both back with the others.

"Go on," urged Suzie to me. "Tell him what you've found."

I explained as succinctly as I could who the woman was and who she was here with. "She was here with her husband. I looked at Suzie. I'm sorry I can't remember his name."

"That's okay honey. Neither can I But he's on the official list. Hank will have a printed copy from when he double-checked all the guests onto the island, and I'll have it on my computer too." She turned to Trip. "Trip, I'll get you the complete guest list. You'll be able to find out who the husband is and let him know the sad news, won't you?"

"Don't worry. I'm already on that." He pulled out his cell phone and dialed a number. From the one-sided conversation it became clear he was talking to his colleague Nate to inform the next of kin and ask them to come and identify the body. "And send officers with tape to secure the crime scene will you. Then notify Annie Osborne. She's running the crime scene investigation. Tell her what's happened. We need lights here, ASAP. I'll try to get her additional on-call officers and material for this new investigation. And I'll inform the Captain. Yeah, I know. She's going to be livid. Oh, and call Diane Cowen. Get her to come back. You don't have to tell me, but she is the Medical Examiner. She signed up for it and as you well know, this job is never 9 to 5."

He hung up the call, indicated that we should both stay where we were, then dialed another number. He turned his back to us, and took three steps away, but the brisk breeze carried his side of the conversation to us as clearly as if we were standing right next to him.

"Captain Ortiz, I'm calling with an update on the events at the Wilde Estate. We're going to be here a while longer."

I felt uncomfortable for him as he explained, in what I was beginning to discover was his natural matter-of-fact manner, what had happened. He then requested additional resources, both the human kind and the equipment kind. I never liked going to the dean of the college to request resources either, whether it was for funding or more people to assist at a dig. "Yes. Another death," he continued. "Yes. suspicious like the other victim. Yes, we'll need more resources to work on this crime scene. The victim's next of kin is here and can do the formal identification. Okay. Understood."

"Phew," he said under his breath as he walked back to us. "Okay. Fill me in on what you know."

Just then there was screaming and high-pitched yelling that came from far off to my left, followed by an echo on the right? Or was it another scream and yell and not an echo? I stood rigid, as did Suzie. "What's that Trip?" asked Suzie quickly, grasping his nearest forearm.

"Sounds to me like coyotes howling in the distance. Two packs. One pack howls and the other pack responds by howling back."

"They can't come here, can they?" I asked, wondering if they were able to get here on the causeway?

"Highly unlikely. What with all the noise we're making and the spotlights we've erected. They'd be mighty stupid to come this close to what we're dealing with."

"I'm relieved." I took a deep breath, feeling the weight of the situation we had found ourselves in. "Unfortunately, I don't believe we're dealing with an accident. While we really don't know much, other than Celia alerted us to the fact that there was a body here, we didn't know if the person was alive or dead when we arrived here. I checked for a pulse on her wrist and didn't detect one. She felt warm to my touch. But I did find this." I held up my phone with the photo of the froth clearly visible around Ginger's mouth.

Trip leaned closer and squinted slightly before pulling back. "Same type of frothing as on the other body. Hmm. Poisoned."

"And likely by the same poison, and by the same person," I said firmly.

"But we don't know what type of poison. Yet."

"True."

Two uniformed officers arrived carrying police caution tape. "Hey, about time," he called over to them. "Cordon off a twenty-yard area. We'll then need to get a tent erected over the body ASAP as there's a storm coming through in the next hour or so. In the meantime, I'll get a team to search the area beyond where the crime scene officers will be working when they get here, although with the impending rain and wind, any clues will likely be gone if we don't act fast."

He turned to Suzie and me. "Right, you two should head back to the marquee and think about getting everyone over to your house Suzie. It's not safe for either of you to be around here. Or anyone else for that matter."

"But if the murderer is one of the guests," I asked, "doesn't that mean we're isolating ourselves with them?"

He deftly ignored my question. "Nate and I will be along shortly to conduct interviews. I'll also post officers inside and outside of the house to ensure the safety of everyone."

"Understood," I said, grateful for his concern for our safety, but disappointed that the murderer had apparently struck again.

As we made our way back to the others to encourage them to move along to the relative safety of Suzie's house, I wondered who would want to do something like this. Who would want to harm Ginger? Or Amber? Was it personal, or was it a random act of violence. There were a myriad of possibilities, but from my experience in archaeological digs I knew that I needed to focus on the facts in order to find out the truth. I sensed that apart from what had been left at the sites of both murders, I was missing obvious clues.

As we entered the marquee, the atmosphere was tense. People were whispering and looking around nervously, unsure of who to trust. Helene had returned after her being interviewed and was deep in conversation with her son Max.

We made our way straight to Celia who was sitting at a table with a worried expression on her face. Her husband Bernard was beside her, holding her hands in his.

She looked up at us, her eyes filled with tears. "Is it true? Is it Ginger?"

I nodded slowly.

"Is she…" she whispered.

"Dead? Yes, I'm afraid she is."

She released her hands from Bernard's grasp and held them to her mouth, letting out a sob. "Oh no. This can't be happening."

The truth was, we were all in shock. Ginger was such a vibrant, larger-than-life woman and it was hard to believe she was gone. I looked around for her husband and couldn't see him. "Bernard, have you seen Ginger's husband?"

"He's with some police officers. They left a few minutes before you arrived."

There were murmurs as Trip entered the marquee, accompanied by a group of six police officers. "Everyone, please remain calm," he said, his voice booming across us. "I am Sergeant Trip Brodie, and I can confirm that Mrs. Ginger Maloney has been found dead."

There were hushed murmurs as though the confirmation being given by an official made it real.

"Her husband Ian is assisting us with our enquiries and will be helped by one of our officers specially trained in helping newly bereaved family members."

We all fell silent as he continued to speak, listing the people lucky enough to go home. "The members of the Clammers group, Ms. Wilde's band members, the jazz musicians, the catering company staff, and a photographer and media reporter. These people were all interviewed and released. We have confirmed their alibi's for the time of the murder. That said, we have asked Ms. Wilde's security personnel to remain and continue to assist her with her personal security while the investigation is ongoing. In the meantime, we will continue to conduct interviews with all guests and employees, so thank you for your cooperation and patience."

There were disagreeable mumblings as Trip outlined that we were all to go to Suzie's house immediately, and the officers were to accompany us. Then, he turned on his heel and strode out of the marquee, heading in the direction of the house.

There were rumblings of dissent, but we had nowhere else to go, and a solid house somehow felt more secure and safer than being outside. The once warm glow of the evening sun had given way to the darkness of night. Apart from the sound of the rising chorus of the cicadas and the waves on the seashore and jetty, we were a quiet group as we followed Suzie to her house, each of us lost in our own thoughts. I felt a chill run down my spine. There was something dark and twisted at play here. Something that seemed to go beyond a sudden act of violence.

Chapter Twenty-Six

At the house, we were met by Officer Nan Bundock who instructed all of us to remove our footwear and go into the living room where we would then receive additional information. We all obliged, and I was glad to finally have my feet out of my sandals and have the opportunity to sit in a comfortable chair. The women, and some of the men, appeared to be glad to shed their footwear, and before long there was a relatively neat line of shoes of various sizes and colors lining up along the entrance hallway. That was when I noticed that my sandals had white dust on them from the path, similar to the dust I'd seen on Melissa's sandals and dress.

Cindy, one of Suzie's security people, was waiting for us in the living room with Harry. There was no sign of Sergeant Brodie. The atmosphere was tense as we mulled around the large front room, some of us sitting on chairs, others on the floor with backs to a wall, and waited for the police to arrive and begin more interviews.

Anthony drew attention when he ambled into the room, stuffing his phone back into a pocket in his trousers, and flicking dust off his trousers onto the polished floor. He looked for his brother and joined him beside the wall of sliders that looked out over the lawn and the ocean, the windows acting like a mirror reflecting their bodies so as to create the illusion of there being two of them, like identical twins.

Hank consulted with his colleagues Jerry and Cindy and then approached Suzie. "Ms. Wilde, sorry to disturb, but given the unfolding events of the evening, I feel it would be prudent if Jerry and Cindy circle through the house checking doors and windows, and all the empty rooms to ensure the windows are still locked and no-one has been able to break into the house."

"If you really think this is necessary."

"I do. Until we know who, or how many people are involved in the deaths, we have to be ultra-observant and careful."

She sighed. "Okay. I must admit I'll feel safer knowing that you are all taking as many precautions as you deem necessary."

Hank returned and spoke with Cindy and Jerry, and they quietly left the room without creating a disturbance. It seemed like they could blend into the very walls of the house themselves.

The living room had a magnificent twenty-foot wall of white-edged slider windows that maximized the ocean view, but of course by now it was almost pitch-black outside, except for the eerie glow and long shadows cast by the crime scene spotlights, and there wasn't anything to see except our own reflections mirrored against the window panes. Lush green potted palms were in the opposite two corners. The polished light oak floor was a warm contrast against two oversized and overstuffed navy sofas, a love seat, a wicker rocking chair, and two navy and cream coral-patterned swivel chairs surrounding a cream and blue rectangular rug with a light wood coffee table in the middle.

I was expecting to see Suzie's many awards lining walls or shelves, but there were only numerous vases of pink and white flowers on polished tables, and smiling photos of Suzie and Harry in black picture frames. Large ocean-scape watercolors were artistically displayed on the walls depicting scenes of various harbors and beaches on the Cape. Suzie's awards must be in another room in the house.

"We'll need to be split into two groups," I whispered to Suzie. "There are too many of us to be crammed into the living room."

Suzie looked around the room. "I wish people would stand still so I can count who's all here."

"I reckon there's about twenty of us. Plus your three personal security people and any police officers who are told to keep an eye on us."

"What time is it?"

I checked my watch. "It's almost eight-fifty."

"Have you heard any updates on Gabby?"

"No. It's only been a little more than an hour since she left for the hospital. I thought I'd give it another half hour before I call the ER to see how she is doing. But, it may be hard to get any information given that she's accompanied by a police officer, plus I'm not her next of kin. To be honest, it may be easier if I go there in person, but I don't know when any of us are likely to be released."

"The waiting is unbearable, but this is no longer a celebration. I can't very well start singing and ignore what's happened."

"Was there any food or beverages left over? Make it kind of like a wake or something?"

"Yes. I asked the caterers to bring the food into the kitchen before they left. I believe there were lots of items remaining." She placed her hands on her hips. "In fact, I'll tell everyone right now."

She turned to address the room. "Ladies and gentlemen, I just want to let you all know that there are refreshments and snacks available for you on the kitchen island. Help yourself to whatever you need from there."

There were mumbles of thanks.

She turned to me. "I'm going to get some food. Can I get you anything?"

"No thanks. Perhaps later." And with that, Suzie left the room and went into a hall that presumably led to the kitchen. Seeing as I was now on my own, I spied Kaylee and Sabrina, glued to the hip as always, sitting on the sofa opposite me.

Despite doing such an amazing job helping people, as well as fund-raising and driving awareness to her charity, Kaylee did not appear comfortable mingling with people in large social gatherings. I caught her eye and walked over to join them. I still had to ask her about what she and Amber collaborated on.

"Hey, how are you holding up?" I asked Kaylee, trying to keep my voice low and sound as comforting as possible. I was genuinely concerned as she looked really anxious.

She gave me a weak smile. "I'm alright I guess. Just a bit shaken by what's been happening, you know?"

I nodded sympathetically. "We're all dealing with something that I hope we never have to cope with again." I leaned in slightly and sighed. "When we spoke earlier, you were about to tell me what kind of work you and Amber did together."

"Oh, it was mostly work related to our charity. Apparently she saw our work as an opportunity to expand her company beyond New England."

"Well, Amber may have been invited here because of the good work that her company has been doing, but from what I've been hearing, she's not exactly a saint. I mean apparently she's been seen with one of her organization's advisors in more than just a professional manner." I raised a knowing eyebrow, hoping I was being effective in what I was calling my first ever foray, in any form whatsoever, of the oh-so-subtle art of undercover questioning.

Kaylee snorted so hard I thought her nose ring was going to pop out. "You can say that again."

"So she is involved with Rupert Boyden?"

She rolled her eyes. "Oh, and the rest." She shrugged. "But then again, when Amber sets her mind on something, she goes all out to get it. Nothing will stop her." She gave a half-laugh.

What else did she mean? I thought quickly. Troy's words sprung to mind from when I'd confirmed to him that I was coming to this event. 'The ubiquitous dancing twosome between three people if you follow me.' A threesome. Oh, My Gosh. "So, she was dating two guys at the same time?"

"We just thought it kinda gross as they're all so old," said Kaylee. I felt her and Sabrina stare at me. "Well sorry, but Simon's in his late forties, we think, and Dr Rupert Boyden's not far behind."

Rupert was my age, but I chose not to divulge that I knew how old he was, nor that we were at least fifteen years younger than Simon.

I gave a little laugh. "I hope that one day you both remember what you said about forty being old. I'm not there yet, but chapping at the door, so to speak."

Sabrina turned to me. "I don't like just waiting around. I wish we could do something."

I looked over at Suzie who was chatting with Harry. I was reluctant to share my suspicions regarding Anthony, especially with his brother Rupert being there.

Just then, raised voices caused everyone in the room to be quiet and we all turned as one in the direction of the ruckus.

"Rupert," Simon growled, his eyes boring into him. "You've been suspiciously quiet this whole time. Or do you have something to hide?"

He bristled at the words and stared back at Simon, letting out a shuddering sigh. "Me? Nope. My friend Amber is dead and I'm grieving her loss, and while it's bad enough I'm stuck in this room," he glanced up at Simon as if to say 'and stuck here with you', "I'm too preoccupied by her death to dwell in idle gossip and speculation."

Simon placed his hands on his hips and stepped forward until he was nearly nose to nose with him. "Oh, it's more than speculation, doctor."

Heat surged Rupert's face and it turned red, his eyes narrowing into slits. "What the heck are you implying?" he demanded angrily.

"Oh, we'll find out soon enough when the police drag you and your brother away in handcuffs."

Rupert's hands clenched into fists, then he took a small step back from Simon. "Time will tell, Simon. Time will tell."

Simon sneered then went back to his girlfriend Stella, who appeared very uncomfortable by the entire macho blustering that her date was doing.

Kaylee looked at Sabrina and there was a brief exchange of something between them. I was curious about what they knew and weren't actually saying. "Do you know something about what's been happening between Simon and Rupert?"

Kaylee hesitated before answering. "No. It was Rupert's brother Anthony. He was being a complete jerk to Simon."

I leaned forward, intrigued. "What exactly were they arguing about?"

Kaylee shifted in her seat, her eyes darting nervously around the marquee. "It was something about a deal gone wrong. Anthony was accusing Simon of cheating him out of his share."

"And they weren't arguing about Amber? It was about a deal? Do you know what kind of deal they were talking about?"

She shook her head. "I have no idea. All I know is that Anthony was furious, and Rupert intervened to try to calm him down. But it wasn't working."

I tried to piece the information together. "Do you remember anything else?

Kaylee shrugged. "Not really. It was all just a lot of yelling and accusations."

I leaned back on the sofa, deep in thought.

Kaylee and Sabrina seemed relieved to have shared the information and the tension dissipated slightly. We sat in silence for a few moments, each lost in our own thoughts.

Just then, Officer Bundock, who had been briefly on her phone, tucked it away and stepped into the center of the room, holding a hand in the air. "Ladies and gentlemen, your attention please." There were a few disagreeable comments from some of the people, but quickly everyone became quiet. "I've been instructed to divide you into two groups to ensure a smooth interview process. Would the following people please step forward." She read from some notes she had made while on the call. "Amoy Johnson and Mark Kleinman. Lashawna and Richard White. Bernard and Celia Lazenby. Henry Grant and Benjamin Pearce. Helene and Max Gauthier. Melissa Maxwell, Carrie Abrams, Fiona Gibson."

Each of the thirteen people stood beside the officer when their name was called, each one remaining apart from each other. Some had their arms folded defensively, giving the impression of wanting to avoid any physical contact with any member of their group. "Okay, please follow me to the dining room."

I was relieved that I wasn't in the same group as Melissa, but I was stuck with Rupert Boyden. We watched them leave, and Fiona, who we all knew better as Amber's friend Fee, was the last in the group and turned to look at those of us left in the living room. She wiped her eyes with the back of her hand and slowly trudged from the room to catch up with the others.

All of a sudden, Harry leaned forward from where he was sitting on one of the sofas and fell forward onto his knees, grasping for the edge of the coffee table.

I rushed over to him, trying to help him sit up. "Harry, are you okay? I asked. Rupert was immediately by my side assessing Harry's condition.

Harry groaned and clutched his chest, looking quite pale and sweaty. "I don't know," he groaned. "It feels like my heart is about to give up on me."

Suzie appeared beside us, having heard the commotion from the kitchen. "Harry," she cried, bolting to his side. "What's happened?"

She looked at me and then Rupert for an explanation. "What's happened? You're a doctor. Should we get the paramedics?" she asked.

"Definitely," replied Rupert. "They can check his vitals, establish a baseline of what's going on. His pulse is rapid though, and his skin is moist with perspiration."

"Hank, go find Officer Bundock," directed Suzie. "She can call Trip, perhaps see if any medical personnel are still here?"

"Right-o," he said and hurried off to find the officer.

"I'm okay," said Harry, trying to get up. "I just had a little turn, that's all. Get me a drink of iced water. That'll help."

"I'll go," said Kaylee.

"It's down the hall on the left," said Suzie.

"I'll be as quick as I can," Kaylee called back as she headed off down the hall in search of the kitchen.

Suzie tried to make Harry stay sitting, but he brushed her gently aside. "Suzie, I'm going to be fine, especially if I can get up."

Harry didn't look fine to me. What if something serious happened to him? All of us were already on edge and his collapse could only make things worse.

Kaylee burst back into the room clutching a glass of water and handed it to Suzie, who lowered it to Harry's lips. "Drink this slowly, honey," her voice steady and reassuring.

Harry slowly took a sip of water and closed his eyes. "Thank you," he whispered, his breathing finally starting to calm down. "I think I just need some rest."

Suzie looked at me with concern.

I gave a reassuring smile that I wasn't actually feeling, but thankfully Hank returned with Officer Bundock, plus Sergeant Brodie and Detective Whitney right behind them.

As they entered the room, the tension seemed to double. They looked serious and focused as they made their way to us to check on Harry.

"Trip," said Suzie, both of us standing up to meet her friend. "You need to send for an ambulance. Harry's had a turn. I want him checked out."

"Hey Harry, how're you feeling," asked Trip, crouching down to look at Harry.

"Doing better now that I've had a drink of water. Sorry to scare everyone."

"We've notified the paramedics. They'll be here any moment to at least check you out. You'd do the same if it was Suzie, wouldn't you?"

Harry sighed. "Yeah, you're right."

Trip stood and addressed everyone in the room. "Ladies and gentlemen, we're going to continue the interview process in this room next. It's going to be a long night, but we want to thank you for your patience, and your cooperation."

He turned to Officer Bundock. "I'll need you to escort the guests to the piano room where we're conducting the interviews." Then he looked around the room and called out the first name. "Anthony Boyden. We will talk with you first. Please follow Officer Bundock to the piano room."

Anthony stood up, hesitantly at first. Then he tilted his chin up slightly and sauntered over to Officer Bundock. But first, he leaned over to Kaylee as he passed her and whispered something, causing her to stare at him with wide eyes. Then he followed Officer Bundock from the room.

I looked at those of us who remained. There was Kaylee and Sabrina, Rupert, and Simon and Stella. And of course Harry and Suzie and myself. Hank would stay with us as protection for Suzie and Harry, while Cindy and Jerry continued to patrol the house to ensure it remained tightly locked up.

Then it dawned on me.

Where were Liz and JT?

Chapter Twenty-Seven

I didn't know if I should say anything to Sergeant Brodie or not. For all I knew, Liz and JT had been interviewed and allowed to leave. Just then, two paramedics, one male and one female, strode into the room and immediately headed over to Harry, given that he was the only person that people were making a fuss over. Their presence was welcome, and I felt a wave of relief wash over me. He was getting help and I could only hope that he was going to be okay. Suzie held his hand while his vital signs were checked.

I went over and sat with Kaylee and Sabrina again. I wanted to know what Anthony had said to Kaylee that had upset her so much.

Sabrina smiled and welcomed me to sit beside them. "I wonder which one of us will be next. I'm wracking my brain, but I don't know what I can add. I was too focused on the concert, and enjoying the food, if I'm honest. I didn't notice that Amber was missing."

"Me too," added Kaylee. "I wasn't really paying attention to other people. I was having too much fun. I actually don't know what's relevant to the investigation and what's not. Also, I'm worried in case the sergeant and the other officers jump to conclusions."

"What do you mean?" I asked, my tone laced with genuine concern. "Is everything all right?"

She adjusted how she was sitting on the sofa, looking visibly distressed. "It's a constant battle for me to be clean and sober. Sabrina and I work damn hard every day to keep our lives on track." She looked straight at me. "Do you have any idea what it's been like?"

"Has something happened? Is it because of what Anthony said to you just now."

She nodded and hung her head, before taking a deep steadying breath and looking directly at me. "It was Amber," she said, keeping her voice low. "She tried to ruin everything, for me."

"How? What did she do?"

She gave a deep sigh. "I have a son, Liam. He's eight now. He's been living with my parents. They won the right to be his guardians. Now I've been doing my best to prove that I'm trustworthy."

"So that you can have custody of your son permanently?"

She nodded. "But Amber has been threatening me."

I couldn't believe what I was hearing. However, with the way this evening's events were continuing to unfold, the thought of someone being capable of blackmail didn't seem too far-fetched. Nor was it far-fetched to consider it a motive for killing Amber. But could Kaylee be capable of such an act?

"Oh my gosh. Anthony knows, is that it?"

"Oh, yes. He made sure to let me know that."

"And now that Amber is dead, you're worried that he may tell the police and lead them to think that you had something to do with Amber's death?"

She nodded slowly, tears welling up in her eyes. "I didn't want anyone to know. I was ashamed you see, of what I'd done in the past. Losing custody of Liam was actually what drove me to get clean." She leaned back against the sofa, looking in the direction of the hallway where Anthony had walked through with Officer Bundock. "I just want to be a part of my son's life. And now this has happened."

"What was Amber threatening to do? Was she demanding anything?"

"Oh, you bet. The bitch was threatening to say some pretty damaging things about me that could ruin my chances of ever being allowed to see my son again. If that happened, I don't know what I would do."

I tried to process what I'd just heard. Now that Amber was dead, Kaylee had no need to be fearful of losing her son permanently. "But why did Amber want to do this awful thing?"

"She was intimidating Sabrina and me and was effectively holding us to ransom because she wanted us to close our rehab centers. She saw us as some kind of threat to her own expansion of her charity work. With us out of the way, she could move into the rehab space, be seen as some kind of savior of people, not only through the work that her organization currently undertakes."

"I'm beginning to see now. That's what Sabrina and you meant earlier when Suzie and I were talking with both of you in the marquee. You called Amber 'Mother Theresa'.

"Yup. Our nickname for her. Although what we usually called her was 'the devil incarnate'."

"And somehow Anthony found out. Do you think he's telling the police this information?"

"Probably. It's just the sort of devious revengeful thing he would do."

"Devious, I can understand, but revenge? Why revenge?"

"Isn't it obvious? He had a thing for Amber too. But Sabrina and I think she was only stringing Anthony along."

"Why?"

"Fun? Her ego must have really enjoyed having a little puppy dog drooling after her. And Anthony really knew how to drool after her."

I caught movement at the corner of my eye. The female paramedic was talking with Suzie, while her partner was returning items to their equipment bag. Harry was getting up and smiling. My shoulders relaxed. I hadn't realized how tense I was.

The paramedics left the house and Suzie gave Harry a peck on the cheek. Then with a flick of her head indicated that they should join Sabrina, Kaylee, and myself on the sofa.

We all scooted over to one side and Suzie squeezed in next to me, Harry sitting opposite us in a padded wicker rocking chair that I surmised was his favorite chair, noting the ease at which he settled back into it.

"Phew," said Suzie, settling in beside me. She looked from me to Kaylee, then Sabrina and back to me, clearly reading our faces and sensing something was up.

Then before she could start asking questions, we heard a high-pitched scream. It was Stella. Simon was trying in vain to hold her to him, but she wasn't having any of that. She was shrieking at what I surmised was the top of her lungs and pointing to the direction of the entrance hall. I followed her gaze and immediately saw what she was frightened of.

It was Liz. She was covered in blood and as she staggered into the room, her knees buckled and she collapsed in a heap, her face twisted in pain. Her sandals dragged in pieces of shells from the path and sand from the beach. Her pedicure was severely distressed and her feet were dusty, and even her bag with its pretty gold chain hung loosely across her body and was dusty with detritus from the ground.

Stella's screams only added to the chaos of the moment. We all rushed over to help Liz, but it was Rupert and I who reached her first and helped her to sit on the wooden floor, her back against the wall, my ever practical self keeping her away from the soft furnishings. There was blood on her dress and on her hands and knees. The blood looked dark, almost black in the electric light and smears transferred onto my hands and arms.

"How is she?" I asked Rupert, trying to keep my voice calm and steady despite the rising panic in my chest. I saw that she appeared to have lacerations on her arms and legs, and I couldn't be sure if it was hers or someone else's.

Rupert, his medical skills kicking in, began assessing the extent of her injuries. He leaned back. "You're one lucky woman," he said soothingly, addressing Liz. "Superficial injuries and shock are my initial diagnosis," he said, leaning so close to me I could feel his breath brush my ear. "Someone go and bring the paramedics back."

"On it," called out Sabrina.

Liz sagged against the wall. She reached for my hands and found them, holding them shakily.

"What happened Liz?" I asked.

She took a steadying breath, wincing as she did so. "I'm not sure," she said, her voice barely above a whisper. "Someone attacked me."

Suzie came over and crouched down beside me. "Who attacked you Liz?" she asked, her eyes wide with concern.

"I don't know," Liz replied, her face flushed. "I was with JT down on the cliff walk. It was getting dark, so we were going to turn back, when someone came up behind me and pushed me, hard. When I woke up, it was dark, so I headed here. I followed the lights. They acted like a beacon guiding me here."

I tried to process what she was saying. Who would want to hurt her? And why? "Where's JT," I asked.

Liz looked around the room. "Isn't he here?"

The paramedics who moments earlier had been attending to Harry hurried back into the house and over to our side. Rupert and I took a step back to give them room as they began evaluating Liz, checking the sources of her bleeding.

Right on cue, Trip and Detective Whitney rushed into the living room, followed by Officer Bundock and a much younger uniformed officer.

"We heard the commotion. What's going on?" Trip began. They saw for themselves almost as soon as they came into the room. Trip came over to me.

"Liz's friend JT is missing," I explained. "We need to send out a search party for him." Then another thought crossed my mind. Perhaps Anthony had hurt Liz before he came to the house with the rest of us. Or had he harmed Ginger? After all, he was the last person to come into the house, and after the fracas with Simon I wasn't sure how much I trusted Anthony to remain calm under any situation.

"Nate, I want you to coordinate a search for the man JT. Get a description from the guests and from Liz. They were on the cliff walk so start there and fan out."

Nate moved over to Kaylee and Sabrina and began asking them if they could provide a description of what JT was wearing. Henry Grant and his friend Benjamin Pearce also added some helpful descriptions of what they remembered of JT. Nate left the house shortly after talking to them, issuing orders through his phone to a colleague.

The group of guests who had been taken to wait in the dining room must have heard the commotion because they now re-appeared in the living room, all of them choosing to observe from the periphery.

One of the paramedics came up to Trip. "We've checked her out. Superficial injuries only. She's suffering from shock, mostly."

That was good to hear. Liz was being helped off the floor by Kaylee and Sabrina and onto the sofa to sit.

The paramedics had no sooner squeezed their way out of the room when Bernard pushed his way forward until he was only a couple of feet away from Trip. "What are you lot doing to protect us," he demanded, his voice booming so loudly that I was sure that he could be heard all the way over to the pool house. "How many more people need to die or be maimed before you finally let us go."

I saw Trip's back and shoulders tense with each of Bernard's persistent demands.

Bernard now turned to the other guests and tried to rally them into supporting his cause of demanding action and to be allowed to leave. Murmurs rose up from the assembled crowd that moved like a restless living mass as Bernard stepped forward once again.

"You can't keep us locked up here. It's obvious. None of us were involved in Liz's attack." He was now in an especially determined mood and was getting himself more and more riled up. "We were all here. We are each other's alibi!"

Trip was a few inches taller than Bernard, and he was neither provoked nor intimidated by the man's brashness, instead remaining the competent professional that he was. He stood his ground and seemed to draw himself up even taller. "Right now we don't know when this woman was attacked. Without an accurate timeline it could have been before anyone entered this house."

This was uttered firmly with no room for discussion or argument. There was a brief pause where I swear that time itself stood still before there was a collective sigh and the crowd dispersed themselves to other parts of the room and the dining room. Right now, I don't think anyone was wanting to stray too far lest they fall afoul to whoever was doing the attacking.

I was on sensory overload. Between Bernard's shouting and odor from the blood and the color of the blood on my hands I swayed and felt cold beads of perspiration over my body. In one swift movement Trip caught my left elbow with one firm hand and placed his right hand behind my back for support.

"Deep breath," he instructed. "Let's sit you down on this chair over here and bend forward, that's it, as far as you can go. Take deep breaths."

It only took a few breaths until I felt more like my regular self. Then I looked down at my hands. They were sticky with blood and staring at them seemed to activate all my senses again and I became acutely aware of the metallic odor emanating from the blood. I retched and held my arms out, not sure what to do, how to get rid of the blood on my hands. I realized I was shaking yet couldn't stop.

"Wait here," he ordered.

He didn't know that at that moment I couldn't move. I was fixated on the blood and how the evening was sliding into mayhem. There was a murderer here and they were hellbent on having another victim. With JT missing, perhaps they already had.

Chapter Twenty-Eight

Sergeant Brodie reappeared by my side moments later with a glass of water and a wet towel. "Here, take these. Do your best to wipe the blood off. You can get cleaned up properly in the bathroom next." He stepped away and had a conversation with two of the officers.

I quickly set to work, shakily using the wet towel like a washcloth to scrub away the worst of the blood. It was slow going, the blood already ingrained under my fingernails and the creases between my fingers. It was going to take a while to get the stains out properly. Why Liz, I wondered, and where was JT?

Everyone was now huddled in small groups, whispering amongst themselves. I could feel the tension growing again. Suzie was sitting on a sofa with Harry, who thankfully was looking much better, both of them talking quietly to each other with Hank standing protectively near Suzie. Sergeant Brodie returned by my side, his face uncharacteristically grim. "You're having quite the time of it. First you find not one, but two bodies and now you're covered in someone else's blood."

I looked down and saw red staining on my hands from the blood. The blood I'd wiped off using the wet towel was heavy with the smell of iron and copper. I looked up at Trip.

"You've had quite the shock," he continued. "I reckon it's all beginning to catch up with you."

"I reckon you're right. And this," I held up my blood-stained hands, "brings it all back. We're dealing with a cold-blooded murderer and the thought of more violence scares me."

"That's understandable, but you're actually safe here. I've still got officers guarding the perimeter, jetty, and the entrance to the property."

"What about the garages and other buildings?"

"Yes. those too. We checked them and they were empty, and no-one has tried to enter them, especially, I think, as the buildings are being closely watched."

I was thoughtful while I processed what he was telling me. I leaned in closely to him so that I could keep my voice as low as possible. "You know what you're telling me, don't you?"

His eyes met mine and searched my face. I hoped I wasn't displaying the fear that I was feeling. "Unless someone is hiding in the dark outside," I began, "then the murderer is here in this house."

He continued to look at me, his gaze never straying from mine. "I'm afraid that's exactly what I'm saying."

I sighed heavily. "Thank you for not trying to placate me. And just so you know, I'm not about to engage in a pity party. Not now, not ever."

"Glad to hear it."

"I think I can help."

He narrowed his eyes as he looked at me. "You've found something?"

"I'm not sure. Like any investigation on a dig, it's often not until we've got all the pieces laid out before us that we can understand what happened to the people who lived hundreds of years ago, or what sort of society they lived in."

"And?"

"Well, Suzie and I have been chatting to quite a few of the guests. And it turns out that Amber had made enemies with some of them by going out of her way to stir up trouble. In fact, quite a few seemed to despise her." I paused and glanced away nervously, aware that I could be making a huge mistake by trusting Kaylee, and choosing in that moment to not reveal her name or the circumstances around her warranted dislike of Amber.

He raised his eyebrows. "Hmm. Unfortunately, having a motive isn't usually enough for us to arrest someone, no matter how powerful it is. Lots of people dislike other people but they don't go around killing them." He pursed his lips to one side. "You have to understand that I've got to be able to prove that someone had the opportunity and the means by which to kill either Amber and/or Ginger. Otherwise we'd spend all our time chasing everyone who had a dispute with someone else. And that's precious time that we don't have."

"Do you think there could be more than one murderer?"

"It's possible. We can't rule that out," he replied, all matter-of-fact again.

"Crap. That's all we need." I glanced quickly around the room. "So if there's the possibility that there's more than one murderer, do you think the two deaths are connected?"

He shrugged. "It's possible. But it's too early to say. I'm not sharing with you anything that you don't already know. As you will no doubt realize, forensics will tell us more but that will take time. I need the team working on Ginger's scene to give us some general information that may indicate a direct link to Amber's death."

"There was the same foaming around Ginger's mouth that was on Amber's."

"I know it looked the same. I can't speculate on that though." He paused. "You would do the same in your line of work, wouldn't you?

I thought about that briefly. "You're absolutely right. Speculation may steer me in a specific direction, but I wouldn't be swayed by it. I'd continue digging and searching for some other clue so that when I lined everything up, I'd have a complete, or near complete picture of what had happened in the past."

"But archaeology is different from what I do."

"Agreed, But I don't just do this for a living. It's a passion. In fact, one I've had for a couple of decades. And figuring out what happened in the past is actually something that I'm highly skilled at Trip."

"That's how I work too. Without knowing more about each victim, who they associated with, had pissed-off, that sort of thing then it's an uphill slog to find the person, or persons I'm searching for." He leaned back and rolled his shoulders. "So, to put it in a nutshell, right now we need to know more about each person so that we can put together a timeline of who was where, who they were with, and why."

"And you're asking me to share what Suzie and I have found out?" I wasn't sure about how much I should share without getting someone in trouble. "You said that in addition to a person having a reason to commit the crime, they would also have to have the means and the opportunity in order to potentially be guilty, correct?"

He held my gaze and gave a curt nod.

"There was one person who arrived at Suzie's house later than we all did," I said in an almost conspiratorial whisper. "And he had dust on his clothes too."

"And you know who this person was?"

I swallowed hard before answering. "Anthony."

He stayed silent for a moment, but I could feel tension rising between us. "You're sure?"

His breathing remained calm and steady which was the opposite of mine as I rambled on about how Anthony appeared and acted when he rejoined our group in the living room.

My voice lowered to a hoarse whisper as I posed my next question. "So, what happens now?"

Trip's face was solemn as he listened to my account. Finally he spoke, his voice serious. "We will continue talking to him, but while this is helpful we can't jump to conclusions. I'll need to gather more information on where he might have been and why he wasn't with everyone as you all left the marquee."

I felt a sense of relief wash over me. I'd done my part, and now it was up to the police to take over. Although, one thing bothered me. If Anthony did kill Ginger, he couldn't have killed Amber, because I saw him before the start of Suzie's concert and again when he left to go to the bar for another drink. I didn't see how he could have killed Amber too. Which meant there was another person who was involved.

"Should I do anything else now?"

Trip thought for a moment. "Keep your eyes and ears open for anything suspicious, but don't, and I mean do not, under any circumstances confront anyone with your suspicions. Come directly to me."

I felt his steady gaze bore into me. "I will. Where will I find you?"

"I'm heading back to where Nate is interviewing Anthony. And remember what I told you, no going off and being a heroine."

I watched him as he left the room and then leaned back heavily in the chair. Despite what I told Trip, I had to keep my guard up and gather more information to ensure that I cleared Gabby and prevented anyone else from being killed. I made two fists and stared dismally at my hands that were still stained with splodges of dried blood. I couldn't bear having this on my skin any longer. I quickly made my way to the guest bathroom, however, getting rid of blood is by no means easy, as I found out. It was ingrained beneath my fingernails and in-between my fingers, and I noticed with a sense of detachment that each of my hands were beginning to have wrinkles.

I filled the sink and immersed my hands to soften the grime, the metallic odor wafting up once again. I kept my eyes averted as the water quickly changed color to a reddish brown. Then I refilled the sink and scrubbed my hands in fresh warm water using liquid soap from the dark brown bottle on the sink to remove every visible trace of the offending blood. The scent from the soap was actually cleansing physically as well as mentally, as the odor of blood was finally replaced with the fragrant scent of, according to the description on the bottle, rose and pachouli.

Refreshed, I went back to the living room with a purpose; Rupert was chatting with Simon and a more composed Stella beside the window, Kaylee and Sabrina were sitting either side of Liz on one of the sofas, and I spied Suzie sitting with Harry on a loveseat. Suzie caught my eye and with a subtle flick of her eyes indicated for me to join them. I immediately hurried over and drew an armchair closer.

"We need to talk," Suzie said, keeping her voice low and barely giving me time to sit. "I just found out something."

"Go on."

"I met Helene Gauthier in the hallway earlier when you were talking with Trip," she continued, glancing around the room in case anyone was paying us undue attention. "She said Ginger told her she knew who murdered Amber."

"What!" I hadn't expected that. "Did she say who this person was?"

She shook her head.

I let out a frustrated sigh. Oh how I wish she'd mentioned a name. "Did she at least give a clue?"

"Not really. Only that if she hadn't seen who it was with her own eyes, she wouldn't have believed it."

"Really?" I said, thinking of possible scenarios. "Why did she tell you that? Shouldn't she have gone to the police?"

"She said she wanted a second opinion. That she wasn't sure what to do and didn't want to get Ginger in trouble."

"Trouble? Why would Ginger get in trouble?"

"Helene said she initially thought Ginger was exaggerating and was looking for attention, especially as her Ginglab business needed another round of funding in order to bring the drug they've been developing to market."

I nodded slowly, understanding Helene's hesitation. "Well, it's a bit late now, given that Ginger may have been killed because of what she knew."

"But that's not all," continued Suzie, leaning in closer. "I did my own digging around, being the consummate host after all, and according to at least three people, Rupert's brother Anthony has apparently got a history of aggression."

"We saw that in action. Anthony's currently 'helping the police with their enquiries,' so perhaps they've already heard something. Plus, I have my own suspicions of him." I shared with Suzie and Harry what I'd told Trip.

Suzie leaned back. "Oh, but this is awful. I feel sorry for Rupert. To think his brother could be capable of murder."

"Yes, but I distinctly saw Anthony before and during your concert. Perhaps Helene saw someone who resembled Anthony. Or perhaps she saw someone else entirely?"

"Perhaps, honey. But this could be a crucial piece of information. We should go and let Trip know what Helene told me. Let him decide what to do about it."

"I agree Suzie, yet at the same time I don't think Anthony was able to murder Amber. I don't believe he was near the pool house when she was killed. But I can't explain why he was late in joining the rest of us at your house after Ginger's body was discovered. After all, it was only soon after that, that we found out that Liz and JT had been attacked." I shook my head. "But then again, I don't think we can rule out the possibility of there being two people who have been doing the killings."

"Two?"

I nodded. "It stands to reason. If Anthony wasn't near the pool house, then someone else killed Amber. Yet," I mused aloud, "both Amber and Ginger were poisoned, most likely with the same toxin creating the frothing around the mouth."

Harry leaned in and patted Suzie's thigh. "I told you she was smart at figuring details out."

"But we need a plan of action," I continued. "So far, I feel we've been running in circles chasing our tails, and I can't bear the thought of there being one or more murderers in your own house."

"Good idea hon, but we need to be careful. We can't afford to make any mistakes and I sure as heck don't want anyone else gettin' hurt."

"We need to be pro-active though. And if Anthony returns here to the living room after he's given his information to the police, we will need to keep a discreet eye on him. We can't alert him, or anyone else for that matter, to our suspicions."

"Agreed. Harry, you can keep a watch out for Anthony."

"Oh, yes. I sure can Sooz."

"Tell you what," I said, "I'll start with talking to Liz, see if she can remember anything else that might lead us to figuring out who was where, and who else besides Anthony and the mysterious person that Ginger saw might have a motive and the opportunity for harming one or both women."

"Okay, I'll wait here until you're done talking with Liz, and then we can both go to see Trip and let him know about what Helene told me."

"Actually, I think it would be prudent for the three of us to not tell anyone what Helene said."

"Crikey!" said Harry. "You're right. Whoever this person is, or persons, they didn't plan on someone seeing them kill Amber and I dread to think what they will do if they find out that Ginger spoke to Helene." He held Suzie's hand firmly. "And that Helen spoke to you Sooz."

I was worried too for our safety, but especially Suzie's and hoped that I was successfully hiding what I was feeling. I got up and made my way over to where Liz was sitting with a bandage around her head, flanked on the sofa by Kaylee and Sabrina. "Hey, Liz. How are you holding up?"

She smiled weakly at me. "Feeling fortunate. Although my head still hurts like you wouldn't believe."

"I can only imagine," I said sympathetically.

Kaylee stood up and indicated to Sabrina to do the same. "We'll let you chat. I want to see how Stella's doing, and Simon too I guess." She turned to Liz, and placed a hand on her shoulder. "Take it easy. You're safe here, and I'm sure the police are close to finding the bastard that's responsible."

Once they moved away to join Stella and Simon, I turned my attention back to Liz. "I'm sorry this happened to you Liz. Do you remember much of what happened to you and JT?"

Liz furrowed her brow in thought. "Not really. It all happened so fast."

"Did you see or hear anything before you were attacked?"

"No. Nothing. Why?"

I took a deep breath. "We need your help. We're trying to figure out which person, or persons, might have a motive for harming Amber and Ginger, and now you and JT."

Liz's eyes widened. "You think there's more than one person involved?"

"It's too early to know for sure, but we can't rule it out. Can you think of anything that might help us figure out who was where and who had a motive?"

She closed her eyes for a moment, deep in thought, before turning to look at me. "I don't know if it's relevant, but I remember feeling like someone was watching us."

I could feel the weight of her words, and I gave an involuntary shudder. "Did you actually see anyone?"

She shook her head slowly. "It was getting dark, and I didn't want to stay outside any longer. I wanted to rejoin everyone." She grabbed my hand. "We have to find out who's doing this. Make them pay for what they've done." Her eyes narrowed, then she closed her eyes and leaned her head back against the back of the sofa.

"I'll let you rest now."

"Okay, let me know what you find out," she said, reaching down and removing her scuffed sandals and stuffing them into her copious handbag. "My feet are weary too," she said with a thin smile.

"Oh, I see you like Miss Dior perfume?" nodding at the pretty pink bottle in her bag.

"Yes. I've worn it for years."

"I like Chanel No 5, myself. I'll let you rest."

Everyone is on edge, I thought, as I rejoined Kaylee and Sabrina who were chatting quietly with Simon, Stella, and of course Rupert.

"How is she?" Stella asked, referring to Liz.

"She's holding up, but she has a headache, and she is still shaken up," I replied, taking a seat next to Simon.

"Not surprising," said Simon. "Do you think she remembers anything?"

"Not really. She felt she was being watched but didn't see anyone."

Simon rubbed his chin thoughtfully. "Perhaps she's right. Perhaps there was someone lurking around the property. Maybe there still is?"

Stella touched Simon's arm lightly. "That's what I'm afraid of, Si. That there is someone still out there. Someone we haven't seen yet."

"Don't worry Stella," he said, patting her hand. "I'll make sure you're okay."

"We can't let our guard down Si. Not even for a second."

I was lost in my thoughts, all manner of possibilities and questions running through my mind. How did the murderer escape detection in both murders? What was the poison they used? How did they bring it into the event? I felt like I was missing something vital to the investigation. I needed a break, to be away from people for a while.

I excused myself from the group and headed over to the sliding doors that open out onto the patio overlooking the ocean. There were a couple of comfortable looking armchairs tucked in a nook beside the sliders and plopped myself wearily into the nearest one. I hoped that sitting down might help me piece together the bits of information that I'd gathered yet may have overlooked during the evening so far.

What I knew so far was the police were systematically interviewing the guests, the scene of crime personnel had taken samples of the foam from around the bodies to establish the type of poison used, as well as photographs of the scene surrounding both bodies, and anything else they deemed suspicious or relevant or worthy of investigating further. I'm sure they would literally leave no stone unturned in their pursuit of answers that would help them solve both crimes. So far though, it appeared that the police were struggling to move forward with finding evidence linking them directly to the person, or persons, responsible. This meant that either the murderer was very careful and had disposed of any evidence efficiently or they were someone who was not associated with our group. But if it was someone from outside, who was it, and how did they get on the property?

My musings were interrupted when I saw the reflection of another person approaching me. I didn't need to turn around, I could see who it was. Rupert Boyden. And I could feel his piercing gaze on me as he walked towards me.

He stopped and hesitated like he wasn't sure I wanted him there. "I'm sorry to bother you," he eventually said. "Do you mind if I sit down?"

I shook my head. "Please. It's okay." Why on earth did I say that? I should shun him, keep myself apart from him, and protect myself. He was the perfect embodiment of everything in my childhood, outside of my messed-up homelife, that strived to make me feel scared and small. Why was I inviting him into my space?

I waited until he was settled, curious as to why he had come over to me.

His expression softened as he continued to talk again. "I hope you know I meant every word of what I said out on the lawn earlier. I'm truly sorry for all the things I said to you when we were children."

I looked at him. He meant what he was saying. I had been taken aback when he approached me earlier today, and to be honest I thought it had simply been the alcohol that was making him apologize. But now I wasn't so sure.

His voice dropped to a whisper. "After everything I did to hurt you back then, all the pain I caused you, do you think you can forgive me?"

I looked at him. For a moment that seemed to drag on forever, unsure how to respond. How could I forgive someone who had caused me so much pain? Yet something about his sincerity made me want to finally believe him.

"It was wrong of me and there's no excuse for it." He held my gaze, imploring me to answer him. "The past can stay in the past," he stopped and took a deep breath, "but we don't have to. We can put it behind us and move ahead, with friendship, if you'll let me."

Chapter Twenty-Nine

I was stunned. Rupert was offering me friendship, and possibly something more. Was this really happening? I took a moment to gather my thoughts before answering.

"I appreciate your apology Rupert, and I do believe that people can change," I said cautiously, "but it might take some time for me to fully trust you."

He looked down at his hands, nodding. "I understand that. But I just want to make it right, Marnie." He looked at me directly now. "I've strived over the years to be a better person than I was back then, and I'm willing to prove myself to you," he replied with a hint of determination in his voice.

I took a deep steadying breath. Forgiveness was not something that came easy, especially not for something as traumatic as being bullied. But as I looked at Rupert, I saw a different person in front of me, compared to the one I remembered from many years ago. This man before me displayed a vulnerability and a sincerity that I don't recall seeing in anyone, and against my better judgment, I felt myself starting to soften towards him. Maybe it was the apology, or maybe the stress of tonight's situation, or maybe it was simply the fact that I wanted to believe in second chances.

"Okay," I said softly, surprising even myself. "But it's not going to be easy."

We sat in silence for a few moments before he spoke up again. "Marnie, can I be honest with you?"

"Of course," I said, feeling a little nervous about what he was going to say next.

"I had feelings for you, back when we were in school," he confessed.

I was taken aback by his admission, but there was a nagging voice in my head urging me to be cautious. "I'm flattered, but right now I'm not sure I'm ready for that type of relationship," I said honestly.

"I understand."

I felt a glimmer of hope that maybe, just maybe, Rupert Boyden had truly changed.

Then I saw Suzie's reflection in the window. Perfect timing for me to get away from Rupert. "You'll need to excuse me," I told him, hurriedly. "I need to talk to Suzie about something."

"Later then."

"Sure." There wouldn't be any 'later' if I had anything to do with it though. I smiled briefly at Rupert and he smiled back, holding my gaze, his eyes never leaving mine until I turned and hurried after Suzie who had already left the room.

"Suzie. Hold up. Have you got a minute?"

"For you honey? Absolutely. Although I thought you'd be spending a bit more time with Rupert. He's quite the catch, by the way."

I remembered Celia telling me the same thing at the yacht club.

"Shh," I said softly, and lowered my voice. "We need to be mindful of our voices carrying. Anyone could eavesdrop on us."

"What's up? Do you think that someone is watching and listening to everything that we're doing."

I nodded.

"What do you propose, honey? I'm just so fired up I want to get this solved so we can send everyone home to their own sweet bed. Well, not the murderer or murderers obviously."

"Two things. First, what happened to the video surveillance footage that you have on your premises. Trip hasn't seen it yet, has he?"

She shook her head. "I forgot he asked for it. We can take a look at it first before we hand it over to him," she winked. "What else?"

"Helene. We should talk to her. Now's the perfect time to find out more about what Ginger told her."

"Ah, yes. Ok, let's go."

"Wait. I have an idea. Here's what I think we should do." Conscious of the potential for our voices to be overheard, I leaned in close and whispered.

"I love it. Let's do it."

I pulled out my phone and sent a quick text hoping that when Helene received it, she would understand and play along.

Chapter Thirty

We reached the dining room from the hall. It had no door, but was instead a large open space facing the kitchen. We could see everyone sprawled throughout, sitting in small groups where they'd dragged the dining chairs from their place around the table. Bernard was sitting with Celia, Fee, Max Gauthier, Henry Grant and Benjamin Pearce, and Melissa and her friend Carrie Abrams. Huddled in the opposite corner were Amoy and Mark, Lashawna and Richard, and Helene Gauthier.

We entered the dining room, Suzie by my side, and walked over to Helene, everyone in the room pausing to watch us. "Helene," said Suzie in a reverent voice. "I'd love to chat with you about that special family recipe you promised to share with Marnie and me."

"Of course, *ma cherie*. It has to be for you and Marnie's eyes and ears only, though. It is a secret recipe after all."

"Well, I sure do love family recipes. Heck, I think we can even do a swap, if you're interested."

Helene stood up tall and followed us without a backwards glance to the rest of the room. Her son Max watched us with a curious look on his face. If he suspected anything, hopefully he was savvy enough to know that his mother was helping Suzie and me and he wouldn't give anything away to the other guests.

Suzie led us out of the dining room and into a butler's pantry adjoining the kitchen. From there, we went into a side room decorated with dark red walls and an informal bar with high-backed wooden stools in front of a granite counter. The walls of this intimate space were filled with plaques and disks commemorating the many awards Suzie had earned during the course of her lengthy career.

"Have a seat, Helene. You too Marnie," said Suzie. Suzie leaned her elbows on the counter in front of us, and spoke directly to Helene. "Thanks for acting so well."

"No problem, When the text arrived I understood and to be honest I'm happy to be away from those people. Any one of them, apart from my Max, of course, could be a murderer."

"And how was your interview with the police? Why did they not let you leave here."

"Oh, they said I could leave, but I wanted to stay with my son Max. I would be frantic with worry if I wasn't here to keep an eye out for him."

"Ah, I see," Said Suzie. "Now, I shared with my friend Marnie what you told me earlier, Helene. You know," she lowered her voice and looked back toward the butler's pantry in case someone was there and might overhear, "about what Ginger told you."

Heene nodded. "Ginger was convinced that she knew who the murderer was."

"And it's more than likely that she was killed because of it."

"Helene," I said, "we are trying to figure out a timeline of when we last saw Ginger alive, as well as people she spoke with. What can you tell us about anyone she was keen to talk with."

"Nothing really. She mentioned she was angry with a few guests. Some had made promises to help her company with the new round of funding," she shrugged, "and I don't know for sure, but I believe some were trying to renege on their decision to be an investor."

That reminded me of something. "Someone told us earlier this evening that Anthony Boyden was fighting with Simon Stadler over a deal that went wrong. Do you know anything about that?"

Helene gave a wry laugh, her wrists jangling with her silvery bangles. "Simon Stadler is a shrewd man, but he's not one to be trusted."

"Is that who I saw you looking at in the marquee earlier? You didn't exactly look pleased to see whoever you were staring at."

She nodded. "I have done a good job at staying out of his way, and thankfully we are not in the same room together."

"Why? What has he done?"

"The man is not dependable. He is only looking out for himself. My Max is going to be a famous chef. He is going to have his own cooking show on television, you know. And this man is attempting to sabotage him."

I looked at Suzie. She was as confused as I was. What was the connection between the two men? "I'm sorry, I'm not following you Helene. What has Simon done to upset you and your son?"

"Max has plans, big plans. He is going to have a chain of restaurants throughout New England. And that's just the beginning. Once his cooking show on TV is aired, people will travel from all over the country to taste for themselves the gastronomic delights that none other than Max Gauthier can produce."

"And Simon is somehow involved in this?"

"*Mais oui,* he is supposed to be building the restaurants. Max and I have paid the man a great deal of money, and what do we have to show for it? *Rien*! Nothing!"

Now that we had uncovered why Helene disliked Simon so much, it was hard to stop her from expressing how much disdain she had for the man.

"We paid Simon Stadler good money," she continued. "He has only excuses as to why the project is stalled and not progressing. I want to sue the man, but Max says doing so will only reflect badly on him himself. He said it will show that he makes poor business decisions. No, No, No, he does not want to have bad publicity. Max doesn't want to do anything that will jeopardize his career."

"So Simon took your son Max's money and is full of airy promises. I wouldn't be happy with the man either," I said. "It does explain why he has been seen around town with new and expensive toys. Like a new boat," I added, thinking back to what Celia and Lashawna knew of the man's spending habits.

"I'd like to talk a bit more about what Ginger told you," said Suzie. "Do you know for sure that she was going to talk to the person she believed was the murderer?"

Helene nodded slowly. "Sadly, I do. She didn't mention any names. Only that she was going to talk to this person. Oh, now I remember. She said she would be able to kill two birds with one stone." She looked at both of us. "Is that how you say it?"

We nodded.

"Good. We have a similar expression in French."

Suzie looked at me excitedly. "Helene, I was going to suggest you stay in the living room with Hank, my bodyguard, but given that there is no love lost between you and Simon, perhaps you'd best stay with the others in the dining room."

"Yes, I do not want to see that man. And I want to be near my son. I can trust him to protect me."

"I don't blame you honey. C'mon, let's get you back to the others."

"And Helene?" I said sincerely, "don't be alone. Stay with a group. There's safety in numbers."

We left Helene safely ensconced in the dining room seated next to her son Max at the dining table. I was glad that neither Bernard nor Melissa decided to ask us any questions.

"We need to tell Trip what we've found out," I said. "C'mon."

We headed to Suzie's piano room which was located halfway down the hallway on the left. We marched determinately up to the young officer standing guard outside the door. His nametag identified him as Officer Reynolds, and he looked to be in his early twenties, with a shock of dark hair, buzz cut at the sides. His eyes were dark brown, his skin swarthy and smooth over his cheekbones. A dark stubble was already forming around his lips and chin.

Suzie put her hands on her slim hips. "Tell Trip it's Suzie, and it's important. I need to see him at once."

"I'm sorry, Ms. Wilde," said the officer, shifting from one foot to the other while staring at her. "He said he wasn't to be disturbed. By anyone."

"Listen to me. This is my house and I'm doing your boss a huge favor by letting him turn my home into some damned interrogation center. Go in there, right now, and tell him that I have urgent information for him, or so help me, I will barge straight in there. Do I make myself clear?"

I wouldn't want to be the officer making the decision, but after a few seconds hesitation, clearly deciding whose wrath was going to be worse, he sidled up to the door, gingerly opened it, and stepped inside.

"Crikey, Suzie," I said in a whisper.

"What?" she said with a wry grin.

"You're fierce."

"In my industry, you have to be."

Right then, the door opened, and Trip stepped out into the hall alone. "Suzie. Marnie. How did I know it would be one or both of you? What's up?"

We both turned and looked behind us to ensure that no-one from the group in the dining room nor the living room could hear what we were saying. As succinctly as she could manage, Suzie went first, keeping her voice low and filling Trip in on what Ginger told Helene before she was killed. "Ginger also said that in addition to confronting the murderer, she was going to kill two birds with one stone. What do you think it meant, Trip?"

"To be honest Suzie. I haven't had time to process it. I'm hearing this for the first time, remember."

A memory of what someone said during the initial gathering in the marquee when we all first arrived, flashed into my mind. "I might know," I said. "Ginglab."

"Her company," asked Trip. "What about it?"

"She needed another round of funding. That's what she may have meant when she said about killing two birds."

"You're thinking of blackmail."

I nodded. "Without another wealthy investor, she wouldn't be able to bring her product to market."

"So now we need to make a list of everyone here who is wealthy enough to provide that chunk of money." He raised an eyebrow. "Can't be that many, right?"

Suzie sighed. "Actually, it's practically everyone. I can count on one hand who it's not."

She looked at me when she said it, and I was actually relieved that there was another potential vindication of my innocence. Even though by default I wasn't in the same financial league as many of the other invitees. And I'd no idea how I could ever change that scenario, but given that I had a successful career, my own home to return to, and good friends, well… I caught Trip's expression. His face was stoic, not giving anything away.

"Oh, and there's one other item, Trip," said Suzie. "The video surveillance footage from around the perimeter of my house."

"Yes. I was going to remind you of that. Can you bring me the data on a jump drive so that I can look at it?"

"Sure. I can do that. It's all on an app on Harry's and my phones, but I've got the ability to upload or transfer the data from a specific time period."

"Okay. Officer Reynolds, let me know when Suzie gets back with the footage."

"Yes sir."

Suzie turned to leave then paused. "Are you still interviewing Anthony?" she asked.

"Yes. And after him, we've still got a few more guests to talk to. I'll leave a word with Officer Reynolds to let you know when we're done."

Suzie gave him a hug and pecked him on the cheek. "See you in a bit, Trip."

We left Trip to resume talking with Anthony and I followed Suzie down the hall to the room at the end.

"This is my office," she said, opening the door and stepping inside.

Then I remembered. "Suzie. I need to check in on Gabby. See if there are any updates. They must know by now if she's going to be okay or if they've found something that concerns them."

"Sure. Go ahead, although they may not say much, especially as you're not a family member and she's got a fine police officer with her."

"I'll say I'm her sister. That should do the trick."

"Fingers crossed she's doin' okay darlin'. And don't feel rushed. I'll be on my computer."

On a whim I tried Gabby's phone, rather than call the hospital, but her phone just rang and rang. It was so frustrating trying to call someone who you know may need help, only to have no direct way of communicating with them. We're so used to just being able to talk to whomever we want, whenever. I first had to find the website for the hospital though, then scroll through it to find the central phone number. After a few minutes, I found what I was looking for and called the number, and it was professionally answered after three rings. I then asked for ER and was put through, but the phone rang, and rang, and rang. I was about to hang up when a male voice answered the phone. It was a nurse, I didn't catch his name, but I explained who I was and that I was enquiring after my sister, Gabby Martinez, who had sustained a head injury at the Suzie Wilde event."

"One moment," the voice on the other end of the line said. There was a muffled conversation on his end then he came back online. "I'm sorry, we can't give out any information at the moment as this is a police investigation. Please contact the officer in charge for updates." He hung up as I was about to ask him to tell Gabby I had called.

I felt so sad. Tears welled up in my eyes, but I blinked them away. It was hard to reconcile the fact that just a few hours ago, we were having a good time together, and now she was in hospital, with a murder accusation hanging over her.

I opened Suzie's office door. This was where some of her awards were displayed, on the wall as well as in glass - fronted cabinets.

Suzie glanced up at me and caught my eye. "Bad news?"

I took a deep breath and explained what the nurse had told me.

"Then grab a chair and pull it next to me and let's see if the video footage shows whoever killed Amber."

Chapter Thirty-One

Suzie quickly brought up the application on her computer and the video feed from her estate flashed up on the screen, from fifteen minutes before the concert started. "There's sound as well, but I doubt if we'll hear much because of the music playing."

"There has to be a clue in here somewhere," I said. I could see that there was video feed available from cameras placed around the estate, a map of their location flashing up on the screen, but right now we were only interested in the footage from the path to the pool house. She increased the scrolling feature to speed up the rate at which we could view the images as we tried to catch any suspicious movement.

For the first ten agonizing minutes there was no sign of anyone. No one. I hardly dared move in case I missed something, or someone, lurking just out of sight, ready to pounce on Amber and Gabby. We sat, hunkered down in front of the surveillance footage, scanning the images with laser focus for anything that would point us in the direction of the murderer.

And then suddenly, we saw it. A shadow moving in the corner of the frame. "Rewind, rewind," I said to Suzie, trying not to shout with excitement.

Suzie rewound the footage and pressed play again.

Sure enough, our patience was rewarded, as not one, but two people came into view. "Look, there. It's her," I pointed at the screen. Amber's silhouette was unmistakable; the flowing blonde hair against a cream-colored dress was her for sure. And she had an arm around a man's waist. After a brief conversation, she pecked him on the cheek and strolled toward the pool house path.

"Who's she with?" mused Suzie.

"I can't tell from his back." The man watched her until she disappeared from view then he turned around in the direction of the lawn, his fists clenched. His face was instantly visibly, and also unmistakable. "The quality of the recording is good, Suzie. That's Anthony Boyden. Rupert's brother."

He disappeared out of the camera view, and just then, another figure appeared near the path. They were keeping to the shadows and entered the path between two large rhododendrons, their face averted from the camera.

"Stop the video Suzie. Go back a couple of frames."

"Hold on a mo. I was just about to do that."

I held my breath while Suzie went back a minute and we rewatched Amber pecking Anthony on the cheek, and walking onto the path. Then we saw Anthony disappearing from the camera angle. Then the other person slid into view. "Stop it there!"

We both peered at the screen, tilting our heads and squinting. A person had indeed followed Amber, and they had stayed away from the entrance to the path, instead keeping close to the shadows on the left side.

"Damned if I can make out who that is," sighed Suzie. "Oh, this is so frustrating."

My heart sank. "I can't even tell if it's a man or a woman. The police may be able to enhance the images, make them clearer. Perhaps they can even do something to reduce the background noise."

"Yeah, but how long is that gonna take. Despite what Trip may think, we haven't got all night. People need to get home. We have to figure out who the murderer is, 'cos that person there is sure acting all suspicious."

"Let's keep watching. We might see the suspect leave." We settled down again. The minutes ticked by, and no one reappeared.

Then Gabby hurried onto the path towards the pool house, but it seemed like she was alone and unaware of anything untoward going on around her.

"What time is it when Gabby appears?"

"Let me see. 6:48. So that's twelve minutes before the start of my concert."

"If only I hadn't waited so long to go and find Gabby, I might have been able to stop whoever killed Amber."

Suzie shook her head vehemently, her blonde curls shaking. "Now don't you go all wistful on me. What's done is done. You can't change what's happened."

"I know. But to think that I was having a good time, while Amber was being killed and Gabby attacked."

We let the surveillance roll on until the footage arrived at 6:53. "Another person!" exclaimed Suzie and we peered at the screen as a busty silver-haired woman stepped hurriedly onto the path.

She stopped the recording.

"I recognize who that is!" I said excitedly. "It's Ginger Maloney. She must have seen the murderer after all."

Suzie resumed the video until 7:00, then she scrolled faster until another figure appeared on screen.

"That's me," I whispered as loudly as I dared. The footage shows 7:16."

We looked at each other in silence, realization hitting us that we had a strong timeline of when Amber was killed. Then Suzie began to make a copy of the footage from when the guests arrived and the police appeared on the property.

"I think it's unlikely that Anthony was the person who murdered Amber," said Suzie.

"I agree, but he could have murdered Ginger. Perhaps he saw her go in and thought she was the murderer. He's definitely shown us tonight what he's like with that short temper of his."

"So, he's still a prime suspect?"

"In one of the murders, yes. Amber was distant with Anthony in public, but in your video she gave the impression that she was offering him false hope. Either that or they were in a relationship and didn't want others to find out."

"Like his brother Rupert."

"Exactly. And that may also explain why Anthony was so angry tonight."

Suzie held up the thumb drive that she'd transferred the surveillance footage onto. "Let's go talk with Trip and trade what we've found for information on how Gabby's doing."

Still, I kept turning over all the possibilities, opportunities, and what-ifs as we hurried down the hallway to talk with Trip again and hand over the recording.

There wasn't any problem this time in getting to talk with Trip. He hurried out of the piano room, gently closing the door behind him.

"Here," said Suzie, handing him the thumb drive. "I know you guys will look at every minute of the footage, but Marnie and I can save you some time, related to when Amber disappeared."

He raised an eyebrow. "Oh? Go on."

"You tell him Marnie."

I outlined the facts of what we'd seen on the recording and at which point on the footage to start looking, just as I would if I was teaching a class of students. A sense of relief washed over me. At least I'd been able to contribute something to the investigation.

"Well, that's helpful Marnie," he said with a hint of a smile. "And you're right Suzie, we will look at all the footage," he said, holding up the thumb drive. "But what you've both found out will give us a jump start on where to focus the investigation, as well as giving us a clearer idea of the timeline."

Trip was all business as he spoke, and a flutter rose in my chest as I looked at him. There was something intense about his commitment to the case and the way his eyes narrowed when he focused.

He opened the door of his temporary office. "Thanks again," he said to us, giving us an appreciative smile. "We're nearly done here with this guest anyway."

Suzie and I exchanged a knowing glance before she cleared her throat. "Just a moment Trip. There's one more thing." She looked at me to take over.

"It's about my friend Gabby. She's the one that Detective Whitney was suspicious of. He sent an officer with her to the hospital."

"I remember what happened. And why."

"Well, she's innocent of anything you think she's done. What's on that thumb drive will prove it."

"Okay. We'll bear that in mind."

Dammit. I wasn't making myself clear. "It's just that, I was wondering if you could call the officer who's with her.

Find out if there is any news on Gabby's condition. I tried calling the hospital and they wouldn't tell me anything because they said she's involved in a police investigation."

I waited for his response.

He sighed deeply, and I could see exhaustion etched into his features. He looked from me, to Suzie, then back to me. "I'll make the call. But," he lowered his voice, "this doesn't necessarily mean that your friend is cleared of any wrongdoing. We need to check everything out. Plus there was a witness who saw her involved with the deceased."

I pressed my lips together, I didn't want to say or do anything that would compromise proving Gabby's innocence, but I was fuming inside at the damage that the so-called witness, Melissa Maxwell, had done with her lies. Was there no end to what the woman would stoop to? Instead I controlled my response. "Thanks for your help Trip," I replied, as professionally and calmly as I could muster. My heart sank. It wasn't fair that Gabby, who had done nothing wrong, was now lying in a hospital bed because she'd been in the wrong place at the wrong time. That, and damned Melissa Maxwell. I wasn't sure if I could control myself if I saw her again.

"Trip," said Suzie. "Do what you can, please."

I turned to leave and felt a hand on my arm. It was Trip, and he had a serious expression on his face. "I'll let you know as soon as I know anything."

I thanked him, but had the gnawing feeling that we were missing something crucial about the identity of the murderer. Crucial, yet also simple.

He returned to the piano room and the young, uniformed officer came out once again to stand guard, making eye contact with Suzie and giving her a big grin. He was clearly a fan.

Without missing a beat, Suzie gave him a warm smile. "How are you doing Officer Reynolds?"

"Fine ma'am. Glad to be helping out." He looked around the hall.

"Yes, you're doing a fine job."

"I was at your concert in Boston two months ago."

"I hope you enjoyed it."

His eyes widened. "Oh, you bet. It was amaaaazing."

"I'm so happy. Now, what can I get you? Water, cans of soda, a sandwich, some cake?"

He hesitated, giving a slight glance towards the closed door behind him.

"Go on," she urged. "It's been a long evening and it could be a longer night. There's plenty of food for all the guests, plus your boss." She nodded to where Trip was sequestered. "Leave it with me. I'll have something sent to you shortly."

"Thank you. Thanks very much."

"Suzie," I said as we walked away. "We should go to the dining room and talk with the other guests there. See who else has had any interactions with Amber."

"Sure honey. You go on ahead. I'll catch up with you. I'll just go raid the kitchen for food for Officer Reynolds. Plus, I want to give that nice young officer a little extra special surprise."

I was curious what that would be, but right now I was trying to put all the pieces together, but even with the new information we'd gathered from the surveillance footage, I knew I was still missing crucial facts that would help me form a final theory as to who had killed Amber, then Ginger. And what about Gabby? Despite being attacked so brutally, she hadn't seen anyone.

I was still trying to put the pieces together when I went into the dining-room. I felt all eyes turn to look at me but I kept my eyes averted. I avoided looking at Melissa who was chatting with her friend Carrie, as well as Amoy and Mark. I looked at each of the other guests. There were so many people here tonight who attended Suzie's soirée, each one potentially concealing dark secrets behind their veneer of polite conversation and light-hearted laughter. Any one of them could have snuck away before the start of Suzie's concert, killed Amber, before returning to join the other guests, largely unseen.

I remembered that according to Kaylee, Amber was blackmailing her. Who else might Amber have been blackmailing or have grossly upset? Any one of the guests could be the murderer. But without solid evidence, I couldn't just accuse anyone. I needed more facts.

Bernard was with Celia and Amber's friend Fee. Bernard, for once, was subdued. I decided to offer my condolences to Fee.

She looked up at me with tear-filled eyes when I approached her and the Lazenby's.

"I'm so sorry Fee. I can't imagine what you're going through right now."

"Thank Marnie," she said, her voice hoarse with emotion. "She was such a fun friend. I can't believe she's gone."

"I know, it's hard to wrap your head around it. Did you see anything unusual, or anyone acting strange before Amber disappeared?"

She shook her head. "No, I wish I had. I didn't even realize she was gone. I was so wrapped up in watching the concert."

I turned to Bernard and Celia. "What about either of you? Did anything or anyone seem out of place or displaying different behavior?"

Before either of them could answer, Melissa strutted over and pounced. "Why are you able to just walk freely around the house without anyone with you?"

I was kind of expecting this question from one of the guests, but of course, if anyone was going to demand an answer, it would be BobCat herself. "Actually, I'm with Suzie. I'm helping her with some things." I didn't want to share too much information about what we'd been doing, because while I didn't want to suspect one of the guests, one of them was the murderer. "She's in the kitchen laying out some snacks left from the caterers." I tried to put on a smile, given that everyone in the room was now staring at us. "She'll be here any moment."

"Well, I think it's a bit off, you know. Especially as your friend is involved."

My eyebrows shot up at that last remark. She just wouldn't give up, would she. She was relentless in her determination to cause me harm.

"Please direct your concerns to Sergeant Brodie," said a strict voice behind us. Suzie to the rescue!

I swiveled around to look at Suzie, grateful for her intervention.

Melissa looked taken aback for a moment. Her jaw was firmly set and her eyes bug-eyed and that was when I saw a bead of sweat dribbling down her forehead from her perfect hair. "No offense Ms Wilde," she stammered, "it's just that everyone saw her friend Gabby being escorted from your event with a police officer guarding her."

"Then I suggest you take the matter up with Sergeant Brodie," she repeated firmly. "He's the person in charge of the investigation. Now if you'll excuse us, I need to discuss something with my friend." She smiled her lovely wide Suzie grin, instantly putting everyone at ease.

Melissa wasn't to be stopped though. She was in her stride and now she pounced.

"She's the daughter of a druggie," she called out, pointing at me. "She shouldn't be trusted."

The room fell silent, everyone was waiting for her to continue. Or for me to respond.

Chapter Thirty-Two

I bristled with rage at Melissa's revelation of my past. What was worse, she was insinuating that I couldn't be trusted. That I was different from everyone in the room. Well, I *have* been living a different life since I left here. I had moved on literally and figuratively and I had a successful career, good friends, and a wonderful, adopted family.

"That's quite enough," said a voice from the hallway. It was Trip. He was standing outside the entrance to the dining room and from the dark look on his face I'd say that he had heard everything that she had said to me.

Melissa immediately straightened up when she saw him.

Trip stepped into the room, his presence commanding everyone's attention. He walked towards us. "Melissa, may I have a word with you, please?" His voice was low, but stern.

She nodded and followed Trip in silence. I watched as they walked out of the room together, her face pale and expressionless.

I sat there feeling grateful that Trip had intervened, but at the same time feeling a little lost. I turned back to the group, the awkward tension palpable. "I'm so sorry about that," I said, breaking the silence. "I had no idea that my past would come up like this."

"It's alright Marnie," said Suzie, placing a hand on my shoulder. "I'm here for you. We all are."

"Thanks," I said to Suzie, feeling my shoulders relax a little. "Melissa can be a little… intense."

Suzie looked at the assembled group, and then out towards the hall where the group from the living room had heard the commotion and were now standing in the hall, unsure if they should enter the dining area. Suzie inclined her head and they stepped forward to join the rest of us.

Rupert came up to me and drew me aside. "I can't imagine how hard that must have been for you."

"I've come to terms with my early childhood. It was tough, but I've moved on from it," I replied.

"I've had my own share of struggles, and I'm here for you, no matter what."

I looked at his eyes and only saw kindness reflected back at me. A weird warmth spread through me. "Thank you," I said, feeling tears prick at the corner of my eyes.

He cleared his throat before speaking again and took my hand. "I know it's not much Marnie, but I want you to know that I meant what I said earlier."

I shook my head, startled. "You don't have to say anything. You were never as bad as Melissa."

"Maybe not, but I was still part of the group that made your life difficult. And, like I said, I'm sorry."

I looked down at our hands, amazed at how warm and comforting his touch was. It felt like everything else in the room had receded into the background, leaving just me and Rupert.

"I forgive you," I said softly. "If you're really sorry, then I forgive you."

He smiled, and I saw a glimmer of happiness return to his face. "Thank you Marnie."

We stood there in silence for a few moments, lost in our thoughts. I was grateful for his company, grateful for his sincerity. I had finally let go of something that had been weighing me down for years.

Suddenly, there was a commotion and Trip Brodie strode in, his expression serious. I felt Rupert's hand slip out of mine as he rose to his feet.

"I need to speak with you Marnie," Trip said, his eyes flickering towards Rupert before returning to me.

I nodded, feeling a sense of unease settle in my stomach. Whatever it was, it couldn't be good.

I followed Trip out of the dining room, wondering what could have happened now. We walked down the hallway in the direction of Suzie's office. He opened the door to let me in and as I passed him, my arm brushed lightly against his. I was startled by the spark that jumped between us and hastily apologized. "I'm sorry. There must be too much static or dry air."

A rumble of distant thunder made me jump. The storm that Amoy and Mark mentioned was approaching. I gave a little smile to Trip. "I guess I'm more on edge than I realized."

He entered the room behind me, leaving the door slightly ajar.

"Have a seat," he said, pointing to a navy and cream striped armchair.

The chair looked comfortable and welcoming and I sat in it gladly, feeling my spine relaxing against the pillowed backrest.

Trip pulled out the padded desk chair, similarly upholstered to the armchair in a complementary stripe in coordinating navy and cream, and a contrast to the solid navy sofa with cream cushions. He rolled it along the bleached wood floor until it was about three feet from where I was sitting.

"Marnie, I've got something to tell you."

My eyes widened. What was going to happen now?

As if sensing my worry, he leaned forward. "It's about your friend Gabby."

"Gabby! What's happened to her?"

He shook his head, then he gave a hint of a smile. "According to the hospital, Gabby is going to be okay. She has a concussion which will require monitoring, especially given that she was unconscious following the assault on her. And she's apparently got quite a few stitches in her head wound, but apart from that, no serious injuries."

"It's a good job I'm sitting down. That's great news." Then I remembered that there was another issue which had a potentially harmful outcome. I gripped the arms of the chair. "What about the false accusations by Melissa Maxwell?" I demanded. "What's going to happen? Don't tell me you're trying to soften the blow by giving me a piece of good news only to slam a devastating criminal charge against her!"

He raised an eyebrow, and his expression grew serious once again. "That's the thing Marnie. My team has conducted an investigation into the matter and we believe that Melissa's allegations need not be pursued any further.

I didn't think I'd heard him correctly. "What?"

"Gabby is no longer considered a suspect. In fact she's free to go home from the hospital once they give her the all clear."

"Oh, thank goodness," I said, feeling a huge weight lifted off my shoulders. "I knew Melissa was lying all along."

Trip nodded in agreement. "It seems that way. However, we still need to find out who really attacked Gabby. The investigation is still ongoing, but I wanted you to be aware of the situation."

"Of course, thank you for letting me know," I said, feeling a sense of gratitude towards him.

"I just have one question," he said.

I waited. I knew this had been too easy. "What is it you want to know?"

"Melissa claims to have witnessed you and Gabby having an argument before Amber was killed. She says that Gabby appeared to be quite upset with you."

"That's ridiculous," I exclaimed. "Gabby and I never had an argument. We were getting along just fine. We always do."

He wasn't fazed in the least by my outburst trying to defend Gabby. "I'm sorry to have had to ask you that Marnie. But I need to investigate all potential leads in this case, and that includes Melissa's claims."

My mind was racing. There was no way Gabby and I had argued. Had Melissa made it up to further implicate me in the attack? Could she in fact have been Gabby's attacker. And then by default be the murderer?

Trip noticed my agitation. "We'll get to the bottom of this Marnie. I won't let you take the fall for something you didn't do."

I looked at him, grateful for his support.

"Or Gabby, for that matter," he added.

There was something in the way he spoke that made my heart skip a beat. "Thanks for all your support, and for keeping me informed," I said.

"Don't mention it," he said, getting up from the chair. "I'll keep you updated on any developments."

I didn't know whether to shake his hand or hug him, so I did neither. But inside I was jumping for joy. With Gabby cleared of any wrongdoing and being able to be sent home soon to rest, I was determined to put all my energy into finding out which one of the guests was responsible for the unthinkable murders.

I followed the sound of voices through the hallway. The dining room was empty and so was the kitchen. So I made my way to the living room. I looked for any signs of Melissa so that I could avoid her when I saw a man talking with Rupert. It was his brother Anthony!

I thought Anthony was a likely suspect in at least Ginger's death. What had happened. What did Trip know that he made the decision to release Anthony? With Gabby also out of the equation, who else could be a likely suspect?

I really wanted to share the good news about Gabby with someone and spied Suzie chatting with Helene and her son Max next to the fireplace. I went directly over to where they were and was greeted by Suzie.

"Hey Marnie, darlin', everything okay?"

"I just got some great news about Gabby. She's going to be okay," I replied, smiling at her.

"Hey, that's great to hear. I was so worried about her."

Max's face lit up. "I've met Gabby at business bureau networking events. I never doubted her innocence for a moment.

Helene also said how relieved she was. "That's good news. It's a worrying time for all of us."

"Did you get a chance to talk to her?" asked Suzie.

I shook my head. "Trip told me."

Suzie raised an eyebrow and gave me a little smile. Instead of acknowledging her not so subtle insinuation, I gave a quick glance over at Rupert and his brother. "Any idea what happened with Anthony? I thought he was under suspicion?"

Suzie's expression turned serious. "He was, but according to what he told all of us before you returned, they couldn't find any evidence linking him to the murders. He's decided to stay here so he can leave with his brother." She shook her head slowly. "It's frustrating, I know, however we have to trust that the police are doing everything they can to solve this. And more importantly, accept that Anthony is not involved."

I nodded, despite my feelings of uncertainty. Every lead was a dead end.

"Hey, don't worry y'all," said Suzie, sensing my exasperation at the lack of progress. "I'm just glad that Anthony's not involved in this awful affair. His brother doesn't deserve that. It would be a terrible distraction from all the good that Rupert does for the community. Plus, Trip's a great detective. One of the best. I'm sure he'll solve the case very soon."

I smiled at her. It was comforting to know that we had someone like Trip working to solve the horrendous crimes especially as Suzie thought so highly of him. And with Gabby out of danger on two fronts, I was starting to feel like a huge weight had been lifted off my shoulders.

Helene spoke up then. "It's just hard not to let our emotions cloud our judgment in all this. How are you managing Marnie, after this shocking confrontation with that awful Melissa."

I groaned inwardly. I had been hoping to avoid any mention of Melissa for as long as possible. "Yes, she's made some pretty awful accusations, all without merit. But it's more a reflection on her. And anyway, Trip didn't take anything she said seriously."

Suddenly, a loud clap of thunder shook the room, followed by a bright flash of lightning that illuminated the darkness outside. Everyone jumped in surprise and let out various gasps and shrieks, followed by embarrassed laughter. The mood in the room lightened a bit, and we all resumed our conversations.

"Would you excuse us?" Suzie asked Helene and Max. Of course, they didn't mind and Suzie took hold of my elbow nearest her and guided me over to two empty chairs next to the entrance hall. I leaned back and relaxed my shoulders. My feet were aching.

Suzie leaned towards me and sighed heavily. "It's said there's no such thing as bad publicity Marnie. Trust me, that's a pile of baloney. These terrible events need to be solved, and fast. My charity can't survive this type of publicity."

"I'm trying to figure it out, Suzie. There're a lot of clues and I have this nagging feeling that the solution is simple. I'm overlooking it when all along it's staring me in the face. But I'm curious. What was the surprise that you gave Officer Reynolds?"

"It turns out he's a huge fan and was at one of my concerts recently. So, in addition to providing a tray of food for him, I gave him some signed photos and two t-shirts, and two back-stage passes to my next concert which will actually be in North Legacy Cove."

"Wow! Is that allowed? To give gifts like that?"

"Of course," she winked. "He's one of my friends now. But back to business. Tell me how you got on earlier this evening."

I filled Suzie in on what Trip had shared, as well as my conversation with Fee. I was aware of some people quietly leaving the room and crossing the hall to the kitchen where their voices picked up as they gathered plates of food and beverages.

I felt a presence behind me and turned quickly, surprised to see Celia and Bernard standing beside my chair, Bernard sporting a strange expression on his face. "I have a question for you," he said to Suzie.

"Yes? How can I help?"

"The guest list. How were people selected?"

"Well, this is a surprise. I didn't expect that. Actually, it's a lengthy process, one that involves researching possible people from successful businesses, receiving recommendations from charities and doing checks to ensure they meet our strict criteria for eligibility. Then we have three people in reserve in case of last minute cancellations. The following year we carry those people over to the guest list, if they've not attended, of course." She looked at him steadily. "Why do I get the impression that you're not asking a general question, but instead enquiring about a specific guest?"

He crossed his arms over his ample abdomen and huffed out a long sigh that caused his jowls to wobble. "You're pretty savvy, you know that?"

"Takes one to know one Bernard. After all, that's one of the reasons you were invited to my event this year."

"Simon Stadler. Why on earth was that man invited?"

She straightened slightly in her chair. "As I said, how people are invited is a long and serious process, and I can assure you that everyone here deserves to be here. You and all the other guests."

Celia intervened. "Well, you see Suzie, Bernard and Simon have known each other since high school and they stopped being friends when Simon got a football scholarship that Bernard deserved."

Ah, I thought, so that's what was actually behind their dispute. It wasn't a lost romance, it was a sports scholarship that caused them to be so divisive and exhibit so much animosity towards each other. I had thought that Bernard was much older than Simon, but I guess his days of being a sportsman were long over and that had contributed to him appearing older than he actually was.

"It's okay Celia," said Bernard, patting her hand. "There's no need to mention it."

Celia ignored him and continued. "Simon caused the accident that prevented Bernard from pursuing his dream. So, Bernard, being the wonderful man that he is, he started his own company after college with his master's in business administration. And because of his success, he continues to help others."

"Yes I know," remarked Suzie, turning to Bernard. "You have not only built a considerable empire but you recently donated several millions of dollars to the Surfside Family organization."

Bernard puffed up slightly at the mention of his impressive financial donation. "Thank you for mentioning it, and for inviting Celia and myself to your annual event, even with the unfortunate events that have transpired."

"You are both most welcome. In fact everyone is. But I have to reiterate that I cannot give specifics as to why people are invited to my event, except to say that each one deserves to be here."

"I see," he said slowly. He now looked a little deflated as though the events of the day, plus being in the same space as his nemesis, were now too much to bear.

Suzie looked at them sympathetically. "Why don't you and Celia go get a bite to eat and a refreshment? It's a simple spread of small sliders and different salads but I hope that socializing over food will take everyone's mind off what's happening right now." She smiled graciously to them. "I'll talk to y'all later."

"Good idea," said Celia, tugging at her husband to let us resume our discussion.

I was relieved when they left as I needed to chat with Suzie privately. I had had an idea earlier and it required her help.

"What's up?" Suzie asked.

"Something that you said to Trip earlier seems especially important, as it may in fact narrow down the list of potential murderers."

Suzie's brow furrowed. "What do you mean?"

"You mentioned that Ginger would require significant funding if she was to launch her product. We speculated that she may in fact have approached the murderer and attempted to blackmail them. You remember she told Helene about knowing who the murderer was and killing two birds with one stone?"

"Yes. I remember. And we told Trip and he said we need to find out who the wealthiest attendees are."

"Exactly. The more I considered each attendee, the more I found myself thinking this could be a significant clue. I didn't consider the importance of this at the time, but this can really help us. Ginger saw whoever it was who killed Amber and had tried to kill Gabby. Then Ginger, needing money for the next wave of funding for her company, threatened to blackmail the murderer. From what you were saying to Bernard moments ago, you have a fairly in-depth knowledge of each guest. This means that we should find out exactly who the wealthiest are. You know Trip's going to ask for it."

Suzie paused. "You're right. Oh my gosh. I can't say off the top of my head. They're all wealthy, to some extent or another, but in order to provide the capital that I suspect she needed, it would be a lot, in the tens of millions. And from what I understand, there's typically not just one investor. The risk is spread between several investors."

I nodded. "I've heard some of my colleagues talk about this during lunch breaks whenever there's a big breakthrough or launch of some new product. Even some of our departments are involved in collaborating with other organizations and developing new products."

"C'mon Marnie. All the info is on my computer in my office. Let's go sift through the data.

We rushed past the kitchen down the hall towards Suzie's office when we saw Trip coming out of the piano room, his shoulders slumped, his head slightly down.

"What's up Trip? What's going on?"

"I've just been taken off the case."

Chapter Thirty-Three

My heart sank as soon as I heard Trip's words.

"What? Why?" Suzie and I asked him simultaneously.

He let out a deep sigh. "Captain Ortiz doesn't feel I'm making progress fast enough. I told you when I arrived that this was a high profile case and that results would be demanded quickly. She's bringing in officers from another town and she'll be here with them within the next hour."

I couldn't believe what I was hearing. From what I knew of Trip so far, he had a good work ethic and seemed to be following everything by the book, so to speak. Plus, according to Suzie, he was the best detective in the Legacy Cove police department. I had been hoping that we would be able to solve the case, but now it seemed like that was never going to happen. "That's insane," I said. Can't we do something about it?" I looked at Suzie.

She patted Trip gently on the arm. "You don't deserve this. I'll call Captain Ortiz," she said decisively.

He shook his head. "I appreciate it, Suzie, but it won't make any difference. It's out of my hands now."

"Hmm, if there's one thing I dislike doing, it's using my name to get an advantage. But for you Trip, I'd do it."

"Like I said, I don't think that even you can change the Captain's mind about keeping me on the case."

I could see the disappointment in his eyes and felt his frustration. This was a huge setback, not only for him personally, but for the investigation too. "We'll keep on working to find out who the murderer is," I stated firmly.

"Absolutely," he said, a small smile appearing on his face. "At least until the captain arrives. Until then, I'm still here and I don't plan on stopping the investigation."

Suzie grabbed him by the shoulders and reached up and planted a big kiss on his cheek. "That's more like the Trip Brodie I know. Don't you dare think of giving up now."

"Thank you, Trip," I said. "I appreciate everything you've done so far."

"You're welcome," he said, a thin smile breaking out on his tanned face. "I just want to see this case solved as much as you both do."

"What now?" Suzie asked. "With the new officers coming in and all?"

Trip let out a sigh. "I'll need to review the information I've already gathered and check in with Annie Osborne as she's managing the crime scene and those officers. See if she's been able to find anything else that might help me discover who the murderer is before the new team arrives to take over from me."

"Let's hurry up then," she said, moving quickly past him to her office. "Marnie and I might have another piece of information for you."

She sat in the chair in front of her desk and used her forefinger to unlock her computer and started scrolling through folders. Trip and I stood behind her to see the screen. "Got it," she said, opening a folder and one of the files contained in it. It was a list of names, companies, and financial data, all color-coded in red, blue and green.

"What are we looking at," Trip asked.

"This is a high level confidential overview of the guests we considered for this year's event," she explained. "We broke them down into groups based on how much they have contributed to the community, and I don't mean by writing checks. They had to have done something constructive with their time as well as either raising money for specific items, rather than money disappearing into a charity's fundraising pot."

"Which names are the wealthiest or have donated the highest amount?" asked Trip.

"The ones in red are the biggest contributors," she said, indicating the grids at the top of the file. We leaned in closer to look at where she was pointing. There were seven names. Amber, Bernard Lazenby, Simon Stadler, Rupert Boyden, Amoy Johnson, Liz Tanner, and Julia Musto. "Julia was injured and unfortunately was unable to attend this year's event."

Trip took out his phone and snapped a photo of the list of names.

I realized that Suzie didn't know about Julia's death. Nor the fact that her death was being pursued as a crime. Now didn't seem the time to mention it. There had been way too much death already tonight.

Trip glanced at his wristwatch. "I'm going to call Nate and Officers Bundock and Reynolds. They can help me talk to the people on this list and see if we can determine if one of them is hiding anything."

Suzie turned off her computer and stood up. "I guess you'll be wanting to use my piano room again?"

He grinned at her as he pulled out his phone to call his colleague Nate when his phone rang. He checked the name of who was calling and answered. He listened intently and then leaned on the desk and took a pen from a jar on the desk and a square of light blue paper from a multi-colored block, quickly writing on it. "Check the spelling of that again will you?" He listened as the caller spelled out a word as he used the pen to follow against what he had written down. "Great thanks."

He looked over at both of us. "That was the lab with the result of the toxicology from Amber. They've confirmed it was poison."

"No big surprise there. That's what we suspected all along," I said. "But I'm curious about what type of poison was used. It might give us a clue as to who might have brought it here and how they used it."

"I agree, but I'm not sure that it helps us much. Turns out it's a native plant of North America and quite prolific too." He glanced down at the notes he had made. "Spotted Water Hemlock." He raised an eyebrow and glanced at each of us. We shook our heads. "Me neither," he said. "But what makes this particularly interesting is that apparently it's the deadliest plant in North America."

Suzie gasped and I gave an involuntary shiver. "How did Amber come in contact with it? Is it growing in my garden?"

He shook his head slowly. "I doubt it. Every part of this plant, from the stem to the leaves is highly toxic with the roots being the deadliest. And not only to humans, but animals too. The toxicology levels indicate that she was exposed to a high level of the active toxin derived from the roots." He looked at his notes again. "It would also be bloody hard to miss. It's anywhere from three to six feet tall."

"But that doesn't make sense, Trip," said Suzie. "There's none of this type of plant in my garden."

"Any idea how she came in contact with it?" I asked.

"Perhaps. According to the report there was a high level of the toxin not only in her bloodstream, but in the tissues of her lungs too."

"So you're saying she inhaled its toxin and that's how it got into her bloodstream?"

"Yep."

We all let this sink in. "There's only one way that she could have been affected by this Spotted Water Hemlock. Someone meticulously planned it and brought it with them."

"But how?" asked Suzie. "Every bag was searched and every pocket wanded. Nothing unusual was found."

"If this plant, the Spotted Water Hemlock was inhaled," I said quietly, an image forming in my mind, "there's only one way it could have been administered."

Suzie looked at me thoughtfully. Trip, on the other hand, leaned forward slightly. "Go on," he said.

I shared what I was thinking. "The way I see it, this murder was meticulously planned. The murderer chose this specific method of killing knowing full well that the plant was hugely toxic. They would have had to have known where the plant was, and handled it extremely carefully in order to transport it to a place where they could wear protective clothing to prevent cross contamination."

"It was inhaled," said Suzie. "Did Amber sniff the plant?"

"I doubt it. I think the murderer must have been able to crush, dehydrate, or distill the toxic roots and other elements of the plant to make a liquid or powder. That way they could easily transport it here. It would look perfectly normal. Then they could sprinkle it or spray it onto Amber's body or into her nostrils then stage the scene to make it look like Amber had an anaphylactic reaction to peanuts and was unable to reach her lifesaving EpiPen."

Suzie shook her head. "But my security team didn't find anything weird. I mean, I have a drug free environment in and around my house and Hank and his team know that. They are skilled at identifying anyone who might try to smuggle something onto my property." She looked to Trip. "My background checks can only dig around so much, you see."

We all sat in silence, contemplating the various scenarios as to how someone could smuggle the poison into the event and administer it, without harming themselves. A tangled thread began to unravel.

"What is it?" asked Suzie. "You've got some kind of weird look on your face."

"As I said, the murderer expected Amber to have a reaction and die. What they didn't expect was the white frothy saliva appearing on her lips. It would point to murder, rather than the seemingly unfortunate accident that they had planned."

"Then Gabby appeared," continued Trip, "and the murderer panicked. They had to get rid of Gabby and then you appeared and they didn't have time to remove the froth from Amber's lips."

"Exactly."

"But how did they bring it to my event?" asked Suzie.

"A medicine bottle," I blurted out, "or something small like a nasal antihistamine bottle. I don't think it would take much of the poisonous product to kill someone."

"I'll go and check with Hank," Suzie said, starting to stand up. "I'll have him ask the security team to see if they remember seeing something like that in anyone's bag or pocket."

"Yeah," said Trip. "In the meantime, I'll go check with Nate, have him get the uniformed officers to check the guests' personal effects. Hopefully we'll get lucky if the murderer is still hanging on to the container that the poison was in." He paused. "I'll warn my team, and I'm warning you too. That poison is lethal. If you think you've found the container, don't touch it. There's no telling how fast the poison can kill, and if it can be toxic through touch as well as via inhalation. Be careful."

I was relieved that they were both onboard with my theory as to how the murderer had been able to distribute the essence of the poisonous plant. Now, it gave me the boost I needed to divulge the remainder of my theory; how the murderer had been able to access the poison in the first place. I held up a finger, still concentrating, my eyes focusing externally yet inside my thoughts were gaining speed. "I think I know how the murderer did what they did. It was well-planned and well-executed."

Suzie sat down again.

Now it was Trip who did the questioning. "I'm listening."

"Like I said, a small vial or bottle seems the obvious container. The murderer didn't have enough time, or inclination, to do the same to my friend Gabby, but Ginger was a different scenario. She had to be silenced permanently because she had seen the murderer kill Amber. And after what happened to Ginger, I think the murderer very much wants to stay alive."

"And do whatever it takes to stay alive," whispered Suzie, wrapping her arms around herself. "But I still don't get it. How would they prevent it going onto their own skin?" asked Suzie. "Surely if it's that poisonous, they would need to prevent overspray from landing on themselves?"

"Go on, Marnie," urged Trip. "What else are you thinking?"

"Disposable gloves." I stated. "They're thin, small, and easily concealed either in a bag or on one's body. Tucked in a pocket, for example. I think that's how the murderer was able to administer the poison to each of their victims at close contact and ensure their own safety from the potential risk of back spray on their skin."

I cleared my throat. Presenting my ideas in front of Suzie and Trip, was akin to the first time I had to deliver a presentation to my peers at college where it was important for me to get their agreement, or acceptance. Shoot, every time I had to give an important speech relevant to my career I was nervous. This wasn't part of my career though, yet somehow what they thought of my summation was important to me. It mattered.

"Of course!" said Suzie excitedly. "Those types of gloves wouldn't be detected by the metal detector wand that Hank and the security personnel use."

"So hear me out on this next idea. Swimmer's nasal clips."

Both Trip's and Suzie's eyes widened. "Damn it," he said. "That way the murderer could avoid inhaling the poison, especially if droplets were in the air."

"And many people wear them, even here on the Cape, when swimming in the ocean," added Suzie. "I've seen them!"

"It's a lot of if's though," said Trip. "Although it makes a whole lot of sense."

"I know," I continued. "Think about it. Amber was sprayed and inhaled the poisonous solution up her nostrils and voila, the dastardly deed was done." I opened my bag and pulled out my phone. "I'm going to find out more about this plant and what specifically it does to the body." I quickly typed in its name and scrolled past a couple of sites until I found the national poison control center and opened the link. "Okay, it says here that ingestion or skin contact may cause convulsions, delirium, and death."

"But neither of the victims ate it," stated Trip. "They inhaled it."

"I agree," I said, closing my phone and replacing it in my bag. "The murderer could have made a concentrated liquid, perhaps by boiling it."

"But they would need to have access to special equipment to protect them from contamination."

"Like in a lab. Something a doctor would have access to," I said slowly."

"Not Dr Boyden, surely," gasped Suzie, shaking her head so insistently that her hair bounced. "Rupert helps children. He's not a murderer."

I glanced quickly at Trip. He was chewing on his bottom lip, mulling over the idea that Dr Rupert Boyden could actually be the murderer. His gaze held mine. It's possible, he seemed to say. I looked quickly away. Could we have discovered the actual identity of the murderer? I thought for a moment, trying to recall the many conversations I had had, as well as what I had overheard at the party. "Well, we know that both victims were involved in medical research, and the murderer seemed to have access to special equipment and knowledge about how to make a concentrated substance in liquid form."

Suzie's eyes widened. "That's true. But Dr Boyden is a doctor who specializes in pediatric oncology."

"He would still have access to the kind of equipment required to safely distill the poison," said Trip.

"But why would he do it?" I asked. "What would be his motive?"

Trip shrugged. "Maybe he had some kind of grudge against Amber."

Suzie stood up again. "I'll go talk with Hank and see if he or the security team saw anything unusual like gloves or a medicine bottle, or spray bottle, or nasal clips." She reached the door and paused. "Oh, and Trip, say hi to my new friend Officer Reynolds," she called back as she breezed out of the room.

He shook his head and laughed.

I stood up too, thinking I would go and chat further with the other guests and made to follow Suzie.

"Marnie, wait a moment."

I turned back to face Trip. He approached me and placed a hand on the doorframe. "How are you doing after what happened earlier?"

"Earlier?"

"With Melissa. I know it wasn't fair that she made those accusations against you, especially in front of everyone." His voice was low and filled with sincerity.

"It's fine. I'm just glad it's over and done with." I tried to sound nonchalant, but I couldn't help feeling a little grateful for his concern. His eyes locked with mine, and I felt a sudden jolt of electricity pass between us. But I quickly glanced away, remembering that he was in a relationship as I'd overheard him tell someone on the phone that he loved them too. We stood there for a moment, neither of us saying anything. The only sound was the rain tapping against the office windowpane and the distant roar of thunder in the background. Then I remembered something from a long time ago, when I was a child.

"Do you have a brother?" I asked him.

"A brother. Yes. John."

"Did he ever go by the name of JJ?"

A hint of a smile passed across his face. "Yes. When he was at school. But he never uses it now. Except when I tease him and call him JJ. He gets annoyed at that because he's an adult now."

"I remember you too. You were much older than me and JJ. He and I were in the same year at school and you helped stop the bullies. Then I was adopted and moved to Boston and never found out what happened to you or JJ."

"The bullying ended. They never bothered him again, even when I left school and went to college, and was no longer an immediate threat to them."

I cleared my throat nervously. "I'm glad. So, what happens next?" I asked, trying to keep my voice steady and matter-of-fact.

"Next?"

"With Rupert Boyden."

"Oh, yes, Rupert." He drew his hand away from the door frame and raked his fingers through his hair. "I'll need to talk with my colleague Nate Whitney first, bring him up to speed with what we know. Then we'll have a serious interview with the good doctor."

"Do you really think Dr Boyden could be the murderer?"

Trip sighed. "I don't know. It's a possibility. But I also don't want to jump to conclusions without enough evidence. We need to keep all options open and gather as much information as we can. Maybe he was pressured into it, blackmailed or threatened."

"You're right," I said, feeling a little disappointed. I had been hoping that we had finally cracked the case, but it seemed like we still had a long way to go. "I'll let you get on with the investigation then. I'll be in the living room if you need me for anything."

I was quiet as I returned to the living room, passing by half of the guests assembled in the kitchen. I saw Suzie chatting with Hank in the dining room. I needed to process what we'd just found out. I was bothered by the names on the red list. But there was something else niggling away at me and I needed time to process it. On a physical dig site I would lay out what we'd discovered and stare at it until I formed an idea of what exactly had been unearthed. Except the clues from today's events were not physical objects but pieces of information swimming randomly in my head and I needed to bring them in to shore.

But in this case, I didn't have the luxury of time to analyze information. I needed to go back to the beginning from when Gabby and I first arrived on Suzie's island and itemize what I knew, and fast. The answer was there, I just had to sift away the crap that was swirling around and masking the identity of the murderer.

Suddenly, Suzie came back into the room. "Are you going to be alright, honey?" she asked.

I gave a thin smile. "Definitely. I just need some time alone to lay out all the pieces, so to speak. There are clues and I just need to figure them out."

"Go sit in my office as no-one is in there at the moment. Hank and I have had a chat and he's off to talk with Jerry and Cindy, see if they saw anything unusual when checking in the guests."

"Sounds like a good idea. I need some alone time to sort out all the thoughts tangled up in my brain."

"I'll come check on you soon. Hopefully you'll get some peace to separate them out."

Safely ensconced in Suzie's office, I sat down heavily in her chair and leaned my head against the heels of my hands, while resting my elbows on my upper thighs. I was tired. I wanted to go home. My nerves were fraught, yet there was this nagging niggle between my eyes. The answer to who the murderer was, was right there. I simply had to filter out the distractions and figure out what was real and what was speculation and rumor.

I thought about the boat trip over to the island, the guests in the marquee, searching for Gabby, finding poor Amber, the fights between Bernard and Simon, and Anthony and Simon.

And then there was the dispute between Helene and Melissa where Helene stood up to her and refused to be drawn into one of Melissa's disagreements.

It seemed that everyone I came across had an alibi, or a reason they weren't seen for a moment, or a reason they disliked Amber. Could I determine though who was telling the truth and who was lying to me about themselves or other people?

Then there was Ginger's tragic demise, followed closely by the attack on Liz and her friend JT's disappearance.

And moments earlier Suzie shared the information on who were the wealthiest attendees who Ginger would likely have approached in a failed attempt to blackmail.

Finally there was Rupert. A doctor who had the means and knowledge to create a poison, as well as having access to the protective equipment that were found in hospitals.

And that was when it dawned on me. I'd become so caught up in reading the clues that I'd ignored one of my basic tenets; to always be doubtful when I was so sure of myself. I glanced around the room and shivered violently. I was alone, thankfully, but I needed to find Trip immediately.

We had just made a terrible mistake.

Chapter Thirty-Four

I needed to find Trip fast.

I hurried out of the office and headed straight to the living room. Suzie was standing near the fireplace with at least eight people around her and laughter erupted as she was just finishing her story about the time she met Mick Jagger. Everyone was laughing and clapping but I could sense the tension brewing below the surface. Rupert Boyden was eyeing me from across the room, his expression inscrutable.

I rushed straight to Suzie's side. There was no time to waste. "Suzie, have you seen Trip."

She raised her eyebrows at me, her eyes searching mine. "Trip? Not since the three of us were in my office earlier. Although didn't he say something about going to find his colleague Nate Whitney?"

I chewed my lip as I looked towards the window. "Is he outside?" The raging storm appeared to pound against the windows with more strength as the seconds ticked by, billowing beyond the windows, and I dreaded the thought of searching for him out there in the darkness in the middle of a thunderstorm.

Suzie's phone pinged. "Oh crap!" she muttered through clenched teeth as she read a text. "It's from my manager." She held up her phone to show me.

"Oh crap indeed!" I agreed.

The text included screenshots from several social media sites all with trending hashtags and accompanying images connected with the event, Amber's death, and even Gabby's assumed guilt, despite the fact that she'd been completely exonerated by the police and was no longer a suspect but another victim. The comments and photos were posted by guests on their own pages. It was easy to see who was to blame for posting them. People who had left their moral compunctions behind before they landed on the island.

"Here's one from earlier when the news helicopters were circling overhead and the boats were approaching my island," continued Suzie. She held her phone up to show us. "It's from none other than Celeb Nooz."

"The paparazzi site?"

She nodded. "It says here that the photo shows two guests out for a stroll."

I squinted closer. "It's black and white and really grainy, but I'd say this is an image of Liz and her partner. I can just tell it's them."

"It was taken with one of those super long-range lenses," she explained. "The ones that would probably show the great wall of China if used on the International Space Station."

We all gave a little laugh at the lengths these people would go to. "But looking at the level of clouds it surely would have been around the time that they were attacked." I closed my eyes and groaned. "How stupid of me."

"What?"

I took out my own phone and held it up. "I forgot that I have Trip's phone number when I exchanged photos with him earlier this evening. I'll try calling him. See if I can reach him."

I walked over to the rain splattered sliders, keeping my eyes averted so that I wouldn't engage anyone else in the room. I stared out into the night and the garden which was eerily illuminated by the distant floodlights from the crime units, while the storm swirled relentlessly around the world beyond the sanctuary of the house. I had no intention of being reckless and putting myself in danger, but I'd learned since I was a child that you have to be resourceful if you're going to survive. The moon was obscured by the storm clouds, and I dialed Trip's number, willing him to pick up when the call went through.

However Melissa had other ideas.

"What are you doing Marnie," she asked sharply as I pressed the call button, her voice laced with suspicion. Her green eyes glinted in the light of the room.

"Making a private call," I replied, unable to keep the annoyance out of my voice. I hung up making the call as I needed privacy and the last thing I needed was BobCat listening in and causing trouble.

"Don't be ridiculous," she scoffed. "You can't just go off doing your own thing, snooping around like you're a detective. I've seen you, spreading lies to Detective Brodie. It's a good job his colleague Nate knows what you're like. He's keeping a close eye on you."

Just then the front door flew open and Trip Brodie scrambled inside the hall, rain dripping off his jacket. The water dripped from his face and hair onto the polished wood floor. Sensing my opportunity to break away from Melissa, I hurried over to Trip. Suzie joined me at the door.

"You're soaked," she said. "And you're dripping all over my floor."

"How observant of you," he replied, shaking his hair deliberately so it would sprinkle rainwater over her.

"Enough of the flippant talk. Come with me and I'll get you a change of dry clothes. At the very least a towel to dry your hair and a white tee."

"I'm coming too," I insisted. "We need to talk. It's urgent."

Suzie addressed the guests in the living room. "We won't be long. I'm sure there'll be an update soon."

Murmurs and mutterings followed us as we hurried out to the hall, swiftly moving past the dining room and kitchen, turning right at the end of the hall past Suzie's office and moving along the shorter corridor to a set of double doors.

Suzie placed her hands on both door handles and swung the doors inward, revealing an expansive bedroom. The lights were dim, a gas fire flickered in the furthest corner, flanked by cream colored curtains that were closed against the storm battering the island. A large bed, draped with a white quilt and white sheets and pillows stood against the right-hand wall. To the left was a large walk-in closet and what appeared to be a luxurious bathroom.

Pictures of Harry and Suzie over the years were on the walls. None were of Suzie in concert. No, these were personal photos of Harry and Dottie, a happy couple far from the bright stage lights and adoring fans. The settings were varied; they were smiling at each other, relaxing on a beach, the rolling hills of Tuscany, the colorful houses of Cinque Terre, skiing in the Alps, selfies at the Grand Canyon. Each photograph told a story of a shared life well-lived.

At the far left corner of the room was Harry, sitting on a cream colored sofa with his feet up, a bottle of red wine and a half-filled stem glass resting on a coffee table. He glanced up from the book he was reading and he laughed. "You found me. What took you so long."

"Enjoying some peace and quiet?" asked Suzie, heading straight into the adjoining bathroom.

"You know me so well honey. I needed to get away from all the drama." He looked closely at Trip. "What on earth happened to you?"

Suzie returned seconds later with a large fluffy white bath towel, which she promptly thrust into Trip's arms. "Here, dry yourself quickly before you cause any more problems."

"I needed to see something in person," he explained, rubbing his hair and bare arms with the towel. "And of course, the storm was at its heaviest when I headed out twenty odd minutes ago."

Suzie meanwhile was busying herself in the large walk-in closet that was as big as two of my guest bedrooms combined. She sifted through one of the drawers on the left side of the closet eventually pulling out something that she was happy with. "Here," she said, handing the T-shirt to Trip. A plain white tee. You'll be glad to get out of the wet one you're wearing."

"Thanks. My jacket wasn't exactly waterproof." He pulled off the wet shirt he was wearing and threw it on top of the bath towel that he had thrown on a nearby chair. Suzie swiftly scooped the wet items from the chair and promptly plopped them into a modern style bathtub in the bathroom. I was slow in averting my eyes from his muscled bare chest as he slipped on the fresh tee, the fabric clinging to his torso. I couldn't help but notice the way his biceps bulged as he pulled the shirt down. "Okay," he said, turning to me. "What is it that's so urgent?"

I took a deep breath, hesitating for only a moment. "We made a mistake," I began. "We've been so focused on trying to figure out who could have synthesized the aerosol version of the poison that we failed to look at all the aspects in front of us."

"Go on," he said. Suzie sat beside her husband and they leaned forward, eager to hear what I had to say. For the second time this evening I was front and center in sharing my thoughts on where the clues were pointing at.

"Previously, before we knew about the type of poison used, we were focusing on the motive." I checked their faces and Trip gave a brief nod to continue. "Despite Anthony having a temper, he was in the marquee, having a drink when Amber was killed. We also know that Ginger shared with Madame Gauthier that she saw the actual murderer, and we believe she then tried to blackmail the murderer, only it backfired on her."

"You're not suggesting that Helene is the murderer, are you?" gasped Suzie.

I shook my head. "No, the clue that helped me tie it all together was the list of the wealthiest guests. Ginger was in desperate need of another round of funding for her company. She'd already gotten as far as testing and approvals, she only needed another round of funding prior to the launch of the skincare products."

"So, we look at the list again," asked Suzie.

"We can, however there's something else that separates one name from the others. You see, while we were focused on how the murders were done, and who would have the opportunity to sneak away without being seen, I kept having this niggle about why. What had Amber done that warranted her death?"

"Motive," suggested Trip. "We're working through her contacts, business colleagues to find out if there was a deal that went south, someone who may have a grievance, perhaps for being passed over for a promotion they felt was theirs, but in fact it went to Amber."

"All very logical," I agreed, "however this was methodically planned. It took careful planning and preparation to source the poison, to distill it, to smuggle it in here today in an everyday container. And then there was the incident a few weeks ago at the yacht club."

Trip sat down on the chair where he'd previously discarded the towel and his wet shirt. "The yacht club. What's that got to do with what occurred here?"

"The events of that day have been bothering me since it happened." I explained about Amber's peanut allergy and the fact that she'd somehow been exposed to nuts and had it not been for me recognizing what had occurred, and hoping that she carried a life-saving Epi-Pen, then she may not have lived. What had occurred that day may simply have been recorded as an unfortunate, yet deadly accident."

"So you think that whoever caused the allergy attack is the murderer?"

"I do." I sighed heavily, and clenched my hands together realizing that I was shaking slightly. I had laid out the facts and could come to only one conclusion as to who the murderer was. "There were other things that happened that day, small things that I didn't realize were important clues to the murderer and their warped sense of vengeance, but once I sat quietly this evening and thought through everything that happened today, and at the yacht club, I realized that we had a clever and desperate murderer. And Amber was the second person they had killed, not the first."

"What!" all three exclaimed.

"Yeah Marnie, who is it?" said Harry.

Just then, the bedroom door flew open and Nate Whitney rushed in. "Quick Trip, you better come now!"

Chapter Thirty-Five

Trip and Nate rushed out of the room, leaving Suzie, Harry and I behind. I'd hoped that the murderer was done killing. That they were planning their escape. I had a sudden burst of energy at the thought that we were so close to catching the murderer and that my deductions were correct.

They were the only things that were logical.

Feeling like I'd just had a double espresso I bounded to my feet. "Are you coming?"

Suzie and Harry looked at each other and then turned to me as one and nodded.

I had a feeling that this was it. That everything was finally going to fall into place.

"Let's go then."

I ran from the bedroom with Suzie and Harry a few steps behind me. Raised voices emanated from the living room and I hoped that the murderer hadn't struck again.

I stopped abruptly when I entered the room, Suzie and Harry almost crashing into my back. All the guests had crammed themselves into the space in a huddle, their voices filled with suspicion and dread. I pushed my way through the throng, feeling a knot forming in the pit of my stomach. What had happened in our absence? The tension in the room was palpable, like a thick fog that refused to clear. I scanned the room looking for Trip or Nate, then I saw Trip emerge from the crowd, his face grave.

"Give us some room to work here," he called out, raising his arms, encouraging the crowd to back away.

Suzie and Harry pushed forward and I followed right behind them.

I gasped aloud when I saw why Trip was calling out for space. Slumped in one of the chairs beside the fireplace was none other than JT. He was soaking wet and shivering and had red welts the size of my palm on his cheeks. His forehead was gashed and his arms scratched and bleeding. His head slumped forward onto his once pristine pale blue polo shirt and matted blood tangled in the hair at the back of his head. His cream chinos were torn in the left knee where he'd struck the ground hard. He looked exhausted, but he was alive, and that right now was what mattered.

We had all feared he was dead and now he was here. Alive. My knees almost buckled with relief and I felt a surge of happiness that the murderer had failed to chalk up another body.

A collective sigh of relief filled the room and for a brief second everyone seemed to forget why we were here. We all just stood there looking at him, feeling relieved that he was safe and accounted for. But then reality set in again, and the questions started rolling off everyone's tongues in a flurry.

"Who did this?"

"Where has he been?"

"How did he get here?"

JT groggily opened his eyes and mumbled something unintelligible before lapsing into unconsciousness.

"Thank God, he's alive," exclaimed Liz.

She looked ashen and drawn. I hoped she wasn't having a relapse.

Nate and Trip were in a huddle, Nate no doubt bringing Trip up to speed with what had transpired. They broke apart and Detective Whitney made a beeline towards Melissa, while appearing to glower at me. They immediately began to talk privately, Melissa's eyes flicking towards me with a smirk on her face. Trip gently squeezed JT's shoulder in reassurance and then turned to us all with a determined look on his face. "Detective Whitney has informed the medical personnel who are still here on the island and they are on their way here as I speak."

I glanced at JT again. Time was running out. I had to finish telling Trip what I knew about who the murderer was.

I glanced around quickly for a private space but there was none. This place was as busy as a Christmas market.

"Trip," said Suzie, touching his arm firmly. "I'll stay with James until the medics arrive."

Trip nodded in agreement, and then turned to me, and gripped my elbow. "We need to talk," he said softly so as not to draw attention. He led me quickly away from the living room and down the hall to Suzie's office where we could talk without interruption. I mulled over that I hadn't thought of JT as anything other than JT. When I was first introduced to him he said his name was Jim, but that everyone called him JT. So why did Suzie call him James? Thinking quickly I surmised it was because she had a list of all the guests and partners and the list would have been necessary to give to her security people in advance, so that paparazzi or gatecrashers weren't able to gain access to the private party. After all, Gabby was addressed formally as Gabriella when we arrived.

Keeping the office door ajar so that we could both see and hear either anyone approaching us or the arrival of the medics, I wasted no time in being straight with Trip. "I need to tell you about the murderer. Before they strike again."

"Go on. You mentioned that they had killed someone else before."

I nodded. "Julia Musto."

"Musto. I don't know the name."

"It was a car accident several weeks ago."

"A car accident?"

"Yes. Except it wasn't an accident. Julia is, or rather was, a friend of Rupert's. She was invited to today's party, but because of the accident, she was in a coma and obviously wasn't able to attend. Then, she died from her injuries a week or so after the supposed accident."

"How do you know it wasn't an accident, and why was she targeted?"

"Rupert told several of us today that her car had been tampered with. Then, earlier tonight, when Suzie showed us the list of wealthy attendees, Julia's name was also listed as one of the wealthiest."

"But if she wasn't here, why was she on the list?"

I sighed inwardly. He really needed to keep up. "Suzie also mentioned that when drawing up a list of attendees, she always had some spare names who would be invited if anyone couldn't attend. Then if they remained surplus, then they would be invited the following year. It's a good way of getting a jump start on who to invite, don't you think. But, back to the importance of the list, and Julia."

"Suzie found someone else to replace Julia."

"Exactly!" I could barely contain myself.

"I need that list." He checked his watch. "Damn, my replacement will be here any moment."

"Perhaps the storm will have delayed them."

"Possibly, but it won't gain me much time."

"No need for the list." I smiled grimly at him. "Suzie should be able to tell us who was the last minute replacement. C'mon. Let's go."

We ran from the office and were plunged immediately into darkness. Screams erupted from the living room and that's where we were headed. Wasting no time I reached for my phone to switch on the flashlight app.

"Are you okay?" asked Trip.

"Yes," I said, illuminating my home screen and pressing the flashlight icon. White light shone brightly and ahead of us I saw other guests doing likewise. "Was it the storm or do you think someone did it deliberately?"

His jaw was clenched as he spoke. "I'd say without a doubt it was deliberate."

"How can you be so sure?"

In the gloom, shadows cast weird shapes on his face as he looked at me. "This house has a generator. It should have kicked in after only a couple of seconds. Someone has switched the power off at the main panel in the kitchen."

"Crap."

"Well said. Let's hurry."

The screams ahead of us died down and a man's booming voice ordered everyone to stay calm and switch on their phone flashlights. Bernard!

Trip and I reached the living room. All of the guests had complied and the room was filled with a soft white light. The guests were huddled in groups near the entrance or near one of the couches, their eyes darting nervously as they waited for whatever was to come next. Without doing a headcount I reckoned that all the guests were here, including the murderer. I was glad that Trip was by my side.

I saw Suzie and Harry crouched beside JT who was now awake. Suzie had her arms wrapped protectively around her torso like a shield to protect herself from whatever was heading our way.

The front door bell rang and the door flew open. A few people screamed in shock, but I sighed with relief as two paramedics entered, their medical bags in hand, and trailing mud from their shoes into the hall floor while dripping rain from their jackets. Detective Whitney broke away from Melissa and spoke to them, guiding them to where JT was seated. They immediately motioned for some lights to be shone in their direction so that they could get to work checking JT's vitals and assessing his injuries in the shadowy conditions.

As the paramedics tended to JT, Trip and I made our way over to Suzie and Harry. Suzie's eyes were filled with tears and Harry's face was etched with worry. I placed a comforting hand on her shoulder and squeezed it, giving her a reassuring smile.

The tension in the room was almost unbearable as we waited for any news, good or bad. Finally, one of the paramedics stood up and turned to face us. "He's got a concussion. He has a nasty bump on his head, but we need to take him to the hospital, run a CAT scan and some x-rays just to be sure." They began putting their equipment away. "We'll be right back with a gurney."

A wave of relief washed over me. The thought of losing another person was too much to bear.

Trip crouched next to JT, his face a mask of concern. "Can you tell us what happened? Do you know who did this to you?"

JT's eyes flickered open and he looked up at Trip. "I don't know," he said hoarsely. "I don't remember. I found myself in the ocean near the jetty. Fortunately it wasn't deep as the tide was out. I climbed out onto the jetty and I think I passed out again. The next thing I remember was an almighty loud clap of thunder followed by a bright flash of lightning. Then the rain began, pelting me hard. I followed the lights to the house, rather than the lights in the distance at the little tents."

"Those are where my colleagues are. One of them would have helped you."

The paramedics returned with the gurney and set to work transferring JT onto the thin mattress and elevating the frame. They rechecked his pulse, blood pressure, and breathing. Once they had him stabilized, they began to move towards the door, giving instructions to Detective Whitney about where they were taking him as they went. Everyone in the room stepped aside so that the paramedics could get through, thanking them for their help. With JT and the paramedics gone, the room seemed eerily quiet. The flashlights from the phones cast eerie shadows up the walls and ceiling and across everyone's faces. We all looked around at each other nervously waiting for someone to make a move or say something but no one did. It was Trip who finally broke the uneasy silence by taking charge.

"Detective Whitney will complete the interviews. If you have not been called previously, please listen for your name to be called. We want to know your version of tonight's events and whether you noticed anything out of place or suspicious during your conversations with each other."

I was in need of some much-needed respite from this whole terrible ordeal but we still had a murderer to catch. Then my jaw dropped and I clamped a hand over my mouth. I stopped in my tracks and spun around in alarm. A chill ran down my spine as I glanced fervently around the room, quickly evaluating each guest's behavior and facial expressions. One of them was missing. That was when I knew for sure who the murderer was.

Chapter Thirty-Six

"We need to act fast," I hissed as I grabbed Trip by the arm. "Now!"

Detective Whitney gave me an intense glare which told me he knew that something was amiss.

I grabbed a man's jacket from the hall coat cupboard. I recognized it as one that Harry wore at the dig site and threw it at Trip. "Here. Put that on. And your shoes. We have to catch her!" I said.

I grabbed a mid-length Burberry raincoat which I assumed was one of Suzie's and tugged it on. My dress hung below it so I turned my back to Trip and hitched my dress up, tucking it into my knickers. It hung down like a balloon skirt but at least it wouldn't get sodden by the rain.

"Hold on. Catch who?"

I shone my phone into the cupboard and spied what else I was looking for. A pair of welly boots. Green Hunters. Perfect.

"Liz."

I slid my bare feet easily into the boots. There was no way my dainty sandals would cope with the weather.

"Liz Tanner?"

"Yes," I called back as I opened the front door. "Are you coming?"

Trip didn't wait. Shrugging into the jacket, he slipped his long arms into the sleeves. It was at least one size too small for his muscular frame but at least it would keep the worst of the storm off him.

I hurried outside, desperately searching for any sign of the woman. The wind howled, making it impossible to hear anything above the roar of the storm with the rain pouring down relentlessly. The twinkle lights were still lit and swayed violently in the wind. The tiki lights had been extinguished but the floodlights from the two crime scenes where Amber and Ginger had been murdered helped illuminate those areas of the property, their glow spreading upward and outward through the trees and across the lawn and the area leading to the jetty. I couldn't remember how long the storm had been going. I thought that Amoy and Mark said it was only meant to last about an hour and a half, or maybe it was two hours at most. I wish I'd paid more attention. If this storm continued much longer we could struggle to find her.

I squinted into the darkness and thought I saw a light moving along in the distance. "Did you see that?" I called out to Trip, pointing into the darkness.

Following my gaze he squinted to get a better look. "There. I see it," he exclaimed. "It must be her!" He pulled out his phone, struggling to stand against the howling wind and battering rain. "I'm texting Nate." After a few seconds he stuffed his phone in a pocket in the jacket. "Let's go!" he shouted, moving steadily towards the wavering light as fast as he could.. "I've filled him in on what's happened and where we're heading."

I struggled to keep pace with him, his long legs pulling away faster than I could muster, especially as I was clumping behind him in rain boots that were a size too large for me and I wasn't wearing any socks. The raging storm didn't help as there were moments when I was being blown backwards, rather than making forward progress. I surged on regardless as I realized the direction we were heading.

The jetty. Was she trying to take a boat? Or was she planning on throwing herself into the ocean?

The gravel path beneath our feet proved treacherous as we dashed through puddles and pushed against the driving rain. The rain was now coming down with fierce determination. With each step, I could feel the relentless downpour beat against my skin, but I refused to let it stop me. We ran to the jetty as fast as we could. Only when we reached it did we finally slow down, cautiously navigating through the slippery terrain caused by the fierce combination of rain and crashing waves, braving the slick wooden planks that threatened to send us crashing into the churning waves below.

Trip took out his cell phone and checked on the status of the much needed police backup while I peered frantically around us, my eyes adjusting to the gloom, searching to see if Liz was nearby. Relentless waves crashed against the jetty, their force amplified by the storm.

"She must be here," Trip called out. "She can't have gone any further."

"A dinghy!" I pointed at it as I saw a dark bedraggled shape clamber into it.

I clumped forward in the welly boots and almost reached the dinghy when its little engine sparked into life and Liz took off, leaving me and Trip behind on the jetty beside the ocean's edge.

We watched in horror as she navigated the treacherous waters, dodging a nearby Boston Whaler and heading towards the open sea with reckless abandon. I watched helplessly as huge waves tossed the tiny vessel around. It looked like it was part of a roller coaster, riding up and down, side to side. The waves violently tossed the small craft with ease and I heard Liz screaming over the roar of the storm.

Suddenly she was clinging to the side of the boat, all hope of steering it gone as it struggled to fight the raging waves. An enormous wave swelled up and in the blink of an eye it overturned the dinghy, tossing Liz into the air like a ragdoll surrounded by oily darkness and sea spray.

I didn't see or hear her land in the choppy water. But she must have, because one minute she was there in the air, the next she was gone. Trip and I stood on the jetty, silent and shocked.

We turned at the sound of running feet and voices calling out to us. I immediately felt relieved as I saw Nate and four other officers arrive: Nate panting heavily. Trip quickly filled his colleagues in on what had transpired. "She was here a few minutes ago, but then she jumped into a dinghy and tried to escape across the ocean. A huge wave knocked her overboard and she disappeared beneath the surface."

Nate swore under his breath and scanned the murky waters surrounding us.

"I've also notified the coast guard," Trip informed us. "They should be here in a few minutes. They'll fly overhead in one of their helo's and search for her. And the fire department responded with their heavy rescue truck and their rescue pumper, as well as a dive team. An ambulance is heading here too, but I think they'll all have a wasted trip."

The storm appeared to ease momentarily and my hopes rose. We could possibly attempt a rescue, but I knew with a sinking heart that that was a hopeless task. Even if Liz had managed to stay afloat she would have been swept far from shore by now.

The storm was now finally drifting off to the west just as Amoy and Mark had said.

If Liz had waited another fifteen or twenty minutes, she might have escaped.

Trip looked at the rest of us, a bedraggled crew certainly, and sighed heavily before turning slowly away from the jetty. "Let's head back. I'll need Marnie to fill us all in. Plus, there'll be a lot of anxious people who can finally go home."

We followed him back to Suzie's house mostly in silence. Her house was lit up like a guiding beacon, the power having been restored. I paused at the front door with my hand on the doorknob and looked over my shoulder one last time at the moonlit ocean before entering inside. Our investigation had come to an abrupt end; Liz likely gone forever beneath the ocean's murky depths.

I had so much to share about Liz and why she committed these heinous crimes.

Inside the warmth of the house, I realized I was shivering from being out in the cold rain for so long. Suzie brought all of us bath towels to dry off on and blankets to snuggle under. Trip accepted the towel but refused the blanket. Also, Harry had restored the power to the house by simply flipping the master switch in the basement. Liz had snuck off down there earlier, flipped the power switch, then exited the house from the basement door.

Trip placed the damp towel on the hall floor, which was wet with our footprints. Then he addressed the guests. "Those of you who have been interviewed may call a cab or a family member to come and take you home." Cheers erupted from everyone in the room. "The others of you will still need to complete your interview with us, then you too will be free to leave." There were groans from the three remaining guests.

I went over to Suzie and spoke quietly to her. "Suzie," I said, my voice tinged with urgency, "could I use your office. I need privacy to share with Trip the information about Liz."

"Of course," Suzie replied, her eyes widening. "I'll come along as well. And Harry too. We'll both want to hear all of the details."

"Trip," I said, touching his elbow lightly to get his attention. He leaned down to me. "Come with Suzie and me to her office. I need to tell you about Liz."

"Let's go," he said.

The four of us quickly made our way to Suzie's office, Harry making a brief detour into the kitchen. "I'll be with you all in a moment. Once inside the office, I sat on the guest chair, Suzie behind her desk, and Trip on the navy sofa. Harry joined us next, awkwardly carrying four stemmed glasses and a bottle of red wine which he then placed on the desk. From a pocket he produced a bottle opener and opened the wine and poured. Harry sat beside Trip and each of us, except Trip, had a glass of red wine in front of us.

"How did you manage to figure it out?" Trip asked me.

"Yes, honey. Harry and I are bursting to know too."

"Well," I said, savoring a sip of the wine before settling into my reveal of what happened. "It was the shoes."

"Shoes?" they all asked at once.

I nodded and explained. "My feet were aching when we arrived at your house this evening. My sandals are flat, but they're also new and were pinching a little. I sat down with the intention of removing my sandals when I saw Amoy take off her sandals. Her feet were also aching in new sandals. I didn't think anything of it at the time until later when I saw Liz in the process of removing her sandals. Her sandals were dusty and she was the only one with a larger bag. She dropped her sandals in the bag and it made me wonder. The bag seemed a little out of place, but then I remembered that the place where Ginger was killed was dusty from the seashell path."

"So you saw the dust on her shoes and you figured that Liz had been there?"

"Not at first. But not long after. It niggled me. You know what happens when there's an idea, or a name, or a song that you can't quite remember and it's on the tip of your tongue? Well that's what this was like." I wiggled my toes and looked at them curiously. "My feet were aching and I sat down wearily. That's when the penny dropped and I began to quickly put the pieces together. But first, there was the sad case of Julia Musto."

Trip pulled out his phone and looked at the photo he took in Suzie's office. "And there she is. She's on the list of wealthiest attendees. But she didn't actually attend."

"No. Because she was dead. Liz tampered with Julia's brakes causing the fluid to leak out. She tried to make it look like an accident but the police were able to figure it out fairly quickly."

"But why Julia?" asked Suzie.

"Liz was desperate to get to this year's event because she knew that Amber had been invited. By taking out one of the wealthiest guests, she could have herself inserted in her place. And she had help from JT."

"JT. Why does everyone call him that? His name is James," insisted Suzie.

"And you know that because?"

"James is on my event committee. He's been working on it for four years. I see him occasionally when we have team meetings but I didn't know he was here as a guest."

"Liz knew he worked for you. He'd mentioned that they'd recently met. She must have targeted him to ensure that when a vacancy arose, she would be able to persuade him to let her attend, with him as her plus one."

"We always have a backup as life does happen," Suzie explained, "and sometimes, not often though, someone either can't attend or has to drop out because of other commitments or illness. That sort of thing. James recommended another highly qualified individual to attend in Julia's place, to make the numbers up."

"Liz Tanner," said Trip.

She nodded silently.

"Then once here," I continued, "and everything started to unravel, she decided that JT was a loose end. It was dusk when they went for a stroll. If JT wasn't suspecting anything, then it would have been easy to lure him out onto the ocean path, then trip him up and whack him from behind with a rock or something."

"Supposition. Not fact," said Trip. He ran his hands through his thick dark hair, deep in thought. "We'll ask JT in the morning once he's finished at the hospital. See if he can remember more of what happened."

"I want to know about the poison," said Harry.

"Ah yes, the poison," I said with a faint smile. "We thought at first it was someone who had access to medical equipment and safety clothing, however, Liz mentioned that she loves hiking in the woods, looking for ideas for her company. She would have seen the Spotted Water Hemlock and, with her experience, known what it was."

"But how did she extract the poison?"

"Disposable clothing is available at any large hardware store, but to ensure that she didn't inhale it, required a different set of skills."

They all looked at me.

"Liz was a certified SCUBA diver. She told me how much she enjoyed diving when I met her at a fundraiser at the yacht club. At that point, she hadn't been invited to your party Suzie. However, she had her own breathing equipment and could safely ensure that when she boiled down the hemlock she was safe. Then she transferred it into an innocent little perfume bottle. One with a spray where she could direct it into the victim's nostrils."

"But why?" asked Trip. "I can understand why she retaliated against Ginger, but why target Amber?"

"Liz and Amber were allegedly close friends when they were in high school," I said. "Liz left the area soon after and returned about a year ago."

"Do you know if they kept in touch?"

I shook my head. "From the way they greeted each other at the yacht club it didn't seem like it. Amber was surprised to see Liz, but Liz on the other hand appeared to be expecting her."

"So Liz has been planning this for a while," Trip said with realization. "Hmm...she obviously had the means and opportunity." He crossed his arms thoughtfully as he continued speaking. "But what about the motive? What drove her to want to kill Amber?"

"Revenge."

"For what?

I sighed. "She mentioned at the yacht club that she was unable to have a child because of an accident. Well today when we were arriving at Suzie's event, Fee mentioned that she thought it lovely that Liz didn't hold any grudges against Amber for an accident that they had in their late teens." I think that the accident impacted Liz's ability to have a child, and it's something that she never forgave Amber for. Especially as she does so much with her own charity helping mothers and babies."

"I'll have that checked out," he said.

"Rejection, jealousy, grudges. The whole myriad of human emotions leads to no end of cruelty and pain and ultimately punishment," I said as I finished my glass of wine. "And then there are secrets. We all have them, but there's one that can cause a rift between friends, lovers, family."

"Guilt," said Trip.

I nodded.

The front doorbell chimed. "I'll get it," Harry said, standing up.

"I think we're done here," said Trip, also standing up.

We all followed Harry down the hall. He opened the front door, and we were surprised to see at least ten uniformed officers and half a dozen detectives waiting outside. "Come in, come in," he said cheerfully, stepping aside to let the men and women enter. "But there's only room for a couple of you, at the moment."

"I'm Captain Ortiz. What's going on here?" demanded the senior officer.

"Ah," said Trip. "Good to see you, Captain. We're in the process of wrapping up the case. Let's go into the kitchen and I'll fill you in on what happened tonight."

"You've got a lot of explaining to do."

"That is true."

Fifty minutes later, with interviews complete, the house was quiet as the last of the guests and the replacement officers had all departed. I was anxious to leave too.

"I need to call a taxi and get home to my bed. I'll be up early to collect my dog Duke from my friend Troy's house. Or 'The Hairy Beast', as Troy likes to call him."

We all laughed.

"No need for a taxi. I'll drive you," said Trip.

Chapter Thirty-Seven

Sundowners

I was sitting on Gabby's front porch, sipping sundowners with Gabby and our friends Troy and his partner Patrick. Gabby had made us all tall, iced Cape Codders. It had been one week since the shocking events of Suzie Wilde's party, and the news had settled down to the point that we deemed it safe enough for Gabby and myself to go outside for a bit of a break.

Duke lounged lazily on the wooden porch, his eyes tracking the graceful movements of an osprey soaring high in the vibrant blue sky. The bird's broad wings sliced through the air with effortless precision, searching for its next meal in the shimmering waters below. Duke's right ear pricked at the distant cry of a seagull while his droopy left ear twitched.

The warm sun beat down on his fur. Every now and then, he let out a deep sigh, content to be with me and my friends.

He'd had quite the sleepover at Troy and Patrick's when they'd picked him up last week and I swear this dog was still exhausted from the long walks they had given him that evening, not to mention the bacon they'd provided as a tasty treat for him the following morning when I went to their house to collect him.

They spoiled him. And I loved them both even more for it.

My life was back on track and I felt good having stood up to Melissa and shed the past. Quite what I was going to do about Dr Rupert Boyden I wasn't sure. We were sure to meet again at one of Troy's soirees.

Plus, I'd scheduled the massage I'd promised myself and was looking forward to a luxurious spa day next Saturday.

My mum and dad were relieved as they were now currently in Scotland on another dig, this one north of Inverness where they were part of a team digging beneath standing stones. I was excited for them, and who knows, maybe one day I'd join them again as I used to as a young adult, only this time perhaps with some of my students, and even Harry.

And then there was Trip Brodie, Suzie's friend. I enjoyed his company when he drove me home after Suzie's event. Would it lead to anything though? I doubted it as I was pretty sure he was seeing someone, based on the conversation I'd overheard him having during the investigation.

We were all deep in conversation when my phone rang. It was Suzie's number. "Have you seen the news?" she asked.

"No. What's happened?"

"They found Liz's body. You need to turn on your TV right now!"

"Quick," I told my friends, explaining what Suzie had told me.

We all scrambled inside Gabby's house.

Turning on the TV, we saw a breaking news report that battered human remains had been spotted by Nature Reserve Guards, washed up on an island inhabited by seals and gulls. Dead sand was taking on new meaning as the anchorwoman described in detail what was being seen from drones circling around the island.

Then the footage went live to a reporter at Legacy Cove Harbor, interviewing Sergeant Trip Brodie, confirming that it was Liz's body that had been found after she had been thrown off of her boat during the storm.

"We're watching it right now, Suzie."

"We couldn't have solved the case without you. You're a genius. Even Trip said you're a genius crime solver."

He mentioned me, I thought. "Well, when you asked me to help you out I should have asked for more details before jumping in and saying yes. But I guess that's a lesson learned for another time."

"And now we have some closure. Talk to you soon, honey."

"Before you go Suzie, remind me to always ask for more information before committing to your random requests," I told her. "Unless I'm certain of the consequences."

She chuckled. "Don't you worry darlin'. That type of drama will never happen again."

"I won't worry," I laughed, putting my phone away. The breaking news report ended and Gabby turned off the TV and we all traipsed outside onto the porch once again. I sat and took a sip of my Cape Codder.

Suzie's words replayed in my mind. *That type of drama will never happen again.*

Never say never, I thought.

The End

THANK YOU

Thank you for reading! I hope you enjoyed getting to know Marnie, Suzie and their friends as much as I enjoyed writing about them.

If you have any feedback, please consider leaving a review on Amazon or Goodreads.

Be one of the first to know when the next book is published.

Sign up for my occasional newsletter and extracts of future books at Margaret stockley dot com

Join Marnie and her companions in their next thrilling adventure in the series: **A Concert To Die For**

Made in the USA
Las Vegas, NV
18 February 2025